MONEY MAKER.

GET RICH
Investment
Guide

**The Get Rich Investment Guide:
Volume Three, Number Four
(ISSN 0730-692X)**

Money Maker Magazine (ISSN 0730-692X) is published bi-monthly with an extra issue in May, by Consumers Digest, Inc. with executive and editorial offices at 5705 N. Lincoln Ave., Chicago, IL 60659. Second class postage paid at Chicago, Illinois, and additional mailing offices. Printed in U.S.A. All rights reserved under international and Pan-American copyright conventions. Reproduction of any part without prior written permission from publisher is strictly prohibited. Subscription prices: In U.S. and possessions $19.95 for one year, $35.00 for two years, $50.00 for three years. In all foreign countries add $10.00 for one-year subscription. Postmaster: Send form 3579 to MONEY MAKER, 112 Tenth St., P.O. Box 10770, Des Moines, IA 50340. All subscription inquiries, including renewals, billing, expiration date, non-receipt of materials, change of address, etc., must be sent in writing to MONEY MAKER, 112 Tenth St., P.O. Box 10770, Des Moines, IA 50340.

All editorial and reference requests correspondence must be sent in writing to MONEY MAKER, 5705 N. Lincoln Ave., Chicago, IL 60659. Reference requests must be accompanied by $2.00 for postage and handling. Address editorial: Attn: Editor. Address reference requests: Attn: Reference Dept.

MONEY MAKER Get Rich Investment Guide is designed to provide opinion in regard to the subject matter covered. It is sold with the understanding that the Publisher is not engaged in rendering legal, accounting or other professional service. If legal advice or other expert assistance is required, the services of a competent professional person should be sought. The Publisher and/or authors specifically disclaim any personal liability, application, either directly or indirectly, or any advice or information presented herein.

TABLE OF CONTENTS

Authors' Credits

Philosophy of Trading and **Gold** by Philip John Neimark: Doctor, Business Management; SEC registered investment adviser; CFTC registered commodity adviser; member or former member of International Monetary Market, Chicago Mercantile Exchange, New York Mercantile Exchange, Chicago Board of Options; Financial Editor, MONEY MAKER magazine.

Economic Indicators and **Foreign Markets** by Gregory Rossie: Free-lance writer, formerly with E.F. Hutton, the Commodity Exchange, Inc., and National Association of Security Dealers.

Stock Market and **Investment Clubs** by Bernard D. Brown: Managing editor, *The Stock Market Magazine;* former associate editor, *Financial World* magazine; former senior editor at the Research Institute of America.

Penny Stocks by Jerome Wenger: Publisher, *Penny Stock Newsletter*.

Bonds by Morris Gartenberg: Business and financial writer.

Options by Stephen A. Kerns: Chicago Board Options Exchange, Public Relations; and by Penny Dolnick: Floor broker on the CBOE and the Exchange's first female member.

Mutual Funds by Nancy Dunnan: Financial analyst and writer of *The Market Letter*, a stocks and bonds newsletter; author of three books.

Commodities by Warren Moulds: Former public relations director of the Chicago Mercantile Exchange and feature financial editor for *Chicago Today*.

Foreign Currencies by Robert Z. Aliber: Author of *The International Money Game, Exchange Risk,* and *Corporate International Finance,* plus numerous other books and articles; Professor of International Trade and Finance at the Graduate School of Business, University of Chicago.

Banking by Donald R. German: Co-author of over 14 consumer and banking books.

Coins by Don Bale, Jr.: Publisher of *The COINfidnetial Report,* coin and stock market newsletter.

Diamonds and **Gemstones** by Kurt Arens: Editor, *Gem Market Reporter.*

Real Estate by Samuel T. Barash: Real estate investor, appraiser, and author of *How to Cash In on Little-Known Local Real Estate Investment Opportunities* (Prentice-Hall) and other books on real estate appraising and taxes.

Money Market Funds by William E. Donoghue: Excerpted from *William E. Donoghue's Complete Money Market Guide,* revised edition, by William E. Donoghue with Thomas Tilling (Harper & Row; paperback, Bantam Books). Reprinted with permission.

Strategic Metals and **Silver** by Paul Sarnoff: Vice President with Paine Webber Futures; former Research Director of Rudolf Wolff Commodity Brokers, Inc.; MBA in finance; author of 27 books, including *Trading in Gold* (Woodhead-Faulkner).

Tax Shelters by Walter B. Lebowitz: Editor and publisher of the *Tax Planning Newsletter;* author of *Year End Tax Planning* and *Tax Shelter Guide;* and by Marvin B. Seidman, JD, CPA; assistant editor, *Tax Planning Newsletter.*

Insurance by Barry Kaye, CLU: Insurance agent since 1962; author of *How to Save a Fortune on Your Life Insurance* (Carol Press).

IRAs by Mary Holm Ansley: Financial reporter, *Chicago Tribune.*

Chapter One

Introduction

People are now using their money in ways they never would have believed they could, ten years ago. The financial world has changed tremendously for ordinary savers, shifting such people quickly from the safe realm of "savers" into "average investors," as they strive to remain secure in a changing world.

The initial cause, of course, was inflation. It drove individuals from well-known savings vehicles—where they saw they were *losing* money—into risky, only partially understood investment areas. And the profitable avenues have expanded geometrically, as have the risks.

Inflation is no longer the "Great Decimator" it once was, and if the Federal Reserve's tight money policies continue to get considerable help from the worldwide oil surplus, inflation can be expected to abate further. In its place, however, average investors are now confronted by the various ramifications of Reaganomics and supply-side theory. In the end, even though the ravages of inflation have eased somewhat, the future remains every bit as uncertain as it has been for the past five or ten years.

A single question has plagued Ronald Reagan ever since he announced his intention to embrace the untested supply-side theory: How could he reduce taxes, increase defense spending, and balance the budget all at the same time? The answer has turned out to be, of course, he *can't*. Not only will he fail to balance the budget, but the biggest federal deficits in history will be thrown into the bargain.

It is possible that President Reagan's bold new systems will prove disastrous for the nation. At the same time, they could eventually work. And this has created the uncertainty of the day. In any event, Reaganomics has ousted inflation from its position as the number one threat to financial security. In its place, interest rates have emerged as the most crippling force in the United States economy.

Reagan's deficits will force the government to compete ever more vigorously for money in the marketplace to finance the federal debt, so interest rates could remain high enough to choke off any general recovery from the recession before it can really happen. If this continues long enough, it could plunge the nation into a 1930s-style depression. On the other hand, the Federal Reserve could inflate the currency in an effort to prevent such a catastrophe, which would again force investors to try to beat inflation.

In both cases, the investment world remains risky and baffling. While high interest rates have created a few safe investments that offer a real return, such as money market funds and some bank vehicles, those same rates are proving destructive to business, the stock market, and on and on. Yet even in the era of nervous uncertainty, opportunities and alternatives exist on every side.

Clarifying this confusion is the goal of this book. First, you need to understand the many possibilities in today's investment world. Once you become familiar with those alternatives, you must be able to choose among those which match your lifestyle and desires. Second, you must have some direction, some assistance in selecting among the many investments available.

Simply, this book exists with a dual purpose, to educate in a confusing, unstable world, and to offer guidance. We attempt to run the gamut of viable financial investments to help you prosper in extremely uncertain times, with the specters of inflation and depression both real threats.

We have attempted to explore financial arenas in two broad groups: Those which are widely used, like banks, stocks, and money market funds; and those which offer realistic opportunities for success in the coming year, whether they are widely used by the general populace or not. We assess risks and potential rewards, always with concern for the uncertain future of the American economy—so that you can choose which are best for you. Other areas, such as whole life insurance, are omitted because we feel they are not viable in any way—while most people may be under-insured, for example, we do not feel they should buy whole life policies.

You need to know the basic rules of each investment medium, where and how to participate in the areas which appeal to you, and even whether or not a given investment arena is within your means. Of course there are investments other than those discussed in this book—the financial alternatives facing each American multiply every year. Some are worthwhile; many are not —you need to know which of the legitimate alternatives best suits your objectives. The financial savvy of United States citizens has increased dramatically in recent years, and in our constantly uncertain world, that understanding must continue to improve, if people are to prosper.

Our analyses explain each investment area, weighing risks against possible rewards, and we provide strategies for gaining security first, then wealth. Complex though everyone's financial life now is, you *can* achieve your hopes—all it takes is some homework and initiative.

Chapter Two

Philosophy of Investing

P eople have always asked questions, ranging from the simple to the profound. Perhaps the most basic questions ever asked by human beings are, "What shall I eat?" and "Where shall I sleep?" From these elemental foundations, new questions have arisen—every answer provides more questions (or the time to ask them).

As food and shelter are obtained, a primal security fosters some natural extensions of the basics along with some esoteric questions. One dilemma lying somewhere between "Where is my next meal coming from?" and "What is the meaning of life?" is, "How can I retire comfortably?" In agrarian areas of the world that are less affluent than the United States, this question is answered by a "bank account" of offspring. In the United States, the same question has traditionally been answered by a literal bank account.

And, of course, the question has a direct corollary: "How can I get rich?" It is this single bit of information that most people yearn painfully to obtain—in America (and elsewhere), wealth is universally viewed as a golden panacea, offering comfort, security, and luxury for the rest of one's days. With such widespread intensity focused on a single question, many people have found their own answer in selling "how to" letters and books to the questing public. Most do the public little good, of course, but they certainly have provided the desired wealth for those who sold them.

Just as I started my market letter seven years ago because I was annoyed with the theoretical letters then available to the public—I felt that a "pragmatic" letter by a professional trader, rather than a professional writer, would better serve the public need—so, too, I feel, there is a tremendous void in the "how to make money" books.

In my opinion, the essential error of such books is that making money is more a matter of a person's state of mind than of any particular technique. The books focus on the basic strategies of investment in a variety of fields without ever addressing the primary element of making money, which is the basic desire and purposefulness to do so. I am convinced that becoming rich is more a matter of how you do something than of what, specifically, you do. If your mind and personality are geared toward making money, then you can do it successfully in stocks, commodities, foreign coins, artwork, real estate, or anything else that offers an opportunity. Making money is an attitude, a way of thinking—not a secret set of rules or techniques.

Rather than try to obtain this information from somebody who has "yet to make it" or from a psychology text, it seems to me that the public's only genuine chance of learning how to get rich is to look inside the behavior, thinking, and personality of an individual such as myself, who started with virtually nothing and ended up a rich man. Speculative sources of this information may be accurate in some way, but speculation remains speculation.

As opposed to what might be said in a "psychology of wealth" book, I have nothing magical to impart. I'd love to be able to claim special powers and instincts, but to be honest, I don't see myself as being particularly unique, and I wouldn't claim to have an inside line on various money-making vehicles. Very simply, if I could do it, you can too.

How to Make Money

The "passive" investing of the past has been proven to be a failure. We have seen "passive" investments not only fail to provide us with the rewards of our life and livelihoods, but actually waste our savings and squander our futures. We have been asked to believe that 5 percent interest on savings accounts is acceptable, despite an inflation rate that is currently running about 14 to 17 percent. We have been asked to accept the concept that there is something wonderful about the Dow Jones averages returning to their level of a decade ago. Yet, no one offers a solution to the question of "how to cope" with the fact that everything else costs four times what it did ten years ago, and that inflation runs at three times our rate of savings return.

We are living in a world where the price of gasoline and automobiles have taken us off the roads, and where it is often unsafe to walk the streets. We are offered two political choices—one that has proven to debase our money, and the other which threatens our freedom to enjoy it. We are threatened with fears of hyperinflation on one side, and a devastating depression on the other, and, yet, we are asked to "accept it."

Well, the time has come, once again, for the greatest people in the greatest nation on earth to stop accepting. The solution is to "Get Aggressive"—with investments and ideas that have potential for providing you with the rewards of your labors and certainties for your future. That's what this book is all about. We examine the flaws in "passive investments" and the implementation of alternatives. We show you where, why, and how. The rest is up to you. But, if you refuse to sit there and take it anymore and "Get Aggressive", join us in survival and prosperity.

Why Investors Lose Money

Statistics indicate that 90 percent of the people who engage in speculation lost money. This includes people who trade in stocks, commodities, precious metals, foreign currencies, options, and so on and on. If you were to ask this 90 percent what caused their failure, the vast majority would respond with one of the following answers: "I didn't have enough information;" "I was given bad advice;" "I didn't have the time to devote to studying the market;" "I didn't have enough money to stay with my position."

These explanations for failure not only seem totally logical to the people who give them, but in great measure they are provided in advance by the investment establishment itself. In each and every case, these excuses serve to remove personal blame or responsibility for losing money and instead allow the investors to view themselves as victims of circumstances beyond their control. Both the excuses themselves and the rationale behind them are false and self-destructive. The simple truth is, people lose money because they have no concept or understanding of money.

We are all taught a host of incorrect concepts beginning in earliest childhood. They range from the ridiculous, but nevertheless frightening, concept that the boogie man will get you if you don't behave, to the absurd reasoning that by not finishing your dinner, you are personally hurting some child in China. At any early age, most of us do eventually realize that there is no boogie man, and that even if we fail to finish our meal, there is no way the leftovers will be flown to the starving children in the rest of the world. But at the same time, we fail to challenge the absurdity of other concepts which may prove to be far more destructive.

Specifically, I have in mind the concept of "investment." To invest by definition means to put money to use in something offering a profitable return. But the investment community has added some other connotations to the basic meaning of the term. The implication is that by investing in the common stock of American industry, for example, you are almost certain to realize a profit. Furthermore, it is implied that not believing this and not acting upon it is "unAmerican."

The very rules of the New York Stock Exchange, the primary trading vehicle for most individuals, not only make it more difficult to trade from the "short side" in order to profit from the decline in the price of the stock, but actually make it illegal for their registered representatives to recommend such a trade.

Why? Even the simplest logic tells us that all things do not continually rise, that they go through periods of declines as well as advances. If stocks were to continually rise, each and every stock on the exchange would be selling for millions of dollars per share. Since simple logic and the economic reality tell us this is not the case, why take away 50 percent of the chance to make profits?

If it takes intelligence, research, and education to discover that a company is going to have improved earnings, new products, greater sales, higher dividends, and that therefore you can expect to profit from an increase in the price of the stock of that company by buying it, who is to say that a person with the same intelligence, education, and research who discovers an opposite situation should not be allowed to profit from it? The only explanation is that, by convincing the public that things always eventually get better, the investment community can sustain many prices at levels where they have no right to be, thereby artificially bolstering those companies.

"Selling short" under certain conditions is equally as wise as buying long under different circumstances. But more importantly, those who don't recognize this fact have accepted as "truth" a philosophy which is not false, but downright destructive, if the goal is to profit in the market. The patriotic-sounding call to "invest in America" misses the point of what made this country grow to be great. Rather, the underlying philosophy of American industry and its greatness is using capital to make a profit.

If 50 percent of your opportunities to make money are taken away, the game becomes rigged in a fashion that helps explain why 90 percent of investors lose money.

It would be very much like playing roulette and being allowed to be only on the even numbers. You couldn't hope to win in such a game and you wouldn't play it. But by accepting the philosophy that says to play only the long side, you do play a rigged game unnecessarily in the stock market and make it virtually impossible for you to win there either.

The American public has been taught one thing—buy. The reason you accept this and the reason for your 90 percent likelihood of failure is not that you didn't have the information, not that you were given bad advice, not that you didn't have enough money, and not even that you were told the wrong things. The problem is that you chose to accept all these and the false philosophy behind them. The responsiblity and the blame are yours and yours alone. You wanted a built-in excuse to displace the responsibility for being wrong.

Money Explained

Earlier I said that the reason most people don't make money is that they don't understand what money really is. Let's go back to the issue of what money really is, what it represents, and what it can accomplish.

Most people view money as an entity unto itself, and as something which will magically provide them with happiness, security, contentment, power, and peace of mind. Ridiculous! Money is a tool. If you understand this, you will know what money can do, how it should be used, and what it can accomplish. If you don't, you will continue to depend on it (rather than on yourself) to magically create situations and bring you the things that would make you happy, as if it had a mind of its own and will separate from yours. The results of this type of thinking are all too apparent.

Just what is money? In its most basic terms, it is a value you receive for work or services you perform. You earn money and then use it as a tool to accomplish a variety of goals. To the extent you use that tool effectively, you will benefit. To the extent you expect it to take care of itself, you will suffer.

A carpenter does not expect a saw to place itself on a board and cut the proper length necessary for building a home, or to sharpen itself when its teeth are worn down. While we understand tools like saws and would never expect them to accomplish anything on their own, we fail to understand that same thinking about money.

With money, as with other tools, you have to know what your goal is, and it can't be to accumulate a million dollars and stack it up in your basement, because it will do you no good there. If what you want is to pay for a college education for your children, to live in the style you choose when you retire, to buy a new car or take a vacation, or whatever, it can only be accomplished by your conscious direction of that money to achieve the goals you feel are important. And if your goals require that your money earn more money, you will have to approach it with the same dedication and skill with which the carpenter approaches the saw and board.

But in reality, how have you been approaching money your whole life? You probably have been taking your money and blindly following the advice of so-called experts, and expecting it to accomplish your goals. When the results are failure, you're disappointed, angry, and confused.

If you fail to understand that the money which your abilities and hard efforts earn for you requires the same amount of dedication, work, and understanding as the process that produces the money, if you spend a lifetime learning to excel in your trade, but then take the monetary rewards for that excellence and waste them, lose them, disregard them, then you have short-circuited the entire process. You might as well not be paid if you are going to fail to use that payment effectively to accomplish your further goals.

The money you receive for your skills is not separate from the entire process of living your life, accomplishing your goals, and realizing your ambitions and desires. Money is part of it all. You worked to earn it, but once you have earned it, you must work to make it work so that you can have the satisfaction and security, the happiness and peace of mind, that comes with achieving the life you wish to live. If you show no respect for the rewards of your efforts, you show no respect for your efforts.

Why don't you apply the same common sense that you know is necessary in your occupation to the money which that occupation produces? Why don't you throw out the individuals, the ideas, and the advice which don't work and devote the time, effort, and energy necessary to discovering those that will? For only in so doing, can you complete the process and make your abilities worthwhile and your future fulfilled.

You may be saying to yourself, "What does all this theory have to do with making money in the markets?" The answer is—everything. Philosophy is everything in regard to your personal life and professional life, and it is everything pertaining to whether or not you will make money in the markets. Philosophy is a way of thinking, and in your everyday life you use your philosophy, your values of what are right and wrong, your concepts of what you choose to achieve, and your perceptions of how to implement them to achieve success.

Somehow when it comes to stocks, commodities, bonds, real estate, or any other invesment, you are willing to ignore not only your own personality, needs, and goals, but to blindly take the word of another individual and give him your saw, hammer, and nails to work with as he sees fit. You relinquish a tool, which is all that money is, to a person whose goals, personality, and philosophy probably have nothing to do with your goals. And that's one of the critical parts of understanding the philosophy of trading.

Using Money

You've been brought up to think that money is an end, that somehow accumulating stocks, large bank accounts, or whatever will automatically provide you with happiness, fulfillment, safety, and security. Ridiculous! If you had a million dollars and chose to run out and buy yourself a $500,000 yacht, a Rolls Royce, mink coats, diamonds, etc., it could be gone in a matter of 24 hours. Unless you have the capacity to continue to earn that kind of money on a daily basis, rather than deriving happiness, security, protection, and fulfillment, from it, you would actually only give yourself anxiety, unhappiness, confusion, and self-disgust.

Many people have gone through that process, and they've only gone through it because they view money as an end product. It is not. Money is simply one step in the process. Your occupation allows you to be rewarded with value in the form of money and the next step is to take that value, that money, and use it with discipline, understanding, knowledge, and foresight to achieve your real goals.

If you view money this way, you will be a hell of a lot more careful about how you invest it and you will be a great deal more confident regarding what you can expect it to do. You will recognize much more quickly when it is not performing its task and when new analysis and methods are required.

Just as the painter who finds himself painted into the corner realizes that he has approached the task incorrectly, so, too, you must realize that wrong results in trading cannot be attributed to some vagary of the universe or the deck being stacked against you. Rather, bad investments are the result of your own failure to understand money as a tool and use it as such.

But the philosophy of trading is much more even than recognizing that money is not an end, but a means, not a guarantee of happiness and security, but an opportunity to create these. It's also a way of life and a way of thinking.

Being a Realist

If you fool yourself in life, you'll fool yourself in the market as well. While your losses in the market may be much more obvious, the losses or unhappiness in your personal life will exist at some level as well. If you don't enjoy your job, if you don't enjoy your marriage, if you recognize you've accepted incorrect values or assumed too many responsibilities, and yet proceed in the same fashion and pattern convincing yourself you're "trapped," "didn't get a break," "never had a chance," or whatever, personal fulfillment will be as unobtainable as financial fulfillment.

What's the point of staying on this earth working at a job you don't like, living in a situation that makes you unhappy? Why just tell yourself that's the way it is? Why feel trapped? Why play the victim? Because you don't want to have to face the reality of change and with it the possibility of success, and that's where you sell yourself short. You've convinced yourself you're a loser, and by convincing yourself you've made it come true. Losers aren't born, they're made—and they make themselves.

Almost invariably, the winners are those individuals who constantly reevaluate, examine their values, and adapt or change to what they perceive are new conditions and needs. Sure, they'll be wrong some of the time, because they have chosen to act, to change, to take a chance. But the winners know that even when they are "wrong," they can change and take the chance again, until they are right. If you accept the fact that there are no new opportunities and that you are the victim, there is no chance whatsoever. If that is your view of life and yourself, you should not be trading in the various markets.

The fault is not all yours. The fault is the false philosophy that has been taught by or inferred from observation of the investment establishment in the last hundred years. The rich get richer, the poor have babies; it takes money to make money; the big guys run the market, you have to have inside information—all these time-honored clichés imply that unless you fall into one of those groups, you don't have a chance.

If you can sit down right now and say to yourself—I want to be rich; I want to make money; I have the choice to make money or not to; I choose to take that choice, that chance; I recognize the risk, but I also recognize the rewards; and more important, I recognize that if I don't take that risk, that no meaningful reward will ever be possible—if you can do that, believe it, mean it, and act upon it, there are no limits to what you can accomplish.

Assessing and Setting Goals

To specifically discuss the philosophy of trading requires an understanding of a thought process. The first step of the process is to identify your goals. The tens of thousands of people who wanted to invest, to speculate, to make money, have all claimed that their goals were exactly the same, regardless of their education, position in life, social stature, or monetary possessions. They may have phrased it in different words, but they always meant the same thing. They wanted enough money to be able to do the things they wanted to do and to say "no" to the things they didn't want to do—enough money to be secure and comfortable. Enough money, they assume, to be "free."

But that's not an answer, that's the avoidance of a specific answer. Perhaps it takes half a million dollars a year to satisfy the needs and values of one particular lifestyle. On the other hand, for a writer or painter who simply wants to be able to express his or her art form and be able to eat and exist at the same time, $5000 or $10,000 a year might be a meaningful figure. For people with two or three children whose values dictate a college education, the money required becomes much different than for those with no children or those whose values do not include a $30,000 education for each child.

Even more difficult on top of defining specific goals, there is the problem of assessing what will be needed in the future to achieve those goals. At one time, most people felt they could plan for the future because they knew basically what the future would be, but that luxury has disappeared. A man who, 20 years ago, figured accurately and concretely that he could live comfortably in retirement on $10,000 a year, now faces the reality of a world beset by inflation, shortages, and increasing prices. The $10,000 that he once viewed as adequate for a comfortable and satisfying lifestyle will now provide him only with the ability to survive, if even that.

For those of you setting goals for five, ten or 30 years down the road, you must recognize that the security of being able to plan for the future and set a dollar figure for it no longer exists. Instead you will have to continually re-evaluate, analyze, and use your tools (money) in a constantly changing and shifting pattern to match the changes and shifts in the economic, social, and political situation in the world.

In one sense, retirement becomes impossible. Unless you amass a truly incredible amount of money—many, many millions of dollars—you can't be sure of supporting the qualitiative style of living you desire by continuing to follow one set of investmment procedures.

The $350 a month that ten years ago seemed to be a significant payment from a pension fund, may not even pay your electric bill by the time you retire. The automobile you thought you could purchase for $4000 or $5000, today costs $10,000 or $12,000, and by the time you retire, it might be $15,000 or $20,000. Worse yet, it may not be available at any price and you may have to make contingency plans for that. It's important when you set goals not to fool yourself in this area as you have fooled yourself in others. Don't think it's going to be a certain way because you want it to be that way. You don't know how it will be.

Survival Tactics

Okay. You sit down and devote the same time and energy that you put into your business and your personal life to honestly analyze your needs, values, and qualitative desires—and do it realistically. Once you have established what your obligations will be and what the monetary requirements to fulfill them will be, then and only then, can you embark upon a course of action that can make them come true.

A person's survival depends not just on instinct, but on the ability to identify reality and develop ways of dealing with it. We must perceive things as they are, and then take those facts, those perceptions, and form them into conceptions — usable, workable, meaningful, productive actions to ensure our survival. Our survival on every level from simply staying alive to being personally happy or economically secure depends on this ability.

A small boy sees a flame on the stove and perceives it as beautiful and attractive; left alone, he will invariably touch that flame with his hand. What he then will perceive is pain. If he is to survive, he must take that perception of pain and form it into a useful conception. That conception will be that the pretty, beckoning flame is not to be touched again. If instead, he decides that the pain he felt was a singular occurence that will not happen again, he will continue to stick his hand or body in the flame, until he either forms a rational conception or perishes from his burns.

Remember, though, and this is critical, your perception of reality does not make or define reality. Perceptions of reality are sometimes faulty. To the extent we perceive reality correctly and accurately and form conceptions to use it, we will prosper emotionally, intellectually, and financially. To the extent we perceive it incorrectly, we will suffer in all the same areas. This is the crux of what makes a successful individual and a successful trader.

Understand that to make money, you must first want to make it; second, understand there is no reason you cannot make it; third, realistically and honestly identify your values, needs, and goals; fourth, use your money as a tool to help achieve those values, needs, and goals; fifth, perceive the reality of whatever speculative situation it is as rationally, clearly, and accurately as possible; and sixth, implement your conception within realistic parameters that can provide you with the results you seek. Understand that you cannot follow anyone else blindly, anymore than you could blindly let anyone else tell you how to perform your occupation.

Understand, too, that the stock broker, the real estate broker, and the commodities, bonds, and insurance brokers all make their livings on sales commissions. And, understand that because of that they can survive financially only if you, and people like you, buy what they sell. Consequently, they are quite prone to twist their perception of reality in order to make the situation appear to be something that it is not. They will always tell you that things will get better, things are going up, the time is now, you should act.

Sometimes they will be correct, but often they will not be. You must rely upon your perceptions to validate theirs, and when the two conflict, you must withdraw as quickly as the child withdraws his hand from the flame that seems so beautiful and rewarding. If you do not, the pain will be as great financially as the burn is physically.

Sure it requires homework, studying, dedication, analysis, time, and effort, but then there is no such thing as a free lunch. You had to learn your trade, profession, or occupation. It takes the same dedication and motivation to use your money as a tool to achieve your honest and realistic goals.

Understand also that it is not a one-time decision. Understand that constant reevaluation is necessary. Because of the rapidity with which this world changes, the incredible volatility in economic, political, and social situations, things that used to take decades to happen can now happen in months, weeks, or even days. You must perceive reality as it is, as it is changing, and recognize how those changes will affect you. Determining what new tactics, avenues, and implementations are necessary will be an on-going process and will be critical to your success.

The opportunity is there. It has always been there. The problem is you've been convinced that you couldn't do it. You can. Thousands of others have. There is no reason you cannot. The only possiblity of failure will be either that you let yourself be convinced that success wasn't possible, or you perceived reality incorrectly and refused to change and adjust your view of it.

It's a scary, frightening world where security, stability, and the safety of the future no longer exist. It isn't necessarily pleasant, but it can be made pleasant by recognizing it, dealing with it, and knowing you are capable of coming out on top.

The choice is yours. By acknowledging that the choice is yours, that all choices are yours, have always been yours, you at least have a chance. If, instead you deny the concept of choice, you deny yourself the hope of success or of any chance at all.

MONEY MAKER

Chapter Three

How To Read Financial Pages

Dangerous uncertainty underlies all of the United States economy for the next twelve months, and the only defense any individual investor has is education. This isn't as difficult a goal as it may sound—everyone in the country has access to at least one virtual fountain of investment information: A newspaper with accurate financial listings. Even those living far from a large city can receive *The Wall Street Journal*. And a paper with good financial listings is probably the best basic information source going.

They are a primary reference that is updated every day—the only more reliable, more current source available is a quotation tape at a brokerage.

Unfortunately, many new (and even seasoned) investors are stymied by this basic tool. The financial pages *can* be confusing at times, but once you know what you're doing, their value is immeasurable. The key is simply disciplined reading, so that you monitor the same listings from day to day.

The Stock Market

Here is one recommended routine based upon three questions you might ask when reading the stock listings each day, and the time it will take to answer them. 1. How did the market do in general yesterday? (five minutes); 2. How did my investments (or certain investments I am following) do? (five minutes); 3. What new possibilities exist in the market today that didn't exist yesterday? (ten minutes).

The market in general. A quick glance at a few indices and "indicators" puts the day's stock market activity in perspective. The most widely reported and followed index is the Dow Jones Industrial Average (DJIA).

The DJIA of thirty widely traded industrial stocks is the oldest of all the indices, dating from 1928. (Before that it was an average of 20 stocks.) On most Mondays, *The Wall Street Journal,* which is published by Dow Jones, Inc., lists the 30 stocks composing this index, as well as the 20 stocks in the Dow Jones transportation average, and the 15 in the utility average. Down through the years, the ''Dow 30'' has been an exclusive and relatively stable club. Fifteen of the stocks have survived since 1928. 3M (Minnesota Mining & Manufacturing) replaced Anaconda, and in 1979, IBM and Merck supplanted Chrysler and Esmark.

The role of the DJIA is to provide a baseline for the United States economy as a whole and for stock-oriented investment performance. Investment advisers and funds often boast of their track record in beating the DJIA. To provide uniformity, Dow Jones revises the formula for computing the average whenever one of the component stocks declares a stock split.

The DJIA once was important because many Wall Street securities analysts ascribed to ''Dow Theory''—a system which attempts to discern basic trends in the market by charting upward and downward swings. Dow Theory is not so widely followed today, but the DJIA is perhaps even more important for another reason. Many institutional investors, such as pension funds and bank pooled funds, invest heavily in DJIA stocks when they feel the market as a whole will rise. Investors watch the Dow carefully today for evidence that large pools of money are once again ''back in the market.''

In looking for such a trend, you should not take any movement in the DJIA of 5 percent or less (for example: a 50 point move from a base of 1000) too seriously. In recent years, a movement of 10 percent has usually signaled a major market rally or slump. The Dow Jones Industrial Average is computed every half hour during the day.

The other Dow averages are not as widely followed, and generally tend to track the ups and downs of the DJIA. Dow Theory proponents often use the transportation average to verify the industrial average direction.

Events of the past few years have encouraged investors to follow other indices. The Standard & Poor's index of 500 stocks has gained in popularity as a result of sophisticated portfolio theories, which consider the Dow 30 Index too narrow for proper diversification. Institutions follow the S&P 500 and attempt to duplicate its performance, through ''index fund'' portfolios containing a cross-section of the component stocks.

The American Market Value Index, reflecting the group performance of stocks listed on the American Stock Exchange, has gained attention recently because of its performance. In the past two years, the index has almost doubled. Similarly, the NASDAQ Over-the-Counter Composite Index, a compilation made by the National Association of Securities Dealers, of stocks listed on its automated quotation system, has increased about 30 percent in the past year.

Specific stocks. Before you focus on specific stocks, find a newspaper which at least prints full New York Stock Exchange (NYSE) listings—fully, legibly, and in some intelligent order. It is nearly impossible to include full NYSE quotes on one newspaper page, and unlike news copy, stock exchange listings can't be cut to fit the space. Again, *The Wall Street Journal* is a model for formats, and for its comprehensive over-the-counter and foreign stock listings.

Of the 50,000 or so government and corporate securities in existence, less than 5000 are listed in any general circulation newspaper. If it is important to you to monitor your stock's progress daily, you should buy one listed on a major exchange or an "over-the-counter" stock widely traded and carried on the NASDAQ. Since this automated reporting service was initiated in 1971, it has grown to include more than 3000 securities.

For purposes of explaining the stock listings, we have enlarged an actual listing on these pages. If you have never invested in stocks, you might find it interesting to follow daily one section of 10 or so stocks in the alphabetical listings, like the section we have reproduced, from *The Wall Street Journal*. (Table I)

Table I: STOCKS

52 Weeks High	Low	Stock	Div.	Yld %	P-E Ratio	Sales 100s	High	low	Close	Net Chg.
18⅜	9½	GtWFin	.88	8.4	..	284	10⅝	10	10½	– ⅛
12⅞	11¼	GMP n	1.48	12.	6	2	12⅛	12⅛	12⅛	– ⅛
20¼	13½	Grevh	1.20	8.6	5	2808	14	13¾	13⅞	.....
4¾	1⅜	Grey wt		..	.	262	1½	d 1¼	1⅜	.....
10½	5⅞	GrowG	s.36b	5.6	7	45	6⅜	6¼	6⅜	.....
5½	2⅜	GthRty		..	29	20	2¾	2⅝	2⅝	– ¼
39¾	21⅝	Grumm	1.40	6.6	15	85	21⅞	d21¼	21¼	– ⅜
23	17¾	Grum pf	2.80	15.	..	43	19	18⅞	19	+ ¼
21⅝	14	GlfWst	.75	5.0	4	1319	15¼	15	15	– ¼
58	54	GlfW pf	5.75	11.	..	2	52¼	d52¼	52¼	– ¼
53	35⅝	GlfW pf	2.50	6.8	..	7	37⅜	36⅞	36⅞	– ⅛
41⅜	27¾	GulfOil	2.80	9.4	5	5997	30⅛	29½	29¾	– ⅜

Prices as of March 12, 1982. The stock market listings provide a wealth of information about many securities—past and present prices, dividend, yield, price-earnings ratio, volume, net change, and more.

Here, squeezed into about one-inch of newsprint, is the daily chronical of stocks capitalizing two of the largest corporate giants in America, Gulf Oil and Gulf & Western, right beside one struggling real estate investment trust, Growth Realty Investors. This particular listing shows that not all securities listed on the NYSE "stock page" are actually stocks—note the Greyhound warrant—and that not all of the companies listed are operating companies. Real estate investment trusts such as Growth Realty are listed as well.

The most important column in the listing for your quick review is the last one, "Net Change." This signifies the change, up (plus) or down (minus), in a stock's price from the preceding day's closing price, expressed in fractions of a dollar. From the listing, it would appear that this was not a volatile day in the market. Grow Group and Greyhound did not change in price, as is reflected by the blank space under net change. Because of a continuing market slump in March, 1982, most of the stocks shown are down fractionally.

The "daily trading range" can be determined by comparing the high and low prices at which the stock traded during the day. Note that this range is usually greater than the net change. The closing price reflects the price for the last trade of the day.

Sales volume, in hundreds, is quoted to the left of the trading range. Note the great difference in volumes of stocks listed here—from 599,700 shares of Gulf Oil to the 200 shares of GMP. This indicates that Gulf stock probably changed hands often in "block trades" made by institutions.

Naturally, investors like to "buy low, sell high" in the market, and the 52-week historic high-low range at the far left of the column is helpful. The range not ony shows how well a stock is doing in regard to the past year's performance, but also suggests the relative volatility of the stock. For instance, during the preceding year, GMP has traded in a very narrow range, while Gulf & Western has traded in a broader range. Greyhound is trading near the bottom of its 52-week range, while GMP is trading closer to the top.

The first column after the company name, "Div.," is often misunderstood. It means dividend, of course, but a more exact title is "indicated dividend rate." It indicates the expected annual disbursements from the stock based on the last dividend paid.

Special dividends are reflected by initials, such as the s.36 of Grow Group. The company regularly distributes a five percent stock dividend—five shares of new stock for each 100 you own. Stock dividends are more akin to stock splits than to cash dividends and have a tendency to keep the quoted price low, while rewarding investors.

Preferred stocks are usually required to pay a regular dividend if the company has after-tax earnings. (Shareholders also have preference, in a liquidation, over common stock holders.) The Gulf & Western preferred pays an annual dividend of $5.75 or $2.50. The Grumman preferred pays $2.80.

Other initials are usually explained in explanatory notes at the end of the stock listings. This varies from paper to paper and does not follow a regular pattern of daily appearance.

Strategic analysis. When you move into the Yield and P-E Ratio columns, you enter the realm of more sophisticated analysis, in which you answer the third question, "What opportunities exist in the market today, that didn't exist yesterday?" Yield indicates the percentage of the share price that you can expect to receive in dividends within a year. Yields vary widely, depending upon the capital needs of the company and its investors. Growing, technology-oriented companies often need all their earnings for expansion. They pay low dividends and have low yields. Utilities and preferred stocks traditionally have high yields.

Earnings, or "profits," reflect the general health of a company more than yield. The P-E (Price-Earnings) Ratio is the current price of the stock dividend by the earnings in the previous year. This is probably the most valuable indicator in determining whether a stock is selling "expensive" or "cheap."

Why? Consider this analogy. John owns a lemonade stand and he wants to sell it to Fred. Neither knows how much the stand is worth. However, Fred feels that he should earn 10 percent on any money he invests in buying it. John tells Fred that in the past year, the stand has earned $100 for him, after all expenses. Fred does a quick calculation, and decides that if the earnings hold up, he can afford to pay $1000 for the stand and have a 10 percent return on his money. The P-E ratio of the stand is $1000 divided by $100.

For a typical company, a P-E ratio of less than 7 or 8 often signals that the price of the stock is depressed. Stocks which are in hot demand frequently sell at "60 times earnings" and higher. P-E ratios are also referred to as "multiples."

One popular investment strategy seeks out stocks which are selling at low P-E ratios on the assumption that such stocks are a bargain, temporarily underpriced. Of course, some stocks which are selling at depressed multiples represent truly depressed companies.

The actual earnings of the company are not listed in the newspaper, but you can calculate them: Earnings = Price divided by P-E. Gulf Oil, you can tell, earned about $5.95 per share last year. Once you know earnings, you can then determine the "pay-out ratio," or the amount of all earnings paid out in dividends. Gulf paid out about one-half of its earnings in dividends, a pay-out ratio of slightly over 50 percent.

Bonds

There was a time, up until about 1970, or so, that all you needed to know to stay on top of your investments was how to read and interpret the stock listings. But today, to choose and monitor a well-rounded portfolio, you have to dig deeper into the daily financial pages. You need to understand the listings for several other major investment areas, including bonds, mutual funds, stock options, and commodities.

Background and Basics. Bonds, like stocks, are traded in auction bidding each business day at major stock exchanges and in the over-the-counter market. In general, the bonds you will find listed under the exchange names in the newspaper are corporate bonds issued by private companies. "Corporates" are a major source of funds for new investment and for refinancing old debt in capital-intensive industries. By issuing a new bond, a company borrows assets from those who buy the bonds, and then repays the loan with interest to the investor.

In the early part of this century, railroads were the major issuer of corporate bonds. Now, the major issuers are public utilities, finance companies, and industries that spend large sums on research and development or plant and equipment. Many companies that once relied solely on the stock market to raise new capital have been driven to the bond market in recent years by depressed stock prices.

A company is allowed to have only one class of common stock, but it may float as many bond issues as its credit allows. (The quality of each bond issue is rated by the two influential rating services, Moody's and Standard & Poor's.) General Motors Acceptance (GMA) has 33 bond issues listed on the New York Stock Exchange. To the novice, they may all look alike. However, each bond has two unique personality traits—the coupon rate and the maturity date.

The "GMA 9s of 84" carry a nine percent coupon rate and mature in 1984. For each $1000 bond you buy of this issue, you can expect to receive 9 percent interest per year, or $90, until 1984 when GMA will redeem your last coupon and retire the bond by paying you the face amount, $1000. Your $90 interest is claimed by clipping a coupon attached to your bond twice each year and sending it to the company. Or, the company may have your name registered as the bond owner and automatically send you $45 twice each year.

Keep in mind that you do not necessarily have to pay $1000 to buy the bond. You bid for it in open auction and pay a going rate, which is influenced mostly by current interest rates but also by the health of the company, supply and demand for the bonds, investment trends, and so on. Just as the broad trend in stocks is tracked by the Dow Jones Industrial Average and other indexes, bond price activity is tracked by three Dow Jones bond averages, one for utilities, one for industries, and one broad average of 20 bonds. The 20-bond average fell about 13 percent during 1979.

Table II: BONDS

Bonds	Cur Yld	Vol	High	Low	Close	Net Chg.
IBM 9½86	11.	203	88	87¼	87⅜	– ¼
IBM 9⅜04	13.	446	72¼	71	71½	+ ⅛
IntHrv 4⅝88	11.	9	42⅛	42⅛	42⅛	+ ⅛
IntHrv 6¼98	21.	2	30	30	30	– ⅛
IntHrv 8⅝95	24.	19	36	35	36	– ⅜
IntHrv 9s04	25.	307	35½	35	35⅜	– ⅛
InHvC 8⅝91	24.	25	39	36½	36½	–1⅝
InHvC 9s84	16.	115	59	57	57⅝	– ⅜
InHvC 8.35s86	19.	31	43¾	42	43	– ¾
InHvC 13½88	25.	43	53¾	53⅜	53⅜	– ¼
IntSilvr 5s93	cv	6	70½	70½	70½	+ ½
IntTT 8.9s95	13.	15	66	66	66	–1

Prices as of March 12, 1982. Bond listings on the financial pages resemble stock listings—but the prices are quoted as a percentage of the bond's value ("90" means a price of $900 for a $1000 bond).

Table II is one actual section of the daily bond listings from the New York Stock Exchange. The listings are similar to the stock listings in several ways. The days high, low, and closing prices and the "net change" column are in the same format and reflect the same basic auction activity. The only difference is that stock prices are quoted in actual dollars. Bonds are quoted as a percentage of the bond's face value.

Since most corporate bonds are bought in $1000 denominations, another way to look at it is this: Multiply the price quoted in the paper, whole numbers and fractions, by $10 to determine the price you will pay for a bond. For example: You buy an IBM 9½ of 86 at a price of 87⅜. The price you pay is (87 × $10), or $870, plus (⅜ × $10) or $3.75, for a total cost of $873.75. The difference between this amount and the $1000 face amount is called a discount. If you paid more than $1000, the difference would be called a premium.

If you owned one of the IBM bonds above on the trading date shown, your investment lost ¼ of a point on the open market. This translates into a loss of $2.50 per bond, using the same formula for calculation (¼ × $10 = $2.50).

As you can see, bonds fluctuate in price each day, just as stocks do. In the same day that the IBM 9½s of 86 lost, International Harvester's 4⅝s of 88 gained ⅛ ($1.25) per bond. Why? Supply and demand probably. Trading was heavy in the IBM issue, with 20,300 bonds traded; only 900 bonds were traded in the International Harvester issue.

Types of Yields. The one column in which bond listings are not like stock listings is "Cur Yld"—the abbreviation of current yield. Each bond has three different kinds of yields, all of which are expressed as a percentage. The first kind, nominal yield, is the simplest—the amount of the coupon printed on the certificate. The nominal yield—9.50 percent per year in the case of IBM's 9½s of 86—does not change over the life of the bond.

The current yield is the yield based upon the actual buying price, and it can change every trading day. The formula for calculating it is: Nominal yield ÷ Buying Price = Current Yield. When the current yield is less than the nominal yield, bonds are said to be selling at a discount. When the current yield is more than the nominal yield, they are selling at a premium.

Bonds of about the same rating and maturity should have roughly similar current yields. IBM and International Harvester both have bonds maturing in 2004; however, the Harvester issue is currently yielding 25 percent while the IBM issue yields 13 percent. The reason for the difference is that International Harvester has recently had trouble meeting its credit obligations, and its bond ratings have been lowered. Assuming that the company bounces back into good health, this bond could become a good long-term value.

Current yields, when charted over a period of time, tend to parallel long-term interest rates, but two types of bonds do not follow this rule. They are convertible bonds and bonds nearing maturity. You will see examples of both in the newspaper section reproduced. International Harvester Credit has a bond coming due in 1984. In this case, the current yield is much less than bonds issued by the same company with longer maturities. Why is this so?

The answer is obvious if you know how to figure the third kind of yield—yield to maturity. Remember that when a bond matures, the company must pay the full face value, a price of $1000 for your bond. If you pay 57 for the Harvester Credit bond and two years from now the company redeems it at

100, you have a gain of 43 points, or $430 per bond. Not only does this increase your yield to maturity, it may also allow you to declare the 43 point gain as a capital gain and have it taxed at a lower rate than the interest you receive.

Yield is not listed for convertible bonds because it is usually a minor factor in the investor's analysis of the bonds. A much more important influence is the price of the security which the bonds may be converted to at the owner's option—usually the same company's common or preferred stock.

The International Silver 5s or 93 are an example of a typical convertible bond. In this case, each bond could be converted by the owner into about 33 shares of common stock in the same company. The issue rose ½ point on this particular day, and you can be sure that it was due mainly to an increase in the price of the underlying common stock. (While these bonds are traded on the New York Stock Exchange, from which this listing was taken, the common stock of Insilco is traded only on the Boston Exchange.)

Mutual Funds

Of all the investments quoted in the newspaper, mutual fund listings are the sketchiest. The listings do not tell you what kind of fund you are reading about, its past performance, or its dividend payments. Many papers simply quote "NAV" (Net Asset Value) and "Offering Price," so it is safe to assume that these are the main concepts to know.

However, a little background is necessary to understand both.

A mutual fund is one form of investment company, and all investment companies have been granted special tax status by Congress. Unlike other corporations, investment companies do not pay tax on their profits. Instead, they pass the profits to the investor, who then pays tax just as he does on other investments.

A mutual fund is specifically an "open-end" investment company. Such a fund has the right to issue new shares constantly, whenever new dollars are invested. When an investor wants to "redeem" his shares, the mutual fund must buy them back, and the price it pays is called the net asset value.

At the end of each day, each fund totals the value of all its investments and subtracts overhead and expenses. It then divides this net asset figure by the total number of shares outstanding and posts its net asset value. This figure is applied to all sales and redemptions made by the fund on that day.

But the investor does not always buy or sell at the net asset value. Another column in many papers lists the offering price. The offering price is unique among all financial data listed in the newspaper, because it tells you what commission you pay for your fund shares in addition to net asset value.

The difference between offering price and net asset value is a sales commission, and it usually runs about eight percent. Some funds also charge a redemption fee, which is subtracted from net asset value when you sell your fund shares, but this is rarely more than two percent.

If you have followed mutual funds for several years, you will have noticed a growing number of funds which carry the initials N.L. in the offering price column. These are no-load funds. They do not deploy salesmen to distribute their shares and they do not charge commissions. To place an order or make a redemption, you call or write the company directly. The popular new money market funds are all no-load funds.

Most newspapers regularly list 400 or so of the most active mutual funds, and this adds to the bewilderment that many investors feel about funds. How do you select one? How are they different? How do you know when to redeem your shares? Why pay a load if you can avoid it?

Actually mutual funds are based on a simple premise. If many investors with common objectives pool their money, they can afford to hire professional management and achieve diversification—a portfolio with many different investments. The first key to selecting a fund is the concept of "investors with common objectives."

Unfortunately, newspapers don't attempt to explain the objectives of each fund. The most common types of funds are these:

1. Money market fund (also called cash management funds), which invest in safe, short-term debt instruments such as U.S. Treasury bills and certificates of deposit issued by major banks.

2. Growth funds, which invest mainly in blue chip stocks.

3. Bond funds, which invest in portfolios of corporate and Government bonds. Two offshoots of this type fund are high-yield bond funds, which invest in lower-rated bonds, and municipal bond funds, which offer tax-free interest.

4. Income funds, which may either invest in bonds or stocks paying high dividends.

5. Specialty funds, which invest in specific areas such as gold stocks or stocks of small companies.

Several of the larger mutual fund companies now offer each of these types of funds. These fund "families" are usually grouped together in the newspaper under a common heading, and their names describe the fund's unique objective.

For example, under Kemper you will find an Income Fund, Growth Fund, High Yield Fund, Money Market Fund, etc. Other fund companies use letters or numbers to designate different objectives. For example, Keystone has four bond funds (B1, B2, B3, B4) and four stock funds (S1, S2, S3, and S4). The numbers in each fund name signify to investors how aggressively each fund is managed and how much risk is involved.

Each time a mutual fund is sold to a new investor, the investor must be given or mailed a prospectus, which includes the fund's investment philosophy and track record. Just as informative is the fund's most recent quarterly report. Such reports often show exactly which investments the fund owns and which it has recently sold.

Stock Options

Options are one of the few areas left in which the "little investor" can own the equivalent of considerable shares of stock, without putting up much money, and with measured risk.

Table III: STOCK OPTIONS

Option & NY Close	Strike Price	Calls—Last Apr	Calls—Last Jul	Calls—Last Oct	Puts—Last Apr	Puts—Last Jul	Puts—Last Oct
I B M	.. 45	r	r	s	1-16	5-16	s
57⅞	... 50	8⅜	9½	s	3-16	1	s
57⅞	... 55	4¼	6⅜	7⅝	1 1-16	2¼	2 13-16
57⅞	... 60	1 7-16	3½	5	3⅛	4⅛	4⅞
57⅞	... 65	5-16	1⅜	2⅝	7	7¼	8
In Har	.. 10	r	r	⅜	4⅝	r	r

Prices as of March 12, 1982. Stock options may be listed in different ways. In this example, six options (three calls and three puts) with different expiration dates but the same striking price are shown in each line.

Options may be listed in two different ways in your newspaper. Table III shows the method used by *The Wall Street Journal*. Six different options contracts are listed on the same line—three calls and three puts—with the same "striking price" but expiring three months apart. The currently offered options of IBM and International Harvester are shown as they are quoted on the Chicago Board Options Exchange (CBOE), the first and still the largest of the options exchanges.

Most options, like most stocks, are listed on only one exchange. A few are "dually listed" due to competition among the various exchanges for volume. The CBOE and American Stock Exchange are well entrenched as the largest exchanges in option volume, but three competitors, the Philadelphia, Pacific, and Midwest Stock Exchanges, are growing rapidly. As yet, no options are traded on the New York Stock Exchange.

If you want to buy or sell an IBM option, you will have to do so through the CBOE, because these options are not listed anywhere else. In practice, you simply call your broker to place an option order, just as you would place a stock order. Some brokerages are not yet members of the three smaller options exchanges, but almost all are represented on the CBOE and American. All of the exchanges process or "clear" their options through a company they own mutually, the Options Clearing Corporation.

Call Options. Let's look at the first IBM listing, which is identified by the first number to the right of the company name—45. All six options listed on this line are identified as "IBM 45s." Reading under the boldface headings, the options are identified specifically as an IBM April 45 (call or put), and IBM July 45, and an IBM October 45. This means that the option has a "striking price" of $45 per share and expires in the month mentioned. (Specifically, they expire on the Saturday following the third Friday of the month.) There are three calls and three puts on the IBM 45s line. In this case, no trades were made on the date shown for the April 45 and July 45 calls—the premium, at this point, is so high that no one is trading it (noted by the "r"). No October 45 call was offered (designated by the "s").

Let's take a closer look at the IBM July 50 call option, the center option listed on the same line of calls. On this trading day, the closing price ("last") was 9½. Under this format, you are not told what the gain or loss from yesterday's closing price is, and you will have to remember to go back and look. In the far left-hand column, you can see that IBM common stock closed the same trading day at 57⅞, or about $57.87 per share.

If you bought one of these options on the day shown, March 12, 1982, just what have you bought? What is your bet?

Each call option you buy conveys the right to buy 100 shares of the underlying stock at the striking price any time before the expiration date. In this case, you have the right to buy 100 shares of IBM common stock at $50 per share before July 16, 1982. In return for this right, you pay 9½ dollars per share for the 100 shares, or a total of $950. This is called your "premium." It is the total amount of money you have at risk. While you can't lose more than this amount, options buyers frequently lose every penny of their premium.

When you buy an option, you pay this premium through the Options Clearing Corporation to a seller of the same option, a person whom you never see. If you exercised this option immediately after you bought it, you could demand that the seller deliver to you 100 shares of IBM at $50 per share, for a total of $5000 which you would pay him. You could then sell the same shares for the going market price of $57.87 and make a profit of $787.

However, you have paid $950 in premiums plus a commission, so you would lose money on the deal, as you invariably would do if you exercised an option immediately after buying it. You are betting that IBM stock will rise in price between now and June. You are buying time. (In practice, options are rarely exercised. If you buy a call, you would normally liquidate your position by reselling it in the "secondary" market.)

The July 50 IBM call is already "in the money," meaning that the underlying stock is already selling above the striking price. You almost always pay a higher premium for an option in the money than one out of the money.

Obviously, the options of a company are more valuable if the stock price tends to fluctuate. The other value you buy in an option is time value. Look at the difference in price between the July and October IBM 65 call options. The July is selling for 34 cents per share. You can say that the time value of the October option is more than four times that of the July option. If the price of the stock stays the same over the next three months, the buyer of the October option will probably see the resale value of his option reduced. Assuming a stable price for the underlying stock, time works against the buyer of a call option and in favor of the seller.

Now, let's examine the "upside" potential. If the IBM stock price jumps to 70, the buyer of the July 65 call will see his investment five points in the money. For his 50 investment, he will receive at least $500 in return. The holder of an October 65 call will receive the same $500 return, but his percentage gain is not as great. Option traders say the June buyer has less "leverage" at work. The smaller the premium you pay, the more leverage you have.

Put options. Remember that every option has a buyer and a seller, a winner and a loser. However, not all options reward the buyer when the underlying stock goes up. In addition to call options, exchanges make markets in put options for a select few companies. A put option conveys the right to sell 100 shares of stock at a given price before an expiration date. If you buy a put, you benefit when the price of the stock goes down.

Strategies. It has long been the dream of some Americans to own 100 shares of IBM, and yet they lack anything near the $5800 needed for such an investment. But with options you can in effect, buy thousands of shares of IBM and be paid for the privilege. Of course, you must accept the same risk as any other holder of IBM stock.

Here's how this works. Find a striking price close to the current market price (in this case we will select July 65) and (a) buy a call at that striking price, while (b) selling a put at the same price. You would earn a 4⅛ premium, or $412, by selling the put. (Your broker would probably demand some collateral or evidence that you will indeed honor your obligation to sell 100 shares of IBM, if you do not actually own the stock. Selling a put when you don't own the underlying stock is called uncovered selling.) You would pay a premium of $350 (3½) in buying the call. So, you would earn $62 for the right of owning an investment which would very closely track the performance of 100 shares of IBM.

You would pay brokerage fees, of course, and IBM stock would have to rise for you to reach a "break even" point, at which the net premium you earn offsets the current loss on your put position. After that, the fortunes of this pair of options will rise and fall almost exactly like the underlying stock. This is much like buying stock on margin, except that you pay interest on money you borrow from your broker to buy margin stock, and you pay none here.

Commodities

Commodities are like options in several important ways. They are a volatile investment medium in which fortunes are made and lost overnight. They are traded back and forth by financial speculators but rarely are exercised. (In commodities, it is quite obvious why speculators do not exercise contracts. Who wants 38,000 pounds of pork bellies?)

The risk question. There is one major difference between options and commodity futures contracts. When you buy an option, you can never lose more than your premium. The "downside risk" is limited. That is not the case with commodity futures. Such a contract is not an option to buy, but a definite commitment to buy a fixed date in the future. The only way to limit your loss is to "hedge" with commodity futures—that is, to have 100 troy ounces of gold in your vault before you make a contract to sell 100 troy ounces.

Precious metals, like agricultural products, are priced according to supply and demand. As many unfortunate silver traders have discovered recently, the intrinsic economic value of a commodity futures contract may bear little relationship to the ultimate value of a contract when a temporary short supply or "squeeze" develops. The prudent trader knows that all commodities are subject to the same market forces and require the same degree of caution. They all follow the same basic format in newspaper listings.

The listing reproduced in Table IV shows one day's trading on the Chicago Mercantile Exchange (CMX) of 100 troy ounce gold futures. (There are 12 troy ounces in a pound.) Individual contracts are identified by the month in which the contract becomes due. You read the contract, "March gold, April gold," and so on. As you can see, the contract delivery dates extend well into 1983.

Each contract is an agreement between two parties to exchange a given quantity of a commodity (100 troy ounces of gold) at an agreed price on the delivery date. That price is the one you read in the first four columns of numbers. The columns represent (in order, left to right) the opening price or price at which the first sale of the day was made, the high price of the day, the low price of the day, and the last or "settle" price.

Table IV: COMMODITIES

	Open	High	Low	Settle	Change	Lifetime High	Lifetime Low	Open Interest
GOLD (CMX) — 100 troy oz.; $ per troy oz.								
Mar	321.00	323.50	319.00	317.80	−10.30	410.00	319.00	30
Apr	324.00	326.00	317.50	319.60	−10.40	898.00	317.50	43,074
June	330.00	333.30	324.50	326.50	−10.70	925.00	324.50	32,300
Aug	340.00	341.00	332.00	333.60	−10.90	887.00	332.00	16,309
Oct	343.00	348.00	339.00	340.70	−11.10	842.00	339.00	17,607
Dec	354.00	355.50	346.00	348.10	−11.30	666.50	346.00	10,587
Fb83	361.50	364.00	355.00	355.80	−11.50	642.00	355.00	17,746
Apr	370.00	370.50	361.50	363.70	−11.70	604.00	361.50	9,653
June	....	....	....	371.80	−11.90	596.00	379.00	2,012
Aug	386.00	386.00	380.00	379.90	−12.10	515.50	380.00	680
Oct	....	....	....	388.20	−12.30	500.00	392.00	566
Dec	....	....	....	396.50	−12.60	495.00	405.00	61
Est vol 70,000; vol Thu 52,274; open int 150,715, +629.								

Prices as of March 12, 1982. Prices quoted in commodities listing for gold futures contracts represents the per-ounce price. Multiply by 100 for the per-contract (100 troy ounces) prices.

The next two columns to the right show the high and low prices which have been paid for that same contract during its lifetime. Notice the tremendous trading range on the June contract, from a low of $324.50 to a high of $925. That means that a person who bought the contract at its low point would have made a vast profit on each contract.

Margin requirements. Obviously, these are big numbers for the average investor to consider. However, until very recently investors of modest means could take a risky fling in the commodities market with not much initial capital.

They did this by using the considerable margin brokerage firms were willing to extend on commodity contracts.

Because few contracts are actually delivered, the full value of the contract is rarely exchanged. Instead, the brokerage firm might have asked you, in the past, to put up only $800 to control a 100-ounce gold contract worth $30,000. If the contract gained $10 per ounce, using this leverage, your initial investment had the potential to double in a very short time. The opposite was also true: If the contract which you controlled for $800 lost $10 per ounce, your whole investment would have gone down the drain, and your broker would require a "maintenance" investment to sustain your position.

As markets have become more volatile, exchanges have increased the daily trading limits which serve to keep the commodity markets orderly. These limits govern all contracts except the one nearest to delivery. A $19 per day limit on gold meant that, once a given gold contract had sold at a price $10 higher or lower than the previous day's closing price, trading in this contract would be suspended until buyers and sellers agreed to resume trading within the $10 range, or until the end of the day.

Open interest. The one column in the commodity listing which may be confusing is the last one—"open interest." This does not tell you how many pairs of buyers and sellers exist in a given contract. Let's look at an example: On Monday, two people decide they want to buy March gold, and two want to sell. They arrive at their agreed prices and produce two open interests. On Tuesday, two more investors "go long" and two more "go short," and this produces a total of four open interests. On Wednesday, there are no new buyers or sellers. However, one of the original buyers decides he wants to liquidate his contract by selling, and one of the original sellers becomes his buyer. The open interest is now three.

The volume of all gold contracts sold on the Chicago Mercantile Exchange on this day is listed at the bottom of the tabulation, along with the previous day's volume, the total open interest, and the net change in open interest from the previous day. As you can see, commodities markets fluctuate drastically in volume.

As the change column reveals on this particular day gold contracts generally lost value, and by about the same amount. The later contracts lost slightly more.

Chapter Four

Economic Indicators: What They Mean

W hen a TV anchorman announces that housing starts are in the worst slump since the Commerce Department started keeping statistics in 1959, or that the Gross National Product in 1982 exceeded 0.0 trillion dollars. What does that mean to the average television viewer? Do these esoteric statistics have any real bearing on your life? Maybe so. Do you have any immediate point of reference with which to equate these ominous-sounding media pronouncements to your day-to-day existence?

Probably not. Economic indicators such as these are generally regarded as just more examples of bureaucratic list-making that have developed gradually over the years to label occurrences in the confusing world of business, but which mean relatively little in realistic terms. Actually, this isn't the case. These and similar indicators have a vital and immediate impact on almost every United States citizen (with the exception of the very rich and the very poor), regardless of his or her lifestyle, occupation, or standard of living.

The Dow Jones Averages

T he Dow Jones Industrial Average (DJIA) is undoubtedly the most often quoted and practically-used market average in the world. This is due, in part, to the fact that it has been around for so long. Charles Henry Dow, a business analyst and co-founder of the Dow Jones financial empire, first published the Index on July 3, 1884, in a two-page bulletin called *Customer's Afternoon Letter*. The average was comprised of 11 stocks, nine of which were railroad issues, the most prominent securities of the day.

Over the years, other stock market indices have come and gone, but the DJIA continues to reign supreme. Many people (market professionals and otherwise) cite the Standard & Poor's 500-Stock Index as much more representative of stock trends, and there are numerous other indices that vie for national prominence. But for whatever reason (and it is mostly emotional), the DJIA has retained its premier position in market analysis.

Although the DJIA is the most well-known, there are actually four Dow Jones Stock averages (not including the bond averages, which will not be treated here). They are the DJIA, the Dow Jones Transportation Index, the Dow Jones (Public) Utility Index, and the Dow Jones Composite 65-Stock Index (a combination of the other three).

The Dow Jones Industrials. Charles Dow's original 11 stocks became an occasional feature of *The Wall Street Journal* when the paper began publishing in 1889, and as time passed, many of the original stocks were dropped while others were added. The overall number of components increased with the growth in market volume and general business activity and now stands at 30 companies.

Efforts were made to include those issues that had a substantial market following. The index reached its present form (in size, method of calculation, and so on) in 1928.

Changes, of course, have continued over the years due to mergers, acquisitions, and other factors, although Dow Jones is extremely traditional in its thinking and tries to maintain continuity whenever possible. The last change in the DJIA occurred on June 29, 1979, when IBM and Merck were added, and Chrysler and Esmark (formerly Swift and Co.) were dropped.

The Transportation Average. Railroad stocks predominated in early Dow Jones listings, but the first average containing exclusively railroad stocks was published on October 26, 1896. Except for name changes, mergers, and the like, it remained an all-railroad index until January 2, 1970. It was this kind of stubborn sticking with tradition that often got the compilers of the Dow Jones Averages accused not only of hidebound and fuzzy-headed thinking, but of a Neanderthal approach to the realities of the marketplace.

Be that as it may, in January, 1970, the name was changed to the Transportation Average as airlines, and later freight forwarders, truckers, and mixed transportation companies were added. The index presently includes 20 stocks.

The last changes occured in 1980. On November 6, Seaboard Coast Line Industries was merged with the Chessie System, Inc., to become CSX Corporation, and Delta Air Lines was added. On December 1, the St. Louis-San Francisco Railway was merged into Burlington Northern, Inc., (already a component) and replaced by Ovenite Transportation Company.

The Public Utility Average. The Utility Average was first published in December of 1929, and consisted of 20 stocks. Five issues were dropped from the listing on June 2, 1938, and the total has remained at 15 ever since. In subsequent years, stocks of certain operating companies were substituted for those of holding companies. This was because the holding companies acquired other interests outside of the utility business or because they just became investment companies, with sales revenue being generated by the operating utility. As evidence of its traditionality, there has not been a new addition or deletion in the Utility Average in over ten years.

Just how good are the Dow Jones Averages in reflecting total market performance? Probably no better or no worse than the other major averages or indices. Dow Jones officials will admit that their averages are somewhat biased in favor of large, blue-chip companies, with huge capitalization and a long, solid track record. This is true, in contrast to the New York Stock Exchange Composite Index, which includes all Big Board issues and is therefore biased by its very nature in favor of the smaller companies.

The Transportation and Utility Indices are much more representative, obviously, of their market segments, and generally are an excellent barometer of what is happening in their areas. The DJIA's record is less precise, but one thing cannot be forgotten. The DJIA is an emotional, at times, almost Messianic, market indicator. When it is moving up, brokers and salesmen contact their customers pleading "You just can't miss out on this market!" or some such call to arms. In this way, the DJIA becomes almost a self-fulfilling prophecy—people buy because they're *supposed* to buy.

The components of all three averages are published every Monday in *The Wall Street Journal*, usually on the next-to-last page under the Dow Jones Charts.

Standard & Poor's 500-Stock Price Index

This market indicator was first introduced in January, 1981, with 200 securities representing 26 industry subgroups. Ten years later, S&P produced a different 90-stock index including 50 industrials, 20 railroad, and 20 public utility issues. The similarity to the Dow Jones Averages is obvious, not because of plagiarism, but because this organization of stocks realistically reflected market activity at that time.

The next major change did not occur until 1957, when the previous averages were abandoned in favor of the now-famous S&P 500 Index. At that time it contained 425 industrials, 25 rails, and 50 utilities. Because of recent attrition and mergers in the railroad industry and other factors, it now contains 400 industrials, 20 transportation stocks, 40 utilities, and 40 financial issues.

The S&P list does not comprise the 500 largest publicly-traded companies—much as the *Fortune* 500 does. The index is composed of 90 subgroups, representing the broad pattern of industries in this country. Some of these industry groups are characterized by companies of relatively small capitalization. Still, the total market value of the S&P 500 as of January 1, 1981, represented 76 percent of the aggregate market value of all stocks traded on the NYSE. A more recent figure has not been calculated, but the market value of the index has traditionally fluctuated between 75 and 78 percent of the aggregate market value of all Big Board issues.

One of the major advantages of using the industry group concepts is as a standard of comparison of the performance of individual stocks within each group. Standard & Poor's contends that care is taken to avoid the construction of a group index in which the movements of a single, dominant stock would determine the movements of the group index.

While the S&P Committee that is responsible for all additions and deletions from the Index is specifically charged with adhering to the basic principal of stability of composition and avoidance of excessive turnover, any market indicator that includes 500 stocks in today's volatile marketplace must always undergo regular revision.

Since it is a far more comprehensive index than the Dow Jones Averages, and has been around for about the same time, why haven't investors and professionals used it as a more definitive market indicator? Part of the answer has been the psychological impact of the Dow and the latter's wide distribution throughout certain influential media.

Many technical analysts, however, will promote and use the S&P 500 as a more useful market tool, and indeed, the company has considerably more research data on file than any of its competitors. One might describe it as the ultimate broad-based market tool in the hands of serious researchers looking for long-term investment opportunities vs. the more emotional barometer of the Dow, which invites more short-term trading and speculative possibilities. At the very least, the S&P 500 should be used by informed investors, in conjunction with other market indices, to determine courses of action.

The London Gold Fixing

Gold has been considered, since the earliest times, as the ultimate exchange medium between individuals, tribes, peoples, nations, and governments. The "science" of alchemy existed far beyond the Middle Ages and subsequent centuries to which it has been consigned by history. Even the recent extraordinary interest in gold prices—which saw the yellow metal travel from under $300 an ounce to over $850 and back to under $400 in less than two years—is deceptive.

The price volatility of the metal derives from two facts:

1. There is more or less equilibrium between the 45-million ounce annual world-wide mine production and the unpredictably variable 20 to 30 million ounce yearly consumption. Some of this gold consumption represents stockpiling by hoarders, investors, and central banks, but in any event, the difference between the "more" and "less" results in an uncertainty that gives rise to very volatile prices.

2. Although the world's gold bullion stocks are enormous (approximately 2.5 billion ounces), factors unrelated to mining supply or indus-

trial demand play an inordinately great role in the metal's day-to-day price. The most important of these causes are the impact of inflation, the depreciation of paper currency, and the instability of markets due to unpredictable events such as war, natural disaster, and the like.

In order to bring consistency to such a potentially uncertain market arena, the London Metal Market—at the behest of the Bank of England—established the London Gold Fixing in 1919.

Twice a day, at 10:30 A.M. London time (5:30 A.M. Eastern Standard Time here) and 3:00 P.M. (10:00 A.M. EST), five of the most influential broker/dealers in the metals market convene to establish the "morning" and "afternoon" London Fix. These world-renowned houses are: N.M. Rothschild & Sons, Mocatta & Goldsmid Ltd., Sharps, Pixley Ltd., Samuel Montague & Co., and Johnson Matthey Bankers.

1. The most important influence (as we have indicated) is on the spot price of gold—that is paid between dealers, or individuals and dealers, for the physical metal.

2. Also influenced is the price of gold futures, as traded on the Commodity Exchange in New York and the International Money Market of the Chicago Mercantile Exchange. There are many days when prices are "up" or "down the limit," meaning that the price has risen (or dropped) to such an extent that no trading can take place until the next day.

3. Gold-related stocks that trade on various exchanges are affected. Included among the widest-price swingers and volume leaders are Homestake Mining, ASA Ltd., Hecla Mining, Newmont Mining, Benquet Consolidated, Campbell Red Lake Mines on the New York and Dome Mines and Giant Yellowknife on the American Stock Exchange.

4. The price of other precious metals (either in the spot or futures market or in related stocks) such as silver, palladium, platinum, and so on, are affected by the gold fix.

Foreign Exchange Rate

This is defined as the price of a nation's unit of currency (money) in terms of that of another nation. Foreign exchange rates (FERs) directly affect the prices of foreign and American goods and services as well as the currency markets and commodities futures markets (where foreign currencies are traded). A knowledge of FERs helps Americans buy some foreign goods directly for cheaper prices since dollars can easily be converted into the proper currencies and payments made. It also affects the selling of American goods.

Exchange rates are important, therefore, because they are the vehicle that translates prices measured in one currency into prices measured in another. Changes in FERs that affect the prices of imports and exports will, as a result, influence the rate of inflation, export sales, and competition from imports. Similarly, FER changes affect international borrowers and lenders by changing the value, measured in one currency, of assets measured in another.

The movement of FERs will often make the difference between a profit and loss for international trades and investors. Wide fluctuations in FERs suggest a greater degree of risk; high risk, in turn, will either discourage people from entering into international transactions or cause prices to rise substantially.

In the long run, the underlying forces that determine the exchange rate between two currencies are supply and demand from commercial and financial transactions. This is influenced by the government's monetary policy and the private sector's attitude toward thrift, efficiency, and the work ethic. In the short term, however, supply and demand is most strongly influenced by the *expectations* about the direction in which the FER is likely to move. This more immediate effect will reflect the day-to-day or even moment-to-moment impact of favorable or adverse economic and political news.

One of the most obvious effects of FERs on Americans in recent years has been on travel abroad. When the dollar has been strong, Americans get more for their money when vacationing or conducting business overseas. When the dollar has been weak, it would have been better to stay home.

Balance of Trade

This is the difference between the value of the goods that a nation exports and the value of the goods that it imports. The balance of trade differs from the balance of payments in that the former excludes capital (money) transactions, payments for services, and shipments of gold. When the U.S. has a trade (export) surplus, the balance is favorable. When it has a trade deficit, the balance is unfavorable. The balance of trade concept is losing much of its usefulness because of the growing value of capital transactions and payments of services.

For example, in every year during the 1950s and 1960s, the U.S. enjoyed a surplus in its balance of trade but suffered an almost uninterrupted succession of deficits in its balance of payments. By 1971, both the balance of trade and the balance of payments were in deficit, and in December of that year, for the first time in modern history, the U.S. dollar was devalued relative to other currencies by order of President Nixon. It has been downhill ever since.

The balance of trade is intrinsically entwined with FERs (Foreign Exchange Rates). If the U.S., for example, has a balance of payment deficit, market forces will cause its FER to fall because dollars will pile up in the hands of others. Since the supply of dollars will be greater than the demand, the price of the dollar will fall, and the price of other currencies will rise. The opposite scenario occurs when the U.S. runs a trade surplus, and the dollar becomes stronger against other currencies.

The balance of trade and foreign exchange rates have such a direct bearing on each other that an examination of one will lead to an examination of the other. While the balance of trade is normally considered to be a rather esoteric economic indicator, it should be seriously considered by the average American, since it will *directly* and *immediately* affect his or her consumer purchases and sales, both here and abroad.

The Gross National Product

The GNP is the most comprehensive measure of a nation's total output of goods and services. In the United States, the GNP represents the dollar (or monetary) value of all goods and services produced for sale, plus the estimated value of certain "imputed outputs," that is, goods and services neither bought nor sold.

These "imputed outputs" include such things as farm products (like produce and livestock) consumed on the farm and not brought to market, the rental value of owner-occupied housing, and other factors. GNP is generally expressed over a set, given period of time, most often a quarter of a year. In 1980, it was $2,626,000,000,000 or 2 trillion, 626 billion dollars.

The GNP includes only the cost of final goods and services. For example, a shirt that costs the manufacturer $3.50, the retailer $7, and the customer $10, is counted as $10 in the GNP, the amount of the final sale, not $20.50, or the total of all the transactions.

The GNP may be calculated by adding either all expenditures on currently produced goods and services or all incomes earned in producing these goods and services. Calculated from the expenditure side, it is the sum of: 1. consumption expenditures by both individuals and non-profit organizations, plus certain imputed values; 2. business investment in equipment inventories, and new construction (residential as well as commercial); 3. federal, state, and local government purchases of goods and services; and 4. the sale of goods and services abroad (exports) less foreign purchases (imports).

From the income side, the GNP is the sum of all wages, interest, and profits before taxes and depreciation earned in the current production of goods and services.

GNP is a "gross" measure because no deductions are made for capital consumption allowances, or depreciation of the capital goods used in production. The indicator is a key measure of the overall performance of the economy and a gauge of the health of important sectors.

Used principally to compare national output from one year to the next, or decade to decade. GNP is considered to be the most comprehensive single barometer of a nation's overall economic well-being. It is also used to compare the contribution to the economy by various sectors (consumer, business, government) or various industries (auto, health services, construction).

The Consumer Price Index

The Consumer Price Index (CPI) is a monthly statistical measure of the average change in prices over time in a fixed market basket of goods and services. It is compiled by the Bureau of Labor Statistics (BLS) and is announced during the last week of the month for the preceding month. It was first published, interestingly enough, to help set new wage levels for workers in the ship-building industry in 1919.

Beginning with January, 1978, the BLS began publishing CPIs for two population groups: 1. a revised version of the traditional CPI for Urban Wage Earners (a misnomer that really means production workers) and Clerical Workers, which represents about 40 percent of the total non-institutional civilian population, and 2. a new CPI for all Urban Consumers that covers twice as many people, approximately 80 percent of the population.

One of the worst significant changes ever to be made in the CPI will occur in January, 1983, when a rental equivalence measure will replace the present complex formula based on home ownership. Critics have argued for years (with much merit) that the home ownership method was not representative and extremely more inflationary than necessary because a home purchase is usually a once-in-a-lifetime occurrence. This change will be made in the CPI for Urban Wage Earners in January, 1985. The reason for the two-year difference is that the latter index is used as the basis for most union negotiations, and the BLS wants to give all parties plenty of notice so that they can adjust their demands and bargaining positions accordingly.

The CPI is based on the prices of food, clothing, shelter, fuels, transportation fares, medical services, drugs, and other goods and services that people buy for day-to-day living. It includes approximately 400 items, from magazines and insurance to pet supplies and haircuts. All taxes directly associated with the purchase and use of the items are included. The Index is expressed as a percentage of average prices during the base year 1967. The U.S. Government uses 1967 as a reference year for almost all its price indices and statistical information. The BLS was in the process of changing this base year to a more realistic 1977, when the Reagan budget cuts were imposed last fall, and the government now says it does not have the funds necessary to implement the change (it was supposed to be made in January, 1982), and has not set a future date when it could be done.

The relative importance given individual items is based on periodic geographic surveys. Prices of goods, fuels, and a few other staples are obtained every month in 85 major urban areas. Prices of all other commodities and services are also collected every month in the five largest urban areas of the country (New York, Chicago, Los Angeles, Philadelphia, and Detroit) and every other month in 23 other major locations.

The quantity and quality of items measured is kept essentially unchanged between major revisions so that only price changes will be measured. This is extremely important since the CPI is used as an indicator of inflation to evaluate economic policy, as a deflator to adjust other economic indicators (such as the Gross National Product), and as a monitor of how well income payments keep up with the cost of living.

Of more importance to many individuals and unions in America is the third use of the CPI—to escalate income payments. Almost two-thirds of all major bargaining contracts now contain some kind of escalator clause (commonly referred to as COLAs, or cost-of-living adjustments). This often includes pensions as well as wages. In addition, the Index now affects the income of approximately 60 million other Americans, largely as a result of statutory action. This includes about 35 million people on social security, 3 million retired military and federal civil service employees and survivors, and well over 20 million food stamp recipients.

Also, the official poverty threshold estimate, which is the basis of eligibility in many health and welfare programs of federal, state, and local governments, is periodically updated vis-a-vis the CPI. Additionally, the "low income" standard under CETA provisions, which determines distribution of revenue-sharing funds, is kept current through adjustment to the CPI.

Finally, escalator clauses in an increasing number of rental, royalty, and child support agreements automatically increase payments to an undetermined number of people. It is obvious, then, that the CPI is probably the most important of all the economic indicators we are discussing, at least in terms of the number of people affected and the immediate impact on their personal lives.

Despite any drawback, however, the CPI is very useful in determining not only price changes in individual products, but also changes in real income (the purchasing power of the dollar). In short, it fills the needs of many different users and is the nation's principal measure of price change, probably the most important statistic affecting most Americans

The Minimum Wage

The Fair Labor Standards Act of 1938 established minimum wages, overtime pay, recordkeeping practices, and child labor standards that today affect well over 50 million full-time and part-time workers in the United States. According to the latest amendments to the Act passed in 1977, it has risen on January 1, of the last four years to the following: 1978—$2.65; 1979—$2.90; 1980—$3.10; and 1981—$3.35.

In order for it to increase sometime in the future, further legislation would be required by Congress. Presently, overtime of at least 1 1/2 times the employee's regular pay rate is due after each 40 hours of work in a week. Additionally, an employer may consider tips as part of wages, but such a wage credit may not exceed 40 percent of the minimum wage. There are some exceptions to the minimum wage. Part-time students under certain circumstances can obtain a youth differential. The whole question of a reduced rate for teenagers is under intense study in Washington. One recommended plan with considerable support would allow younger people to work below the minimum scale for a six-month period before requiring an increase to $3.35. Mayor Koch of New York City (with probably the greatest number of unemployed teenagers in the country) has proposed a specific decrease to $2.50.

In addition to students and teenagers, so-called "sheltered workshops" for handicapped workers may get permission for a wage differential. However, they must get certification for this from the Department of Labor, and this is very difficult to do since the department actively discourages the practice.

The question of the minimum wage is intricately bound up with the whole subject of the Employment Rate, inflation, etc. To take an example, an increase in the minimum wage can decrease marginal employment (especially by the non-skilled) as employers find that they just can't afford to pay certain workers a wage they feel is too much for certain tasks. At the same time, an increase can lead to rising inflation as higher wages are translated into higher prices for goods and services. This would be reflected in a rising Unemployment Rate, Consumer Price Index, and so on.

Employment/Unemployment Rates and Compensation

According to the Department of Labor, employed persons include: 1. all civilians who worked for pay or profit, or for 15 hours or more without pay in a family business or farm, and 2. those who were not working, but were temporarily absent from jobs because of illness, bad weather, vacation, labor management dispute, or for various personal reasons. The civilian labor force consists of all those not in active military service.

Persons not in the labor force include retirees, homemakers, students, those unable to work because of long-term illness, seasonal workers not looking for work in an "off-season," those discouraged from seeking work because of personal or job market circumstances, and the voluntarily idle.

Full-time workers are those employed at least 35 hours a week. Workers on part-time schedules for economic reasons (such as slack work, terminating or starting a job during the week, material shortages, or inability to find full-time work) are counted as being on full-time status, under the assumption that they would be working full-time if conditions permitted. Persons working at more than one job (about five percent of the population) are counted at their primary occupation.

Total employment is measured each month by Current Population Surveys (CPS) conducted for the Labor Department by the U.S. Bureau of the Census. CPS measures people 16 years of age or older, available for work during the calendar week including the 12th of each month. A series of personal interviews is undertaken in 629 areas comprising 1133 counties and cities in all 50 states and the District of Columbia. It includes some 60,000 housing units including over 135,000 people 16 or older. Although these surveys have nothing to do with the decennial census, from time to time adjustments are made to the CPS figures to correct estimating errors made during the preceding years. The Bureau also compiles payroll data, civilian employment figures for all non-agricultural businesses, excluding sole proprietors, the self-employed, and servants.

Unemployment insurance (UI) coverage for those out of work varies considerably from state to state. All requirements concerning who qualifies, waiting periods, maximum and minimum coverage, duration of coverage, and all other relevant factors are determined by the individual states. UI in each case is funded solely by the employers in each jurisdiction, while the cost of administering the program is borne by the Department of Labor.

Although the unemployment rate is thought of most as a very *personal* economic fact of life (are you out of work?), it is also extremely useful as a measure of the cyclical performance of the economy. The main reason that the unemployment rate and the national income are useful statistics is that they serve to measure changes over time. They are also useful in measuring the relative economic performance among different nations.

Housing Starts

A housing start is defined by the Department of Commerce as the beginning of construction of a new residential unit for housekeeping (no commercial buildings allowed), usually counted when excavation for the foundation has been done.

Representatives of the Bureau of the Census, the agency that compiles this statistic, estimate the number of starts on the basis of building permits issued each month for housing units, as adjusted for the time lag that occurs between the issuance of the permit and the actual start of construction. Apartment buildings are counted per their number of "dwellings units," so that a high-rise structure with 500 units is, in reality, 500 housing starts.

The Bureau makes surveys to determine the pattern of these time lags and the number of construction projects that are canceled after permits have been issued. However, an examination of random reports during various months reveals not only a great deal of variance as to what is projected and what actually occurs, but also as to the margin of error in what the final statistics report.

For example, the "average relative standard error percentage" for new housing units for one month recently, showed a "preliminary margin of error" of between four and 20 percent, and a "revised margin of error" of four to 17 percent. We say "between" because housing starts are broken down into many categories, including publicly-owned units, privately owned dwellings, (depending on the number of units), by condominium and townhouse ownership, mobile homes, geographic area, and the like.

Notwithstanding this analysis, Housing Starts statistics are viewed with great authority by those in the construction industry (whether they be general contractors, plumbers, electricians, or carpenters) and to a lesser extent, by those consumers wishing to buy or sell a new or used home. The main reason is that, for lack of a more precise indicator, no developer, worker, owner, or prospective homebuyer can get a better handle on what is happening in the housing market in his section of the country.

Chapter Five

Finding the Right Broker

Most people exercise great care in choosing their doctors, lawyers, dentists, accountants, or even their barbers or beauticians. Yet, when it comes to selecting a broker or investment adviser, most individuals use no more discretion than they would in picking a tailor, a laundress, or a gardener. The potential loss, however, from the failure to select an effective broker is far more devastating than whether your suit is properly pressed, or your bedsheets are pearly white, or if the tulips in your garden burst forth in color every spring.

If you have a good broker, it's likely your income will increase. If you have a mediocre broker, chances are you will win some, lose the rest, and watch your investment money being slowly whittled away. If you have the misfortune of linking yourself with a bad broker, you will have the agony of watching the decimal point on that line of zeros in your "portfolio value" column move quickly to the left, until all that remains is a solid line of zeros.

So the given element in investing is the need for a good broker; the fear element in investing is that even the best-intentioned broker may be inept enough to slaughter your savings—with or without the dubious achievement of lowering your tax bracket—and the question is this: How on earth do you choose a capable broker?

To answer that question, we offer a series of effective criteria for the right brokerage house and representative to handle your needs.

Initial Criteria for Choosing a Broker

Briefly, let's review some considerations of what any prospective investor should seek from his broker:

1. Image of the firm: Even though the client/broker relationship becomes personalized as it develops, the progression of the relationship after the initial contact may depend on the reputation and the resources of the broker's firm. The public does "buy brand names," and this is just as true when choosing a brokerage firm as when selecting a blender or a pair of blue jeans. A firm that has a proven (and well-advertised) reputation for stability, financial solidarity, and high business ethics will receive easier acceptance.

2. Management: Two important factors in the evaluation process of a potential brokerage house are the quality, depth of knowledge, and the background of its management, as well as the commitment of higher management to financial excellence. There are firms who claim they are dedicated to financial planning, but in reality they have a definite product bias. No one product or investment vehicle can be the solution to every problem confronting prospective investors. They must have access to a wide variety of choices.

The only constant factor in the brokerage business is that it changes continuously. An investor must seek to be aligned with a far-sighted firm that is both sensitive and responsive to changes. Management must include experienced individuals with a reputation for integrity and innovation. In short, the relationship between the broker and the customer must be open and forthright; characterized by a mutual desire to initiate courses of action that benefit the client first, and the broker secondarily.

It is of prime importance for both the investor and the broker to learn about the personal and professional backgrounds of each other. The caliber, philosophy, and capabilities of top management will directly affect broker performance.

Both parties must understand what will be expected from each other. It is imperative that the client ask questions about business philosophies, backgrounds, and future intentions of the brokerage. But be aware that it is human nature for brokers to be supportive of the organizations and to laud its capabilities and potential. So, while listening, you have to be discerning enough to separate the facts from the fantasies.

3. Training: A quality firm recognized the need for putting in time, talents, and capital into continuous training for its personnel. The training curriculum must be well organized, encompassing every aspect of the financial services industry, and be competently conducted. It must originate with an orientation and familiarization program designed to acquaint the broker with new products and ideas, as well as the different capabilities the firm has in the area of the planner's expertise. Don't be reluctant to ask a prospective broker how much experience he has, and what kind of training the firm provides in new products and new investment techniques.

4. Product (type of investment) Selection: Some brokerages do a minimal amount of review in their selections process while others conduct intensive and extensive research ranging from projected financial data to qualitative evaluation of the principals. The better brokerage firms pride themselves on this facet of their business and are anxious to demonstrate their capabilities to the client.

The most diverse product line is of little benefit to anyone if the investments selected are fraught with legal or economic peril. It is difficult for brokers to maintain their clientele and build a solid business by selling product just for the sake of a sale.

In the matter of tax shelters, for example, which are the most perilous investment vehicles with regard to due diligence, extreme caution must be taken to ensure that the various shelters chosen for sale by the firm have been thoroughly investigated. Some firms sell all manner of tax shelters, and customers cannot be certain they are not dealing with an undercapitalized, or fraudulent investment vehicle. Don't be reluctant to inquire as to what efforts the firm makes to check every aspect of every investment for the protection of the clientele. And if an investment, like a tax shelter or commodity position, begins to go sour, find out what process the firm has to sound an early warning so that investors can bail out before their losses become too serious.

Some Specific Steps

In selecting a broker initially and evaluating his performance, a customer would be smart to follow these guidelines:

1. Start with your other financial advisers—your attorney, accountant, tax preparer, etc. If you have a long-term relationship with them, you will probably get some good advice on brokerages to consider.

2. Investment philosophies must be compatible to your needs and lifestyle. If the broker is a wheeler-dealer trader, who usually speculates, while you are a conservative investor who is interested only in blue-chips, you are going to have a problem. You must be comfortable with your investment adviser; the relationship must be personal to a certain extent. But above all, he should be in tune with what you are looking for in your investment portfolio.

3. Continually review your broker's performance, but by the same token, give him a chance. He will not be right every time, but he needs time to establish a track record. How do you evaluate results? Well, in a bad market your stocks may go down, but did they decline less than the market in general? That is a good sign. However, if they went down more than the market averages, you're in for stormy weather.

It is not so easy to recognize your broker's effectiveness in a bull market. Your stocks may be going up, but are they going up as fast as the market averages? If not, your broker is underperforming the market—and that's not a healthy sign. On the plus side of the ledger, if your portfolio is achieving better results than the average, you've got a winner.

4. How long should an evaluation period be? Obviously, if a broker starts losing money for you from the start don't stick around long enough to find out if he's going to win the "comeback of the year" award. A reasonable approach is to let him go through one full market cycle, which would encompass at least one up and one down market. A generally accepted benchmark is that any broker whose performance resulted in a loss of 25 percent or more of your assets should not be retained. Keep in mind that a good broker will not keep you in the market all the time. In an uncertain market, he will have you sitting on the sidelines, with your cash gaining interest in a money market fund.

5. Finally, the client should focus his attention on total portfolio results. Individual issues should be ignored when reviewing performance. Investors have a tendency to focus on problem issues rather than the aggregate results because every portfolio will have some mistakes. The results of a total portfolio, or the "bottom line," should be calculated quarterly. Percentage changes should be compared with Standard & Poor's 500 Stock Index for the month, year-to-date, since the inception of the account. Frequent comparisons are useful in recognizing the formation of dangerous trends. Cumulative losses in excess of 15 percent in a few months period should alert the client to the possibility of larger losses later.

Long-term results should be calculated on a compounded rate-of-return basis. A reasonable rate of return over several years is accepted as 1.2 times the 90-day Treasury bill rate for the period measured. Expressed another way, a 12-15 percent compounded rate, or any rate that actually beats the rate of inflation, is considered a very respectable performance.

Choose Brokerage House First

First, there is the choice of a brokerage house to be made. Within each firm, there are good, bad, and indifferent brokers (some firms call them customers' men, registered representatives, brokers, or account executives). The man or woman is important; so is the firm. The wrong firm can snarl up your orders and your accounting of holdings so badly that it nearly takes a court order or a CPA audit to get things straight.

To find the best broker (another person's tastes and financial outlook will be different from yours, so well-meant advice from friends is not always the thing to go by), consider this question:

Do I want a giant firm, or will I do better trading with a regional or local brokerage house?

The giant firm has gigantic facilities. This *may* mean better and quicker executions for you, but not necessarily. Big is not always the same as efficient. Efficiency comes from both large and small brokerage houses. Big *does* mean that the brokerage can employ research specialists in more fields than the regional firm. It doesn't mean better research, however, for frequently, the size of a big national house precludes its making buy or sell recommendations in stocks or bonds of smaller companies lest the large number of people who follow those recommendations cause an unnatural run-up or run-down in the security.

The conventional brokerage firm renders a variety of useful services. It will advise you (but you'll have to be discerning enough to evaluate that advice). It will hold your securities for you, but this is less a service to you than a benefit to the firm since those securities are counted in its balance sheet for meeting the SEC's minimum debt-to-capital ratios. It will send your dividends and clip your coupons, or hold these in your account pending your instructions (thus getting the interest-free use of your money).

Although they also benefit the brokerage firm, these services do help small investors, as well, if they don't want to take the trouble of maintaining a safe deposit box or depositing checks for interest and/or dividends.

A regional house frequently specializes in securities of firms that reside in or serve its area. The brokerage research people can get on closer, first-name terms with corporate executives. But the disadvantage is that few regional firms have that sort of relationship with the big, national companies.

It is therefore, the *quality* of the research that most often uncovers the best buys.

Types of Research

A n investor should be aware that there are two basic kinds of research offered by brokerage houses. The first is called fundamental. It consists of a research analyst studying all the facts about a company—its incoming orders picture, its products both under manufacture and in development—and, after adding the spice of hopefully well-informed conjecture about the coming state of the overall economy and of the industry under study, deciding whether a stock or bond is a buy, a sell, or a hold.

The second kind of research—technical analysis—seems esoteric, but it is highly useful. It is usually done by means of charts and increasingly with the help of computers. Its aim is to study the internal market conditions for an investment—what the trend of price fluctuations tells a technical analyst about the state of demand and supply. This kind of study is more complicated.

Within brokerage houses are found honest (the majority) and dishonest (fortunately a minority) individual brokers. Some brokers give out only their firm's recommendations. That is a safe (for them) procedure, since any losses can be blamed on the firm's research people. Other brokers—there are fewer of these—like to recommend favorites of their own along with, or even instead of, the company's. Regarding this group, MONEY MAKER recommends a broker who asks the correct—as opposed to standard—questions of a new investor. But what are the questions that a broker who can make money for you asks?

For openers: (1) What are your real values, and which goal do you want to achieve first; (2) How much money do you have; (3) What would happen if it all went down the sewer through what I recommend; (4) What would happen if you invested it in 11 percent municipal bonds; (5) What kind of a life style do you want; (6) What's your physical condition; (7) How much do you earn a year; (8) What tax bracket are you in; (9) How many children do you have to send to college and do you have alimony payments to make; (10) How much life insurance do you have?

Discount Brokers

D iscount brokers came into existence on May 1, 1975, when fixed commission rates were abolished by the Securities & Exchange Commission. Since that date, approximately 150 national and regional discount firms have sprung up around the country. More than 20 of these are now members of the New York Stock Exchange.

Just like other broker/dealers, discount firms base their commissions on the number of shares traded and the price of the stock involved. Similarly, those firms that deal in options (and not all do), base their charges on the prices of the options and the number of contracts traded. With regard to bonds, it is the price of the bond and the number traded. If you are interested in commodities, tax shelters, and other so-called "exotic" investments, a discounter is not for you since they don't handle such investments.

Some have flat rate per share—usually about 12.5 cents—with bigger discounts for larger orders. Since the brokerage business has become highly competitive in the last few years, many discounters are willing to "work with clients" to arrange higher discounts based on the volume of business transacted. Major investment firms will not offer this advantage if you are a small fish in a big pond, but discounters, who are beating the bushes for new clients, will.

As with full-line investment houses, whether they are members of an exchange or not, discount brokers are covered by SIPC (Securities Investors Protection Corporation) insurance. Accounts are insured up to a value of $500,000, which can include $100,000 cash in the event that the brokerage firms fails. However, there has been no significant failure of any discount broker in the seven-year history of this facet of the brokerage industry.

Today, discount firms offer savings of from 25 percent in commission to, in some rare cases, 90 percent for big customers, with an average savings of about 45-55 percent. Discounters account for 10-15 percent of all New York Stock Exchange trading volume, and this percentage is increasing.

When should you use a discount broker? Basically, the decision depends on what type of service you require. If you make all your own investment decisions and need no advice on buy or sell recommendations but just want someone to execute your orders—you should consider the discount broker. If you need, or would like, investment guidance, research reports or other information, and services available only through a full-line investment firm—then the discounter may not be the answer.

This does not imply that the discounter will not advise you at all; they will give you quotes, general advice, and specific information that has come across the ticker. Some, such as PARR Securities Corporation in New York, will keep you on the phone while they get specific quotes from the floor, execute your orders, and relay the sale and commission figures to you.

But discounters are not in the business of portfolio analysis, and they cannot discuss your particular investment aims and objectives, or advise you on personal financial management.

Questions To Ask Broker

When you believe you've found the right broker, here are some questions *you* should ask: (1) Have you made money in your investments in the last year and would you send me a record of your personal trades; (2) What specific facts about this particular investment lead you to believe it will go up; (3) If it goes up, at what point should we sell; (4) How long do you expect it to take to go up that much; (5) And again, if it goes down, at what point will you believe that you were wrong and recommend selling?

You see, the broker is touting you on a stock that's going to go up, right? And if it does, fine. But if it goes down, how far down should he let it go? Has he even considered that possibility? If he doesn't give you an absolutely specific answer, and a firm one, to the question of exactly where you should sell to cut your losses, you had better cut him off. Otherwise, when it goes down, he might tell you to buy some more and get it even cheaper.

Once you get the answers to these questions, you will still have to decide for yourself. You have to weigh each answer to see whether they make sense and add up. Ask yourself—once you look into things yourself—whether the investment really will appreciate.

The best kind of adviser is the individual who has no set philosophy at all, but is guided by a policy that is suited to the times and his client's needs, and who possesses a willingness to change as circumstances do.

Two examples of the broker who does not change viewpoints and recommendations when they need to be changed are exemplified by separate executives working in different cities. Both favored the Real Estate Investment Trusts when those were riding high in the early 1970s, and favored them right down to zero in some cases because of an inability or unwillingness to perceive changed conditions.

Will the broker give you the names of other investors who have done well with him? Better still—will he let you choose a few names at random from his records?

Don't let the broker get you on the defensive by asking more than the needed queries. Put him in the position of proving *his* abilities by being the questioner.

What Brokers Say—And What They Mean

How do you spot a winner other than through questioning? The first thing in spotting winners is to eliminate the losers. There are three key questions by which you can spot the broker who will make you a loser. The first question is: "What are your investment goals?" A variation is: "What would you like from investing?"

What is the broker really saying? What does he mean?

Put simply, we all want to make money from investing. So what is the broker really asking? He's asking you what your fantasies are. Since he already knows what your goals are—what everyone's goals are—what he's actually doing is playing into your dreams of glory, your illusions. He's setting you up. Everyone welcomes a chance to talk about what they'd ideally want, and if somehow that can be anchored to reality—wow!

A second type of statement which a broker—or anyone who wants you to blindly invest in something—will make is: "We only want you to invest risk capital." That's what the broker is saying. But here's what he means: "How much have you got?" Or, more exactly, "How much are you willing to lose?" A person who makes this kind of statement to you is thinking of anything but protecting you. He can always say later that he told you only to risk what you didn't need.

What's the alternative to this statement? "We want you to invest what you need for emergencies and to live on." At face value this is totally nonsensical. But the broker's doing something else, too. He's intimidating you, subtly. Just as a minute ago he was playing into your fantasies, now he's playing into your pride. Partly because of the myth that you've got to be fairly wealthy to make money investing, and partly out of false pride, people who call up a broker wanting to put in $700, may answer with two or three times that much. And lose it.

The third statement the broker makes which can cause problems for you, goes something like, "I'm conservative when it comes to investing," or "We favor conservative investments—don't you?" Does the term "conservative" really tell you what he'll do with your money? Does it literally mean he prefers to put you in the institutional, venerable stocks? If that's the case, run from him like the plague. Those have gone down, or at least underperformed against the market, for years now. Maybe he means that he wants to take your money and invest in in the best municipal, tax-free bonds? No way. That would be one commission for him and one commission only, while you sit with those bonds in the safety deposit box and draw the interest. A broker could never make a living that way, and besides, you don't need him to buy bonds.

So what does conservative mean? The answer is that it means nothing. But the implications of the word "conservative" are many. It's the closest word to "sure thing." The broker can't say "sure thing," because the SEC won't let him. So he uses this next best word to make you feel emotionally that, although you're in the market to make money and that's what it's all about, somehow what he'll do will involve little or no risk. Great gain with almost no risk—that's what he wants you to feel when he says "conservative" or words to that effect.

There's no limit to the evasive language a broker will use to try to sell you something. They'll appeal to your emotions, and the only way you can check them out is to make them translate the emotional into the tangible.

Here are a few key phrases which can help you spot a potential loser:

Special situation—What's special about it? Is he the only broker who knows about it? Do the other 1000 brokers in his firm know about it? Is that special? Again, it's obviously special to the brokerage firm. They're not going to push a stock or commodity or whatever on which they'd make less money than usual. You never want any special situations. You want real ones.

Candidate for a takeover—This is used to describe companies which, in the magical and mysterious world of mergers, you will automatically think are on some most desired list because "everyone's fighting to take them over." Though this happens once in a while, the chances are slim that you'll hear about it from your broker. In the case of so-called takeover candidates, what he really should be saying is: "You've got a lousy stock, selling at $6. No one has seen the Board of Directors for five months (except at their country clubs), but because they own a lot of machinery, some other company with good management might come in and try to revive it—if they can get the stock at $3 a share."

Even if the broker is playing it straight, the takeover game is a real crapshoot—an investment you want to stay away from. But let's say it is good—or rather, was—because do you think the broker was the first one to hear of it? And once he's heard of it, don't you think he's going to get in before he gets you in? So in those unusual instances where a company is a real candidate for a profitable takeover, the profit has already been taken out by those on the inside.

Inside information—And speaking of "inside," this is one of the most used and most meaningless words in the broker's language. First, the chances are overwhelming that he doesn't have inside information. Let's say that he does—again, do you think he's going to give it to you? Not until he's made every penny he can out of it by buying in, and not before telling those to buy in who can return the favor in kind some day if it goes up. So, on those rare occasions when the broker really is on the inside, that's where he is. You are still on the outside.

Fashionable words, from "growth" to "gambling stocks"—First, last, and always, the broker is a salesman—and sometimes the best way to sell you something is to tie it in with a current trend that's capturing everyone's imagination. "Growth" was one that lasted a long time and is still used. You'll hear brokers start off with, "This is a great growth company."

Well, once you're sure it's a good growth company, it's probably no longer growing much. Take McDonald's as an example. They opened a fast-food chain and the growth was 200 percent in one year. The next year they opened even more franchises. Finally, they had thousands of restaurants and you can't have that much growth forever. There are only so many towns, so many streets. So the word "growth" by itself—unless you develop new products or new markets—really means problems.

Another fashionable word which a lot of people sank money into and which then sank, was "technological"—particularly anything that ended with "-tronics." If a new issue came out called Something-tronics, there was a period when it would be bought up almost overnight. It didn't matter if the company was in the computer field where there were already 10,000 companies competing. It was a fashionable key word—or actually, half-word.

It'll come back—Obviously the most dangerous time for you, except when you get into the wrong investment in the first place, is when it goes down. It was supposed to go up, wasn't it? It's time to get out—unless you have set a certain number which the stock or whatever has to hit on the down side before you'll sell. But when you call the broker, is he going to tell you to sell? Chances are overwhelmingly against it, for two reasons. First, he's got to protect himself legally, and protect his reputation. He's the one who said it would go up: obviously, he didn't think it would go down and therefore tell you to buy it; so he in all likelihood would stick with what he said and advise you to keep the stock. Just about the only way he can get out of it is for you to say something—like you need the money right then and there—which allows him a loophole.

But secondly, he really doesn't know any better. Maybe he thinks it will go up again. Since chances are he had no good reason to think it would go up in the first place, a good reason such as the fact that it's gone down isn't going to change his mind much. He's human and would rather not admit he's wrong. Sure, he may like to get you out of one stock and into another quickly because of the commission—but you won't go on paying him a lot of commissions if you keep getting out with losses, will you?

Other Cautionary Clues

Beware of the broker who is a "churner." This is the Wall Street term for generating extra commissions by too many buy and sell orders. There is no practical, hard and fast way to tell if an account is being churned. The broker may have a good reason for advising the sale of a security whose purchase he had recommended only two weeks ago. But such transactions should not number many, and if an investor even suspects that his/her account is being turned over in order to generate commissions for a broker's benefit, the investor should immediately transfer the account elsewhere. In addition to the lure of the churner, one should beware of offerings that come "net without commission." These often hide a sizable mark-up. And they apply only to new or secondary offerings the broker wants to push.

Inquire about how much the broker tries to get investors to employ "leverage." Leverage is the use of margin and/or options to increase the opportunities for money-making. These are not inherently bad practices; just remember that in using leverge you are increasing your opportunities by a degree comparable to the opportunity for loss and that you are increasing the broker's share of the firm's commissions. The broker wins whether you do or not. Keep those facts in mind and then judge as best you can whether leverage is recommended for your good or his gain. Think also in terms of whether you are the kind of person who can preserve his/her contentment and cool when fluctuations occur—as they will.

You will, of course, pay interest on all the amounts you borrow through a margin account. The interest rate is determined by the "broker call rate"—the rate banks charge brokerage firms for money lent—and this rate rises and falls with the prime rate. The brokerage firm charges you, the customer, two or three percent above the broker call rate for the privilege of loaning you money with which to buy more stock. (Don't kid yourself; brokerage firms are in the lending as well as selling business.)

As the prime rate has reached record levels and kept right on rising in the past year, many investors have had to rethink the logic of margin accounts. Not only have margin rates hit record highs of 23-24 percent interest; it is impossible for the customer to know what rate he will be paying. Here is a record of rates paid by one margin account during a particular frantic period of 1980, when rates were rising almost daily:

November 16	17%
November 17	17¼%
November 18	18¼%
November 19-27	18¾%
November 28-December 4	19½%
December 5-15	21%

December 16-17	22%
December 18-22	23%

When you open a brokerage account, the person behind the cluttered desk will ask you certain questions. Know which questions are required by various federal, industrial, and sometimes state bodies under something called "Know Your Customer." They are in the rule books of the firms themselves. The aim is to help you and to avoid putting you into investments which are not suited to your circumstances and/or your investing objectives. But from the answers the broker can learn—if he or she is a perceptive and scrupulous person—much information that is useful to him/herself as well.

One trend you might note and take advantage of: Most brokers are still basically stockbrokers. That is all they know about and care to sell. However, a few have taken interest in providing a full range of financial services for their clients. This includes commodities, options, mutual funds, tax shelters, and even life insurance. Since most tax shelters must be bought through licensed securities dealers, it is a convenience to buy them through the same brokerage house which has your stock account. In many cases, the life insurance offered by stockbrokers is cheaper than that offered through full-time insurance agents.

What does a broker have to do in order to qualify legally as a publicly perceived expert? Usually a brokerage house will give six months training at first. Part of that time is served in New York, actually working on the floor of the stock exchange, learning the ropes and observing market operations—the total mechanics of the brokerage business. Basically, trainees are instructed to follow company recommendations for a number of reasons. Then the trainee has to pass the N.A.S.D. (National Association of Securities Dealers) test and the New York Stock Exchange exam. All brokers have to be registered with the Securities and Exchange Commission and comply with any individual state requirements. If the company is then satisfied, they'll give the new broker permanent status.

The directory of SEC Registered Investment Advisers (annual) published by the Source Securities Corporation in New York City, is a good research tool. For further information (not advice or tips) regarding any firm you plan to do business with, there is a toll-free number for inquiries: (800) 424-9839; Alaska and Hawaii call (800) 424-9707; Washington, D.C. residents can call (202) 254-7837.

Chapter Six

The Stock Market & How It Works

G iven the queasy state of the nation's economy as it stumbled through the first quarter of 1982, the pervasive atmosphere of nervous uncertainty prevailing in the stock market was completely understandable. Most economists not affiliated with the Reagan Administration were sharply critical of the President's policies, despite the fact that inflation was slowly abating.

The price (ten million unemployed) was considered much too high—at least, as far as economists without a Republican axe to grind were concerned. They blamed Reaganomics, the tight money policies of the Federal Reserve Board, the shifting (or nonexistent) policies of the Administration, the worldwide economic uncertainty, the baffling arithmetic of a massive military buildup on the heels of a tax cut and in the face of $100 billion-plus anticipated federal deficits, and a growing lack of confidence throughout the American populace that "Our Man in the White House" is on the right track or, for that matter, even knows what he's doing.

The growing belief that Ronald Reagan is, after all, out of his depth—campaigning against budget deficits and then creating the largest deficits the nation has ever seen—has the stock market as skittish as a new colt. Why, then, should anybody want to become involved in the anxious auction at the corner of Broad and Wall Streets in New York?

Actually, there are many good reasons. For one, the stock market remains the most popular investment arena among the widest number of Americans. For another, even in the worst of markets—and 1981 was a bad year—those who pick the right stocks, bucking the general trend, still make money. And even in a market that is bumping down a long flight of stairs, hefty profits can be made.

But mainly, the deadly fascination of the Wall Street game is simply too great for most investors to resist.

Life After the Fall

The great stock market crash of 1929, which preceded the Depression of the 1930s and led, by circuitous routes, to the election of Franklin D. Roosevelt and the New Deal, seems to have been forgotten by all but those who lived through it. At the depth of the Depression, 17 million workers were idle. Today, some ten million are unemployed. In the 1930s, banks were failing, unable to meet their obligations. Today, savings and loans are struggling to keep from going under, merging with sounder institutions in an effort to keep their facilities operational.

In the 1930s, Roosevelt and his New Deal rescued the nation from total disaster, regardless of revisionist views today. Who will save the economy now? Roosevelt closed the banks until legislation could be passed that would enable them to become profitable again. He created a Works Progress Administration so that the jobless could be put to work building roads, bridges, public schools, post offices, and other useful projects. For this he has since been condemned—and one criticism, that he was essentially a dictator, if benign, is accurate enough—and Wall Street has never forgiven him for rescuing it from its own excesses.

Reagan's approach is somewhat different, a variation on handing the country over to its biggest businesses in an effort to re-stimulate it, but Wall Street isn't taking a particularly favorable view of him, either. In fact, almost every time he makes a new economic announcement, the market falls, hard.

While the final word has yet to be written on Ronald Reagan's influence, Roosevelt's works remain in a variety of forms. One of the most effective innovations of his tenure was the Securities and Exchange Act of 1934, which put an end to the dishonest practices of brokers which had helped bring about the 1929 crash. Today, the Securities and Exchange Commission (SEC) is one of the most effective agencies in Washington, charged with protecting the interests of investors, large and small.

Ten years ago, its hand was strengthened by the creation of the Securities Investor Protection Corporation (SIPC), a nonprofit organization supported by member firms. Your investments in the stock market are now protected fully up to as much as $500,000 by some brokerages—worries about the consequences of a crash are, to a large degree, no longer necessary. In fact, your money on deposit with a broker is now safe, even if the brokerage fails.

Tangible Benefits

The SEC and its godchild, the SIPC, are only two of the long-term benefits of the New Deal. The Glass-Steagall Act of 1933, which regulates banking practices, was a third. The Federal Deposit Insurance Corporation, which guarantees payment of your bank deposits, was another.

The point is this: Largely as a result of New Deal legislation passed in the 1930s, the money you deposit in a bank or leave with a broker is protected.

This is only important because more and more people are drawing analogies between the 1920s and 1930s and current events. It gives them confidence to know that only the outright bankruptcy of a bank or brokerage will cost a portion of their deposited funds. But with an eye toward a real crash in the market, or toward a deepening depression that might wipe out businesses, people are avoiding the stock market—if the company in which you own stock goes bankrupt, you, as a partial owner, don't get a thing out of it.

Yet the stock market is a valid investment arena, especially now. There is plenty of risk, of course, especially in a troubled economy, but an intelligent approach, tailored to your goals and needs, can pay off handsomely.

How the Market Functions

Publicly-owned companies must register with the SEC before they offer stock for sale, providing detailed information concerning their businesses, their officers, and their assets and liabilities. This information is published by the SEC in the form of a prospectus.

However, the prospectus may be difficult to understand—it is couched in technical language that may force you to seek the advice of a professional investment adviser to guide you in making your decisions as to which stocks to buy and sell.

To most people, "the stock market" means the New York Stock Exchange, located at Broad and Wall Streets in the heart of New York's financial district, accurately considered the financial capital of the United States. However, there are many other regional exchanges along with the American Stock Exchange (Amex) in New York and the flourishing over-the-counter (OTC) market.

In fact, there are now more than 3000 stocks traded on the OTC market, listed on the National Association of Securities Dealers Automated Quotations System—the NASDAQ—which is more than the total number of stocks listed on the NYSE and Amex combined. In its 11th year, the NASDAQ System is booming, and the low-priced issues it lists are definitely worth consideration.

The New York Stock Exchange, or Big Board, as it is called, remains the most prestigious of the stock markets. Accordingly, its requirements for membership are stiffer than those of the Amex or the regional exchanges. To be listed on the Big Board, a company must have at least one million shares "outstanding" (available to the public). It must be owned by no fewer than 2000 individual shareholders who own a minimum of 100 shares apiece. It must have made a pre-tax profit of more than $2.5 million in its most recent year, and the pre-tax profit for the two preceding years must have been over two million dollars. The Amex also has requirements, as do the regional exchanges, but there are no such restrictions for stocks traded over-the-counter.

In general, companies that grow steadily move toward membership on the NYSE. Some who cannot meet the Big Board requirements will seek a listing on the Amex, but many large and powerful corporations are still listed on NASDAQ. Obviously, there is no stigma to trading on the OTC Market —which in 1980 boasted a dollar volume of $68.7 *billion*, or almost twice the dollar volume of shares traded on the Amex. In fact, some very well-known companies are traded on the NASDAQ system, including Apple Computer, Adolph Coors (beer), Hoover (vacuum cleaners), Mallinckrodt (chemicals), and Sotheby Park Bernet (art auctioneers). Included are some 79 banks, among them the Mellon National, 96 insurance companies, and 37 transportation companies, including Roadway Express and Yellow Freight Systems. The point is that many OTC stocks are no riskier than those traded on the Amex or even the Big Board.

Some new issues are quite risky, of course, but the prevailing mythology about soaring risks and rewards on the OTC market is a bit off base, and the OTC stocks deserve your consideration.

The giant institutional traders prefer to do their trading on the NYSE, where they will often exchange blocks of shares amounting to millions of dollars. Some analysts follow this block activity with great success, others discount its importance. The "institutional investors" (banks, insurance companies, pension funds, trade unions, and universities) are closely watched, in any case, and their activities can have a marked effect on daily market movements. For example, early in 1982, a single block of *one million shares* of Texaco caused a late rally in what had been a down day on the market. Since the institutional investors account for perhaps two-thirds of all the trading done on the NYSE, their influence cannot be ignored.

Where does this leave the individual investor, who may have only $10,000 or $20,000 to gamble on stocks? In a better position than it might appear, providing he or she does some research.

How Prices Move

What determines the price of a given stock? There are a lot of different theories, but in practice the stock market is an open auction. "Specialists" representing broker members of the New York Stock Exchange stand at posts on the trading floor, matching buy and sell orders delivered by public outcry—meaning the floor brokers are shouting their buy and sell orders. The specialists are charged with maintaining an orderly market, guaranteeing that every buyer will find a seller and *vice versa*.

To do this, they match the buy and sell orders they receive from the floor and from the firms they represent. Thus, if you place an order for 100 shares, 500 shares, or 1000 shares of a particular stock with your broker, that order is phoned to the floor of the NYSE (or the exchange on which the stock is listed), where the specialist can quickly determine if the shares you want are available at the price you have bid.

If, for example, you order 1000 shares of XYZ stock for 20 (or $20 per share), and the specialist has an order on his books to sell 1000 shares at that price, your order will be executed. If, however, the seller has placed an order to sell 1000 shares of XYZ for 20½, your order will not be filled. If there are more sell orders than buy orders on the specialist's books, he will drop the price of the stock. The converse is also true.

In order to maintain an orderly market, the specialists are allowed to buy and sell for their own accounts, and for this they have been criticized. The theory is that when they stand to gain or lose by the movement of the stock's price, they have the incentive to manipulate stock prices to their benefit—which it is within their power to do—if they so desire.

Brokers prefer that their customers place their buy and sell orders "at the market"—meaning whatever price prevails at the particular time the deal is struck. This, obviously, makes life considerably easier for everyone involved, but it does not assure you of the best price. However, if you are convinced that a stock will be rising substantially from its current level, the half or one-eighth of a point difference in price won't matter.

How to Trade

To open an account with a broker, you must place on deposit with him an amount of cash sufficient to cover your purchases. Standard brokers often require fairly sizeable deposits, depending upon the amount you wish to risk. Thus, you may deposit $5000, $10,000, or $50,000 with your broker, but when you place an order to buy shares of any stock, you should have enough cash in your account to cover the transaction. However, there is a short period of float, if you do not have sufficient funds with your broker—payment is due five days after the purchase is made.

Margin trading is a different story, requiring only half the purchase price to acquire the shares. In this case, however, the brokerage will require a certain balance in your account, as is discussed in detail later.

Over the past few years, discount brokers have enjoyed rising popularity. Discounters charge a lower commission than the so-called "full service" brokers, such as Merrill Lynch, Bache, or E.F. Hutton. However, the discounters do not offer the research reports or recommendations of the full-service brokerages—the discounters are in business primarily to execute your orders, and nothing more. In some cases, the savings in commissions can be dramatic, ranging from 20 to 50 percent. Also, discounters often tend to take a more favorable view of the small investor than do the large, national brokerages. However, you should be careful when you open an account with any broker for the first time. Read the literature carefully, so you will know in advance what the fees will be and what services you can expect for those fees.

For beginners, a standard, full-service broker is probably best. You pay for the advice and information you will need, but since this makes intelligent decisions possible, it is probably worth it. Once you are making all of your investment choices yourself, then a discounter may be a better choice. In addition, some of the discount brokers are now offering research services and advice to clients who want to pay for it—in other words, many discounters are now becoming full-service brokers for some of their customers.

As the market conditions have changed since fixed commission rates were abolished by the SEC in 1975, the discount brokerage has grown at the expense of the old-line brokers. Now, the two camps are tending toward middle ground, and the distinction may eventually disappear.

If you feel a discount broker is for you, some of the best are Charles Schwab & Co., which is national, Rose & Co. in Chicago, Stock Cross of Boston, and Kenneth Kass & Co., based in Florham Park, NJ. Schwab is the biggest, and although it was absorbed by Bank America, it operates independently. It is headquartered in San Francisco, but there are offices in most major American cities.

Do Your Homework

Too many newcomers to the stock market do not bother to acquaint themselves with the fundamentals of stock ownership, or even with the procedures of trading. These are the people who provide everyone else with profits.

There are no armchair investments, and stocks can move too rapidly to take excessive chances. Ignorance is deadly when you trade stocks. Obviously, newspapers such as the *New York Times, The Wall Street Journal*, and so on will give you much useful information. In addition, you should read leading business and financial magazines, such as *Business Week, Barron's, Forbes, Fortune*, and others which regularly analyze stocks or industry groups.

It is also a good idea to obtain annual and quarterly reports from any company whose stock you are considering. These reports give basic information about revenues, earnings, dividends, assets, and liabilities, and they also shed light on the company's policies in a constantly-changing business environment.

During the past few years, daily newspapers throughout the country have expanded their business news coverage, simply because interest in investment has been growing steadily. Read the appropriate chapter in this book to be sure you understand how to read and interpret the financial listings.

Make sure you learn how to read the tables, especially dividends, earnings per share, and price/earnings ratios. Many people advise beginners to avoid the high-flying issues whose P/E ratios bear little or no relationship to the actual book value (value of total assets, including plant and equipment and in-ground reserves, in the case of minerals companies) of the stock. A rule of thumb that is often applied, in this case, is that P/E ratios of 15 or higher should be avoided. This approach gets sticky, of course, with the stock of a very strong company that is having serious difficulties at a particular time. For example, at the end of February, General Motors had a P/E ratio of 34. Does this mean it is a bad stock to buy? Not necessarily. But for the novice stock investor, yes, it should be avoided.

You have to determine what kind of stock investor you will be. If you have more of the gambler in you than the long-term investor, and wish to trade rapidly for profits, you may be interested in stocks that pay no dividends at all, whose managements claim to be reinvesting profits into the company itself. In this case, it really doesn't matter whether they are doing what they say they are or not; you are planning to profit from short-term rises. This is an entirely different ball game—most of the people involved in the stock market are there for the long haul.

Buying Stocks

Whether you use a full-service or a discount broker, the procedure is the same. You place an order to buy a specific stock at a price you name, unless you are willing to pay whatever the market price may be. From there, everything is handled by the broker.

You may, if you wish, buy stocks on margin. In such a case, you pay only half of the actual price for the shares you buy—say you wanted to buy 10,000 shares of Exxon stock at $30 per share, you could purchase them on margin for $15,000. The gamble, of course, is greater, but the potential profits are commensurate, because you're being allowed, essentially, to buy two-for-one. However, the brokerage will require you to keep enough cash in your margin account to cover the cost of the shares themselves, in case the stock drops.

Margin buying is an excellent way to buy shares, when you are sure a stock has reached its bottom, or nearly its bottom. You won't face a margin call unless the stock loses half its value, and you can write options against the stock you have purchased on margin (see the chapter on options). However, if your margin account is not quite healthy, and the stock drops suddenly, your broker has the right to sell your shares for whatever he can get, in order to protect the brokerage.

Obviously, buying on margin is a bit more exciting than buying stocks outright, but it isn't recommended for beginners—you can lose too much, too quickly.

In addition to common stocks, there are also preferred stocks. A preferred stock is simply one which the issuer must redeem before he redeems the common stocks, in the event of a company's liquidation. Preferred stocks are considered safer investments than common stocks for this reason, and many, especially utilities, offer higher dividends (and therefore, higher yields) than the common stocks. However, common stocks generally trade more actively, so profits from sale are usually faster and better.

As was mentioned earlier, a stock trade usually takes five days from the time it is traded for ownership to actually change hands. This float can be used to your advantage, but this is chancy—it should only be done when you have the cash to cover the shares, anyway. However, when the market is really volatile, it is possible to buy and sell several thousand shares of a given stock without ever taking possession of the certificates.

A stock will go "ex-dividend" five days before the dividend is due to be paid. This means that anyone purchasing the stock within those five days will not receive the dividend until the next quarterly distribution. In the newspaper, this is declared by a small "x" next to the stock's name. Obviously, one strategy is to know when the stock will go ex-dividend and buy a day or two before the cut-off. Then you receive the dividends, and you can sell the shares as soon as you have. However, many stocks drop slightly in price when they are ex-dividend, and this approach can backfire.

Many people buy stocks for their yields—if you hold a stock that returns hefty dividends for long enough, you will have effectively brought the stock's price down to 0. Long-term investors sometimes view stocks in this way, but the best profits come to traders—you would have to hold most American stocks for a good number of years before the dividends would reduce the purchase price to nothing.

How do you calculate the yield of a stock? Many novices are puzzled by this term, and there is no reason for the confusion. If your stock is selling for $25 per share and the total annual dividend is two dollars per share, then the yield is eight percent. The yield, in other words, fluctuates with the price of the stock. At $30 per share, the yield would drop to 6.67 percent, and at $20 per share, it would rise to a gratifying ten percent. In short, yield is a simple percentage—total dividends paid as a portion of the total price for the stock—and is meaningful only to those planning to derive an inflation-beating income from their stock holdings. Bear in mind also that yield is a figure that can be manipulated by the board of directors of a company—if they want to raise the yield figure in their stock's report, they will simply raise the final dividend of the year.

The concept of a "stock dividend" deserves some additional discussion, because a variety of alternatives are used. For example, if a company's board of directors announces a five percent *stock* dividend, you will receive five free shares of stock for each 100 shares you own. You can keep the shares for further appreciation or sell them for a profit on a "when issued" basis. However, if the stock would ordinarily pay a dividend of a dollar per share, or $100 for each 100 shares owned, you would have to sell the stocks for more than $100 (for the five shares) to earn a profit on the deal.

In addition, the board of directors might choose to raise extra capital by offering additional shares to present stockholders. In this case, "warrants" are issued, giving the shareholders the "right" to buy a specified number of shares before a certain date, usually offering a discount to entice buyers. Warrants can be used quite advantageously, and there can even be brisk trading in the warrants themselves. However, they lose their entire value on the specified expiration date, so it is best to take quick action with them.

If the market price of the stock moves up, the value of its declared warrant increases. To use a purely hypothetical example, suppose Eastman Kodak gave its shareholders warrants allowing them to buy five shares of Kodak stock for $65 per share by September 1, and the stock was currently trading at $68 per share. You could exercise the warrants immediately, and take a three dollar per share profit. Or you could wait to see if Kodak stock went higher. If the market price slips, though, the value of the warrants will diminish, or even vanish.

Finally, you can ask your broker to sell something you do not actually own. This procedure is called "short selling." It is a useful, profitable technique if you decide correctly that a stock is going to decline. For example, you may decide that a stock which is currently selling for $25 per share is going down to $20. You could then ask you broker to sell 100 shares of the stock for $25 per share. Your broker will borrow the stock from someone else and sell it, and you are responsible for replacing the shares you borrowed. If the stock drops, then you buy 100 shares with the proceeds of the short sale and replace the stock you borrowed at a lower cost—your profit is the difference. In other words, you can profit from selling a stock without ever having owned it.

However, there is substantial risk in selling short. You sell the stock, and no matter what happens after that point, you are responsible for the shares you sold short. If the stock moves up suddenly, you still have to replace the shares you borrowed. If you sell 100 shares short at $25 per share, and the stock moves up to $30, you will have to pay $3000 in order to replace the 100 shares. In addition, you are responsible for any dividends that might be declared while you are holding a short position. In the end, there is no reason for an investor without a lot of money to ever hold a short position in a stock which also trades put options (see the chapter on options). Selling short is discussed in greater detail below.

Market Orders

So far, we have only discussed buying and selling various types of securities "at the market," which means whatever price the stock is at when your order reaches the floor of an exchange or an OTC dealer for action. You can, however, be more specific with your broker, by asking that a stock be purchased at a specific price, even though it might be selling for more or less at the time. This is called a "limited order," and you will not get the stock until it reaches your price.

You can also specify how long your order is good for. Your limit order is "good until canceled." Or you can make it a "day order," good only for that day, or any other reasonable period of time you specify.

Another type of order is referred to as a "stop," or "stop-loss order." This is used to protect yourself against the possibility that your stock will drop below a pre-determined level. If the price of your stock falls to that pre-determined level, your stop order is immediately converted into an "at the market" order and your shares are sold.

This process can be tricky, however, due to the systematic way exchanges operate. If two orders reach the floor at the same time, each bidding or offering the same stock at the same price, the bigger order takes precedence and is executed first. When two orders are the same size, a coin is tossed and one of the two traders is told he was "matched and lost."

Your 100-share stop order for, say, $22.50 might be smothered by a 1000-share order at the same price. If there were, at the moment, only 800 shares offered at $22.50, the 1000-share order would get them all plus 200 shares at the next price offered. Meanwhile, your "stop order" has automatically become an "at the market" order. When its turn comes for execution the going price might be, say, only $22.25 and the sale would be made at that price.

Selling Short

A major market downturn signals trouble for most investors, but thanks to the growing popularity of an old investment technique, investors can protect themselves against loss and even profit from a downturn. The technique is "short selling"—the sale of borrowed stock, loaned to you by your broker.

By using this technique, you stand to gain a dollar per share for each point the stock drops. If you "short" 100 shares of IBM at $70 per share and it drops to $60, at which time you "cover your short," you will have earned a profit of $1000, or $10 per share (not counting brokerage fees).

Let's examine how a typical short sale works in practice. For this example, let's say you phone your broker and place an order to sell short 100 shares of IBM, at a time when IBM is selling for $70 per share. Your broker will place an order to sell 100 shares of IBM, just as if you had the shares in your possession.

However, when the time comes, five business days later, to deliver the stock certificate to the buyer of those shares, the broker will deliver 100 shares belonging to someone else. In most cases, the shares are borrowed either from the brokerage house inventory or from a client who has left his shares in "street name." In this case, the client does not know his shares have been sold short. It really doesn't matter, because you are responsible for delivering to him the same economic benefits he would receive if he actually had physical possession of the shares.

If IBM declares a dividend while you are short—that is, before you replace the borrowed stock—you must pay that dividend to the lender through your broker. If IBM stock splits 2 for 1, you must eventually deliver 200 shares instead of 100.

How much money do you pay your broker when you make a short sale? Bear in mind first, that a sale is taking place. In this example, the sale of IBM at $70 produces $7000, which your broker holds as collateral against your obligation to replace the stock. You are also required by Regulation T (which governs margin requirements on securities transactions) to pay an additional 50 percent of the sale price as the broker's protection in case the price goes against you.

The Long Term Versus the Short Term. How long can you maintain a short position? The answer is indefinitely. Theoretically, short-selling is a short-term strategy which enables investors to hedge against losses during brief downturns in the market. In an inflationary age, stock values are supposed to rise over the long-term. Even if all stocks stayed at about the same price, but paid a regular five percent annual dividend, a long-term short position would be a losing proposition.

In recent years, however, long-term shorts occasionally have proven quite profitable due to the lackluster performance of the market. For example, two years ago it would have been possible to sell IBM short at $80 per share and cover your position at this writing for $57. Even after paying dividends, your return would have been almost 20 percent per year.

You would liquidate your short position by having your broker execute a buy order for 100 shares of IBM and then transfer the newly purchased shares back to the original lender. For tax purposes, the brief time between the purchase of this stock and the delivery constitutes your "holding period." In a straight short sale, this holding period is almost never a year long, which is needed to qualify for long-term capital gains or losses. Thus, as a rule, all short sales produce short-term capital gains or losses.

There is one important exception to this rule. Suppose you have owned a stock for more than one year and then sell that same stock short. If you then cover your short position by delivering the stock you originally owned, and if this transaction produced a loss, that loss will be treated as long-term. Traders say that short selling has a "tainting effect" for tax purposes, meaning that it is hard to come out ahead. Your gains will all be short-term, taxed as ordinary income, while a loss might conceivably be long-term (only 40 percent deductible).

Tax Deferral Tactic. Even so, there is one important tax planning technique made possible by short selling. It is called the "short sale against the box."

Suppose that ten years ago you bought 100 shares of XYZ company at $10 per share, and you now find that those shares stashed away in your safe deposit box are worth $50 each. Furthermore, you think that now is the time to sell. XYZ's prospects do not look so good. However, you can't afford to pay the capital gains tax on the appreciation of $40 per share in this tax year. You would rather defer the tax until another year.

By selling short against the box, you can have your cake and eat it, too. Here's how: You keep your 100 shares "in the (deposit) box" and also sell short 100 shares of XYZ at $50. This protects you against a drop in the price of the stock. Let's suppose that when the new tax year rolls around, XYZ has dropped to $30 per share. You then deliver your shares "in the box" to close out your short position. The proceeds of your short sale, $5000 ($50 per share) are reduced by the original basis of $1000 for tax purposes, and long-term capital gain rates apply. By selling short against the box, you have thus avoided a decline of $20 per share and deferred taxes into another year.

When Can You Sell Short? There is one other technicality governing short sales. A short sale must be made at a rising price, which is defined in broker parlance as a sale on either a "plus tick" or a "zero-plus tick." A plus tick is a sale at a price above the previous sale price. A zero-plus tick, is a sale at the same price as the preceding sale, but at a price above the last different sale price.

For example, if the last four trades in XYZ stock were made at 22⅛, 22, 22⅛, and 22⅛, the seller in the third trade could have sold short because the stock sold on a plus tick. The seller in the fourth trade could have shorted on a zero-plus tick. However, the second trade (at 22) was made on a minus tick and could not have involved a short sale. This rule prevents short sellers from adding to the velocity of a sharply downward market.

Here are a few general rules which brokers recommend for a successful short selling strategy:

● As in "long" investments, don't follow the impulse to get every last dollar that you can out of an investment. Don't anticipate that the market will hit an absolute bottom. Set goals and stick to them.

● Don't be intimidated by suggestions you will hear, that short selling is "unpatriotic." It's not unpatriotic to bet that the market will go down. Like any other trade, a short sale has a winner and a loser. Everyone can't win.

● Don't be too concerned with the short interest theories that hold that short sellers could fuel a market boom if they all rushed to cover at once. The total short interest is currently only about one healthy day's trading volume on the Big Board. It is not higher mainly because short selling is still the reserve of the "little guy." Most major institutions and funds are prohibited from shorting.

Decide How You'll Invest

One question each stockholder must answer before buying any stock is this: Are you buying stock for income purposes or to achieve capital gains? Most people will answer that they are in the market to make money. Fine, but the question remains—do you need income or do you want to wait for a profit?

What you must decide is whether you are an investor, a trader, or merely a gambler who likes long shots. It's like betting on horses: There are the "chalk players" who habitually bet on favorites and the gamblers who prefer to play the long shots.

Naturally, if you buy the so-called "blue chips," such as American Telephone & Telegraph, your risk is far less than for those who buy Siwash Sizzle at 10 cents per share, hoping for a killing. But there is still an element of risk involved, as many conservative investors have discovered—no one would have predicted that an industrial powerhouse like General Motors would slip from $45 per share to almost $30 in a matter of two or three months. The stock market never stands still, and it adheres to laws all its own—and it changes those laws at will. It defies the predictions of legions of newsletter-publishing, self-appointed experts, to the chagrin of their many followers.

Before you plunge into the uncertain waters of the stock market, you must decide whether you are looking for quick profits or income. If short-term profits are your goal, prepare to spend a great deal of your time talking with your broker, and diving out of the market as soon as you have a five point gain. This is a fine way to make money, although it is nerve-racking. If you require income, other than from a savings vehicle of some kind, then you should plan to buy stocks with healthy dividends that are paid on a regular basis—preferably quarterly with a 10 percent overall yield. Countless stockholders follow this policy—it's no way to get rich, but they receive their steady return on their investments for many years. Such investors should concentrate on large, powerful stocks, like AT&T, Union Carbide, or IBM. Even these people get burned occasionally, when they are holding stocks like Chrysler, Lockheed, or International Harvester. But generally, such long-term investors get what they want out of their purchases.

Of course, there is also the outright gambler, who plays the "penny stocks" (stocks selling for less than a dollar per share on the OTC market) and sometimes makes money at it. Actually, betting on the pennies is a lot of fun, and the payoff can be staggering, in terms of percentages. (See the chapter on penny stocks.)

What Lies Ahead for the Stock Market

The overall picture for the stock market in 1982 is not much better than it was in 1981, when the usual year's end rally never materialized and the Dow Jones Industrial Average hovered around 840-850. Of course, it is dangerous to attempt forecasts. For example, the behavior of the market can defy all expectations and predictions by professional analysts, as when the DJIA suddenly burst up for 21 points on January 26—without any noticeable cause.

However, economic facts weigh against a strong year for the market. The explosive burst on January 26 came two days after President Reagan's State of the Union message to Congress—which said nothing while some 10 million jobless Americans were wondering where their next meal would come from, or how they would pay the next month's rent. The bellwether industries of the nation, automobiles and housing, are mired in their worst depression in 20 years, and this bodes ill for the stock market. Although the country is likely to survive the "supply side" experiment—although various sectors will fare very poorly—1982 does not look like a good year for playing the upside of the stock market.

However, 1982 is also an election year. Faced with the prospect of losing their jobs on a wholesale level, the Republicans will undoubtedly do something to at least give the appearance of economic recovery. Even President Reagan will eventually realize that his Congressional support is eroding fast, as his would-be proponents recognize their own danger. He may even become aware that those would-be proponents are no longer in Washington, come November. So it is reasonable to expect some sort of governmental action that would have a positive effect on stocks, although it might be temporary.

There are, of course, certain industries that will grow in 1982, and these are worth stock consideration. Chief among them, of course, are companies that feed on defense spending—that's where most of the federal government's money is going. High-technology industries, such as electronics and computers, and drugs and medical supplies, also show promise for 1982.

If interest rates and inflation continue to decline, we may witness some kind of stock market recovery, and those who pick their stocks carefully will be able to profit from it. You will have to investigate each potential company with care, though, and you will have to keep a close watch on national and international events. Even some of President Reagan's warmest admirers on Wall Street have lost their confidence in his game plan, so the road is sure to be rocky for at least the first nine months of the year.

Chapter Seven

The Basics About Bonds

The hackneyed term "market bloodbath" applies to nothing in recent years so aptly as to the beleaguered bond market, yet countless investors continue to place conservatively-gathered hoards into these securities, mutilated though their faith should be. The funny thing is, those "Granny" investors are right, especially today. Few markets are offering equal opportunities for spectacular capital appreciation and high current yield *at the same time*, and the bond market is resurging.

How can this be? Everyone knows the bond business has never been more bewildering than it has in the past two years. Rapid changes in interest rates have delivered alternating periods of tremendous profits on declining yields and devastating losses as yields rocketed to new highs. Many investors who were forced to sell their bonds during the market's rocky passage through the last two years made the appalling discovery that their investments had shrunk hideously in only 12 months.

So why consider bonds as investments? Because today's yields are so staggeringly high that the investor is actually compensated for almost every conceivable risk. For example, yields on 30-year Treasury bonds, or for top-rated telephone issues, are so far above the basic inflation rate that the bond investor can earn a real, positive return for the first time in years. And like all depressed markets, a wide variety of excellent bonds are going for bargains.

Background on Bonds

The concept of bonds has been around in one form or another since ancient days. The instrument became more formalized in the Middle Ages, when a rich nobleman doubted a king's word and wanted a contract. Bonds have been on the American scene since the Revolution, when bonds were sold in New England for an industrial development project. Government bonds were issued by the young Republic. As the Industrial Revolution progressed and railroads began spanning the land, bonds came into further use.

In the 20th Century, the evolution of tax-exempt bonds increased to the extent that about 8000 issues are sold each year. In the corporate market, an investor can choose from over 5000 issues.

What is a bond? A bond is an interest-bearing certificate of debt which is basically a written contract by the issuer to pay the lender a fixed principal amount on a stated future date, with a series of semi-annual interest payments during the life of the contract.

The acid test for inflation is to assume a "real rate" of interest should be added to the inflationary rate. For instance, if the inflation rate is 12 percent, then 15 percent is needed (before taxes) in order to equal the inflation rate. In the area of tax-exempts, an investor in the 37 percent bracket could equal the 15 percent rate by purchasing a bond with a 9.50 percent exempt yield, bettering the inflation rate plus the real rate of return.

In this chapter we will be considering United States government, corporate, and municipal bonds. Certain features are the same in these instruments. They all have a type of payment, interest rates, and certain denominations. Most bonds are sold in $5000 denominations, although many U.S. government securities can be purchased in $1000 increments. Many older tax-exempt bonds are also in $1000 denominations.

Although interest rates are set by bidders, the issuer may set the type of fraction (ie: ⅛ or ¹⁄₁₀th). However, there is a difference in the figuring of interest. Corporate and municipal bonds (tax-exempts) have their interest figured on a 360-day basis; while U.S. government bonds are figured on a 365-day basis.

In the matter of interest payments, the investor can usually choose between a bearer or a registered bond. In some government issues, the Treasury keeps a record and sends out interest payments and the ultimate principal. This is called a "book entry" system.

The most common bond is the bearer bond. Most tax-exempt bonds are bearer bonds. This preference is fostered by the fact that registered bonds are difficult to convert and bring a lower price in the secondary market. It seems that public bodies have a difficult time issuing registered bonds and re-converting them to bearer securities. However, this is not always the case in the corporate area, where many investors prefer registered bonds, and debentures because of the increased protection against loss or theft. It is also true that the conversion of a registered bond to a bearer-type is much less complicated in the corporate area.

One of the most important documents in a corporate or tax-exempt revenue bond issue is the indenture. The indenture states the promise to pay, the rate of interest, and the maturity date when the issue is to be repaid. It outlines any property to be pledged or revenues that belong to the bonds. It lists the various covenants that the issuer must observe, and the restrictions on further indebtedness. It sets out redemption or call provisions. The indenture sets up a three-way situation.

The arrangement is between the issuer and the investor; however, a Trustee Bank functions as the protector of the investor and the enforcement agent of the indenture provisions. U.S. Government and General Obligation State and Local Government issues do not have indentures. The understanding is that the full faith and credit of the issuer is behind these bonds.

A document which is peculiar to tax-exempt issues is the legal opinion. However, corporate issues basically have opinions, too; but, they do not become part of the transaction as found in tax-exempts. The legal opinion is just what its name says. It is an opinion by a recognized bond attorney that the bonds are legally issued. Most legal opinions are now printed on the bonds; when they are not, a sales transaction cannot be completed unless the legal opinion accompanies the bonds.

Many investors are just as interested in the redemption of call provisions of a bond. Of course, there are many municipal issues which are non-callable, basically because they have serial maturities (ie: 1982 to 2000). Investors usually have rules of thumb regarding how much protection they want from the possibility of bonds being redeemed by the issuer. Five-year protection is usually the minimum, although some investors insist on 10 years in certain corporate and tax-exempt revenue issues.

Another feature that bridges both the corporate and tax-exempt revenue bond areas is the sinking fund. Sinking funds are used when there is one maturity in an issue. Most corporate issues (except rail bonds, which are serial maturities) have one maturity and large tax-exempt revenue issues have a term maturity which is similar. These issues are mandated by their indentures to set aside specified sums of money which will eventually "sink" the debt, thus, the name. The sinking fund can either be used to retire bonds when they are ready for redemption or to purchase bonds before their retirement date. Actually, the sinking fund is a protection to both investor and issuer.

Corporate and tax-exempt revenue issues have another common property. This concerns the matter of debt coverage, which is extremely important to investors. With corporations, the debt coverage is arrived at by ascertaining the amount of earnings over the debt that must be serviced annually. In tax-exempt revenue issues, the revenues collected on issues are used to compute the coverage. Again, it is the indenture that prohibits an issuer from marketing further debt when debt/service ratios fall below a certain level.

Here is an example of debt/service coverage: Let's say that an issue has 2½ million dollars in interest payments, sinking fund payments, and principal redemption, versus 6¼ million dollars in revenues or receipts. This means that the coverage is 2½ times (ie: $6,250,000 ÷ $2,500,000).

The Trading Market

There are three separate and distinct markets for trading U.S. government bonds and agencies, corporates, and municipal tax-exempt bonds. The first two are basically professional markets where large institutions trade. The tax-exempt trading market is geared for both the institutional and individual investor. It was not too long after the Civil War that corporate markets were established to trade the bonds created during the Industrial Revolution.

The tax-exempt market for trading is fairly new with the real expansion taking place after World War II. However, the secondary trading market is much more sophisticated than other markets because of the number of maturities and issues that must be traded. One of the misconceptions regarding tax-exempt bonds is that there is no resale market available. This is not true. The secondary market of the tax-exempt area is vast, with computerized communications systems extending to all parts of the nation via the municipal brokers. These brokers can only act between themselves and do not deal with investors—either institutional or individual.

It could be said that the bond markets are only as strong as their secondary markets because investors must have the assurance that they can sell their holdings at a fair market price whenever they choose.

An important factor in considering particular bonds is the rating that they have received. It does not apply to U.S. government securities, which are automatically AAA. Therefore, consideration of ratings and their implications relate to corporate and tax-exempt securities. There are three raters. Two are considered major—Moody's Investors Service and Standard & Poor's Corporation. Fitch Investor's Service is less of a factor, but rates many corporate issued. The rating agencies have established the following classifications and symbols:

Credit Risk	Moody's	Standard & Poor's	Fitch Investors' Service
Prime	Aaa	AAA	AAA
Excellent	Aa	AA	AA
Upper Medium	A-1 and A	A+ and A	A
Lower Medium	Baa-1 and Baa	BBB+ and BBB	BBB
Speculative	Ba	BB	BB
Very Speculative	B and Caa	B,CCC,CC	B,CCC,C
Default	Ca and C	DDD,DD,D	DDD,DD,D

The first four grades are considered investment quality, although many advisers restrict their parameters to the first three and even the first two.

The question is whether the issue under consideration will make timely payments of interest and principal. However, the process of determining the rating of a particular issue is understandably different at each agency.

It is interesting to note that the speculative and very speculative ratings are numerous in corporate issues. The "street" refers to these issues as "junk" bonds. Actually, most of the companies which are rated in these categories are of medium size and usually well regarded. It is also interesting to note that a tax-exempt bond issue rated in these categories could not find a market. It is an established fact that tax-exempt issues lower than Baa or BBB cannot sell.

Ratings affect price and yields, although the raters profess to have no interest in the pricing of bonds. However, bonds are subject to comparisons. Investors and even traders feel that the rating has to be the principal factor in determining the value of the bonds.

Of course, there are many cases where the raters have a difference of opinion. When this happens, the trader or new issue underwriter must make decisions as to which rating the bond deserves. Historically, the Moody's rating has often been the criterion; although this is changing as S&P increases its prestige. The fact that there is a definite pattern of yield levels for each rating bracket is proof that a definite connection exists between ratings and yields.

All exchanges have bonds listed. The requirements for listing are vague. If a security is already listed as an equity, listing the bonds becomes relatively simple. Each exchange maintains the right to evaluate the security of the bond to be listed. However, listed bonds are a small part of the overall bond market. Actually, you could say that bonds are basically an over-the-counter security.

The bond market is dominated by three major kinds of bonds: Corporate, municipal, and government. Each has its own advantages and disadvantages, depending upon individual investment goals and strategies. In addition, each has sub-categories, and each enjoys mutual funds dedicated to its collection along with *unit trusts*.

Corporate Securities

From straight debt contracts, many variations have evolved. However, the principal means of financing debt are basically mortgage bonds or debentures. While we refer to both bonds and debentures as "bonds," there are some important differences.

Mortgage bonds are usually issued by utility companies and are secured by a claim or a lien on certain properties of the company. The indenture comes into play by specifically setting forth what is mortgaged. The mortgage is given to the Trustee who represents the bondholders and can foreclose if the contract is not kept.

Some bonds can be second lien or subordinate. Thus, the lien is most important because it sets up the "packing order" of bondholders in case of foreclosure. The senior lien holders are always the first to be paid. The property that is mortgaged is real property, such as land, buildings, equipment, and the fixed assets used in operating a company. Cash, inventories, and receivables are usually excluded.

A debenture means "owing," but has no pledge of property. The American Telephone & Telegraph Company uses debentures as do many manufacturing companies. The plus point in a debenture is that the companies using this security are strong. The use of debentures is growing.

Years ago, bonds exceeded debt by a wide margin. Now, investors are willing to rely on the covenants contained in that all-important indenture to prevent the company from taking unnecessary risks. There is also the subordinated debenture which is relatively new.

Aside from these two principal means of selling corporate debt, there are several other types of corporate securities:

Convertible Bonds attract many investors. The interest rates are usually lower than other bonds. The *quid pro quo* here is that the company gives the investor the right to convert the bonds into its common stock under stipulated conditions. It should be noted that convertibles can also be converted to preferred stock. Convertibles are typically favored by those companies which fall into the "speculative" category. Of course, the investor can keep the bonds; but, the lower rate of interest usually does not favor this course.

Convertibles are one of those securities which hold great fascination for investors. The problem is that too many investors do not understand them, although there is not that much "mystery." The best way to look at convertibles is to only buy those issues where you like the common stock of the company.

Equipment Trust Certificates are securities issued by railroads. They are unusual because each certificate represents ownership in a railroad car, locomotive, or other rolling stock. The certificates are sold as serial maturities and are non-callable. While they are usually purchased by institutions, there is nothing that should dissuade an individual investor from purchasing these certificates if the interest rates are comparable to other securities.

"Junk" Bonds are bonds which are usually rated in the speculative and very speculative rating brackets. Do not be misled by the name "junk" given by Wall Street trades. This type of bond has come into its own since 1975.

The issuers are typically medium-sized companies which do not have $75 million in stockholder equity like most other companies that sell bonds in the market. Again, the *caveat* is to know the company that you are buying. Today's Ba and B bonds can be tomorrow's A rated bonds.

In seeking to find some new areas of investment, some companies that are involved in mining or manufacturing certain commodities such as silver or petroleum are beginning to offer bonds where the repayment is connected with the price of the commodity at the time of maturity.

Income Bonds are rare, but interesting. The interest is only paid when earned. These are recommended only for the most sophisticated investor.

Bonds with Warrants are similar to convertibles. The price of the stock is higher than the market value. The idea is for the bondholder to resell the stock or the warrants at a profit.

Bonds with Stock in Units is a device that is used quite often. It is the unproven company that uses this way of issuing debt. The bonds are usually subordinated and cost $100 or less. Yes, it is *speculative*.

Collateral Trust Bonds are rare. These bonds are generally backed by specific assets such as the securities of a company and pledged to a Trustee who can sell them in case of a default. The security here has to be measured by the assets pledged.

Yankee Bonds are foreign bonds paid in United States dollars. Canadian issuers have been users of this type of bond for years. Now, we have many European countries and cities, plus authorities in South America and Asia in this market. The strength of these bonds is that the funds needed to pay out are deposited with an American trustee.

Mortgage-Backed Bonds are an interesting security issued by banks and savings and loans. The security for the bonds are government-backed mortgages which make them AAA with Standard and Poor's.

Floating Rate Notes have a spotty history. They seem to fit in tight money market periods. These are debt instruments with interest rates that readjust every six months in accordance with the 6-month Treasury bill rate.

Corporate Notes have maturities of ten years and less. They are used in times of market fluctuation or when the issuer believes that rates will move down during the period of the notes. Notes have the same components as bonds and debentures such as call features and sinking funds.

Do not forget that the idea here is to wait until the market is thought to be more receptive to the issuer's long-term debt. Therefore, be sure to understand the call features.

Commercial Paper is the device that corporations use to finance short-term working capital for periods ranging from one to 270 days. The fact that the denominations are usually $25,000 eliminates many small investors. Historically, the rate has been below that of the prime rate; which means that an investor looking for yield can do better.

U.S. Government Bonds

There are many types of bonds and notes grouped under the heading "U.S. Governments." Some have stronger claim to the credit of the United States than others. For instance, all U.S. Treasury bonds, notes, and bills are direct obligations of the U.S. government—even savings bonds are. However, there are many issues of agency bonds which have U.S. Treasury guarantees or are supported by the agency's right to borrow from the Treasury. In essence, the difference in security might be minute. Yet, it is the basic Treasury issue which is referred to when you read about U.S. Governments in the financial press.

First of all, some salient facts about Treasuries and Agencies. They are taxable by the Federal government, but not by states. They are issued in various denominations from $1000 up. Interest is computed on a 365-day basis and delivery of government securities is one day. Pricing is expressed in dollars and ½nds. A ½nd is equivalent to .3125. Subscriptions for U.S. Treasury obligations are accepted at the various Federal Reserve Banks. There are 12 districts which are headquartered in Boston, New York, Philadelphia, Cleveland, Richmond, Atlanta, Chicago, St. Louis, Minneapolis, Kansas City, Dallas, and San Francisco.

Every Monday, the U.S. Treasury auctions off 13- and 26-week bills. Every four weeks, usually on Wednesday, 52-week bills are sold. Bills are issued at a discount and the investor receives 100 percent at maturity. This means that no interest payment is made. For instance, if an investor pays 95 for $10,000 (the minimum amount), he or she will pay $9500 and the $500 discount is investment profit. Bills are very marketable and it is easy to get a quote.

The Treasury also issues notes and bonds. Notes are due from one to 10 years. Anything longer is considered a bond. Individual investors can subscribe to new issues of notes and bonds via the Federal Reserve Bank in their districts and are usually allotted what they subscribe for. The most frequently issued note is the 20-year variety. However, the issuance depends on the Treasury's need to "roll over" (This refers to debt coming due). The issuance of bonds depends on various conditions such as the state of the market and, again, the need to redeem certain issues that are outstanding.

Investment by individuals in U.S. Governments had been relatively unimportant until rates rose and made this market interesting in comparison with the return offered by savings accounts. Quotes in most government bonds can be found in *The Wall Street Journal* and major newspapers.

While the Federal Agencies that are available for investment issue about half of the Treasury debt, it is a vast market. There is a misunderstanding about the security and, therefore, these are often passed over. The market is dominated by the farm credit system which includes the Federal Land Banks, Federal Intermediate Credit Banks, and Banks for Cooperatives. There is a consolidation of all these credits under an issue called the Federal Farm Credit Banks.

Also important in this area are the numerous issues that finance various U.S. government mortgage programs such as the Federal Home Loan Mortgage Corporation and the Federal National Mortgage Association— better known as "Fanny Mae."

In the agency area there are also World Bank bonds and those of various regional develoment banks in which the U.S. government has an interest. These bonds do not have U.S. guarantees, but the United States has voting power which makes the bonds secure in the minds of most investors.

Mortgage-Backed Bonds are one of the newest types of securities in the market today. It is basically a "pass through security" which means that an investment is made in a group of mortgages and the interest and principal collected is passed through to the investor. The principal in this case includes both the regularly scheduled amortized payments and also the prepayments made by the mortgagees.

The most prominent of these securities is the Government National Mortgage Association issues—better known as "Ginnie Maes." The most important point to understand is that the Government National Mortgage Association does not issue securities. The "Ginnie Maes" are issued by mortgage bankers located in all parts of the nation.

The safety valve for investors in dealing with these bankers is that the U.S. government *unconditionally* guarantees these securities. The issuer (Not GNMA) mails checks to holders. However, GNMA stands ready to make up any payment that is missed. There are various types of GNMA securities in the market and several ways to invest. This security has an attraction for people who like the mortgage market with the added safety of a U.S. guarantee. The $25,000 minimum investment, however, makes it difficult for some investors.

The other "pass through" security available to investors is issued by the Mortgage Corporation, another name for the Federal Home Loan Mortgage

Corporation. This organization issues guaranteed mortgage certificates and mortgage participation certificates. While these securities do not have a United States government guarantee, the organization is a U.S. government entity where all the stock is owned by the 12 Federal Home Loan Banks. Added to that, it is a successful organization, making fine profits. It is an atypical government organization, run like a profit-motivated, private business.

Savings Bonds, despite their safety, are not attractive to serious investors. Any individual who has sufficient funds to purchase marketable U.S. government bills, notes, or bonds (and understands the elements of risk involved) should do so. The non-marketable savings bonds just do not offer enough income in today's economy.

Municipal Bonds

T he bonds of state and local governments have become an important part of the securities market in the past three decades. There are now $343 billion in bonds outstanding. The reason for this popularity is the tax exemption these issues have. The income on interest need not be reported on your Federal tax return nor on the state return (as long as bonds have been issued in that state).

The question here depends on whether the tax-exempt yield is equivalent to, or better than, a yield that can be earned in a taxable security. It is an easy question to resolve by using the following equation: (the 32 percent tax bracket is used as an example: 100 percent less 32 percent equals 68 percent).

Divide the tax-exempt yield (use 7) percent by the 68 percent and you will find that the resulting yield is 10.3 percent. If you can get better than 10.3 percent in a taxable security, then you should not buy this tax-exempt bond. There is one factor, however, that might change your decision. State tax might increase the 32 percent bracket to as much as 40 percent; then the equivalent yield moves to 11.65 percent.

Before getting into the various segments of the vast tax-exempt bond market, let us examine some of the misconceptions about the market and the bonds. The biggest misconception is that there is no resale market for the bonds.

Another misconception is that you do not have to pay a capital gains tax on bonds purchased at a discount. It is not so. This means that when you purchase a discount tax-exempt bond, you should find out what the yield is after the capital gains tax is paid. There is also the misconception that an investor can borrow money or mortgage his or her home to buy tax-exempt bonds. This too, is not so.

Transactions such as this would cause the tax-exempt interest to be taxable if the facts were uncovered by the IRS. They find out because these people usually claim deductions for interest payments on their loans while claiming tax-free interest on their municipal bonds.

There are many investors who worry about tax exemption being continued. We are not sure that tax-exempt bonds will continue to be issued. However, we are certain that any bonds that are purchased as tax-exempt bonds will continue to have the tax exemption on the interest honored until maturity or called by the issuer.

The municipal market is basically broken down into two segments: the General Obligations and the Revenues. For many years the General Obligation bonds dominated this market. However, with the "tax revolt," taxpayers are getting more interested in bond issues that can be paid out by using the revenues of the project. Thus, there is a likelihood that revenue issues could eventually surpass GO's.

The General Obligation Bond is one that is secured by the full faith and credit of the state and local government based on either its unlimited or limited taxing power. In the latter case, the bonds are known as limited tax bonds. In the past several years, the fact that a bond is a full faith and credit has lost some of its former luster after the fiascos of New York City, Cleveland, and Chicago. This has caused both Federal authorities and investment banking people to call for the tightening of issuance procedures.

There are now more stringent requirements on the reporting of tax revenues and expenses attested to by accounting firms. The best way to base your investment in GO bonds is to check out the ratings. The rating agencies follow most credits closely and tend to be on the side of the investor.

Revenue Bonds as a category include many interesting issues. When you consider that revenue bonds were a small factor before World War II, you realize the tremendous growth in this segment of the municipal bond market.

Included among the revenue bond projects are water and sewer projects, electric or gas projects owned by cities and authorities, toll roads and bridges, airports, hospitals and nursing homes, industrial revenue projects, baseball stadiums, mortgage revenue for single family homes, college dormitories, and many others.

In addition to the documentation (such as the indenture) covered in the introduction, revenue bond issues have one other document that is important to the investor. This is a feasibility report by engineers (accountants in some instances) on how the project being financed should fare during the years covered by the bond issue. Of course, this is a projection and must be treated as such. It is important to an investor because it provides a neutral opinion as to the future of the project.

Public power issues were really the first revenue bonds. This trend began in the Northwest. Water bonds have always been popular with issuers because of the basic premise that water users will not risk their water being turned off because of non-payment of bills. One of the early users of the revenue concept was the Port of New York and New Jersey with the funding of the George Washington Bridge and the Holland Tunnel in the mid-20s.

In the 1950s, a new concept came along that has become controversial over the years. This, the industrial revenue bond, depends on the rentals paid by a company for whom a factory is built. The bonds are issued by a city or an authority, but the bondholder can only look to the mortgagee as his or her security. In 1976, the amounts of these bonds were drastically reduced. Now, it is permissible to do issues of $10 million.

The *caveat* with industrial revenue issues is to know the company that is the mortgagee. A rule of thumb is that the total amount of the bond issue should never exceed the net worth of the mortgagee. In fact, it is preferable if the net worth is at least 1½ times the bond issue.

Pollution control bonds are an offshoot of industrial revenue bonds because they are the same in structure. There must be a company which assumes the responsibility for payment of the principal and interest on the bonds. By the way, pollution control bonds do not have a ceiling; they can be sold in any amount. Most of the companies involved here are utilities. This could be a deterrent to some investors except that these bonds have a senior position in the debt of the company.

Airports and port authorities have proven to be good investments over the years. The only problem that affects these projects (as well as road and bridge bonds) is a cut in the use of the facilities because of situations like gasoline rationing. However, the Port Authority of New York and New Jersey, which has both airports and toll facilities, has increased their revenues despite recessions and gas shortages.

Hospital and nursing home financing can be difficult (especially the latter) investments. If you are disturbed by rising health care costs and the other problems connected with these projects, you may want to avoid these issues. Yet, using the strategy of looking at each issue separately, you may find one that fits your idea of a well-run health care institution.

Until recently, most housing issues in the tax-exempt market were state housing authorities which mainly concerned themselves with multi-family dwellings. However, many small cities have found a need to issue bonds for single family mortgages. The majority of these issues receive AA ratings from Standard & Poor's, which makes a good rule of thumb to adopt when considering them.

Sports stadiums are risky. Most of them are backed by GO bonds, but that practice is due to be curtailed because of the aforementioned "tax revolt." Most of these issues in the future will be via the revenue route. Demand high debt service coverage before considering a purchase.

There are some cities which would like to take over their utility company and pass the ownership to the city. There are many projects in the public utility area that are excellent money making opportunities; however, the conversion from private to public ownership in these times can be expensive—perhaps too expensive. It pays to examine these issues closely.

There is a bond that is often referred to as a "double barreled bond" because it is secured by a special tax and also carries the full faith and credit of the municipality. These are the Special Tax Bonds; they would seem to be a vanishing type.

Most General Obligation bond issues are serial in structure, maturing in from one to 20 years or longer. Revenue issues have both serials and a term issue. The term issue is usually more than half of the entire issue. These term bonds become part of an active, and, to a certain extent, separate market: the dollar bond market.

This market is quoted in dollars and is very visible. You can get instant markets on the bonds. You can also get quotes in *The Wall Street Journal* and other large dailies. The dollar bond appeals to those investors who need a temporary haven for funds while they make decisions on new investments. They can also earn tax-free interest on the bonds. The *caveat* here is that dollar bonds usually do not match the regular market in yields; thus, the investor is paying a premium for the convenience.

The short term sector of the municipal market is active and the investor has the choice of public housing notices, which are backed by the full faith and credit of the U.S. government, or other notes. Tax-exempt notes are sold by issuers in anticipation of sales; this is why they are called Tax and Revenue Anticipation Notes and Bond Anticipation Notes. When interest rates are high, an investor can do better in U.S. Treasury bills.

Another bond that has received wide attention is the moral obligation bond. They have been denounced as being bad bonds. This is basically true as far as the issuer is concerned. However, no investor has suffered a default as yet. This is another category that will be eliminated because of the "tax revolt."

Insured Tax Exempt Bonds are available from two insurers. They are the Municipal Bond Insurance Association and the American Municipal Bond Assurance Corp. The issues insured by these organizations receive a AAA rating from Standard & Poor's. There are now over $600 billion in bonds insured by these organizations. The bonds do not sell at AAA yields, which can be considered a plus point.

AMBAC (American Municipal Bond Assurance Corp.) also insures portfolios. AMBAC is backed by the MGIC Investment Corporation, while MBIA (Municipal Bond Insurance Association) is backed by four of the top insurance companies in the nation.

The Municipal Bond market is always innovative. The following are some of the new issues that are now available to investors:

1. Floating Rate Bonds. These are issues where the rate received by the investor "floats" with the U.S. Treasury bills and long Treasuries.

2. Bank Credit Municipals. These are bonds whose security depends on the credit of the bank that issues a letter of credit. It is being used in connection with industrial bonds and housing issues.

3. Municipal Bonds with a "put." This is another case where a bank's credit is involved. It is being used in connection with mortgage revenue bonds. It means that an investor can get a yield that is long-term by usual standards, but can turn in the bonds in 5 years. At that time, it would be the bank's obligation to buy the bonds.

4. Municipal Bonds with warrants. MAC in New York recently issued a bond issue with warrants which allows the holder to buy another issue at the same rate within a specified amount of time. The warrants also have their own market.

5. Municipal Commercial Paper. This is another instance where bank credit is involved and is exactly like a corporate security, except that it is tax-exempt.

6. Municipal Leasing. Many municipal issuers are turning to the use of leasing their equipment and capital items.

Interest Rates

Interest rates are what fixed income securities are all about. They are governed by the market, but more directly by the economy. In times of prosperity and inflation, rates are high. When we have periods of recession and high unemployment, the movement is to lower interest rates—although this is not an absolutely hard and fast rule.

The ability to track interest rates as they pertain to bonds is made easier by following the path of the Prime Rate (the rate of interest charged by banks to their top clients). If the consensus shown in top business journals indicates that rates are going up, this means that bonds will go down in price. Therefore, when it seems that rates are moving up, an investor should wait until some "peaking" of rates is foreseen.

Conversely, when rates start moving down, bond prices move up. Thus, interest rates are a sort of lever that goes opposite: Higher rates are lower prices and lower rates are higher prices. Interest is usually paid every six months.

Aside from the *theory* of interest rates, additional factors affecting its movement include the rating that a bond receives and the type of bond that it is. For instance, AAA industrials carry a lesser rate than AAA utilities. In this case, the interest rate is determined by market conditions rather than the economy.

The most important consideration about an interest rate is whether or not the issuer can generate enough revenues to pay the debt service—especially in times of high rates. (For a detailed explanation of how to exploit interest rates, see the chapter on interest rate futures.)

Buying Considerations

The first decision that an investor has to make when he or she has decided to buy bonds is what type. There are considerations that can be used no matter which type of bond is selected.

The interest rate is important because this determines whether the bond will be purchased at a premium, discount, or at par (100). The premium gives the investor more current income. The discount allows the investor to buy more bonds and leaves open the possibility that they will eventually appreciate. The bond purchased at 100 provides an investment at current rates and a return that is usually not much lower than the premium bond.

Yield is the most important consideration (after security and safety) when buying a bond. The various yields confuse many investors. When you see a bond issue advertised, the yield that is shown is a yield to maturity. This yield is based on the assumption that the investor will hold the bond to maturity. It also assumes that the investor can reinvest at the same coupon. Reality dictates that the average investor does not hold a bond until maturity—especially if it does not mature for 30 years or more. Most investors are really concerned about two yields: the actual earnings from a bond for a given year, and current return.

If an investor buys a bond which has an interest rate of 7 percent, a $1000 investment (although the usual these days is $5000) will yield $70 per year.

Current return is one that investors understand (especially those who buy equities). The basic formula for computing current return is the ratio of interest to the actual price paid. For instance, if you purchased a bond at 95 when the coupon was 7 percent, divide the coupon by the price and you find that the current yield is 7.37 percent.

One of the biggest decisions that an investor must make is whether to buy a new issue or one from the secondary market. It appears that the best buys in U.S. Governments can be obtained by purchasing the bonds when they are issued; although a depressed market is a sign to wait for the new issue to settle down and then buy. This is also true of corporates and tax-exempts. The tax-exempt market is a good example of this axiom. There is no doubt that the vast secondary market of the municipal sector is the best bargain for an investor considering choice and price.

The matter of liquidity is always important. Too often, investors reach out for an obscure issue where the yield is higher but the marketability is low. There are some issues which are well secured, but often do not do well in the secondary market. Some industrial revenue bonds, mortgage revenues, and even some pollution control bonds do not do as well as they should. This is usually because many of these issues are all sold in their initial offering and there is no particular effort to establish a trading market. Secondary markets do not create themselves, and some managing underwriters do not stand behind the bonds in the secondary market.

This means that recognizable names (and not necessarily those with the highest ratings), that have had no problems, are the best "bets" as far as marketability and liquidity are concerned. Government and corporate markets are more institutionally oriented; while the tax-exempt sector, with its vast wire systems, can do a fine job for the individual investor.

The process of selecting a dealer or dealer bank from whom to buy your bonds should include insurance by the Security Investors Protective Association and being a member of a regulated organization such as an exchange or National Association of Security Dealers. However, you need even more than that. You should ascertain whether the dealer or dealer bank that sells you bonds is capable of handling a sell order if you want to sell the bonds. A dealer who cannot perform both ends of a transaction is not for you.

An investor must act in an impersonal way with his or her broker or salesperson. The bonds purchased must stand on their own. It is not a matter of "trust." The bonds you buy must meet your requirements as to security, rating, type of bond, and yield. If this job is done well on the initial purchase, the disposal, when necessary, is easier.

Buying bonds on margin is not a big factor in the market. In tax-exempts, it is basically self-defeating because the amount margined is deducted from your tax-free income; thus rendering the tax exemptions useless. Many investors buy U.S. governments via loans from banks and have no problem putting up the bonds as collateral. Most of the margins on corporates are done on the exchange-listed bonds. The margin requirement goes up to 50 percent on listed convertibles.

Commissions on bonds are quite reasonable (except on bond funds where the sales charges can run as high as $40 per $1000 unit). In fact, in many bond transactions there is no commission charge. In this instance (especially in new issue transactions), the seller has a profit built into the selling price.

It works differently on selling the bonds. In the case of tax-exempts, if you ask for the bonds to be put out for bid, you will be paying at $2.50 per $1000 bond to your broker plus $1.25 per bond ($1000). On corporates, you will usually pay a $2.50 per bond ($1000) commission, although most of the trading in corporate bonds—when the amount is small—is done on the exchanges. This is because most corporate trading desks are set up for institutional trading.

The commissions on U.S. Governments are small—about 31¼ cents per $1000 bond. Again, that is institutional trading and based on millions of bonds and not small transactions. Most small trades carry a service charge which covers the cost of clearing and a small profit. The potential problem for the investor is that the charge could reduce your effective yield on a small transaction. This is the principal reason why small investors are better off in subscribing for original Treasury issues.

Selling Your Bonds

N eeding funds is not the only reason to sell bonds. The principal goal is to make sure that you receive the best price possible. Since bonds are in an over-the-counter market, there is no "board," and yet markets are remarkably close in the bids given.

Here are some easy rules to follow when selling bonds:

1. Sell U.S. Governments with a dealer or dealer bank. You may pay an extra handling fee otherwise.

2. The same applies to corporates. Do not deal with a firm that has no corporate bond desk because again you will pay extra.

3. When you sell your municipal tax-free bonds, ask that they be "put out for the bid." This means that your bonds will be looked at by hundreds of dealers via the huge wire systems maintained by municipal brokers. You may have to pay an extra ⅛th per bond ($1.25), but the cost will be worth it because you will be receiving the absolute best bid in the market.

As to when you sell, that is your decision. This means that you do not have to buy bonds based on the maturity. You can buy a bond 40 years to maturity and be ready to sell it in a few years or even months as circumstances dictate.

One reason for selling is "swapping," whereby you sell your bonds and take back similar bonds. Certain IRS conditions must be met in order to set up a tax loss. However, you will be getting more than the tax loss; you will also be establishing a new price base for your bonds. Take a close look at swapping. It is a good weapon in market strategy.

Risks Involved

W henever an investor buys a security, whether equity or bond, a risk is assumed. The idea is to reduce that risk as much as possible. An investor must look further than the obvious possibility that the bonds might default.

There is the risk of not being able to get a decent bid in the secondary market. There is also the risk of having long or short bonds at the wrong time.

The latter possibility brings out the problem of whether an investor should buy short- or long-term bonds. Before you get to this decision you have to define what short and long really mean. To some people, any bond longer than one year is long term. Actually, short-term bonds are defined as those maturing in the first ten years. Corporate issues rarely have serial maturities except in equipment trusts. Thus, you have to be a long-term buyer if you are considering corporates.

The risk problem, as far as maturity is concerned, is difficult to ascertain at the time of purchase. Market conditions determine whether the short- or long-term bonds are the best buy, and therefore the easiest to sell. For instance, in tight money markets, short-term bonds would be in disfavor because investors are waiting for the market to make a turn upward and do not want to invest unless they can do so at a favorable yield which, of course, is unfavorable to the investor owning the bonds. Long-term bonds can be in disfavor when investors feel that inflation is rampant.

Default is a terrible word to any issuer or bond underwriter. It is worse for an investor. Of course, there is no chance of a U.S. Government default and there have been few defaults in both the corporate and tax-exempt sectors. Most of the defaults that have been recorded could have been predicted, especially in the tax-exempt area.

There have been defaults in the corporate area. There have been bonds or debt outstanding that defaulted too. Bondholders should have had seniority in getting what assets were left. In the Penn Central bankruptcy, bondholders did not receive ''senior'' treatment under the settlement arranged, which was designed to ''bail out'' the common stock holders. There should be no question about the standing of bondholders in any default. Settlements like Penn Central's could be harmful to the cause of bonds.

There is one statistic about tax-exempt defaults that is heartening to bondholders. Most of the defaults have a chance of being worked out. The problem with defaulted issues is that the investor who buys the bonds after they default gets the best deal.

Understanding the Bond Business

Once gaining an insight into the varieties of the bond market, other concerns are terminology and rules of thumb. They are as important as sorting out the bond market. One important principle is the relationship between bond prices and interest rates; *bond prices move inversely to yields, so that a decline in interest rates translates immediately into an increase in a bond's price.*

How do prices of bonds behave, particularly if you are seeking capital appreciation? Usually prices depend on the interaction of maturities and coupon rates. That is, low coupon bonds move up faster than high coupon paper when interest rates drop. A bond with many years left in it will swing wider than paper with a shorter maturity.

Another element in the bond market is *call*. Many industrial, government, and municipal bonds have provisions for abrupt retirement (or call) by the issuer whenever the opportunity to refund at a lower interest rate presents itself. Call is undesirable for two reasons. One, you generally lose a high yield security and have to replace it with something else in a falling interest environment. Two, the yield you originally thought you were getting turns out to be illusory.

Why is most of your bond yield lost when your bond is called before maturity? To understand this is to understand that bond yields are figured on yield to maturity—the interest received over the remaining years of the bond, plus capital appreciation if a bond was purchased at a discount on the secondary market, plus interest on the interest figured at the identical coupon rate. So a lot of your yield is suddenly gone.

Today many industrial and municipal bonds have *call protection*, which is a guarantee that the bond will not be called before five or ten years. This can be particularly important if the call is to be funded by issuing new bonds at a lower interest rate.

There are also many devices that are designed to reduce the immediate interest cost to the borrowing corporation. One is the *put bond* (a play on words derived from puts and calls in the stock option market). A put bond is simply the reverse of a bond call. With a put feature, the bondholder has the option of selling the bond back to the issuer for par value after a certain period.

A second gimmick for reducing interest cost to a bond issuer is the *floating-rate bond*. The interest rate for these bonds track current market rates through either a complex formula or the price of some inflation sensitive commodity. The drawback here is that you cannot take advantage of an opportunity for capital gains in the bond market. If rates fluctuate, the prices will remain in a very narrow range because the price mechanism will no longer be needed to adjust yields to current market levels.

Another of the reduced interest schemes for a corporation is the deep original issue discount (OID) bond. Essentially, the issuer sells bonds at about half their face value and pays a minimal interest rate. The payoff to the investor comes at maturity when he or she gets back a lot more than he invested.

A final novel device to corporate bonds in order to keep down the interest rate is the *zero coupon bond*. Here no interest is paid until the debt issue is redeemed. Because face value would have to be paid upon redemption, the company is unlikely to call the bonds prior to maturity; in other words, the rate of return is assured to maturity. What is troublesome about this investment is that zero coupon bonds bought from a company can turn into a complete loss of principal as well as interest if the firm becomes illiquid before the security is paid off.

One way to save on taxes and wring out additional revenue is to consider *bond swapping*. The concept is simple: sell a bond for less than you paid for it if you want to establish a capital loss for tax purposes and at the same time buy a similar bond in order to maintain your portfolio. There's actually no loss. The Internal Revenue Service demands a 30-day period between the time you sell stocks for a loss and buy others almost identical, but bond swapping usually presents no problem as long as the new ones differ in at least two of a bond's major characteristics—quality, maturity, and coupon. One thing to remember is that repeated swapping can cost heavily in broker commissions, so you should know what you're getting into before a swap is made.

It is also possible to buy bonds on *margin*, a strategy that a consumer might undertake if, for example, a sharp drop in interest rates and a corresponding rebound in prices was expected. Margin is simply money borrowed; it can provide more bang for the buck. The percentages of cash an investor must put up to open and maintain a margin account on convertible bonds are the same as for stocks—50 and 30 percent, respectively. On straight corporate bonds, both the initial and maintenance requirements are 30 percent. The initial requirement for Government bonds is eight to 10 percent of the principal amount; thereafter, an equity of five percent must be maintained. If you buy on margin, you should remember two things. One, if the market goes against you, you can lose money faster than you would otherwise and wind up taking a terrible beating. Secondly, if you margin municipal bonds, the margin interest is not tax deductible under the rules of the Internal Revenue Service.

An Array of New Style Bond Products

Not long ago, bonds were a humdrum investment. A customer simply bought them and clipped the coupons. This scenario has changed abruptly because of the turmoil in prices and interest rates. Now issuers keep inventing alternatives to bond deals. Some of the recent innovations in bond products include:

1. The high premium convertible debenture. This is a bond with a long-term package to offer some protection against inflation. Designed primarily for the bond buyer, it carries a higher return than conventional convertible debentures. One drawback for this bond would be a declining price in the common stock (because the bond can be converted to common stock).

2. A bond with an equity advantage. This is a debenture that is sold with common stock. This could mean that the bond is sold at a discount. The ultimate success of this investment depends partly upon the future price action of the common stock.

3. The variable rate bond. This can be a publicly traded bond for a privately owned company. Here the rate is pegged to the yield to maturity on 20-year Treasury bonds and is reset every three months. Thus, the risk to the owner is that if rates decline over the long term, he or she receives a lower indexed return that might otherwise be obtained on another bond.

4. The silver indexed bond. These bonds are exchangeable either at maturity or redeemed for the cash value of certain ounces of silver, if that exceeds the dollar face value of the security. These bonds offer investors a chance to profit from higher prices for silver in exchange for accepting a low interest rate of let's say of 8½ percent. The obvious caveat is that if silver prices fail to rise sufficiently during the life of the bonds, the buyer can be left with a lower return than might otherwise receive from high interest bonds.

5. The original issue discount bond. Mentioned earlier, this security is sold at considerably less than its full value and is designed eventually to be paid off at par. The idea here is to lock in today's high yields without the likelihood that issuing companies will retire the debt before maturity.

6. A sovereign Yankee credit. A bond by a foreign issuer offered in the United States public market with warrants attached. The warrants expire in a relatively short period of time. The caveat here is that if interest rates move high enough, the buyer might not find it advantageous to exercise the warrant privilege.

7. The oil indexed bond. The coupon for this bond is reset every year, depending on the extent the price of crude exceeds or falls short of a 10 percent annual increase.

8. Municipal bonds with warrants attached. These are bonds with warrants exercisable for a period which permits owners to buy at par a like amount of bonds. The aim of the issuer of these tax exempt bonds is to reduce the interest cost and, at the same time, create an appealing new wrinkle to facilitate the bond sale. Investors accept a lower interest rate on the original issue bond because the warrant increases the profit potential if interest rates fall. However, if yields climb above the coupon rate, the warrants could expire worthless.

9. Municipal bonds with a super sinker provision. This is another feature in municipal bonds that is designed to raise mortgage money for buyers of single family homes. These issues are designed to provide a long-term equivalent yield on a short-term holding and to provide an early return of principal. The average life of super sinkers is four to six years instead of the conventional 20 to 30 years.

10. Closed-end bond funds. Although publicly traded bond funds have been around for over a decade, they may be one of the best kept secrets on Wall Street. Unlike open-end mutual funds, which sell unlimited shares that can always be redeemed at their net asset value, closed-end funds have only a set number of shares outstanding; they are listed on the New York Stock Exchange and in the over-the-counter market. These bond funds nearly always trade at a discount from net asset value because individual investors generally aren't familiar with them; the discount tends to widen when interest rates are on the rise (and the underlying bonds become cheaper) and to narrow when interest rates decline and bond prices move up. When buying or selling shares in a closed-end bond fund, you pay the same regular or negotiated commission rate that you would pay on any brokered stock transaction; these costs can be cut by going to a discount brokerage house. You can also buy shares in the funds on margin; the margin requirement is the same as it is for stocks and convertible bonds—50 percent.

BOND STRATEGIES

Dealing in bonds today is no easy chore. After years of soaring interest rates and weeks of erratic rallying, it is easy to understand why bond investors are in a quandary. Unfortunately, advice expert has been equivocal at best.

However, a general consensus of financial planning consultants appears to be that the disarray in the bond market has reached the stage where it is buying opportunity. But bond investors will have to pick and choose the types and maturities that are appropriate for them.

Besides the volatility of interest rates and bond prices, the new tax laws passed in 1981 will have an effect on the bond market in 1982. For example, the rate on unearned income in 1982 is reduced from 70 percent to 50 percent, which is of great importance to wealthy investors who buy tax exempt issues. Also, capital gains rates drop to a maximum of 20 percent, increasing the appeal of stock investment. Tax shelters get a marketing assist from accelerated depreciation. Substantial increases in the ceilings on annual tax deductible contributions to Keogh and IRA retirement plans lessen the need for tax free interest. Some individuals will no longer be dependent on municipal bonds as the basic uncomplicated tax shelter.

In the *corporate bond sector*, professionals see a continuous move toward lower rates and a continuing preference for shorter maturities. Seven to 10 year securities have been the most popular, and the trend is likely to continue. Intermediate maturities are also typical of European debt financing.

One striking thing about corporates is that there appears to be virtually no worry about the quality of corporate bond instruments. This is unlike the experience during previous recessions, such as during the 1974-75 period.

Because the yield gap between taxable Treasury bonds (where the whole fixed-income bond market takes its cue from) and tax-exempt *municipal bonds* has almost vanished, the tax-free bonds could well be the best investment for individual investors today.

Why has the gap diminished? Essentially it is because private borrowing has found ways to slip into the tax-exempt status for things like industrial development, pollution control, and environmental improvement, for privately owned hospitals, and for utilities that supply and compete with investor owned companies. These bonds are backed not by tax revenues but by revenues from the projects financed; they are crowding out the bonds that governments would sell to raise funds for streets, lights, schools and other government services.

A question arises as to why the governments lent their credit so liberally to private corporations? They did it partly to attract private business to their areas, partly to bring home ownership to more people, and in the case of utilities, to help hold down utility rates with less expensive borrowings. Now corporate and private tax exempt borrowing may soon crowd out government borrowing for traditional services.

It was axiomatic in the municipal bond market that general obligations of state and local governments are a better risk than revenue bonds because they are secured by the full faith and taxing power of the issuing government; revenue bonds have the pledge of a specific flow of cash. The general obligations had appeal to investors seeking safe, secure holdings because basically if any credit problem arose, it would only be a matter of raising taxes a little bit further to increase coverage.

Investor perceptions have changed. Municipal bond analysts have learned to prefer revenue bonds to the general obligations because they can analyze the credit quality of a revenue bond. It isn't possible to come up with a good judgment about the ease with which to measure a community's willingness to pay taxes and the quality of general obligations outstanding. Thus a reversal of values is in progress. Once the general obligations were the preferred risk, now the revenue bonds are becoming so.

Two reasons for the volatility in the *governments market* are the Federal Reserve's abandonment of efforts to keep interest rates steady and the spilling over from the financial futures market into the cash governments market. Governments were formerly dominated by investors who would buy and hold securities until maturity. Now speculators in the futures market buy and sell bonds as an alternative commodity.

The consensus on governments is not to get too far out on the long end of the market, which is vulnerable to wider price swings than very short Treasury paper. This means investing in intermediate term instruments defined as two to ten years. Also in the intermediate market are Ginnie Maes—something investors should look at; the pass-through certificates issued in $25,000 denominations are a relative bargain in yield.

Are bonds for everyone? Bonds are not recommended for their stability, because they will continue to be volatile. Bonds are for those willing to take a risk for higher relative total return over the next couple years than they can expect in money market instruments, Treasury bills and even stocks.

Revenue bonds tend to carry higher yields,and prices have yet to catch up with changed perceptions. This lag, along with the current over-supply of revenue bonds and the generally high interest rates, constitutes a rare mix of events. This mix has created spectacular values in tax-exempt revenue bonds.

This may also be a good time to buy tax-exempt electric utility bonds. An unusual kind of market exists for these issues where it is often cheaper to buy bonds on original offering than in the after market, because offerings are so huge that the pricing has to be instantly attractive, as a concession to the present market. The pattern is for most utility issues to come to market cheaper in order to attract a large volume of orders. After the sale has been completed and the bonds settle down in investment portfolios, the price usually starts to rise.

Even for an investor in the 30 percent tax bracket, a 14 percent tax-exempt return is superior to 17 percent on taxable bonds; and it is even superior to common stocks with a total (and taxable) return—including dividends plus capital gains—of 15 percent annually, a return that many think likely during this decade. The political and social issues remain, but the other side of the coin is a once in a lifetime opportunity in tax free revenue bonds for investors who want to lock in aftertax interest rates that exceed any foreseeable rate of inflation.

Chapter Eight

How To Start An Investment Club

Humble people are congregating, unconcerned whether their lives or even their fantasies are mundane, their goals tending more toward visions of security and maybe a little fun than toward dreams of glory or great wealth, people like the bulk of America, who want to keep their lives honest and relatively free from problems, if they can. Once each month, they gather in a middle-aged woman's living room, where she quickly organizes the proceedings, which can become heated, at times. Each of the 18 people assembled knows at least one other person in the room fairly well, but no one would call everyone else there ''friends'' in the usual sense of the word.

No, it isn't a garden club or a civic organization, nor is it a bridge group, the people may not even know one another's religious affiliations, and the click of mah jong tiles will never be heard. These unrelated people are together because they comprise a successful investment club, and the meetings can either glow with relaxed warmth or crackle with the intensity of a corporate board meeting.

Although none of the members honestly expects to get rich through the club, their initial pooled $8000 investment has grown to a little over $12,000 in three years, and they are—collectively and individually—violent about giving up an inch of their gains. And if Norman Rockwell were still alive, he might choose to illustrate this slice of Americana, this combination of modest means, neophytic interest in stocks, general sense of insecurity about the future, and sincere fervor—the components that spark the development of a working investment club, that have caused a rebirth of this informal investment strategy.

Club Idea Not New

Since they date back to about 1900, and since some investment clubs are almost a half-century old, the idea cannot be called new. Investment clubs saw their heyday, though, in the 1960s, according to the National Association of Investment Clubs (NAIC) of Royal Oak, Michigan. In fact, the popularity of investment clubs has been a strange sort of barometer, both of the nervousness of the populace and of the rocky road the economy has crossed in the past decade.

Thomas E. O'Hara, founding member of the NAIC and chairman of its board of directors, estimates the number of investment clubs operating in the United States by multiplying the Association's membership by a factor of four or five. Thus, ten years ago, when NAIC membership rolls included some 14,000 clubs, there were as many as 70,000 investment clubs in the country. The market bloodbath of 1973-74 frightened literally tens of thousands of small investors out of stocks, and investment clubs evaporated like standing water in Death Valley.

On a slow comeback trail, 1981 showed the NAIC's lists at about 3800 members, and O'Hara estimates there may be as many as 20,000 investment clubs nationwide, chasing profits at full speed. Since memberships typically number between 15 and 20 people, this would translate to 300-400,000 individuals throughout the country, with as much as a *billion* dollars invested.

The past year has seen a surprising resurgence of small investor interest in the stock market. This, of course, has led quite naturally to a regeneration of the investment clubs, as people pool their funds and research to diversify investment strategies.

Why this sudden surge in investment clubs? O'Hara answers, "I really think it's just an accumulation of successful investors who have spread the word." Referring specifically to the growth in NAIC membership, O'Hara says, "It's the same thing—people have followed our recommendations, made money, and told others about it. For example, we recommended the old American Cement Company, which became Amcord and was recently bought by Gifford-Hill, about five years ago, when it was below five dollars per share. Stockholders who sold their shares when Gifford-Hill bought the company got $34 per share."

Where was this recommendation made? In *Better Investing*, the official monthly magazine of the NAIC. Club members receive a subscription to the magazine when they join an NAIC club.

How Clubs Work

What makes investment clubs intriguing is the low cost to each member. An average member will put up as little as $20 or $25 each month toward the purchase of stocks agreed upon by the club. At the same time, some clubs invest as much as $100 or $200 per month per member—perhaps even $1000, says O'Hara. Obviously, this would require careful bookkeeping by the treasurer or some other officer of the club.

"The average club portfolio has a value of about $63,000," O'Hara says. Interestingly, he adds that a member's own portfolio is often greater than the club's. In other words, the NAIC estimates that an average club member's personal portfolio value is about $70,000—not exactly in line with the notion of a "small" investor.

However, all kinds of people, with all kinds of means, belong to investment clubs, and the average may be pulled up by some very successful clubs. Obviously, many people belong to a club for the social aspect of the meetings, and concentrate their investing in their own accounts; other people use the club to learn about the stock market; still others may use a club to diversify their portfolios; some exploit a club's conservative policy to protect capital, while taking riskier ventures for themselves.

Whatever the reasons, investment clubs are spread across the country and are found in every economic stratum. Many members are new to the stock market and join a club hoping to learn about investing, but perhaps an equal percentage of club members are sophisticated investors who simply enjoy the exchange of ideas that is part and parcel of a club meeting.

Max. E. Cohen and his wife, Ruth, have been members of a Yonkers, NY, investment club for about 16 years. According to Cohen, a retired educator, they've "done very well." The club meets monthly to discuss market trends and possible investments. They concentrate on solid companies and growth companies, Cohen says. "We don't go in for high flyers. We've been fortunate, but the truth is that we've done better than the Dow Jones averages.

"One of the best choices we ever made was Digital Equipment, which we bought at 20. I think it's up to about 90 now. Another good choice was IBM, which we unloaded at just about the right time."

Cohen's club includes about 20 members, among them a retired judge, a couple of lawyers and dentists, and other professional people. As Cohen describes it, "It's a social situation. We've gotten to know each other well."

Similar but different, the Cleveland Investors Club meets once a month in a church on Cleveland Avenue in Staten Island, NY. The pastor of the church is a member. The club has been in existence since 1965, and, according to R. A. Oman, a retired accountant, it has been doing "pretty good" most of the time.

"Last year was very good," Oman says. "In fact, the last few years have been good. One of our best winners is Dover Elevator, traded on the New York Stock Exchange, which we bought at $25.89 a share about three years ago. It has more than doubled in value, to a current price of $56.75."

The club includes 11 members—three accountants, three telephone company employees, three retired persons, one young woman who only recently became interested in the stock market, and one husband and wife team operating as a single member. All attend the meetings regularly.

As memebrs of NAIC, the Cleveland Investors often follow the Association's recommendations—but not exclusively. "We follow the articles in *Better Investing* occasionally but not all the time," Oman says. "We're all partners, of course, since that's part of the system, and we study the *Better Investing* recommendations. The NAIC advises a 10-minute study of each stock, but we spend 45 or 60 minutes studying and discussing each stock before we make a decision. We don't just jump in and buy because a stock is recommended. We check them out."

Among the stocks they do buy are those that received detailed analysis from *Better Investing* in its regular columns.

The membership of Oman's club has been fairly constant. "Sometimes we lose a member because someone moves away or dies, but then we gain a new member occasionally, so it evens out. Practically all of the current members have been in since the beginning, though."

Not All Clubs Succeed

However, not all clubs are as successful as Oman's and Cohen's. In fact, many are dismal failures—when a group of relatives forms one, when close friends form one, when the structure isn't right, when the people involved can't agree on investment objectives. Some clubs last a few years, during which time the members learn some of the basics of investing in stocks and bonds, but then strike out on their own, perhaps correctly sure they can do better on their own or with the advice of a portfolio manager. After all, an investment club is run, more or less, on a committee basis, and the riskier (and more lucrative) plays are shunned under such circumstances.

But whatever the reason for a club's disintegration, the time spent was surely not wasted.

Sam Schiff is clearly a sophisticated investor, employed on the public relations staff of the Insurance Information Institute of New York and a former editor of a financial magazine. Among his "formers" is membership in a Manhattan investment club that lasted a couple of years before falling apart.

"We didn't lose anything," Schiff says, "but for one reason or another, people began to drop out. Actually, each of us felt pretty confident about our own knowledge of the stock market, and we felt we probably couldn't learn anything more as club members. While the club was operating, most of us invested about $25 a month. By the time we disbanded, our personal holdings might have been worth as much as $1000, but mostly it was penny ante stuff."

So each member went his or her own way, Schiff says. Just the same, the club was profitable—Schiff's organization fell apart because members wanted a higher yield and wanted to make their own investment decisions.

However, his example raises a crucial element of any investment club: Maintaining interest in the club. The NAIC acknowledges that investment club members may lose interest after the first year. The excitement of beginning a club will insure good attendance at first, and later, when each member has a substantial stake in the club's future, interest will be correspondingly high. But when the newness wears off and before the club's assets have grown, or if the stock market is stuck in a long down-trend, a club can dissolve simply through inertia.

Maintaining Member Interest

In order to retain membership interest, the NAIC recommends that two areas in particular be emphasized: Education and a social program. By education, the NAIC means a deliberate educational program, for which some 20 minutes of every meeting are set aside—in effect, regular "lessons."

Subjects can range from general investment and economic issues to detailed studies of specific stocks. Almost anything can be covered in a given

HOW TO CONDUCT A MEETING

While most investment clubs hold informal meetings, it is best to keep them moving purposefully along, ideally along the well-known parliamentary lines (presiding member call the meeting to order, secretary takes minutes, motions are made and seconded, and so on). Generally, one member (called the ''Presiding Partner'' by NAIC) is in charge of controlling the meeting and is responsible for advance preparation, such as determining new stocks to study, discussing the current portfolio with the club's broker or adviser, and so forth.

Since the monthly meeting is the focal point of club activities, it is important to keep it flowing smoothly to allow for adequate discussion and decision-making. The NAIC outlines simple procedures for conducting a successful meeting:

1. After the meeting is called to order, the minutes from the previous meeting are read.

2. Copies of the club's current financial statement are distributed.

3. One member reviews recent conversations with the club's broker or adviser.

4. Each member gives a brief summary of the club's stocks that he or she is responsible for following, with recommendations to buy, sell, or hold the securities.

5. Individual members present reports on specific industries or stocks the club is investigating. The reports are the result of studies assigned at previous meetings.

6. Following discussion, motions are made and voted upon to buy, sell, or hold stocks. Motions are made until a decison to purchase a given security is reached.

7. Miscellaneous matters are discussed, and suggestions are taken for new stocks to study. Each company is assigned to a member for detailed research.

8. Refreshments are served.

Many clubs include an education program within the context of their meetings, and this can be inserted at any point in the meeting agenda.

''lesson,'' such as an explanation of terms used in the stock market, an analysis of a useful financial text, ''book reports'' on any of the hundreds of books in the investment field, studies of different investment theories, specific group studies of individual stocks or industries, and on and on. Many clubs find it advantageous to have two or three members present educational reports (complete with visual aids) at each meeting, often focusing on particular corporations.

Some specific suggestions from the NAIC *Investors Manual* are:

1. Have a committee from the club attend programs presented by the local NAIC council (if one exists in your area) and report to the club.

2. Invite your broker to your annual meeting to discuss your portfolio.

3. Have an NAIC council member (or an experienced investor) attend a meeting.

4. Have a representative of a local corporation in which you own shares—or which you are considering—attend a meeting to discuss his or her company.

5. Show movies at the meetings—any number of good films are available, and your broker may be able to suggest a few.

6. Enter the club in NAIC's annual performance survey. This can be especially entertaining when you compare your club with others.

Of almost equal (or greater) importance, a good social program will often stimulate member interest as well, especially in the club's early years. The NAIC highlights a few ideas that have been successful for member clubs:

● Conduct joint meetings with other clubs.

● Hold dinner meetings, perhaps in a local restaurant.

● If the meetings are held in a plant or office, switch to meeting in members' homes on a regular basis.

● Conduct meetings at which non-members, such as spouses or friends, are invited. If you wish, scheduling guests at every meeting can help spark continuing interest.

● Schedule outings, such as to the local stock exchange or to your broker's office. A trip to a brokerage can be especially interesting, if only because of the wealth of reference materials available there.

● Hold demonstration meetings for friends who wish to start clubs of their own.

The list can continue virtually forever. The purpose is simply to keep the club's impetus high until its profits stimulate interest on their own.

In any case, investment clubs offer an opportunity for thoughtful investing without a great deal of personal risk. Many start small, but none needs to stay that way. Some clubs have accumulated holdings worth more than a million dollars. Even very experienced investors have found clubs to be a way to broaden their understanding of the stock and bond markets. Almost everyone involved learns how to read and evaluate published information—in newspapers, annual reports, and research reports—and most find a great deal of help in developing their personal portfolios, which O'Hara says is, in many ways, a primary goal of an investment club. It also belies the prevalent attitude among brokers, who are somewhat loathe to handle investment club accounts.

"What many brokers overlook," O'Hara mentions, "is that while an investment club may have a relatively small portfolio, some of its members have substantial individual portfolios."

Structuring Your Club

Most clubs consist of 10 to 20 individuals who have banded together in order to learn about the fundamentals of stock market investing. Discussions, obviously, are initially led by the better-informed members, but everyone has a say. And such a setting is generally conducive to having questions answered without embarrassment. People involved also learn to get along together, to disagree without taking personal offense, and how to accede to a majority vote without becoming disenchanted with the investment club concept. After all, the club is a cooperative venture.

Legally speaking, an investment club is a limited partnership, complete with all the advantages and disadvantages of such arrangements. The NAIC has been at this long enough to have identified some guiding principals for those who wish to establish an investment club.

First, the club must have an organizer, who also must understand the principles involved. Every participant must realize that the club is a long-term commitment to making regular investments. The specific amount to be invested each month is set by consensus.

In addition, each member must be aware that the commitment is to re-invest any profits—an investment club is not a "get-rich-quick" scheme. Based on that premise, the organizer should be prepared to propose investments in good, long-term companies.

Second, the club should be gathered from several sources, preferably with three different people promoting it, according to O'Hara. This relieves the burden from any single individual, but more importantly, it insures that the club will be somewhat heterogenous, rather than a close-knit group of friends.

Third, when the group has been established, get some guidance. One of the best places is, of course, the NAIC. Its *Investors Manual* is an exceptionally handy book. About a third of its copy is devoted to setting up a club, but the bulk of the book is a detailed guide to rating stocks for investment purposes, geared specifically to conservative goals.

O'Hara capsulizes his organization's operating procedure as follows:

● Invest regularly, preferably monthly, whether the market is going up or down. Clubs that try to predict where the market is going are often wrong—not always a disaster when investing long-term, but not desirable, either. At best, they are wrong as often as the many market analysts, who seem to be more often wrong than right. Investments in strong stocks can always pay off, because they are not necessarily dependent upon market trends.

● Reinvest the club's earnings, which will make the club's portfolio grow, if only through compounding.

● Invest in growth companies, which are defined by the NAIC as firms with earnings and dividends outperforming their industry average.

● Aim for a 15 percent annual portfolio growth.

According to a recent NAIC survey, member clubs earned money at a compounded rate of about 8.3 percent. Hardly sensational, but in 10 years this will more than double an investment, and clubs are rarely formed with a high yield in mind.

Using the NAIC

One of the easiest ways to start a club is by joining the NAIC. Each member club pays $25 in annual dues, plus $4.50 per member. The dues bring a

DRAFTING AN OPERATING AGREEMENT

The operating agreement of an investment club—the literal contract among the club's members—is as crucial as the club's investment policy. It should be a simple, clear statement of the club's organization and operating procedures while meeting the legal and tax requirements of the members. In other words, an attorney should put it together. Again, though, the NAIC offers very helpful suggestions for the general format of the agreement.

One of the first points to consider is whether the club should be a partnership or a corporation. While most clubs opt for a partnership, the advantages and disadvantages of either organization must be considered in light of the state's laws and each member's goals. Several elements play a part in the decision, according to NAIC; Taxes—which form will require the least in taxes from each member; organization costs—which form will cost more to create; maintenance costs—which form will cost less in the long run; and member liability—what is the financial risk for each member under either form?

Once the structure is determined, then the legal agreement is drafted. As an example of a good partnership agreement, the NAIC uses the Mutual Club of Detroit's contract, one of the oldest investment clubs in the country. The Mutual Club's agreement can serve as a model of a concise but inclusive operating agreement. Remember, though: Each club must review the details of any agreement with an attorney to make sure the member's needs are met.

Like any agreement, the Mutual Club's defines the formation of the partnership, its name, the agreed-upon term of the partnership, and its purpose. Then it details policy and procedures in the following categories:

- Meetings
- Contributions of each member, both initial and regular
- How the club's assets will be valued
- Capital accounts, or the amount of each member's share
- Management structure of the club
- How profits and losses will be shared among the partners
- Accounting procedures, including member access to the books
- Annual accounting requirements
- Partnership bank accounts and brokerage accounts for trading activity
- Compensation to members for their time
- Acceptance of new members
- How to terminate the partnership
- How a person can withdraw from the partnership
- What to do in the event of death or disability of a member
- What things partners are forbidden to do—a clause for the protection of all members

This is signed by all the partners, and it is binding. The intent is to tell each member what his or her share of the club will be, what will be required of each member, how a share may be obtained, and what each partner's limitations are, *vis a vis* the club. Although fraud is rare, such precautions can avoid it entirely.

variety of advantages. One, of course, is a subscription to *Better Investing*. Members also receive model portfolios from the Association, which are updated quarterly by the NAIC stock selection committee—a homogenous group consisting of seven professional investment advisers from the Detroit area. Belonging to an NAIC club also provides each member with $25,000 in insurance coverage, and the *Investors Manual* can be an invaluable tool.

The manual describes how to organize a club, how to keep members' share records, how to prepare the operating agreement, how to report taxable income, and how to manage the club on a permanent basis.

In many cities, an NAIC council is available as well, offering experienced investment club members who can give you personal help. To obtain this and a vast amount of other information, contact the National Association of Investment Clubs at 1515 E. Eleven Mile Rd., Royal Oak, MI 48067.

You don't have to go through the NAIC to get started—by its own calculations, the NAIC includes less than one-quarter of the functioning investment clubs in the the country. However, the organization can certainly help get you on your way.

Nor do you have to focus on stocks. Some clubs play the commodities markets, some concentrate on oil wells, others buy bonds and government securities. In every case, the partnership is designed to increase individual leverage, so that all the members can benefit from investments they couldn't make individually. Given the NAIC's projected goal, you and a variety of friends could exceed their 15 percent ideal simply by pooling enough money to buy one-year Treasury issues.

Regardless of investment strategy, one thing is sure—while you invest together, you'll have a blast, and you may learn a thing or two as well.

Chapter Nine

Choosing Your Options

I nvesting is often a waiting game—waiting for the bottom of a market, waiting for recovery, nail-biting, gut-wrenching pauses in movements in either direction—and, lately, the stock market's new rules seem designed to weed out the impatient. Investors are forced to sit on the sidelines, striving for equanimity, as they wait for some market segments to bottom, for the rapid growth of other stocks to slow, to see what effects new economic policies will have on the future—everyone waiting for the right moment to buy or sell.

But the importance of good timing is nothing new to the investment scene, and the opportunity to buy some time is certainly one of the reasons behind the continuing growth of the listed options market. Because of this ability to buy time, options offer small and large investors alike the ability to *fine tune* their securities investments. And, of course, options offer potential for substantial profits from a relatively small investment, and options allow you to play either direction of the market, both aspects equally appealing.

Stock investors can lock-in a sale or purchase price on a large parcel of shares for as long as nine months, and options investors can profit equally from an increase in a stock's value or a decline in the market price. Finally, and perhaps most appealing to many investors, options allow buyers to predetermine their risks—the most that can possibly be lost is the price paid for the options, which is substantially less than the risk in most stock transactions.

Options of the Future

B efore explaining exactly how options work and how they can be effectively used, it's worth mentioning that the options realm is now expanding beyond just listed stocks. Many of the investment areas discussed in this book will soon include options as part of their overall markets. If these new options programs prove only partially as successful for other markets as they have for the stock market, you can be sure that virtually any investor will have some type of listed option available for any chosen investment avenue.

Currently, only stock options are traded on registered security exchange floors. However, proposed programs for various types of options are being announced across the country for many different underlying "products." Here's who wants to trade options on what and where:

● **The Chicago Board Options Exchange (CBOE)**—Government National Mortgage Association Pass-throughs (Ginnie Maes), Treasury bonds, Treasury bills, Treasury notes, and stock *groups*.

● **The American Stock Exchange**—T-bonds, T-bills, T-notes, certificates of deposit (CDs), and bullion-valued notes.

● **The New York Stock Exchange**—Ginnie Maes, T-bonds, T-bills, and T-notes.

● **The Philadelphia Stock Exchange**—foreign currencies.

● **The Pacific Stock Exchange**—gold foreign currencies.

● **The Chicago Board of Trade, New York Futures Exchange, and Kansas City Board of Trade**—T-bill futures contracts.

● **The Chicago Mercantile Exchange**—CDs futures contracts.

● **The Commodities Exchange of New York**—gold futures contracts.

● **The New York Mercantile Exchange**—platinum futures contracts.

● **The Coffee, Sugar & Cocoa Exchange**—sugar futures contracts.

Like any other investment medium, of course, options aren't for everyone. There is risk, even though it is defined, and the ability to buy time also means you will be running against a clock, if you have chosen wrong. However, options can be a useful, highly versatile tool in meeting a variety of investment objectives. Although options are now only offered on listed stocks, the basic underlying logic of the strategies and general use of options will apply equally to other markets.

Specifically, what are those uses? Some investors are attracted to options because they know the most they can lose is the premium (price) they have paid for their contracts. Others use options to increase the income derived from their stock holdings, either by complementing long positions with calls or by writing options on their stocks. Still others may use options as a means of establishing their purchase price for stocks up to nine months in advance—the "strike" price of the stock option is the price at which you may buy or sell the underlying stock, period. Others use options to diversify their stock investments with a small capital outlay. Still others will use options to protect their long stock positions—they might buy puts on a stock in which they were long, as a hedge against a decline in the stock's price.

Whence Came Options

For many years, a limited number of investors participated in over-the-counter stock options—options to buy or sell stock at a fixed price within a specified period of time. This market was actually a loose amalgam of professional trading firms known as "The Put and Call Brokers and Dealers

Associations,'' and very few public investors ever got involved.

It was only nine years ago that stock options were granted the "legitimacy" of an exchange floor—but it wasn't a stock exchange. On April 23, 1973, in a corner of the Chicago Board of Trade—the nation's largest *commodities* exchange—about 40 Board of Trade members decided to participate in a pilot program called the Chicago Board Options Exchange.

The concept behind the CBOE was to apply the principles of commodities futures trading to stock issues, so its roots are logical. Needless to say, the CBOE was successful—it is now an independent securities exchange. In fact, it is the second-largest securities exchange in the country, behind the NYSE. CBOE's success was great enough to prompt similar programs on the floors of the Pacific Stock Exchange in San Francisco, New York's Amex, and the Philadelphia Stock Exchange.

On the first day of CBOE's existence, 911 options contracts were traded on 16 underlying stocks. In 1981, well over 100 million options contracts traded on the stock of 290 companies listed on the four exchanges. About 90 percent of those contracts—amounting to over *10 billion* shares of stock, in total—was traded by private investors, rather than banks, insurance companies, or pension funds (which tend to do the most trading on the stock exchanges).

The Options Market

The basic concept of "options" has been around for a long time—the option for the purchase or sale of real estate is a familiar example. For a securities (stock) option, the essential components are the same as most other options: A description of the item the option buyer may purchase or sell, the price for which the item is to be purchased or sold (called the "strike" or "exercise" price), the price the buyer must pay for this privilege (called the "premium"), and a specified time in which the buyer must exercise the right to buy or sell the item.

The premium is what the buyer pays the seller for the rights of the contract. The seller keeps this sum whether the buyer exercises the right or not. If the buyer does not exercise the rights granted by the contract within the specified time period, the option expires.

In simpler terms, a stock option normally involves 100 shares of a specific, widely held, actively-traded stock. The strike price is the price at which the option buyer may buy or sell those 100 shares of stock. The premium is what the option buyer pays the seller in order to control the 100 shares. Each option is designated according to a given month, and the option must be exercised by the Friday before the third Saturday of that month.

When an option gives the buyer the right to purchase the 100 shares at a specific price, it is known as a "call option." When the option is to sell the 100 shares, it is known as a "put option." Despite appearances, the workings of calls and puts are relatively simple.

For example, say there is a company called "Manufacturing Co." (MFG), and options are offered on its shares. The options will be traded on quarterly cycles beginning in January, February, or March. Pretend MFG is traded on the

January-April-July-October cycle, and a July/50 call option is being offered. An MFG/July/50 *call* entitles the buyer to purchase 100 shares of MFG stock for $50 per share any time before the Friday preceding the third Saturday of July. However, most brokerages set an earlier date at which the buyer must notify them that he intends to exercise the option.

Conversely, an MFG/July/50 *put* gives the buyer the right to *sell* 100 shares of MFG stock for $50 per share within the same time period.

For any particular stock, there may be trading in several calls and puts with identical exercise prices but different expiration dates. For example, MFG/50 calls might be offered for January, April, July, or October. Generally speaking, the further away the exercise date for a given option, the more expensive the premium will be. It is also possible for options with the same exercise date to have different strike prices, for example, an MFG/July/50, an MFG/July/60, and an MFG/July/70. This is because additional options with higher or lower exercise prices are introduced when a significant change occurs in the market price of the underlying stock. This is true for either puts or calls.

Let's say an MFG option with a $50 exercise price is introduced when the stock is trading at $50 per share. If the stock drops to $47, new options might be introduced with a $45 exercise price. In the case of calls, this would grant the option buyer the right to purchase 100 shares of MFG stock for $45 per share, while MFG stock is currently selling for $47. In this case, the call buyer would obviously believe the stock would not drop much further in price. A put buyer has the right to sell 100 shares of MFG for $45 per share—a put buyer believes the stock's price will drop. If the stock's price should then climb to $56 per share, still more options might be introduced with strike prices of $60 or $70, and so on.

Considering all the possible combinations of exercise prices and expiration dates, it isn't uncommon for concurrent trading in a dozen or more different options on the stock of a single company.

In addition, an individual investor may choose to write (sell) call or put options depending upon his or her analysis of the market and financial objectives at a particular time. At one point, the investor may choose to buy options, at another point, to write them, or to do both at the same time. The flexible uses are simply tremendous, and various strategies can make money, hedge against fluctuation, or both.

Premiums

The premium, in large measure, is what options trading is all about. Simply, you want to pay one premium for your puts or calls and sell the contracts to someone else for a larger premium.

Other buyers, of course, hope the market price of the underlying stock will rise enough above the exercise price (in the case of calls) or fall enough below the exercise price for a put to make exercising the option profitable. In other words, the holder of a call option, say MFG/July/50, would like to see MFG stock selling for $55 or more per share in July. A person holding an MFG/July/50 put would like to see the stock selling below $50 per share in

July. However, unless the difference between an option's exercise price and the market price of the underlying stock is $10 or more, trading for the premium generally delivers a better profit.

For the writers of options, on the other hand, the premium they receive is an additional source of income, or the premium can be a hedge against the possible decline in the price of securities which they own or intend to purchase.

Just as the option buyer may sell the option at any time prior to expiration—realizing a profit or loss on the increase or decrease of the premium—an option writer may "buy in" an option he has previously written (assuming, of course, that the option has not yet been exercised or expired). This offsetting transaction is known as a "closing purchase" and it terminates the writer's obligation to deliver or purchase the underlying stock. His profit or loss is the difference between the premium of the option initially sold and the premium of the option later purchased.

For example, if a writer sells an MFG/July/50 call option when the premium was $600 for the 100 shares, and later buys back an identical, offsetting option at a time when the premium had declined to $200, his profit would be $400 less commissions and fees.

This is a good place to interject the fact that the ability of the option writer to terminate his obligation to deliver or purchase the stock—by buying in an offsetting option, in no way effects the buyer's right to exercise the option he bought. The reason is that the Options Clearing Corporation (OCC) acts as the guarantor of all transactions—the buyer to every seller and the seller to every buyer. This means there is no continuing relationship between the original buyer and seller. The seller knows the money for his option is guaranteed and the buyer knows the underlying security is available if he decides to exercise. This feature helps assure the financial integrity of all exchange-traded options transaction.

The importance of the premium to the buyers and writers of options raises the question of what factors determine the amount of premium and what causes it to increase or decrease?

As is true of any item bought and sold in an open, competitive marketplace, the price is a reflection of supply and demand. During periods of rising stock prices, there is usually increased interest by investors in purchasing call options. On the other hand, individuals who own securities become less interested in writing calls when the prices of their stocks are rising, choosing to hold their stock in anticipation of further appreciation. More people interested in buying calls and fewer people interested in writing them usually results in raising the levels of call premiums.

Conversely, in times of generally weak or declining stock prices, there is greater interest in writing call options, but proportionately less interest in buying them. In this situation, premiums tend to decline. A reverse arithmetic applies to puts—strong stock prices tend to reduce the demand and, resultingly, the price; and weak stock prices generally increase the demand and the premiums for puts.

It should be made clear, though, that just like stock prices, when we refer to "a period of rising prices" we may be talking about a week, a day, or an early morning flurry of buying and selling. So, an option investor and his broker must keep an eye on the market to take advantage of profitable opportunities.

How Premiums Change

There are three other factors that influence option premiums. The first is the current market price of the stock, the second is the length of time the option will be in force, and the third is the volatility of the underlying stock—whether it tends to fluctuate a good deal.

The relationship of the current market price and the exercise price of the option is always a major factor affecting the option's premium. Take our MFG/July/50 call; let's say an investor purchases it in October when the market value of MFG stock is $50 a share. At this point, he is paying for time (nine months) and the possibility that MFG stock will rise during this time. By February, the market value of MFG stock has climbed to $60. The investor who now buys an MFG/July/50 call option—granting the right to purchase the stock at $10 per share under current market value—will of course, pay a greater price for the call than he/she did back in October. With the stock at 60, the MFG/July/50 call is an "in-the-money" option, meaning the market price of the stock is greater than the exercise price.

Time value obviously effects the options premiums during periods of both rising and falling stock prices. However, all else being equal, the more time remaining until the expiration of the option, the higher the premium tends to be. An October option normally commands a higher premium that an otherwise identical July option because the purchaser has three additional months to profit from any subsequent increase or decrease in the price of the underlying stock.

The term for this is a "wasting asset," a harsh-sounding name which simply means that as an expiration date approaches, its time value will decline and eventually become zero. At expiration, the option's only tangible value is the amount it is "in-the-money" in relation to the underlying stock.

The volatility of the underlying stock also influences options premiums. An option on a stock that generally fluctuates widely is likely to bring higher premiums than options on stock that normally trades in a narrow price range.

Plotting just how much a premium will move as the result of a movement in the underlying stock price is difficult; however, there are general principles that apply. Looking again at the first factor influencing premiums, the current market price versus the exercise price, a rule of thumb could state that premiums will neither increase nor decrease point for point with the underlying stock—one point change in the price of the stock usually results in *less* than a point change in the option premium.

Like all rules, there are exceptions, and this one will demonstrate the complexity of options, but the opportunity for rewards to those who invest wisely. Premiums are likely to move point for point with the stock once the option reaches "parity." For a call option, parity occurs when the exercise price *plus* the premium equals the price of the underlying stock. For a put, parity occurs when the exercise price *minus* the premium equals the stock price.

There are three main reasons why premiums prior to reaching parity tend to increase less than point for point with stock prices:

1. Rising prices reduce leverage, making options less attractive to potential buyers. If the price of a stock is $50 and the option is $5, the buyer's leverage is 10 to 1. But if a $1 change in the stock price were to raise the option premium by the same amount, the leverage would be reduced.

2. Increased capital outlay and increased risk resulting from higher premiums can discourage demand for the option. A rise in stock price from $50 to $51 is only two percent, but an increase in a call premium from $5 to $6 is a 20 percent increase in the buyer's capital outlay and risk.

3. The effect of changing stock prices is at least partially offset by the option's decreasing value. For example, a two-week uptrend in the stock price will not be fully reflected in the rise of the premium because the option, simply, is two weeks closer to expiration—bringing the time factor back in.

The Marketplace

The options market is not a dice game, nor is it filled with wildly speculative investors. By studying the marketplace, you can see how options are similar to and different from other kinds of investments.

Options are a listed security, so they share many similarities with other securities traded on exchange floors. Orders to buy and sell are handled through brokers in much the same manner as orders to buy or sell stock. The exchanges are regulated by the Securities and Exchange Commission, and the trading floor is an open, competitive "auction" market.

Another similarity is the opportunity to follow price movements, trading volume, and other pertinent information minute by minute or day by day. The buyer and seller of options, like his stock market counterpart, usually has access to the latest market information through his broker and can know almost instantly at what price his order has been executed.

Most people visiting an exchange trading floor for the first time wonder how business gets done with all the hurrying and shouting. Of course, it does get done. Most exchanges have some minor variation in their trading system which somewhat differs from other exchanges. But using the CBOE floor, the most active options marketplace in the world, as an example, we can see the basics of how orders are executed.

To begin, the CBOE does not have the traditional specialist handling incoming public orders, but instead has an "Order Book Official" system. The Order Book Officials (OBOs) are full-time employees of the CBOE and, unlike specialists, cannot trade on the exchange's floor. Their sole responsiblity is recording and executing all orders—public orders and bids and asks from the trading crowd—for the option classes at their posts. Public orders are executed chronologically and have priority of execution over any orders from the floor at the same price.

Let's say you tell your broker in Dallas to buy ten MFG/July/50 call contracts at the current premium asking price of 6¾. If your order is placed on the book at 11 a.m. and an order for 150 of those same contracts at the same price is listed at 11:01 a.m., your order would be executed first.

As for activity in the trading crowd, CBOE rules require that bids and offers be made by public outcry. Highest bids and lowest offers have priority. If two or more bids represent the best price, priority is determined by the sequence in which the bids were made.

Traders on the floor are: Floor brokers who handle public orders, acting as agents and charging a brokerage fee for each order executed (they may be independent businessmen or employees of a brokerage firm); and Market-Makers trading only for their own accounts, at their own risk for their own profit.

Acting as investors' agents on the trading floor, floor brokers, in consultation with brokers in a branch office and consequently the investors, employ strategies through various types of orders. The most common are:

Market orders—to buy or sell at the current market premium for a specific option; or if a better price is available, it will be executed at that price.

Limit orders—to buy or sell at a specified price or better. For example, the current market premium for a call option is ¾. A limit order would mandate that the floor broker execute the purchase of the option when and if an asking price of ⅝ is offered. Of course, if the floor broker can execute the order at ⁹⁄₁₆ he will do so.

Contingency orders—are limit or market orders that are executed upon some condition being satisfied. These are executed on the floor, not through the OBO's book. An example of a contingency order would be to execute the sale of a put option if the price of the underlying stock rose to a particular, predetermined price.

Not-held orders—give the floor broker discretionary control as to the price and the limit at which an order may be executed—generally used for large orders.

Discretionary orders—give the floor broker some flexibility regarding the price at which an order may be executed. For example, an order to buy at 2⅜ with an eighth discretion means the broker is to buy at 2⅜, but under no circumstances is he to pay more than 2½.

A spread order—is an order to buy one or more contracts of a given class, at the same time one or more options of the class are sold. Orders for spread positions occur in a variety of combinations. For example, an order to sell two July/50 calls and purchase two Oct/50 calls of the same class would be a *calendar spread* order. An order to buy five May/80 puts and sell five May/70 puts of the same class is a *price spread* order.

Straddle orders—to buy or sell the same number of put options and call options covering the same underlying security and having the same exercise price and expiration date.

OPTIONS STRATEGIES

Before you study the various strategies for options and their uses, bear in mind that hypothetical transactions can only give a general idea of the profit and risk involved. The real thing requires a sound understanding of options and, most important, the underlying stock. To correctly gauge price movements in an option, you must consider such factors as past stock price fluctuations, the economic standing of the company involved, the outlook for its dividend payments, and, of course, the general trend in stock price movements. If you don't do your research and charting, then you must have faith in the brokerage's research department and your broker, just as you would in stock transactions.

The following scenarios don't include commissions, margin treatment, or taxes (except where such consideration are a part of the strategy), and such figures can, and do, play a part in options trading—they are dropped here for simplicity's sake. Assume that each contract equals 100 shares, as in standard options contracts.

Call Buying: Limited Risk—Increased Leverage

If you feel a particular stock should go up, you may want to use the simplest strategy—buying a call to limit your risk and increase your leverage. Table 1 will show you how your investment would fare over a wide range of stock prices, using an at-the-money call, an in-the-money call, and out-of-the-money call. Assuming XYZ is trading at $30 on January 1, the XYZ April 35 would trade for $1, the April 30 for $2.50, and the April 25 for $6. The following prices indicate values on expiration date.

Notice that the profit/loss of the in-the-money call most closely approximates that of owning the stock, but has the advantage of limiting risk to the amount paid for the call and of realizing a much greater profit percentage on invested capital. The only way in which the stock investor has a clear advantage is if the stock remains at his purchase price (no loss, no gain), while the call buyer loses that portion of his purchase price which represented time value. The out-of-the-money call clearly has the greatest leverage factor. On an $8 move in the stock (to $38), the April 35 would be worth $300, or triple the $100 invested, while the stockholder would make $800 on a $3000 investment.

Substituting a Call for Stock

If the market is declining (or you fear a decline), it may make sense to sell a stock in which you have a paper profit and replace it with an in-the-money call on the same stock. This technique will enable you to protect most of the profit in the underlying security, while maintaining a position to participate in any upward movement in the stock. This may sound like a contradiction, but it is perfectly reasonable to feel nervous about stock market trends in general, while remaining bullish about a particular stock.

For example, let's assume you bought XXX stock at 38 more than a year ago and it is now trading at 50. A six-month XXX 50 call is currently selling for $4 per share. You can sell your XXX stock for a long-term capital gain of $12 a share and then buy the call for $4. This will protect $800 of your profit regardless of any movement in the underlying security ($1200 profit on your stock sale less the $400 purchase price of the call option). If XXX stock

TABLE 1	Stock Price	15	20	25	30	35	40	45
	B 100 XYZ @ 30	1500	2000	2500	3000	3500	4000	4500
	Profit (Loss) on $3000 Investment	(1500)	(1000)	(500)	0	500	1000	1500
Out-Of-The Money Call	B XYZ Ap 35 @ 1	0	0	0	0	0	500	1000
	Profit (Loss) on $100 Investment	(100)	(100)	(100)	(100)	(100)	400	900
At-The-Money Call	B XYZ Ap 30 @ 2½	0	0	0	0	500	1000	1500
	Profit (Loss) on $250 Investment	(250)	(250)	(250)	(250)	250	750	1250
In-The-Money Call	B XYZ Ap 25 @ 6	0	0	0	500	1000	1500	2000
	Profit (Loss) on Investment	(600)	(600)	(600)	(100)	400	900	1400

advances to, say, $60 in the next six months, the option will be worth at least $10 (its intrinsic value), giving you a profit of six points on the call plus the twelve point profit you took earlier on the stock. In addition, the trade would free $4600 of your capital to be invested elsewhere.

This substitution strategy will affect your tax situation. By selling XXX stock at a $12 per share profit, you realize $1200 in long-term capital gain. Your profit or loss on the call will be short-term. Table 2 shows how the substitution affects your profitability and tax treatment over a wide range of stock prices.

TABLE 2 Substituted Stock Price	35	40	45	50	55	60	65
Long-Term Gain on Stock Sale	1200	1200	1200	1200	1200	1200	1200
Short-Term Gain (Loss) on Option	(400)	(400)	(400)	(400)	100	600	1100
Interest on Capital	276	276	276	276	276	276	276
Net Gain (Loss)	1076	1076	1076	1076	1576	2076	2576
Unsubstituted Stock Price	35	40	45	50	55	60	65
Long-Term Gain (Loss) on Stock Sale	(300)	200	700	1200	1700	2200	2700

Short Stock—Long Call

If you sell stock short, you have put yourself in a position of theoretically unlimited risk. If, however, you sell stock short and hedge (protect) your position by purchasing a call, you have set a maximum price at which you can repurchase the stock to satisfy the obligation of the short sale in advance. This is the exercise price of the call. For example, you sell XYZ short at $50, hoping for a price decline within three months. A three-month XYZ 50 call is selling for $2.50. If XYZ rises, you simply exercise your call at $50 per share to cover your short position, thereby losing only $2.50—the option premium.

If, on the other hand, the stock price drops to $40 during the three-month period, you would buy the stock to cover your short position in the underlying market for a profit of $10 per share. The call would then expire worthless, leaving you with a net profit of $750. The transaction could even be repeated if you felt the market had not yet "bottomed out," with you holding your short position in the stock and buying a call with a later expiration date and a lower exercise price.

This long call—short stock position involves risks and potential profits similar to the purchase of a put option and is, therefore, often referred to as a synthetic put. Let's look at the insurance provided by this strategy over a wide range of stock prices (Table 3). For simplicity, we have assumed that if the stock is trading at or below $50 per share, the call will be worthless; if the stock is trading about $50, the call will be salable at a figure equal to its value.

TABLE 3 Stock Price	30	35	40	45	50	55	60	65	70
Short Sale Profit (Loss)	2000	1500	1000	500	0	(500)	(1000)	(1500)	(2000)
Unexercised Call Profit (Loss)	(250)	(250)	(250)	(250)	(250)	250	750	1250	1750
Profit (Loss) on Comb. Trade	1750	1250	750	250	(250)	(250)	(250)	(250)	(250)

Put Buying

Like the call buyer, the person who buys a put can only lose the cost of the put. The put buyer profits fully in a downward movement of the stock except for the amount of time value in the initial purchase price.

Puts are becoming an increasingly important part of the option investor's portfolio for two reasons: First, the options exchanges have been steadily adding puts to underlying stocks on which calls are traded. At the end of 1981, puts were trading on all listed stocks, and put volume during recent market swings has contributed ever increasing amounts to total options volume. Second, many investors are using options to achieve the same benefits as shorting stock at far less capital risk.

Assume ZZZ stock is trading at 35 on January 1, the ZZZ April 30 put would trade for a dollar ($1 per share per contract, or $1000 for 10 contracts), the ZZZ April 35 put for $3.50, and the April 40 put for $6. The prices in Table 4 indicate values on expiration date.

Again, you will notice that the profit/loss of the in-the-money put most closely resembles shorting the stock. However, the put has the advantage of limiting risk to the six dollars per share you paid for the put and of realizing much greater percentage gains. Again, the only advantage for the short seller occurs only if the stock remains at the sale price (no loss; no gain), while the put buyer will lose the portion of the purchase price that represents time value.

Buying Put To Hedge Profitable Long

Let's say you have long-term profit in a particular stock and you are reluctant to sell this year, either because you expect further profits or

TABLE 4

	Stock Prices	20	25	30	35	40	45	50
	S 100 ZZZ @ 35	2000	2500	3000	3500	4000	4500	5000
	P (L) on $3500 Inv.	1500	1000	500	0	(500)	(1000)	(1500)
Out-Of-The-Money Put	B Ap30 Put @ 1	1000	500	0	0	0	0	0
	P (L) on $100 Inv.	900	400	(100)	(100)	(100)	(100)	(100)
At-The-Money Put	B Ap35 Put @ 3½	1500	1000	500	0	0	0	0
	P (L) on $350 Inv.	1150	650	150	(350)	(350)	(350)	(350)
In-The-Money Put	B Ap40 Put @ 6	2000	1500	1000	500	0	0	0
	P (L) on $600 Inv.	1400	900	400	(100)	(600)	(600)	(600)

TABLE 5

Stock Prices	15	20	25	30	35	40	45	50	55
Unhedged-B 100 Shares @ 20	1500	2000	2500	3000	3500	4000	4500	5000	5500
Long-Term Profit (Loss)	(500)	0	500	1000	1500	2000	2500	3000	3500
Hedged-S 100 Sh. @ 35 or more	3500	3500	3500	3500	3500	4000	4500	5000	5500
Long-Term Profit on Stock Sale	1500	1500	1500	1500	1500	2000	2500	3000	3500
Less Cost of Put (exercised or exp.)	(300)	(300)	(300)	(300)	(300)	(300)	(300)	(300)	(300)
Gross Profit	1200	1200	1200	1200	1200	1700	2200	2700	3200

because you don't want to pay tax on your profit in this calendar year. You own XYZ at $20 a share. XYZ is now trading at $35 and an XYZ 35 nine-month put is $3. For a maximum cost of $300, you can protect your $1500 profit.

If the stock goes down, you have guaranteed your right to sell it at $35 per share. If the stock goes up, you will lose your put premium, but continue to benefit from the rise in your stock price. For tax purposes, when a put is purchased against a long stock position which already qualifies for long-term treatment, the stock continues to qualify. If the holding period does not qualify for long-term tax treatment, accrued time is negated when the put is purchased and begins again when the long-put position is closed out.

Table 5 compares unhedged with hedged long stock positions over various stock prices. For simplicity, we have assumed that if the stock is selling over 35, you will sell it in the open market and the put will expire worthless. We have also assumed that if the stock slips under 35, you will exercise your put and deliver your stock at $35 a share. In either case, the put is represented on the table as an expense item.

Buying Put To Hedge New Long Position

When a put and an equal long stock position are acquired on the same day and identified as a hedge, the holding period for the stock and the put begin on that day, computed separately. If the put is allowed to expire, its cost is added to the cost of the stock. If the put is sold, the profit or loss is a short-term item and the holding period of the stock continues. If the put is exercised, the specific stock must be delivered in order to maintain the stock's holding period. Currently, this could not result in long-term treatment because the longest term listed options are only nine months to expiration.

You might want to buy a put (if available) every time you acquire a new long stock position. This would protect you from any downside risk on your stock during the life of the put (except for the cost of the put itself).

Table 6 shows XXX stock purchased at $40 and a nine-month XXX 40 put purchased at $5 per share. The value of the put for protection versus the unhedged position should be clear.

Covered Call Writing

This strategy is commonly used in conjunction with your stock portfolio to gain protection against any downside moves and to generate income. As such, it is probably the most widely used strategy next to the outright purchase of calls. Using out-of-the-money calls, the downside protection is reduced, while the percentage chance that the option will expire worthless is increased. Conversely, writing in-the-money calls offers greater downside protection while increasing the likelihood that the call be exercised or the option will have to be repurchased at a loss.

If you buy XYZ stock at $60 and write a six-month XYZ 50 call (ten points in-the-money) at $13, your margin investment will be $3000 (50 percent of the stock purchase price) less the $1300 you collect for selling the XYZ call—a total outlay of $1700. The premium protects you until XYZ stock moves down

TABLE 6

Stock Price	20	25	30	35	40	45	50	55	60
Unhedged-B 100 Shares @ 40	2000	2500	3000	3500	4000	4500	5000	5500	6000
P (L) on Stock	(2000)	(1500)	(1000)	(500)	0	500	1000	1500	2000
Hedged-S 100 Sh. @ 40 or more	4000	4000	4000	4000	4000	4500	5000	5500	6000
Profit on Stock	0	0	0	0	0	500	1000	1500	2000
Less Cost of Put (exercised or exp.)	500	500	500	500	500	500	500	500	500
Gross P (L) on Married Put	(500)	(500)	(500)	(500)	(500)	0	500	1000	1500

to $47 a share, or 21.67 percent.

On the other hand, if XYZ stock remains over $50 per share, you will receive an exercise notice and deliver your stock for $50 a share plus the $13 paid you earlier for the call sale. This leaves a profit of $3, or 17.6 percent (Table 7).

Now let's take the case of an out-of-the-money call option sale. You buy XYZ stock at $60 and write a six-month XYZ 70 call (ten points out-of-the-money) at $5. You are only protected until XYZ stock moves down to 55, or 8.33 percent. If XYZ remains under 70, your call will not be exercised and you will collect the $5 premium plus any appreciation in the stock from $60, (your purchase price) to $70, you will collect a $10 profit on the stock, plus the $5 call premium, for a maximum profit of $1500 or 60 percent on an investment of $2500.

Uncovered Call Selling

The "naked" call writer has potential risks which the covered writer and the put buyer do not. This is, therefore, a very aggressive bearish strategy. Risks are theoretically unlimited, while potential profits are limited to the amount of the premium. Profitability depends upon a downward or flat movement in the underlying security. Remember that a call may be exercised at any time up to the final expiration date. Because the "naked" writer does not own the stock, he may have to buy it in the underlying market and deliver it at a lower price to satisfy his obligation.

In this example, ZZZ stock is $70 and a three-month ZZZ 70 call is $11. If the stock stays below 70 for the entire three-month period, the "naked" seller would realize $1100 on an investment of $2100. If the stock rises gradually, so that near the final exercise date it is at $75 per share or less, you should be able to buy back your short call for approximately $5 (the intrinsic value) since an in-the-money call with only a few days left until expiration will have little or no time value left (unless the stock has risen precipitously and investors expect the next few days to bring further upside movement). You would then retain $600 of your proceeds.

If, however, the stock moved to $81 within a few weeks of your short sale (your upside break-even point), you could expect to receive an exercise notice at any moment. You would then be faced with the choice of buying the stock in the underlying market, or buying back your short call to eliminate your obligation. If the stock reaches $80 with, say, four weeks until expiration, you might expect to pay $15 for your ZZZ 70 call, for a loss of $400. In an extreme example, where the stock rose to $90, you might lose as much as $1300.

If you write an out-of-the-money call, your upside protection is reduced. With ZZZ stock at $50, the three-month ZZZ 60 call might be trading at $1.50. On any rise above 51½, you will lose on a dollar-for-dollar basis. If the stock dropped or remained unchanged, you would only stand to make $150.

Covered Put Writing

The short stock—short put strategy is designed to let you profit on the short sale of the stock plus collect put premiums. The put premium also

TABLE 7									
Stock Price	40	45	50	55	60	65	70	75	80
Unhedged B 100 Shares @ 60	4000	4500	5000	5500	6000	6500	7000	7500	8000
P2ofl4 (L&33)(2000)	(1500)	(1000)	(500)	0	500	1000	1500	2000	
Hedged B 100 Sh. @ 60, exercised @ 50 or higher	4000	4500	5000	5000	5000	5000	5000	5000	5000
P (L) on Stock $ XYZ 50 @ 13 (exercised or exp.)	(2000) 1300	(1500) 1300	(1000) 1300	(1000) 1300	(1000) 1300	(1000) 1300	(1000) 1300	(1000) 1300	(1000) 1300
Gross P (L)	(700)	(200)	300	300	300	300	300	300	300
Hedged, exercised @ 70 or higher	4000	4500	5000	5500	6000	6500	7000	7000	7000
P (L) on Stock	(2000)	(1500)	(1000)	(500)	0	500	1000	1000	1000
$ XYZ 70 @ 5 (exercised or exp.)	500	500	500	500	500	500	500	500	500
Gross P (L)	(1500)	(1000)	(500)	0	500	1000	1500	1500	1500

represents your upside protection.

Let's assume you short 100 shares of XYZ stock at 29 and sell an XYZ 30 three-month put at $4. If the stock goes up, you are protected to $33 a share, or a 13.79 percent move in the stock. Over $33, your short put should be worthless and your short position would lose on a dollar-for-dollar basis until you bought the stock to cover your position. On the downside, if the stock moved to $25 per share at the expiration date, the put buyer would surely elect to exercise his put by delivering stock to you (the put writer) at $30 per share. Your purchase would cover your short sale at a $1 per share loss, while you collect the put premium of $400 for a gross profit of $300 on the transaction.

The profit potential of shorting stock and selling in-the-money puts is limited to the put premium. If you short XYZ stock at $30 and sell an XYZ 40 three-month put for $12, any close below $40 would result in an exercise. You would effectively be buying the stock back for $40 per share—a $10 per share loss—while collecting the $12 per share put premium for a gross profit on the transaction of $2 per share. Selling in-the-money puts affords greater upside protection for your short position, as you would not lose any money unless the stock closed above $42 at expiration.

Selling out-of-the-money puts offers smaller upside protection and greater downside potential. If you were to short XYZ stock at $30 and sell a three-month XYZ 25 put at $1, you would not have to buy the stock unless it fell below $25 at expiration. If this happened and the put were exercised, your effective purchase price on the stock would be $24 ($25 per share less $1 collected on your sale of the put) for a $600 per 100 share profit. On the other hand, you would lose on any stock price above $31 at expiration.

Overview

After reviewing these options strategies, it should be clear that they are generally sophisticated financial tools. A potential investor should have a clear understanding of the current and projected price movements of the underlying stock, as well as the potential risk versus reward ratio of the buy or writing strategy they are considering. It should also be clear that options are not a cheap way to get into the stock market. Options are a "secondary market" to stocks—options movements are dictated by stock movements.

The year-to-year increase in options use is unprecedented in the securities industry. No one could have predicted the success of the CBOE and the U.S. options market. So, it is natural to be a little gun shy about predicting the years to come. Some things are clear, though. Because of all the new products on which options will be traded, the leverage and hedging aspects of options will be used by investors outside the stock market before this year is past.

Also, the stock options market will undoubtedly continue to expand. Rules that were established for an unknown market prior to CBOE's opening are being re-examined and amended to allow more stocks to be listed, allow investors to hold more contracts (up from 1000 to 2000 contracts on either the buy or sell sides of the market), and foreign (Canadian) stocks will probably soon be listed on U.S. options exchanges.

Chapter Ten

Investing In Mutual Funds

T ired of trying to figure out what to do with your money? What stocks
or bonds to buy, and when? Nervous when it comes to deciding
whether to sell and take a small profit or wait for a bigger killing,
you hope, in the future? If you can answer any of these questions
"yes," or if you're just too busy to follow the stock market closely on your
own time,. then perhaps you should consider investing in a mutual fund.

Yes, mutual funds once enjoyed the dubious reputation of being "widows
and orphans" investments. And yes, they were once held in terrible disrepute,
after countless investors lost more than their shirts courtesy of high-flying
"growth" funds. And now a cycle of sorts is completed—mutual funds are
again considered a good investment.

What are mutual funds and how do they work? In the first place, there is no
such thing as a "mutual fund"—what you are buying into is an investment
trust, actually an investment corporation, and what you buy are shares.
(However, mutual fund is a convenient term, and it has stuck.) Your dollars are
pooled with the investments of others (often thousands of other people), and
these combined resources are used to purchase money assets—stocks, bonds,
notes, and so on—which are in turn professionally managed. In other words,
the selection, purchase, and sale of these stocks and bonds are executed by
people who are paid to know what is best to do in the prevailing economic
climate. The benefit to the investor is this professional guiding hand; if the
assets of the mutual fund increase through good investments, the capital each
person contributed will do the same. Obviously, the reverse is also true: If the
fund's assets decline, so does your investment.

Think of it as an institutionalized investment club. Say you and nine of your
friends decide to pool some money, for example, $1000 each. You want to use
the total, $10,000, to buy common stock. Since the ten of you don't agree on

the best investment for the money, you decide to hire a money manager to make the decisions. After the end of a year, your manager reports that your fund has made money—the value of the stocks the fund owns has increased to $12,000. Each of your shares is now worth $1200.

Now some of your neighbors have heard about your gains, and they want in, too. You and your nine friends have to decide whether or not to allow new shareholders. If not, then you have a "closed-end trust." That means there will be no new shares issued unless one of the original shareholders sells out.

If the group decides to enlarge the trust and take on new members, it is an "open-ended fund." The price for entry would be based on the new amount per share, or $1200. Called the *net asset value per share*, it is determined by dividing the number of shares outstanding into the current market value of the fund's portfolio. Of course, net asset value per share (NAV) is not a fixed number, because a fund's value moves up and down along with their stock (or whatever) selections.

The term mutual fund has come to be synonymous with open-ended trusts, and for most investors, these are the most appropriate choice.

Today, many regulations control mutual funds, but they basically operate as just described. When you buy a share in a mutual fund, you buy a share in a large diversified portfolio whose net asset value per share is calculated daily. This price determines what dealers will sell the shares for and what the owner will get if he or she sells. Clearly, a mutual fund is quite different from a savings account, where the rate of return is set and guaranteed. In a mutual fund, you are an owner; in a savings account, you are a lender. Mutual fund shareholders may also sell out any time they like.

Mutual funds also distribute dividend and interest income from the portfolio to shareholders. When a fund sells some of its investments, any net gain is also distributed among shareholders.

Mutual Funds Advantages

For non-professional investors, mutual funds offer some special advantages:
1. They offer professional, experienced management of your money on a full-time basis. Fund managers, obviously, are better acquainted with the various investment markets than you are—if not, you have no need for a mutual fund. Managers are trained to make decisions regarding what to buy, sell, and hold, thus relieving the average investor from this often-overwhelming task. Professional management, of course, does not mean there will never be mistakes—there have been and will be, but the chances are reduced as much as is possible.
2. Mutual funds offer diversity. Not all of your money will be invested in one stock, one bond, or—in the case of most stock and bond funds—even in one single industry group. This diversity provides a hedge against risk and prevents the old "all the eggs in one basket" dilemma. If disaster hits one area, as it has slammed into the housing and automobile industries, you are protected to the extent that much of the fund's money will be invested in better situated industries.

3. Mutual funds offer a record of their past performance. The successes or failures of any given fund are a matter of public record. In other words, you can decide between the winners and the losers, and the availability of this information will help you make the best possible selection. Since this data is not published for the performance of stockbrokers, bank trust departments, discount brokers, or portfolio managers, the "out in the open" record of mutual funds serves as an assurance, of sorts, that their managers are at least operating in good faith.

4. Mutual funds offer an anxiety-free means to participating in the stock market. Hot tips, takeover rumors, bankruptcy tales, and other "insider" rumblings need not bother you. Nor do you need to read as much about the market or try to assimilate a great deal of facts about particular industries, companies, or bond ratings—mutual funds simplify investing.

5. Mutual funds provide freedom from excessive paperwork and complicated accounting. Instead of keeping track of a stack of stock certificates and market performance, the fund sends you periodic statements and, at the end of the year, data on income and capital gains. This single statement is handy for tax purposes.

6. Mutual funds offer automatic dividend reinvestment plans. If you have faith in a fund's future performance, this is a good way to increase your savings—not that a mutual fund should ever be considered a savings vehicle.

7. Mutual funds allow even the smallest of small investors access to the market. Some funds require a minimum initial deposit of only $250. This small dollar amount buys far more diversification than you could achieve using the funds to buy stocks directly, since most brokers are reluctant to negotiate such small increments of stock. (Most brokers simply will not do so.)

8. Mutual funds offer switching. Some of the larger funds have an umbrella plan, which means investors can switch all or part of their principal from one type of fund to another. This is especially useful for those whose investment objectives change, for those who sense a coming shift in the market, and for those who are considering the use of a mutual fund for an IRA account.

9. Mutual funds offer an easy way out. There is always a market in mutual funds, at least at current asset value. This is especially helpful for those in bond funds, for a small number of bonds is very difficult to sell except at a discount. When you are invested in a mutual fund that specializes in bonds, you can sell your shares any time you want, without losing the bond's value.

So which fund might be for you? Even before trying to select the winners and losers among the approximately 500 mutual funds in the country, you have to decide what your investment objectives are. There are several different types of mutual funds, and it's important that your investment goals and those of the fund managers match.

Read the fund's advertisements carefully, and give special attention to the first page of the prospectus—a full description of the fund which is required by the Securities and Exchange Commission (SEC). Funds may purchase stocks, bonds, precious metals, options, commodities, and on and on. And they may purchase these assets for income, capital appreciation, or long-term growth.

Mutual Fund Types

The major types of mutual funds group into several broad categories:

● **Growth Funds.** These buy common stock in companies expected to enjoy above-average growth in both earnings and stock prices. Dividend payout is generally average to low. Within this area are some which critics have labeled "aggressive growth funds." Such funds specialize in smaller companies and are best purchased when the market is on an upswing. Geared for capital or maximum appreciation, these are only for those who are willing to take a certain amount of risk.

Other growth funds have portfolios aimed at both growth and current income. These pay fair dividends and concentrate on the so-called "blue chip" stocks. Often, such growth funds are called "quality growth funds," and these are more appropriate to investors who want to avoid risk.

● **Growth & Income Funds.** Such mutual funds contain both stocks and bonds in their portfolios. The stocks, usually of solid companies, pay a decent yield. Also labeled "balanced funds," these are designed to deliver both capital appreciation and regular income to investors.

● **Income Funds.** Made up primarily of corporate bonds, government insured mortgages, and preferred stocks, these are designed primarily to return income to investors. They are also known as "bond funds." A variation is the flexible income mutual fund, whose portfolios vary their holdings from bonds to stocks to a combination of both.

● **Municipal Bond Funds.** As the name suggests, these have a limited investment strategy. They are designed for investors seeking tax-exempt income.

● **Special Funds.** These have a high risk factor. The category includes option funds, commodity funds, venture capital funds, gold funds, and so on. They are not discussed here for two reasons: One, several of them require the investor to take a great deal of risk, trusting the portfolio managers to make consistently good decisions against tight schedules, as in commodities and options. Two, specialized funds, like precious metals or diamonds, are dependent upon cyclical markets—they may perform very well at certain times, but a well-managed growth, income, or capital appreciation fund can do it consistently.

With about 500 mutual funds on the market (not including the money market funds), it's not easy to find the perfect one. However, you can make your choice intelligently by following some general guidelines.

First, locate a fund with investment objectives similar to yours. You can do this by reading advertisements in financial publications, by reading the prospectus of each company that interests you, and by glancing through the *No-Load Mutual Fund Directory* (Valley Forge, PA 19481). In addition, the Investment Company Institute, 1775 K St., Washington, DC 20006 can send you a directory.

Second, select a fund with adequate size, somewhere around $100 million in assets. A fund that is too small may not be able to diversify adequately, and it may not have the funds to support a large research staff or be able to pay for first-rate professionals. This is not true, however, of small funds that are part of a larger family of funds—they can share in research and management. There are exceptions to this rule, of course. In addition, small funds should be considered if you are seeking an aggressive fund with a high risk factor—after all, high risk is usually accompanied by high reward, when the choices are correct.

Third, compare fund performances. The August issue of *Forbes* magazine rates the performance of the leading funds. *Barron's* reports weekly on changes in fund performance. And the monthly issue of *Standard & Poor's Stock Guide* has lists of funds and their records over various time periods.

Another source of information, of course, is any of the various professional charts. Copies of the *Lipper Analytical Charts* or the *Wiesenburger Charts* are available either from your broker or at many public libraries.

Fourth, read the prospectus to find the following information:

● The minimum investment required and the minimum amount for subsequent purchases—can you afford the particular fund?

● Management's background and experience.

● How long the fund has been in business.

● The record of dividends paid out.

● The record of distribution from capital gains.

● Additional services offered, such as reinvestment plans, telephone orders, fund switching, IRA and Keogh plans, withdrawal plans, and so on.

● If there have been significant changes in the size of total assets over the past several years. Don't, under any circumstances, opt for a fund that is dropping in size—there are so many alternatives available that it makes no sense to increase any single risk factor.

● If there are any lawsuits outstanding against the fund. If so, find out what they are, and discuss them with your lawyer or financial adviser.

● Review the fund's portfolio breakdown.

After you have studied several funds, there is one more aspect to consider before you write the check—fees. Mutual funds are sold as either "load" funds or "no-load" funds. Load funds are sold through brokerages, like a stock purchase, and you pay a commission of about 8.5 percent. This means the mutual fund must rise by that value before you will break even.

A no-load fund has no sales charge, and is sold directly by the company. Since there is no great difference in the performance of load and no-load funds, it really makes little sense to invest in a load fund. Both variations charge annual management fees as well, usually one-half to one percent. The prospectus will give you this information as well, along with any other fees the company may charge.

And yes, there are taxes. The Investment Company Act of 1940 provided that in order to operate as an investment company and thereby receive tax benefits, a mutual fund must return at least 90 percent of its annual income to the shareholders. By contrast, a regular corporation is not required to pass on any. The remaining ten percent is used for operating expenses and is subject to corporation taxes. Investors owning shares in a mutual fund must therefore pay taxes on the income passed along to them.

At the end of the year, your mutual fund will send you a complete statement, containing an itemized list of the income you received. Of course, your accountant can advise you as to the best way to deal with the specifics, but you will generally need to save the following for your tax preparation: dividend statements, tax exempt interest amounts from municipal bonds, and the capital gains distribution. You will also need to save the amount you received if you sold any shares. The IRA offers a free booklet (#564) that will help you with tax considerations.

For years, mutual funds were completely out of favor. In terms of assets, the funds scraped bottom along with the stock market in 1973-74, but their assets are now 60 percent higher, in total, than they were eight years ago. Over the past five years, the average common stock fund has risen about 105 percent. During the same period, the S&P 500 rose 52 percent—the comparison speaks well for fund managers. So what can you expect for 1982 and 1983?

Mutual Funds in '81

Let's look at last year. 1981 was very tough for the stock market, with the S&P 500 falling about 9.7 pecent and the Dow Jones Industrial Average slipping 9.2 percent. Yet many mutual funds did well. Of course, others didn't. (See accompanying tables.)

As an example of a well-managed fund, consider Lindner Fund of St. Louis. While the S&P 500 was dropping 9.7 percent, Lindner was gaining 34.87 percent. Why did this no-load fund perform so spectacularly, along with a select group of others? Although the fund is relatively small—net assets in the area of $26 million—over the past five years its smallest annual increase was 21.8 percent. Emphasizing low P/E ratios, the Lindner portfolio is fairly conservative. Its turnover rate is low as well, at only about 25 percent. This emphasis on undervalued companies with low P/Es meant that last year Lindner cashed in on several takeover candidates: Iowa Beef Processors, A.J. Armstrong, Page Airways, and Wallace Murray were all in Lindner's portfolio before they were purchased by other companies.

According to Kurt Lindner, the fund's president, the portfolio is also heavy in utilities—15 percent of the total assets—with holdings in such companies as Wisconsin Electric Power, Con Ed of New York, Louisville Gas & Electric, and so on. Such investments provide both safety and high yield.

A strong utilities position also boosted the value of another fund—Franklin Utilities. According to Lipper Analytical, Franklin's assets rose to 21.10 percent in 1981. Their portfolio includes large positions in Sun Belt utilities, where the population is expanding, providing Franklin with healthy earnings growth and solid dividend returns. Franklin's portfolio manager, Charles Johnson, lists Tucson Electric Power, Southwestern Public Service, and Florida Power & Light among the fund's holdings.

The current economic climate, with a fairly promising trend away from higher inflation, has favored what Wall Street calls the interest-sensitive stocks: Utilities and financial institutions, such as insurance companies and banks. And at least one fund, Century Shares Trust, was specialized to capitalize on this trend—approximately 90 percent of its assets are in insurance companies, and about five percent reside in banks.

Value Line's dependable Income Fund still invests in some common stocks with high yields, but in its current portfolio, according to President Tom Sexton, only 42 percent resides in common shares, while over 50 percent of assets have been devoted to Treasury bills and government paper. The Value Line Leveraged Growth Fund is devoted to the "larger capitalized companies" (or what are usually called blue chips). The selection of these companies, says Sexton, follows the Value Line rating system used for its weekly advisory letter. The fund selects only those stocks which have received the desirable, hard-to-obtain 1 or 2 rating for stock market performance. Of course, Value Line investors have the built-in advantage of the company's superb research department.

Still another approach is practiced by Sequoia Fund. Bill Ruane, Sequoia's president, makes portfolio selections based on good, old-fashioned common sense. "Our portfolio holds less than 20 issues right now. We like to buy truly good businesses, those that are sound and very solid. We find that this approach toward companies with low P/Es has paid off. Two years ago, when everyone was involved in the 'flashy' energy and technology stocks, we took advantage of the fact that the market was ignoring the consumer area—Pepsi, Gillette, food and drug stocks. We did very well with that decision."

In the end, a little research of your own can prevent you from picking losers among the many mutual funds. Study each likely fund's prospectus—six months ago, you wouldn't have wanted to invest in a fund that was heavily committed to oil stocks, but it might be a good idea now. However, if you are unsure of which industries you believe a mutual fund should be invested in, then let past performance and overall strategy guide you.

Mutual Funds and IRA

There is another fund play that is gaining popularity—funds for Individual Retirement Accounts (IRAs). Now that all working Americans can shelter $2000 annually in a tax-deferred IRA, the big question nationwide is, of course, where to invest it.

One excellent solution is to place it in a management company that presides over a group of funds, or a "family of funds." These include bond funds, common stock funds, and money market funds, and they generally allow you to "switch" your assets from one fund to another. This technique provides something of a hedge against shifts in the interest rate and stock prices—if interest rates were rising and the stock market falling, you might switch your money from a stock fund to a money market fund. Conversely, if the stock market is beginning to climb, you could switch from the money market fund into the stock fund.

The chief advantages for an IRA investment are that mutual funds are inexpensive to enter, there are various choices available at the outset, and you can switch your money for the best return according to the economic conditions. Some families literally offer every alternative you might want.

If the umbrella approach appeals to you, examine the prospectus of the funds offered by these three management groups:

Fidelity. This group offers 14 funds suitable for IRAs. The Magellan and Equity Income funds each offered top-quality returns in 1981, and percentage gains over the past five years have been 352.46 and 121.28 percent respectively.

Neuberger & Berman. Six funds are geared to IRAs. Historically a well-regarded mutual fund organization, N&B has an outstanding reputation for selecting growth-oriented companies. Its Partners Fund is organized specifically for pension accounts, and the minimum investment is only $250. Also worth consideration is N&B's Guardian Mutual Fund.

Value Line. With six funds specifically available for IRAs, this organization offers unique advantages, especially its research and investment advisory services.

Finally, bond funds should be seriously considered. This may be a very good time to buy bonds—a number of experts feel that with business activity slowing and inflation subsiding somewhat, high-grade bonds are greatly undervalued. Yields on high-grade long-term bonds are now between 14 and 17 percent.

Bond Mutual Funds

If you agree that interest rates are coming down in the Reagan Depression, then you may want to turn to the bond funds. Small investors should not try to buy odd lots of bonds themselves—the bid and ask spreads are often too wide and liquidity can be terrible. On the other hand, bond funds offer both diversity and liquidity. In recessions, with dropping interest rates, bond funds perform well—but they do poorly when the economy is improving. So timing would be important with this investment.

If you think now is the time for a bond fund, there are several good no-load vehicles available:

- Dreyfus A Bonds Plus—767 Fifth Ave., New York, NY 10153
- Fidelity Corporate Bond Fund—82 Devonshire St., Boston, MA 02109
- Lexington GNMA Income Fund—Box 1515, Englewood Cliffs, NJ 07632
- T. Rowe Price New Income Fund—100 E. Pratt St., Baltimore MD 21202
- Stein Roe Bond Fund—150 S. Wacker Dr., Chicago, IL 60606
- Value Line Bond Fund—711 Third Ave., New York, NY 10017
- Vanguard Fixed Income Securities Fund—Box 1100, Valley Forge, PA 19482

TOP TWELVE PICKS

The funds below have shown both good returns over a five-year period (when available), and outstanding returns throughout 1981. There are many other excellent funds as well, but these are all worth additional investigation. For addresses and general information (before you read the prospectus), write to: The No-Load Mutual Fund Association, Valley Forge, PA 19481.

Fund Name	Type	Percentage Gain '76-'81	'81
Oppenheimer Target	CA	N/A	48.23%
Lindner Fund	G	268.10%	34.87
Quest For Value Fund	CA, G	N/A	30.42
Merrill Lynch Pacific	I	107.04	22.02
Sequoia Fund	G	127.87	21.49
Franklin Utilities	G & I	37.85	21.10
Magnacap Fund	G	73.04	20.72
Delta Trend Fund	CA & G	118.22	20.40
Century Shares Trust	G & I	62.87	20.16
Windsor Fund	G & I	92.71	16.76
Valueline Income	I	112.54	16.20
Valueline Leverage	G	266.09	15.88

Abbreviations: CA—capital appreciation; G—growth; I—income.

A DIRTY DOZEN

L isted below are funds which showed a poor return for 1981, along with relatively weak annual returns from 1976-1981. In one case, it's hard to

Fund Name	Type	Percentage Change '76-'81	'81
Kaufman Fund	CA	−67.37%	−56.23%
Centennial Growth	G	+51.23	−20.21
Sierra Growth	G	+64.87	−19.63
Investment Trust Boston	G & I	+42.82	−18.71
Cheapside Dollar	G	+71.16	−18.64
John Hancock Growth	G	+76.06	−17.09
Wade Fund	G	+56.51	−17.00
Steadman American Industry	CA	+47.65	−14.47
Financial Industry	G & I	+68.40	−14.19
Keystone S-1	G & I	+20.65	−13.91
Stein R&F Balanced	B	+29.21	−13.44
T. Rowe Price Growth	G	+31.53	−12.42

Abbreviations: CA—capital appreciation; G—growth; I—income; B—balanced.

believe the fund is still in business. In any event, better returns were, and are, available elsewhere.

Special funds are not included, which means most of those listed were not the absolute worst performers last year. For example, the precious metals funds did exceptionally poorly in 1981, some losing from 25 to over 30 percent in value. However, this is offset to a degree by their outstanding gains over a five-year period.

KEEPING TRACK OF YOUR INVESTMENT

Tables indicating the current price and other facts about individual mutual funds are included in financial papers and many daily newspapers. The sample here is from *The Wall Street Journal*.

Generally, the first column after the fund's name records net asset value (NAV). Next is the current offering price. If the fund is no-load, the offering price is designated N.L. In a load fund, the offering price is NAV per share plus the sales commission; a no-load's NAV and offering price are the same. The third column is usually labeled "NAV CHG." This gives the change in the fund's daily price, either up (+) or down (−), just like in the stock listings. Some reports, such as *Barron's* include columns giving the fund's 52-week high and low, the dividend yield for the latest 12 months, and the capital gains distributed. This is handy if you intend to play your mutual funds as if they were stocks.

COMPARING TOP FUNDS

As economic conditions change, different investment strategies pay higher returns than others. The best funds one year may not be the best the next—they aren't poorly managed funds, but they may invest in cyclical areas that have taken a downturn. A case in point is a gold fund. Below are the ten best funds for the 1976-1981 period and the ten best from last year.

Note that the top three funds for the five-year period are all gold funds. However, in 1981, none of the gold funds even made the "25 Best" list. In fact, they all resided among the worst performers for 1981. On the other hand, some well-managed stock and bond funds have ranked consistently well, which is why those funds are recommended.

1976-1981		1981	
Fund Name	Return	Fund Name	Return
Strategic Investments	493.12%	Oppenheimer Target	48.23%
United Services	464.06	Lindner Fund	34.87
International Investors	434.55	Quest For Value	30.42
Research Capital	410.69	Lindner Income	26.54
20th Century Growth	377.35	Qualified Dividend	22.48
Fidelity Magellan	352.46	Mutual Qualified Income	22.21
20th Century Select	278.65	Sequoia Fund	21.49
Evergreen Fund	270.40	Franklin Utilities	21.10
Quasar Associates	268.65	Directors Capital	20.90

Source: Lipper Analytical

Chapter Eleven

Shopping Foreign Markets

O nce considered glamorous, perhaps bubbling with exotic intrigue and dead-of-night decisions, the notion of internationally diversifying investments has come to shine under the light of austere logic. As more and more Americans have understood that the world is in many ways a single economic community, the idea of an "international investor" has shifted from visions of James Bond to a more realistic image—a normal investor who participates in a variety of financial markets.

In addition, continuing reports of spectacular gains on foreign stock exchanges, successful mining ventures in South America, Africa, and Australia, and record gains by one foreign currency against another have opened a lot of eyes to the world of profits outside the United States.

If you limit your horizons exclusively to the U.S., you will miss half of the investment opportunities available worldwide. The United States market accounted for about 50 percent of the total value of the world's 18 stock exchanges on June 30, 1981—down from 66 percent at the end of 1970.

International investment offers potentially higher returns than investments in U.S. securities as well. In terms of total return, which is a combination of capital growth and income, the U.S. stock market ranked only 15th among the 18 world equity markets for the period between 1970 and 1980. Disregarding the pummeling of 1973-74, the U.S. market still ranked only 9th between 1975 and 1980. In addition, many countries with lucrative markets enjoy a less painful inflation rate than the United States.

Currency differences among nations also offer opportunities to improve the total return. As a result of the dollar's recent depreciation—over the past few years—many foreign fixed-income markets, such as bonds, have provided total returns superior to similar U.S. markets. However, foreign investments involve risk and reward considerations not typically associated with U.S. companies, which can be a drawback.

At the same time, when things go wrong in the United States economically, they often go well in other countries—for the exact same reasons. For example, energy exporting countries are in far better shape than energy-dependent countries, and international diversification can protect you from internal problems.

Finally, specific tax situations in various countries can influence separate markets in important ways. An extreme example occurred in Sweden, when attractive tax benefits spurred a bull market on the Stockholm Exchange that has driven prices up over 65 percent since the beginning of 1981 and more than 100 *percent* since 1980. Although the tax advantages are for Swedish investors only, U.S. investors could still have benefited from the dramatic rise in Sweden's stock market.

Most importantly, global diversification can help reduce investment risk. In short, diversification of investments by market as well as by industries and companies is a sensible way to spread both risk and opportunity. International investors are not at the mercy of a single nation's market cycles, inflation rate, or economic policies. Since it is unlikely that all the world markets will rise or fall simultaneously—with, of course, extreme exceptions—spreading investments among several different countries provides a measure of diversification that is simply unavailable to those who restrict their investments to a single national economy.

So why don't more U.S. investors take advantage of international investing? One big impediment has been a simple lack of knowledge. Another is a lack of funds necessary to achieve adequate diversification. Both problems can be solved through a mutual fund that invests internationally.

However, investors with both the money and expertise could participate directly in foreign markets, through American Depository Receipts (ADRs). Such instruments function as stock certificates for ownership of foreign securities and are held by banks for their customers. Using ADRs avoids the multiple problems of obtaining foreign securities, and, in the case of Japan, no alternative is available—the actual securities may not leave the country. Unfortunately, the selection of ADRs is limited, commonly representing mature companies (in which little growth possibility is left or expected) or extremely speculative ventures. This isn't always the case, but it can be a drawback. Worse, investing directly in ADRs can be fairly expensive.

Generally speaking, investors lacking either substantial funds or expert advice will be better off in an international fund.

Part of the basis for such funds is a response to inflation. In recent years, the U.S. has had a mediocre record of controlling inflation compared to the rest of the world. The U.S. equities markets are not among the seven world markets that produced a higher total return than their domestic inflation rate through the 1970s.

By investing in countries with a lower rate of inflation than the United States, international funds hope to produce a total return which exceeds the U.S. inflation rate. Although there are, and will be, times when U.S. living costs and share values move in opposite directions, the funds strive to provide an effective hedge against inflation in the long term.

Difficulties In International Markets

A sophisticated investor can usually study and select U.S. securities with at least some promise of success. The same investor would run into difficulty in the international market. Among other things, the investor would have to understand the politics and economies of various nations, would need an awareness of the role of currency changes in international investing, and would have to have enough time, knowledge, and resources to analyze foreign industries and individual companies within the industries.

On the other hand, international mutual funds undertake all these tasks for a small annual fee. Of course, favorable results cannot be guaranteed, but analysts and economists devote their energies to improving the fund's total return. They also seek to reduce risks not typically associated with U.S. investments, such as exchange rate fluctuations, the possibility of foreign governmental regulations or taxes adversely affecting the portfolio securities, and the shifting degrees of liquidity in foreign securities.

By necessity, international fund managers have a broader investment focus than U.S. equity funds. The international funds emphasize four basic areas:

1. Flexibility. The ability to respond promptly to changing political and economic circumstances in individual countries is vitally important, and these conditions are constantly monitored.

2. Liquidity. Securities purchased for portfolios are constantly reviewed to make sure they meet "marketability" requirements. This is important because many foreign markets are not as large, as well developed, or as liquid as the U.S. markets.

3. Currency changes. The shifting relationship of a country's currency to the currencies of other nations is reviewed daily to avoid taking losses on the exchange rates.

4. Asset mix. The allocation of assets between equities, fixed-income investments, and cash is influenced by the size and liquidity of each market. Also, the mix is adjusted at regular intervals to reflect changing economic conditions.

Even the most astute individual investor would find it difficult to keep abreast all these facets of international investing, especially if the investments are sprinkled among five or 10 countries. The resources of fund managers enable them to maintain worldwide networks of investment and financial advisers.

Whether or not you participate in an international fund is a matter of choice. But participating in international investments may be a matter of necessity. The shares of U.S. multinational corporations provide some exposure to the economic developments in other parts of the world, but they cannot offer as significant and undiluted a form of participation as direct purchase of ADRs or indirect ownership through an international fund.

For one obvious example, there are many foreign businesses and industries for which there are no U.S. counterparts in existence. The inner workings of every radio and all but one television sold in the United States are made in foreign lands. If you want a stake in the international diamond industry, you have to buy South African, British, or Australian mining shares. If you want to profit from the escalating natural rubber boom—a direct consequence of the high-priced synthetic rubber/oil prices impact—you must invest in the London or Singapore equity markets for shares in plantation companies.

If you want to participate in minerals, the first choice has to be South Africa. In addition, Australia is the waiting treasure trove for minerals—it has abundant reserves of natural gas, coal, uranium, nickel, bauxite, copper, lead, and so on. And the only way to profit from Australian commodity price changes, frontier oil and gas exploration, and increased strategic metals spending worldwide is to participate in the Australian market.

Mainland China is waiting to boom—the only way to participate in it in a large sense is through Japan or Hong Kong, at least in the short term. Japan is now the world's largest producer of automobiles.

Other Japanese companies are outpacing the earnings figures of American competitors in semiconductors, computers, and high technology industries in general. If you want to invest in robotics, you must invest in the Tokyo market.

A Look At European Markets

The major European stock markets also offer exposure to a number of interesting financial and industrial developments. The French market boomed through 1978-1979 because of new government programs encouraging wider public ownership of equities. North Sea oil development has created a number of exciting investments in Norway, Belgium, and Britain. In fact, Norway's oil potential helped send the country's market climbing *174 percent* in 1979.

In addition, rising defense outlays in Western Europe will have a beneficial impact on a variety of defense-related companies in Britain, France, and West Germany. Japan is also studying rearmament after many years of spending less than one percent of its Gross National Product on defense. Given the size of Japan's economy, an increase in defense spending to only 1.5 percent of the GNP would have a lasting impact on Japanese defense industries.

Another advantage of international diversification is that it enables you to capitalize on currency changes. During the late 1970s, the U.S. Government pursued more inflationary economic policies than most other countries. The policies caused a sharp slump in the value of the dollar against such currencies as the Swiss franc, German mark, and Japanese yen. The appreciation of these currencies contributed to the advantageous total dollar returns available through Swiss, German, and Japanese investments.

In 1980, the dollar recovered some of its earlier losses against the mark and the franc, but it remained weak against the yen and the British pound. The pound was boosted by North Sea oil revenues and the British government's inclination—so similar to the U.S. Government's—to strangle its country with high interest rates rather than lose monetary strength. And the yen was boosted by high tides of OPEC petro-dollars flowing into the Tokyo market.

As economic policies and business conditions change, the dollar will continue to fluctuate against other currencies. In the process, it will create new

132   MONEY MAKER

opportunities for improving investment returns in international diversification —but it will have a far smaller influence on U.S. investments.

Currency appreciation can even compensate for mediocre stock performance. For example, Germany accepted slower economic growth in the late 1970s in order to reduce the inflation rate. As a result, the German stock market appreciated at a meager 4.57 percent compounded annual rate in domestic currency terms—compared to a 9.5 percent gain on the Standard & Poor's 500. However, when the German stock market's performance is adjusted for changes in the value of the deutschemark against the dollar, its capital appreciation was 11.37 percent between 1975 and 1979—far outperforming the U.S. market. The same sort of performance ratio exists for fixed-income securities.

More important than any other factor, the U.S. economic performance guaranteed that the U.S. markets would lag behind other nations'. The growth rate of American GNP—the sum of all goods and services produced by the economy—was lower in two different periods than the GNP of many other countries, in which you or an international fund could have invested.

Very simply, while the United States is a highly advanced, industrial nation with an extremely high standard of living, it is no longer the world's growth leader. Even should the country's economic performance improve, the U.S. GNP represents a much smaller percentage of the world economy than it did 10 or 20 years ago.

Industries which have matured in the U.S.—automobiles, household appliances, frozen food, life insurance, and so on—are just hitting their high growth phases in such countries as Japan, Malaysia, and Hong Kong. In free market economies with stable political institutions, high rates of economic growth tend to produce superior stock market performances—and this has definitely been the case in Japan, Australia, and various European countries.

Industrialized Nations Promoting Investments

E ven though the growth rate for the GNP of all the major industrial nations has slowed in recent years, countries such as Japan, France, and West Germany have done far more than the United States to promote investment and to encourage capital formation. Nearly all the other industrialized nations allow for a more rapid depreciation of plant and equipment than the U.S. Most have reformed their tax systems to eliminate double taxation of dividends. Many have either no capital gains tax or a capital gains tax rate below that of the U.S. Because of these pro-capital formation policies, the equity markets of many other industrial nations have continued to outperform the U.S., despite any slowdown in the countries' economic growth.

What does this all mean to global investment strategy? It means you can capitalize on the widely differing correlations between foreign and U.S. markets, as measured by the Standard & Poor's 500. Between 1975 and 1980, for example, the correlations ranged from a high of .66 for Canada (which has close links with the U.S. economy) to a low of .18 for Spain. The lower the correlation between the U.S. market and a foreign market, the greater your ability to reduce risks through international diversification. When the U.S. market is stagnant or declining, exposure to markets that have a low correlation with the S&P 500 could help protect investment portfolios from capital losses.

Moreover, while the unparalleled strength of the U.S. dollar against all major currencies in the last year has, in effect, reduced the value of foreign assets, it has not in any way undermined the arguments in favor of investing part of one's assets overseas. On the contrary, the dollar's strength now opens the opportunity of acquiring foreign assets at lower dollar cost. Certain countries, particularly in the Pacific Rim, continue to show faster growth than the U.S., thereby enabling higher corporate profit growth and, over the long term, superior stock performance. Some countries continue to enjoy a lower inflation rate than the U.S. and currently provide attractive real rates of return in the fixed-income markets.

One area of optimism in an otherwise gloomy environment is the gradual improvement in the current balance of payment positions of many European countries. The weakness of European currencies against the U.S. dollar, combined with declining inflation rates, has made European exports very competitive against U.S. products. At the same time, weak demand for imports has shrunk the import bills. In time, improved trade accounts will lead to stronger European currencies—particularly the Swiss franc and German mark—which will be further reinforced by any decline in U.S. interest rates. In other words, the dollar will buy more European equities now than it will in the future.

Compared to Europe, the Far Eastern prospects are encouraging. Japan's GNP will probably grow four or 4.5 percent in real terms in the coming year, while its inflation rate will continue to decline. Because it is a net importer of raw materials, Japan is a prime beneficiary of the currently weak commodity prices. In addition, other Pacific nations, like Australia, benefit from the health of the Japanese economy. Furthermore, Japan's balance of payments position has improved continually, and a significant trade surplus is likely to emerge for the island nation over the next year, leading to a recovery in the value of the yen relative to the U.S. dollar.

One other aspect that differentiates some foreign markets from ours, and often provides significant investment opportunities, is the direct intervention of foreign governments in their market systems to achieve certain ends. An example of this is the Japanese convertible bond market in the last few months of 1981. In September, Japanese companies issued $826 million in new convertible bonds, a record for any one month. This was more than the market was able to absorb while stock prices were dropping and the yen was weak. Prices fell sharply, and the Japanese Finance Ministry pressured underwriters into halting almost all new issues for the next month (October) thus forcing numerous corporate borrowers to cancel or delay their financing plans. As a result, stability returned to the bond market, the stock market realized moderate gains, and the yen began to rise.

In addition, the Japanese securities industry is working with the Finance Ministry to establish a means to regulate the flow of issues more efficiently and effectively. Officials from both government and industry have stated that a joint committee will be established in April, 1982, to supervise the timing of offerings so that the situation created by September's overflow is not repeated. This is a far cry from the months (and years) preceding the Great Crash in 1929 and, to a lesser extent, the final days of the ''Go-Go Years'' of the 1960s in the United States, when many corporations issued paper that literally had no backing whatsoever in reality.

Foreign Equity Markets Bullish

What does it all mean? The future is bullish for foreign equity markets, and the strength of the dollar is making them unrealistically cheap. To demonstrate the principles of international investing, a good example is Scudder International Fund—the nation's oldest international mutual fund.

Scudder makes a good example because it is almost totally invested in foreign securities or a combination of foreign securities and cash. Other funds, like the Templeton International Funds, use a combination of foreign and domestic investments, but since American investors can participate in the U.S. markets through the various traditional means, it makes more sense to

GLOBAL WINNERS AND LOSERS — 1981

Best Performers		
Company	Per Share Price 12/31/81	% Change * over 12/31/80
Norsk Data	350.00	Norwegian Krona 452.6
Saba ''B''	98.00	Swedish Krona 192.5
BSR	0.79	British pound 154.8
Dalmine	331.75	Italian Lira 140.4
Toro Assicurazioni	20,750.00	Italian Lira 137.9
Toro Assicurazioni (pfd)	16,390.00	Italian Lira 130.0
Asea	174.00	Swedish Krona 123.1
Novo Industri ''B''	1470.00	Danish Krona 121.0
Berec	1.49	British Pound 119.1
Ericsson (LM) ''B''	219.00	Swedish Krona 114.7
Fortia	83.00	Swedish Krona 112.0
Royal Bank of Scotland	1.95	British Pound 109.7
Lowenbrau	3055.00	German Mark 109.2
Isuzu Motors	444.00	Yen 107.5
Hudson's Bay Oil & Gas	50.75	Canadian Dollar 106.1
Brostroms Rederi	81.00	Swedish Krona 105.0
Hitachi Ltd.	666.00	Yen 101.8
Forenede Bryggerier	515.00	Danish Krona 99.0
Vallourec	103.90	French Franc 97.9
Galerias Preciados	43.00	Peseta 95.4

Based on the 1600 Securities Included in Capital International Perspective.
* *Local currencies*
Source: Capital International, S.A., Geneva

investigate those funds which focus their energies and expertise on the international markets.

Scudder is solidly committed to international investments. It is headquartered in New York City and is a no-load (no commission), open-ended (no limit on the number of shares) mutual fund with a minimum investment of only $1000.

According to Scudder, two major developments in the past 12 months had overriding influence on global economic activity: The U.S. dollar appreciated against all the world's major currencies; and short-term interest rates rose in most countries while inflation started to decelerate, giving rise to widening real rates of interest.

The U.S. dollar has strengthened for a number of reasons:

● It had fallen too far against a number of currencies.

● The U.S. balance of payments position improved.

● There was renewed confidence overseas in U.S. economic policies and political leadership.

● Very high short-term U.S. interest rates attracted capital from foreign financial centers.

GLOBAL WINNERS AND LOSERS — 1981

Worst Performers		
Company	Per Share Price 12/31/81	% Change * over 12/31/80
Central Pacific Minerals	0.95	U.S. Dollar 87.3
Southern Pacific Petroleum	0.45	U.S. Dollar 83.9
Alfa	13.00	Mexican Peso 81.2
Tubaceros	17.50	Mexican Peso 79.4
International Harvester	7.125	U.S. Dollar 72.2
Westland Utrecht	68.00	Dutch Florin 68.4
Cermoc	13.20	Mexican Peso 63.4
Penoles "A"	299.00	Mexican Peso 62.5
Ceramica PozziGinori	186.00	Italian Lira 62.2
Bastogi-Irbs	270.00	Italian Lira 61.5
Imperial Corp	11.75	U.S. Dollar 60.8
Penoles "B"	410.00	Mexican Peso 60.2
Finsider	34.00	Italian Lira 60.0
Pancontinental Mining	2.55	Australian Dollar 58.0
Woodside Petroleum	1.27	Australian Dollar 57.0
Allis Chalmers	15.875	U.S. Dollar 56.4
Thomson-CSF	180.20	French Franc 55.1
Braniff Intl	2.25	U.S. Dollar 55.0
Francaise Petroles	115.20	French Franc 54.8
Maisons-Phenix.	233.90	French Franc 54.8

Based on the 1600 Securities Included in Capital International Perspective.
* Local currencies
Source: Capital International, S.A., Geneva

European Economies' Recovery Complicated

High real interest rates and a strong dollar have complicated the recovery of European economies, which were already struggling to adjust to the aftermath of the 1979 oil crisis. High interest rates have further slowed economic activity, while large budget deficits have prevented governments from introducing counter-cyclical expenditure programs. The strength of the dollar has increased import costs, although the inflationary impact of this has been mitigated, to an extent, by the weakness of various commodity prices, especially oil. Economic activity in Europe has stagnated and unemployment has risen, but inflationary pressures have abated.

The faster-growing countries of the Far East adjusted to the 1979 oil price increases with less difficulty. Heavy capital investment in energy-saving equipment and production rationalization has enabled Japan to outpace the other industrial countries, even while its consumption of energy per unit of output has fallen. Japan's inflation has been on a declining trend since September, 1980, and on a year-to-year basis, the wholesale price index is virtually flat, while the consumer price index is up only about five percent. Real GNP growth in Singapore, Malaysia, and Hong Kong has been between seven and ten percent, and three percent in Australia. Though higher than in Japan, inflation is on a declining trend in these countries as well.

Scudder officials' cautious view revolves around the United States; they believe that the world's industrialists, bankers, investors, and foreign exchange traders "all have their gaze fixed on Reagan, Volcker, and Stockman." So what is a broad outlook for the international investor?

Unemployment and real interest rates world-wide will encourage saving and help finance government's waning profligacy, which will in turn drive interest rates down, albeit slowly. This points to foreign bonds. In addition, if the U.S. rates ease, then one major prop to the dollar's strength will be removed—for foreign bonds, currency gains will be added to high coupons and a respectable capital gain. And the first stage has been set for lower rates, due to recession, and a downward wobble of the dollar. In other words, foreign bonds look very good right now, especially in the disciplined, low-inflation nations—Japan, Switzerland, and West Germany.

Scudder anticipates an upswing in the equities markets in the future, but at present there may be better foreign investments. Lower commodity prices will help countries that import heavily, again meaning Switzerland, West Germany, and, above all, Japan. In choosing equities, it would be wise to concentrate on domestic producers of essentials rather than exporters at present, mainly because of the widespread recession. Exporters will suffer as world trade becomes increasingly competitive and trade friction rises. In other words, a major recovery in the Hong Kong and Singapore markets will not occur soon, but at the same time, their Pacific Basin growth prospects keep them attractive. The United Kingdom economy should be a red flag against heavy investments, and Australia must await a recovery in metal prices. However, if you foresee such a recovery, Australia will be an excellent place to invest.

To sum up, Japan, Switzerland, and West Germany remain strong investment arenas, especially in bonds. As worldwide economic trends dictate, the high-flying Far Eastern stock markets will offer outstanding returns. And always watch the long-term trends, rather than dramatic, highly-publicized events. Inflation or recession, high or low interest rates, stable or unstable oil and commodity prices, worldwide changes in weather and climate, slow-moving but extensive changes in political policy—these are the trends you should watch.

One final point. While it is not our purpose to discuss the relative merits of the domestic stock market, it is interesting to note one point regarding investing in U.S. securities during 1982. Leaving aside predictions of various market analysts and the forecasts of innumerable market letters and other investment advisory vehicles, a look at the most recent survey of The Conference Board is very instructive.

The Conference Board is composed of chief executives of the largest corporations in America. A survey of these 1500 business leaders taken at the end of 1981 revealed that they were quite pessimistic about the nature and outlook for the American economy in 1982. These business leaders, who have their fingers on the pulse of the nation's economy, said their confidence dropped to the lowest point since the middle of the mini-recession during the second quarter of 1980, which in turn was the lowest level since the recession of 1974. On a scale of 0-100, their feelings about present economic conditions were 26, down from 48 just three months ago. Only 42 percent of the nation's top executives felt that their firm's after-tax profits would improve in 1982, down significantly from 59 percent a year ago. The weakest profit expectations were in the areas of paper, stone-clay-glass, lumber, apparel, and insurance. Additionally, the Commerce Department reported in January, 1982, that American businesses plan to spend less in 1982 than in 1981 on building and plant expansion and new equipment.

Should the predictions of these captains of industry prove correct, then it is obvious that there will be many widespread opportunities abroad to make money in investments in 1982, because what is one country's cake is another nation's crumbs—and vice versa.

Scudder Outlook for 1982

Scudder's assessment for improved performance for international markets in 1982 is inexorably tied to conditions in America. Nicholas Blatt, executive vice-president of Scudder, explains that, "The world economic and investment environment is currently more than normally heavily influenced by developments in the United States. Despite the relative decline in the size of the U.S. economy among OECD countries over the last 20 years, its behavior still dominates economic activity in the capitalist world. (OECD is the Organization for Economic Cooperation and Development that was formed in Paris in 1960 to promote economic growth and development, improve world trade, facilitate commercial agreements and encourage economic expansion. It is composed of Western Europe, Greece, the United States, Canada, Japan, Australia and New Zealand.) The current recession in the United States is exacerbating deflationary forces in Europe, which had already been set in motion by the pursuit of tight monetary and fiscal policies by most European governments. High real interest rates worldwide provide a further brake on economic activity.

"Only France is pursuing overtly stimulative policies, and while these may lead to a decline in unemployment, they will also probably lead to an acceleration in inflation. Unless other governments emulate these policies, the French franc will become vulnerable to further devaluations as French exports become increasingly uncompetitive, and the balance of payments deteriorates.

"The British economy, having been the first to move into recession two years ago, may now be the first to recover from a very low base. Unemployment has reached 12 percent, while manufacturing output, having declined in percentage terms by more than 12 percent during the 1929-30 recession, is still below the level first reached in 1973. Prime Minister Margaret Thatcher's policies so far can only be regarded as partially successful, since inflation remains stubbornly stuck at around 11 percent. There are signs, however, that considerable progress has been made in terms of industrial restructuring. Industries have shed surplus labor, with the result that productivity in aggregate has improved even during a period of declining output. Wage demands have become more realistic, and the number of days lost through industrial disputes has fallen dramatically. Therefore, the state is set for a sharp recovery in profits when general economic activity picks up.

"At this point it would seem that there will be a broadly synchronized recovery in the U.S. and European economies during the latter half of 1982, while inflation rates should continue to trend down for a while. Given this overall economic environment, the stock markets of the United Kingdom, West Germany, the Netherlands and Switzerland look relatively attractive. On a historical basis they are cheap, having spent the last six years either declining or trading within a limited range. From a U.S. investor's standpoint, moreover, there is the possibility of some foreign currency appreciation in the German mark, the Dutch guilder, and the Swiss franc. There is very little likelihood that the U.S. dollar will appreciate the way that it did during 1981.

"The Far Eastern markets will continue to be underpinned by the highest real rates of economic growth in the world," Blatt maintains. "Hong Kong and Singapore/Malaysia, even in a deflationary world environment, are forecast to grow at 7-10 percent yearly in real terms. Their stock markets are about 25 percent below the highs reached during the first half of 1981, and are expected to perform satisfactorily in 1982 given continued strong corporate profit growth.

"The Japanese economy has been slowing in recent months, and official forecasts of real economic growth in 1982/1983 have been revised downwards from 5 to 3.5-4 percent. Inflation is well under control with their Consumer Price Index expected to average a gain of less than 4 percent over the next 12 months. In recent months, wholesale prices have been flat. Unlike France, the Japanese government is most reluctant to stimulate the economy for fear of reigniting inflationary pressures. Paradoxically, Japan may be suffering from too high a savings rate, 20 percent plus, since it is consumer expenditure that has failed to mobilize economic activity.

"Much of Japan's growth over the last 18 months has come from the export sector, and while this has slowed recently, reflecting a softening of overseas demand, import costs have fallen faster, leading to a widening balance of trade surplus. Given this macroeconomic background, it is to be expected that the yen will appreciate 5-10 percent against the U.S. dollar over the next 12 months. The Japanese stock market is the second largest in the world after the United States and, unlike many smaller foreign stock markets, it provides a wide choice of investments.

"Japanese export stocks, although they were very weak in the second half of 1981 and now appear attractively priced, may underperform the market for awhile, given investor concern with the ramifications of growing trade friction and the narrowing of profit margins as the yen appreciates in value. The Scudder International Fund has therefore shifted the emphasis of its Japanese portfolio to other sectors of the market to include pharmaceuticals, housing related companies, and domestic consumer expenditure shares (consumer finance companies, retailers, textile firms, etc.) since real disposable incomes are expected to rise as inflation continues to slow and interest rates decline further. Moreover, unemployment in Japan is still only around 2 percent. Those companies that are at the forefront of technological progress in Japan—NEC, Hitachi, Fujitsu Fanuc—have been retained since the bulk of their export sales are relatively immune to protectionist pressures.

"It is probably still too early to make substantial commitments to the commodity-producing countries of the world: Australia, South Africa, and Canada. Given the prospect that inflation is likely to continue slowing, there is no reason to expect a recovery in the price of gold for some time. Other commodity prices will only strengthen later in the global economic cycle," Blatt concluded.

Chapter Twelve

Exploring Commodity Markets

I f you're looking for investments that are more exciting than say, American T&T stock, or with more immediate rewards than collectibles, or sinking your cash into CDs at the neighborhood savings institution, then perhaps the commodities market is just the ticket for your portfolio.

If trading such provocative items as 5000 bushels of oats, 37,000 pounds of coffee, or 12.5 million yens appeals to you, then you can join the mounting millions of Americans who have discovered the commodity futures market, which boomed in the early 1980s, and whose explosive growth shows no signs of abating.

Speculating in commodity futures, however, can be as risky and adventuresome as any investor wants to make it. Big and quick profits are possible, but the dangers are proportionately greater than they would be for someone who is patient and willing to be satisfied with small, steady gains.

Nonetheless, speculating in any of the nearly 100 listed futures contracts in the United States can be reasonably safe, and indeed rewarding, providing the investor takes the time—and makes the effort—to learn the intricacies of this all-too-often misunderstood investment business.

While it is a debatable point, there are many persons who maintain that speculating in commodities is easier to accomplish successfully than speculating in stocks, bonds, options, or what have you. This does not minimize the harsh realities that speculating in futures can be synonymous to one, big crap game. In no way can it be construed as a "can't lose" proposition.

For the unprepared neophyte or novice, commodities future trading—speculating—can be a fast track to financial suicide. A vast majority of the trades do end up in the loss column with seven out of ten trades being wiped out. Because this is a fact of life in the futures market, the maxim that most successful speculators follow religiously is "cut the losses short and let the winnings run."

Lure of Riches

As indicated by the enormous increase in trading volume since the early 1970s, it is obvious that investors in ever-greater numbers are succumbing to the tantalizing lure of riches possible in commodity futures. People talk about it, study it, and plunge into it as a viable investment program for coping with inflation. The more aggressive enter the field hoping to get rich. And those who succeed are the well informed.

Commodity futures come in many forms: agricultural products, metals, petroleum, foreign currencies, financial instruments, and almost anything else that is consumed by the public, business, or industry. Futures contracts can be created so long as there is an agreeable means of standardizing their quantity and quality.

The concept behind commodity futures is a relatively simple one: to offer, for sale or purchase, a temporary paper obligation (a contract) representing a standard amount of goods today for actual delivery or receipt tomorrow. No matter what the commodity, a contract calls for stringent quantity and quality standards. The economic purpose of a futures contract is to offer the producers and users of various commodities a means of protecting themselves against the potential risk of adverse price fluctuations. In futures industry parlance, this is called *hedging*. Without the need for hedging, there would be no economic justification for futures trading.

The counterpart of hedging is *speculating*. It is this area that interests most people who have little commercial use for a herd of cattle, thousands of bushels of wheat, corn, or soybeans—to mention a few commodities.

The speculator is absolutely essential to the operation of a futures market because he is a person who is willing (and able) to assume price risks which hedgers are anxious to avoid. By correctly anticipating in which direction prices will go, the speculator can make a profit commensurate with his risk. In that way, speculating in futures is similar to stocks and bonds, the major difference being the length of time one remains in the market. Futures speculating is a relatively short-term venture.

The enormous success of commodity futures since 1970 can be attributed in part to the economic roller coaster the American consumer is on due to inflation and recession. Working their calamity simultaneously, these modern-day "boogiemen" have driven many investors out of the stock market because stocks have proven to be anything but safe havens for price appreciation.

Through the years, futures markets have chalked up their best performances in terms of volume when the stock market turns bearish, or when uncertainty and doubt cloud the prospects for equity issues and the economy. During the past decade, futures markets have attracted considerable new business and set records in annual trading volume. This performance generally confirms the theory that futures thrive on uncertainty.

Commodity Trading Not New

The bewildering aspect of this dizzying growth is that it took so long to get rolling. To the vast majority of people, commodity futures are relatively new to the investment scene. Nothing could be further from the truth. Futures have been around for hundreds of years and elements of their beginnings can be traced to centuries before Christ.

The concept immigrated to this country around 1848, and manifested itself in Chicago, then the crossroads of the prairie where grain sellers carted their produce to eager merchants. That, in essence, was the origin of the Chicago Board of Trade; organized by 80 local businessmen who saw the need and had the foresight to establish a market governed by rules and regulations that would provide a climate conducive to trade among farmers and merchants.

While the Board of Trade soon became a commercial mecca, it was not until 1865, that the "to arrive" contract was born. It was the first forward contract that guaranteed standardized quantities and quality for commodities—namely grains. Forward contracting, however, was not without problems. Many times there would be defaults due to poor crops, hijacking theft, or other disasters.

Despite these problems, the Board of Trade survived and provided the fundamental concept on which other commodity exchanges would later be founded. Today, there are ten other commodity futures exchanges in the United States and one—the International Futures Exchange (Bermuda) Ltd.—which is being organized offshore for computerized trading that is scheduled to start later in 1982.

Those markets now operating include the Chicago Mercantile Exchange and its International Monetary Market; the MidAmerica Commodity Exchange (Chicago); the Minneapolis Grain Exchange; the Kansas City Board of Trade; the New Orleans Commodity Exchange; the Commodity Exchange, Inc. (otherwise known as the Comex of New York); the New York Coffee, Sugar, and Cocoa Exchange; the New York Mercantile Exchange; the New York Cotton Exchange; and the New York Futures Exchange.

A wide variety of economic variables are behind price movements of the future commodities at any given time. Prices provide only a momentary statement of condition about the underlying commodity and its relationship to supply-demand fundamentals, political issues and actions, weather, the economic climate, and a host of similar ephemeral factors. Futures prices are little more than a reflection of real conditions.

One of the gross misconceptions that has been kept alive suggests that these markets are manipulated by professionals and/or powerful business men who indulge in the game at the expense of the little guy. There have been instances in which the markets were manipulated, but they are few in number.

Recently, there have been serious charges of alleged attempts to control the markets for potatoes and silver. From time to time, the leading commodity exchanges have taken measures to safeguard the public interest when "squeezes" of a particular market occurred. (A squeeze is in the same manipulative family as the corner, in that it forces prices higher to the advantage of a few at the expense of everyone else.) Such actions as forcing the liquidation of contracts in a given contract month (to avert a potential squeeze) have occurred in futures contracts for live cattle, pork bellies, wheat, potatoes, lumber, and foreign currencies.

Several exchanges—most notably the Comex—took such precautionary action in January, 1980, when the famed Hunt brothers (Nelson, Bunker, and William Herbert) allegedly tried to corner the silver market, along with some financially well-endowed friends and Saudi Arabians. It was said that at or near the peak of their silver holding, the brothers had amassed a $4 billion fortune in the precious metal, as the price soared in excess of $50 per ounce from $10 in a matter of four months. Faced with the fact that a small group of speculators were holding almost 60 percent, the Comex board of directors issued an edict that trading in silver would be for liquidation purposes only. In other words, no speculator would be permitted to take a new position as long as the edict was in force.

The result of this one-sided maneuver was the start of a downward drive that snowballed to the extent that silver futures by March 27, 1980, had dropped to $10.80 an ounce and appeared to be headed lower. It was at this point that the market turned around for some inexplicable reason. And, because there has yet to be much logic connected with the reasons advanced as explanations, the government's interest in how exchanges are run has increased immeasurably in the past several years.

One of the biggest issues facing commodity futures trading is whether, indeed, the industry is the best judge of what actions are right and fair when it comes to protecting the public interest. For certain, exchanges today are on their guard as never before. But that has always been the claim of the commodity markets. Leaders of these institutions for years have been rhapsodizing about the integrity and fairness of their markets. The government has heard it time and time again, but skepticism lingers—and even grows whenever a boom/bust, as happened with silver, occurs.

The federal government, through the eight-year-old Commodity Futures Trading Commission, has taken a major, albeit controversial, role in attempting to safeguard the integrity of the marketplace in order to protect the public's interest. The integrity of the market is a touchy subject. Everyone agrees that it must be maintained, but there are many views on how it can best be achieved.

A new non-governmental regulatory body called the National Futures Association, which is sanctioned by the CFTC, is now operating in Chicago. Modeled after the National Association of Securities Dealers, the NFA is designed to augment the CFTC by covering groups of non-floor traders, who previously were exempt from the regulatory process. Included are approximately 135 futures commission merchants, 1100 pool operators (who manage or operate commodity funds similar to mutual funds) and 1300 commodity trading advisers who offer guidance and ideas for stipends of varying amounts.

Winning over a once-skeptical public has taken years, but it still remains a major priority. But judging from the industry's growth since the late 1960s, the industry has convinced an impressive number of investors.

Exchanges—A Closer Look

There are more than 90 contracts in commodities traded on the nation's 11 exchanges. Some exchanges, such as the Chicago Board of Trade,

Minneapolis Grain Exchange, Kansas City Board of Trade, Chicago Mercantile Exchange (via its International Monetary Market), and the Commodity Exchange, Inc.—carry one or more similar commodity contracts. The reason for this overlap is that each operates in a different regional location and serves a different segment of the public; also, each might offer variations in its contracts. Commodities that are listed on two or more exchanges include wheat, soybeans and soybean oil, gold bullion, silver, potatoes, broiler chickens, Treasury bills, live hogs, corn, and foreign currencies.

Exchanges, though fundamentally similar, are different in their personality and rules. Basically, a commodity futures exchange is a marketplace where buyers and sellers meet to do business. Its role is to provide a facility for this activity, establish rules and regulations, and collect and disseminate market information. The exchange does not engage in trading or influence prices. Most exchanges are not-for-profit organizations that are made up of members.

It is not difficult to become an exchange member—providing one has the capital resources and the intelligence to pass an examination. The capital required depends on the going price of a seat (another term for membership) at any given moment; seat values fluctuate in the same fashion as commodities themselves. Because each exchange has a fixed number of seats, demand for them causes their price to change. When markets are flourishing, as they are today, prices tend to be higher. In 1980, for example, prices for a seat on the Chicago Mercantile Exchange spiraled to an all-time high of $380,000—the record for any futures exchange. The low price paid for a CME seat that year was $225,000.

To lend a bit of historical perspective to seat prices at the CME in 1941, they ran from a low of $375 to a high of $800; in 1950, they ranged between $1800 and $2800; in 1960, the spread was from $3000 to $4500.

It was not until the 1970s that seat prices hit the big time, surpassing those of the major stock exchanges. During 1981, the major Chicago and New York exchanges' memberships, or seats, in the futures industry parlance, declined in price from their all-time highs set a year earlier. The high for a Chicago Board of Trade seat, for example, slipped to $320,000 from $330,000; the CME's high in 1981 plunged $60,000 to $320,000; in New York, the high for a Coffee, Sugar, and Cocoa seat dropped $10,000 to $115,000, while the Comex seat dropped to $50,000 from its all-time high of $260,000 in 1980.

Bulls and Bears Affect Prices

What was reflected in 1981 was a general discontent with the futures markets which clearly can be deduced from the decline in trading volume in agricultural contracts. It is generally accepted that a strong public bias exists favoring bull markets, when the investor is more inclined to participate since the prices are upbeat. So too, is the value of a seat more likely to climb, indicating a stronger demand to get close to the action than in times when bears rule the market. According to some schools of thought, making a profit in a bearish market, when prices are going down, carries with it the connotation of opportunism, something wicked or evil.

The larger exchanges now offer "associate" and "limited" memberships. These are designed to restrict the field of commodities a member may trade. For example, an individual might obtain a limited membership to trade lumber, eggs, and pork bellies on the CME, but it would not extend his trading privilege to other commodities. These memberships are relatively inexpensive (compared to full memberships) but they too have greatly appreciated in value during the past year. For example, on the Chicago Board of Trade they went from zero in 1978 to $165,000 in 1981; up from $150,000 the previous year.

Exchanges, which are ruled by a Board of Governors (or directors) elected by the membership, utilize a broad committee structure to establish regulations and maintain a smoothly running facility. One of the key operations in any exchange is its clearing house. At some exchanges, the clearing house is integrated into the overall framework; at others, it is treated as a separate entity. Regardless of its relationship, the clearing house is responsible for several crucial functions: it settles members' daily transactions; transfers funds from member accounts; acts as a depository for members' funds; and oversees the delivery of contracts.

Perhaps more than anything else, the clearing house is the foundation of an exchange's integrity. A clearing house makes certain that all accounts are squared before a trader is allowed to engage in market activities the next day. There is no credit extended and no allowance for carrying unfinished business from one day to the next.

Since every contract traded must have a buyer and a seller, if, at the end of a trading session there is an imbalance, the clearing house sifts through the records to determine which parties were involved in the discrepancy. In its role as a middleman, the clearing house is the entity unto which every trader must account. In other words, after a trade has been completed, the buyer and seller no longer deal with each other; they deal with the clearing house. In severe situations where differences seem irreconcilable, a committee arbitrates the issue.

Investor Leverage

K nowing the mechanics of the exchange is important, but no more so than a knowledge of the fundamentals related to "leverage" which this market provides investors. The term *leverage* is common in markets dealing with stocks and commodities. Essentially, it involves the control of resources (commodities) for significantly less money than the actual value they represent.

When one enters this market he usually opens a "margin"—a term synonymous with credit—account. The individual places a certain sum of money for trading purposes in this account. It is used as earnest money, guaranteeing performance in meeting obligations. In the stock market, the amount initially required for trading is about 50 to 65 percent of a stock's full value; in futures, the initial requirement ranges from less than 1 percent to 10 percent—depending on which commodity is traded.

Margins that are set high offer less leverage: thus, commodity futures afford traders more leverage than do stocks.

Leverage becomes most meaningful when a commodity contract's actual value changes. A small change in price can mean a great deal. In commodity futures, a $250 change in a trading account relates to the margin required to buy or sell the contract. Using a live cattle contract as an example, a $300 change in the required margin of $1200 per contract would translate into a 25 percent change in the trader's account.

Perhaps the greatest leverage available today is obtainable in the 90-day U.S. Treasury bill contract listed on the Chicago Mercantile Exchange's International Monetary Market division. It has a full delivery value of $1 million (in government securities) at maturity; yet, can be bought or sold on margin for $1500. Prices in this contract are quoted on a discount (from 100) index; each .01 unit (a point) carrying a value of $25. If a contract moves up or down the maximum number of points (50) allowed in one day's time, the contract value changes by $1250 more than 80 percent of the contract's required margin of $1500.

There are two basic types of margin requirements. First is the "initial" margin, or that amount required by a broker as good faith money assuring that the terms of a contract bought or sold will be fulfilled. Many brokerage firms require a minimum deposit of $5000 in a customer's account and many others prefer no less than $10,000. Of this minimum, brokers will use perhaps only half for trading purposes, with the other half reserved as a buffer against possible losses.

That brings up the second type of margin. It is called "maintenance" margin and is simply a sum smaller than (but part of) the initial margin. If an account loses equity to the point of "maintenance margin" levels, the broker will call for a replenishment of funds in the customer's account. In such situations, the amount called for—aptly referred to as a "margin call"—is necessary to bring the account up to its original margin.

To illustrate how the system works, we will take a hypothetical person with a $10,000 margin account. If he were trading live cattle, he would need $1200 in margin to buy or sell a contract. His broker, being a prudent businessman, would inform him that he might trade as many as four contracts at a time in this commodity (using $4800 of the funds on deposit). If the customer were a buyer of cattle futures and the commodity's price rose, he would profit (and he could withdraw those profits if he wished). If the price of cattle futures were to decline, however, his account's value would also diminish. If it tumbled too far—beneath the maintenance margin level of $900 per contract or $3600 for four contracts—the broker would necessarily call for $1200 in additional funds to bring the account up to its original level.

Within the limited movement range for each commodity, you can make or lose several thousand dollars per contract in a day's time. There is great potential for fast gain or loss. When considering leverage and margin, fractions of a price movement translate into considerable sums of money for the investor. This inherent market characteristic paints a relatively volatile picture of day-to-day trading activity, not necessarily true when price fluctuations are viewed from an annual perspective.

Of the more than 90 commodity contracts listed on the 11 exchanges in the United States, between 50 and 60 are "liquid"—active enough so that the buyer or seller can be reasonably sure of easy entry and exit on the market.

If a contract starts generating too much volume, as had gold or silver in early 1980, the exchange will stiffen the margin requirements. This is a protective measure instituted when a market becomes too volatile. The exchanges do not want to see traders getting into a position where individual debt obligations cannot be met.

Can Anyone Play the Game?

Not everyone has the qualities to trade in commodity futures. The pressures of trading can be enormous and if one does not have the knowledge or temperament to cope with the tension of making fast, well-founded decisions, this business is not a good one to try. Ultimately, every trading decision will rest on the individual speculator's shoulders. A broker can inform the customer of market trends, important happenings, and even suggest a course of action; but, in the final analysis, the decision is the speculator's own.

Suitability also involves a person's financial position. If he has inadequate risk capital or prior financial obligations that leave him with marginal cash flow or reserves, a reputable broker would not accept his account, finding him "unsuitable" as a customer. This should not be looked upon as an insult; the broker is actually looking out for the potential customer's own best interest.

Commodity exchanges and the Commodity Futures Trading Commission, the Federal agency that regulates futures markets, have specific guidelines covering suitability, and brokerage firms use them in determining the worthiness of customers.

The fact remains that most trades—approximately 70 percent—wind up as losers. To the non-professional trader, this sounds like a quick trip to the poorhouse, and perhaps it can be. If there is one standout characteristic the pros have over the amateurs, it is the sense which tells them not to fight a market trend; to get out of a losing trade fast. Non-pros tend to stick around longer, hoping for a "turnabout" of prices that will convert a loss into a win.

Usually, the loss just gains more momentum and with it comes margin calls and more margin calls. It is a rule of thumb in futures that you should never trade with money you cannot afford to lose. Unfortunately, many people start out with that in mind, but forget it in the heat of battle.

Too often, the public likes to think of commodity exchanges as something akin to Las Vegas East. Gambling and speculating are totally different. As knowledgeable traders will try to explain, gambling involves the creation of risk by itself; there is no risk to anybody until two or more parties decide to make a bet. Speculating, on the other hand, does not create any risk that isn't already there; it simply is accepted by someone wanting to take it for the opportunity of making a profit. Most knowledgeable speculators have a well-grounded feeling with respect to their chances of converting risk into capital gain. There are relationships to what they are doing based on supply-demand fundamentals and other socio-economic and political considerations.

Strategies and Operational Analysis

In the language of the market, a *buyer* is one who takes a "long" position. This position can be closed out with an order to sell. A *seller*, on the other hand, is one taking a "short" position; in essence, because he sees prices declining. This trader enters the market selling the commodity he hopes to buy back at a cheaper price when he closes out his position. A *spreader* might be considered a combination of the two, as he will seek to profit through the fluctuation of differential in two prices. He will purchase January cattle and sell August cattle if he believes the price differential between them will widen—assuming January were at a premium (higher price) relative to August.

If the spreader thought the difference in price would narrow, he would sell January cattle and buy August. Brokers can provide invaluable assistance in working out *spreads,* or *straddles,* as they are sometimes called. To get into this area of trading, one needs the knowledge to interpret price-spread norms between the various contract months—obviously an expertise that takes time to develop.

Fundamental analysis, which the majority of traders use to capture the so-called big picture of the market, involves study of the general economic scene. Supply-demand, price evaluation as it relates to production, carry-over inventory, foreign trade, inflation, and consumption (demand) patterns are among the vast array of measurables used by fundamentalists. There is a wealth of information covering such areas, much of which is created and disseminated by the U.S. government and various leading news organizations.

Technical analysis, which involves the use of bar charts and/or point-and-figure charts, is another popular method of trading. The theory is that prices will repeat past patterns and trends. The chartist who interprets price changes accurately today will have a good chance of predicting what they will do tomorrow or in the near future.

There are other forecasting tools available. Two key indicators are seasonal influences and cyclical patterns. All agricultural commodities are affected by both. Seasonal influences consider changes related to a time of year. Cyclical patterns take longer to form and are better viewed over an extended period of time.

In either case, these two information-bearing agents must be examined in relationship to past behavior. Misinterpretation of them is always a clear and present danger. Wheat prices, for example, are usually highest in the winter and summer seasons; lowest in the fall, during harvest time. Through most of the 1900s, seasonal price patterns have held true about two thirds of the time; prices have remained stable about seven percent of the time. Prices actually worked against the expected trend more than 25 percent of the time. If there is a moral to be learned here, it is not to take anything—especially seasonal influences —for granted.

Cycles work over a longer period. The repeated patterns of production and prices tend to rely on each other. For example, if a bumper crop of soybeans is harvested one year, the price of beans will more than likely fall—more supply being available than demand requires. The next year, farmers who normally might produce soybeans will opt for another crop because of low soybean prices. The low soybean production of that year will more than likely drive up prices—weak supply vis-a-vis constant or increased demand—and lure back producers who dropped out of the production the previous year. And so goes the cycle, *ad infinitum*.

Seasonal influences and cyclical patterns provide the commodity trader with useful direction as to what can be expected in the weeks, months, and seasons ahead. They cannot pinpoint timing with the same degree of precision that technical analysis purports to offer; however, they can signal the technician as to what he should be looking for in day-to-day charting of price movements.

Procedural Guidelines

Opening an account with a brokerage firm is relatively simple, assuming suitability requirements are satisfied. A customer's margin agreement must be signed that obligates the trader to make good on any loses; funds must then be deposited into the customer's margin account. At this point, the customer is ready to participate in the action.

The procedure for trading is also quite simple. A telephone call to your broker instructing him to buy or sell "X" number of contracts in a specified contract month at some specific price gets the ball rolling. That information is relayed to the appropriate commodity exchange where another representative of the brokerage firm (usually a clerk) takes down the trading instructions on an order form. That form is dispatched to the firm's floor broker in the trading pit, who waits for the appropriate moment to fill the order. Some orders, if not filled during the current season, die; if the customer wants to try again, perhaps changing the price, another order must be called in.

If the order is indeed filled, a reverse series of contacts gets underway to inform the customer that his order has been filled as prescribed.

A "market order" can move through the full process within two or three minutes. In other words, a liquid market's action can be quick.

Brokers, of course, do not work for pure enjoyment. For their labors, which might include imparting opinions, doing research, or assisting in the setup of market strategy, they are paid a commission. Brokerage commissions were once based on a schedule that was fairly uniform from one firm to another. Today, commissions are negotiable; trading more contracts generally lowers the per-contract commission rate. Though negotiable, commission rates remain competitive, which is indicative of the keen competition among brokers for new customer business.

Brokerage commissions for commodities listed on the Chicago Mercantile Exchange generally range between $50 and $60 per round turn—meaning entry into and exit from a position in the market. The discount commission firms charge the lowest rates, some less than 50 percent of what full-service firms levy.

As mentioned earlier, there are a number of different types of orders in futures trading. A good broker will offer advice in this connection, but it is incumbent upon the trader to know what he is doing. Some of the more frequently used orders and a brief explanation of what they mean are as follows:

Market orders—By far the most common, they are directives to buy or sell without regard to a specific price. The broker merely buys or sells the number of contracts specified in the delivery month selected by the customer—always seeking to get the best price possible.

Price limit orders—Price is specified in these orders and they can only be filled at that price, or at a better one for the customer. The hazard in using this order is that if the market drops before the order reaches the trading floor, it may not get filled—unless, of course, the market rallies back to a level relevant to the order's price.

Open orders—Price is specified at the point the order is to be filled and it stands as a valid order until another order is made to cancel it.

Day orders—They specify price and must be filled on the designated day or they are automatically cancelled.

Stop orders—They become market orders when a given price is reached. Stops are used as a defensive device to protect a market position from an unexpected and adverse turnaround in prices. They are useful to limit losses, protect profits on previously established positions, and/or to set up new positions because of changed market trends.

It is especially important to understand the nuances and differences between these and other orders. Choosing the wrong type of order can preclude a person from getting into the market or force withdrawal from it prematurely.

There are a number of trading disciplines a beginner should keep in mind when starting out. They are recognized and followed by most successful traders.

1. If you are speculating, use only money you can afford to lose. Speculating is not the crap game some people say it is, but the fact that only 20 to 25 percent of those who try it are successful reveals its risky nature. Fear of losing money can hurt a speculator's trading performance.

2. Test yourself in the market with so-called paper trades—simulated trades—before taking the plunge. When confident and ready, do so in a conservative fashion. Trade in the less volatile commodities such as wheat or oats before jumping on the fast tracks of silver, gold, pork bellies, cattle, or soybeans—to mention a few.

3. Maintain sufficient reserves in your margin account. Use no more than half, or perhaps only a third, of your marginable funds for trading. Being under-margined can force you to do something undesirable such as liquidating a position too early.

4. Make your trading decisions after a market closes and don't follow the crowd. Following or chasing a market can be disastrous, as it is sometimes impossible to catch up. Successful traders frequently employ the "contrary opinion" rule which means that if most people are buying, they will start selling short. Advisory services put out opinions and when 80 to 85 percent of them are bullish, chances are the market will be overbought—an ideal time to sell short. If less than 25 to 30 percent of these analysts are bullish, it reveals the likelihood of an oversold market—ideal for taking a long position.

5. When you are uncertain of what to do, sit on the sidelines or get out of the market. Nobody trades every day and does it successfully.

6. Never build on a losing position. The "averaging down" technique is spoken of in reverent terms by some traders, but it seldom works for beginners. You cannot "hope" the market will work in your favor and those who average down their price-profit point do a lot of hoping.

7. Let profits run; cut your losses short. When one has a profitable situation it is best to let it keep rolling; this can be protected through the defensive stop order. When the market is sour, again, don't hope for a turnaround and hang on. Time and time again, this has done more damage than good.

Offsetting Delivery

R emember, most speculators will want to get out of a position before they are called upon to make or take delivery of whatever commodity they have been trading. When trading in the most active contract month, usually the month closest at hand, you have to make certain you liquidate your futures position before the contract expires.

In a nutshell, that means that a buyer of four April contracts had better sell those contracts before the April deadline or else be forced to take delivery of the commodity. And who want to be faced with the storage problem of taking 5000 bushels of grain (per contract) or 40,000 pounds of live cattle (about 38 head)? Approximately 98 percent of all futures contracts are offset, or liquidated, before this type of action becomes necessary. Delivery acceptance is only profitable when the price paid in the futures market ends up giving the trader a possible profit in the cash market. Because of the way the futures market works in its relationship to the cash market, this eventuality seldom happens. So, it is always best to look for an opportune time to sell out of a buy or buy out of a sell position.

Information and Regulation

T he Commodity Futures Trading Commission is a good source of public information. In addition to its responsibility for safeguarding the public interest in futures trading, it has a toll-free hotline for complaints: (800) 424-9838, and regional offices around the country that can be contacted for information.

The CFTC, an independent government agency, has a chairman and four appointed commissioners. It has a staff of almost 500 employees who judge the economic value of futures contracts, enforce exchange rules and regulations, oversee market position of traders, hear customer grievances regarding fraud or trading abuses, audit brokers, perform a myriad of educational functions, and generally watch out for the public's interest.

Although many industry members take a dim view of overregulation, most agree that a strong regulatory body is necessary. Most will also agree that if the CFTC does the job of allaying public fears about the industry, the industry will continue to prosper.

A second source of information is the Futures Industry Association, whose membership is composed of brokerage firms and exchanges. The FIA is a clearing house for industry statistics and information, as well as one of the industry's resources for training and educational activities.

Future Perspective

The outlook for the futures industry is perhaps brighter today than at any time in history. And, if this is so, it is because of the overwhelming acceptance and growth of contracts in financial instruments. No segment of the industry is growing faster, offers as much potential, or draws more attention from the standpoint of creative intensity. While the traditional agricultural contracts continue to enjoy skyrocketing volume, most of the biggies—corn, the soybean and wheat complexes, cattle, hogs, and pork bellies, and so on—have matured to the degree they are identified with certain exchanges. The Chicago Board of Trade, for example, is THE grain exchange; the Chicago Mercantile Exchange is THE livestock exchange; the Comex is THE precious metals exchange; the New York Coffee, Sugar, and Cocoa Exchange is THE exchange for those commodities, etc.

Financial futures are still in their infancy. Their identification is not so firmly fixed with one exchange or another, although some of the early contracts —namely the Ginnie Mae and the 90-day United States Treasury bill contracts—have become synonomous with the CBOT and CME, respectively. But the field is relatively open, and other exchanges are knocking on the CFTC's door wanting that agency to get with it—specifically, approve contracts in financial instruments they propose to list.

The Kansas City Board of Trade has waited the longest for approval of a stock-based contract. This was granted at the first of the year and trading began in late February, 1982. Contracts based on equities or stock indices also have been submitted to the CFTC for approval by the Chicago exchanges and several in New York. Largely because of the New York Future Exchange's link with the New York Stock Exchange, the Chicago Board of Trade made merger overtures. If, indeed, this alliance ultimately takes place, some industry watchers feel that the CBOT will have the strongest entry among the stock-index based contracts. The CME's contract will be based on the Standard & Poor's index of 500 stocks, while the KC Board of Trade contract is based on Value Line.

All this growth has created problems for the CFTC which, among its concerns, is bombarded with pressure to make highly political (in terms of the futures industry) decisions.

If there are one or two things that bode well for financial futures, it is the uncertainty in interest rates and prices in most commodities. CBOT President Robert K. Wilmouth, viewing 1980's volume, said: "The wild interest rate fluctuations brought many new financial users into the market. Figures more than confirmed this analysis."

The CBOT's Treasury bonds grew 215 percent in 1980, to 6.5 million contracts and more than doubled to 13.9 million a year later, according to FIA records, while the CNE 90-day T-bill volume on the IMM rose 73 percent to

3.3 million contracts in 1980, only to jump another 70 percent in 1981 to 5.6 million contracts.

If significant change took place in 1981 that portends a new direction for the industry, it was substantiation of Wilmouth's remarks the previous year. Financial instruments, including interest rates, foreign currencies, precious metals, and Euro-instruments, are attracting more action than ever before and can be expected to continue to post startling gains in volume so long as prices remain relatively stagnant in the agricultural sector of the market.

There is every reason to believe that the trend away from agricultural futures will continue, with the financial field benefiting, if 1982 market conditions maintain a similar profile as those of 1981. The planting, growing, and harvesting seasons of 1982 will tell the story.

If there is an unusually wet spring that prevents farmers from planting crops on time, or if there is a drought in the summer that threatens crop growth, or if there is a corn blight (or any other grain disease of major proportions), or if for any of many reasons the harvest falls short of expectations, the bulls of agriculture once again will be ready to jump into the pits and, perhaps, lure back some of those traders who have taken to the sidelines or found new life in other financial markets. It is that kind of uncertainty that creates so much excitement and mystique in futures trading. To seize the moment's opportunities, which for the most part have come in the financial pits, is the name of the game.

So successful have been these financial contracts that now London is in the initial phases of setting up a similar market. It is scheduled to open in 1982. And, if it is successful, how many other cities will embark on similar ventures? This, of course, enthralls the brokerage community because it poses an enormous potential arbitrage market—where buying and selling the same instrument (say, T-bill futures) is done simultaneously on different exchanges in order to capitalize on the price spread (or difference).

Such possibilities only underscore the pervasive attitude that financial futures are the wave of the future. It is true that not every financial instrument listed has been successful. Some have failed miserably, even after much hoopla and promotion. But, those that were well conceived have succeeded and today are as liquid as any futures contract listed.

COMMODITY MARKET STRATEGIES

One of the advantages that commodity trading offers is that a generally deflationary cycle hits the commodity markets. Almost the entire grain complex has become severely depressed, due in part to the boycott of grain sales to the Russians. Live stock commodities have become depressed due to large productions of hogs and a competitive effect on the beef and poultry markets. Even the metal markets have had a tremendous retracement. This creates a situation where the risk factor for the investor is proportionately less significant than it would be if these commodities were priced at higher levels.

A good example is the sugar market during the last quarter of 1979. Sugar had declined from price levels of 50 cents per pound to 7 cents per pound. Quite simply what this meant was that sugar futures were selling for less than the cost of production. Therefore, the downside risk, or the potential of those prices going even lower than 7 cents per pound was almost nonexistent while the upside potential remained theoretically unlimited. What happened, of course, was that sugar went from 7 cents per pound to over 20 cents per pound.

This is not a guarantee that anything with depressed prices will provide you with profit on the long side, but it is a strong indication that when any commodity gets down to, or below, the cost of actually producing it, that a number of producers will stop production, supplies therefore will become more limited, and the probability of an upward price movement becomes increasingly greater.

In addition, with almost every commodity, world events and conditions will almost affect that commodity by providing upward movement rather than a downward move in prices. Be it drought, flood, war, famine, or whatever, the prices of commodities tend to go up. Not only that, but with our annualized inflation rate at the present time in the 20 percent range, it is highly unlikely that commodities will stay depressed.

Therefore, even a novice is afforded a highly significant opportunity for taking long-term positions in such commodities as corn and wheat. A significant upward price movement appears much more likely than a further decline.

In addition to the immediate opportunity just described, there are several basic strategies in commodity trading that you should know about and use—no matter what the current market situation. Here are some of the more important ones:

Establish a trading strategy. One thing you absolutely must decide before you trade is how you will approach trading and what your objectives are. After you have analyzed a commodity and decided whether you are going to buy or sell, you have to determine the point at which you will enter the trade and where you will close out the position and take your profit. You must also decide at what point you will get out of your position and take your loss if the trade goes against you. If you set up such a trading plan, and then have the discipline to follow it through accordingly, you've mastered one of the secrets to commodity trading success.

Don't dollar average down. In other words, don't buy something at $70, if you anticipate it going down, with the plan that you'll buy it again at $65 and again at $63 in the hope that prices will go back up to give you profits on the $65 and $63 position.

"If in doubt, stay out," a commodity trading axiom goes. If you think the price is going to drop from $70 to $63, why not wait and buy at $63? Or why not sell a contract short to profit from the downward move? Why deliberately lose money by buying at $70?

Trade with the trend. The most important consideration for commodity traders, no matter what system is followed, is to determine the direction in which prices will move. If the commodity does what the trader thinks it will do, he'll win. If it doesn't, he'll lose and should get out of that losing position quickly to keep his losses small. It is vital for any trader to get in tune with the market trend.

Diversify your account into several commodities, but do not get into too many commodities. No trader can be right 100 percent of the time; consequently, it is not wise to put all your investment dollars into one commodity basket. Rather than bet all your money on one commodity, it's better planning to spread your risk over several commodities. It's difficult enough for even the most experienced traders to guess correctly on more than half their trades, and no one can be sure just which trades will be the right ones until they see some price action after entering the trade.

Don't invest more than you're comfortable with. No one is ever completely comfortable with the idea of losing any money, but the key is to determine at what point you will feel quite comfortable if you should happen to lose. For some people, a loss of $2000 might be insignificant; for others, that might be more than they can stand.

Take some money out of your profits. If you keep plowing all profits back into your commodity account, you're in somewhat the same position as the person who looks upon his house as an investment. You'll wind up with all your eggs in one basket. Commodity traders who have turned, let's say a $3000 account into $30,000, often fall into a trap; they are tempted to take too many or too large positions, or take more risks than normal, and the $30,000 slips away to nothing. By all means, take out some profits and spend the money on something you want.

Look for a three-to-one ratio in your trades. For every dollar you invest or risk in the commodity market, you should expect to make at least three dollars. In other words, when you analyze a commodity, you should expect its price to go three cents in your direction for every one cent you anticipate that might go in the opposite direction. Or, after all your study, you should be convinced that odds are three times as great that prices will move in your favor, as that they will go against you.

Understandably, the three-to-one ratio may not be right for everyone, but it's a good rule of thumb for the highest realistic return any trader can expect in commodities. For one thing, you must consider a reward-risk ratio because you have to allow for being wrong about half the time.

Chapter Thirteen

Cashing In On Foreign Currencies

T he danger of speculative investment in foreign currencies burst noisily into the U.S. consciousness (from a previously overlooked position) with the Franklin National collapse, which was in large part blamed on foreign currency speculation.

However, the appeal of such speculation soared much earlier, especially following President Nixon's history-setting devaluation of the dollar in 1971. Nixon's decision heralded a decade-long frenzy of trading in Swiss francs, German marks, Japanese yen, British pounds, Canadian dollars, and on and on.

Lately, a slight shift in attitude may have occurred: As fears about the solvency of the United States and its currency have escalated, many more investors have sought safer, "harder" currencies, *vis-a-vis* the U.S. dollar, such as the Swiss franc. But the basic drawing power of these investments remains fundamentally the same: The opportunity for high returns is great, because the movements in exchange rates have been so abrupt; and the leverage can be so great—a $70,000 position in a foreign currency can be acquired for an initial margin of only $1500 to $4000.

For most of the 1970s, the U.S. dollar appeared to become weaker, sometimes at a gradual pace, on occasion at a rapid rate especially in 1977 and 1978. In 1979, the foreign currency price of the U.S. dollar was virtually unchanged; in 1980, the foreign currency price increased by about five percent, and 1981, by nearly 20 percent. Since the general move to floating exchange rates in March, 1973, the foreign currency price of the U.S. dollar has increased modestly; the dollar has become more expensive in terms of the French franc, the Canadian dollar, the British pound, and the Italian lira, and less expensive in terms of the German mark, the Dutch guilder, the Japanese yen, and the Swiss franc.

The movements in the foreign exchange price of the dollar have provided large opportunities for gains—and losses—from investments in foreign currencies. At the end of 1970, the Swiss franc was worth a quarter; by the end of 1980, it was worth 57 cents—up over 100 percent in ten years. At the end of 1970, one million Japanese yen were worth $2778 U.S.; by the end of 1980, $4255. An investor who sold the U.S. dollar to buy Japanese yen at the end of 1976 would have earned an annual return of 20 percent by holding the yen until the end of 1977, and an additional 20 percent by the end of 1978.

In 1980, and even more in 1981, the U.S. Federal Reserve Board began to follow increasingly severe contractive monetary policies. United States interest rates began to rise; indeed, on several occasions the U.S. Prime interest rate began to exceed 20 percent. The U.S. rate of inflation began to decline, especially in the latter half of 1981. So investors were increasingly attracted to the U.S. dollar; they shifted funds from liquid assets denominated in various foreign currencies to liquid assets denominated in the dollar. The foreign currency price of the U.S. dollar increased sharply.

Yet, for every buyer of foreign exchange there must be a seller. In other words, for every winner, there must be a loser. In a zero-sum game world, the investors who sold Japanese yen and Swiss francs to buy U.S. dollars would have incurred losses exactly equal to the gains of those who bought the stronger currencies. In short, this is genuine speculation and every bit as risky as commodities.

An investor in the United States can seek profits from changes in exchange rates in the number of ways: By purchasing shares of foreign companies listed on foreign stock exchanges; by investing in the few U.S. mutual funds which specialize in holding the shares of foreign companies; or by purchasing corporate bonds, short-term money market securities, or bank deposits denominated in currencies that are likely to become more valuable. The investor can buy mark-denominated bank deposits in Frankfurt, or such deposits can be bought in London or Luxembourg in the Euro-currency market.

The most convenient way to invest in foreign currencies is to buy either forward exchange contracts or futures contracts in foreign currencies. Forward exchange contracts are available from major banks. Essentially, a bank agrees to deliver a specified amount of the desired currency at a certain future date—almost always within the following 12 to 18 months—at a price determined today. Investors can select the date at which currencies will be exchanged to match the date of payment for imports, or to achieve another business objective.

In contrast, currency futures contracts are purchased through a brokerage firm. The investor can buy a standardized contract amount of any actively traded foreign currency—eight in all—for delivery on the third Wednesday of every third month. Because the down payment, or initial margin, required on the futures contract is relatively small (perhaps as little as two percent of the total amount purchased), an investor can buy a large amount of foreign currency with a comparatively small cash outlay.

In this market, it is possible for a two or three percent price increase in a foreign currency to double an investor's cash outlay. However, any decrease in the price of a currency by the same amount count easily erase the total cash investment. (For more detailed information on margin contract purchasing, see the chapter on commodities.)

Setting the Stage

Opportunities to profit from movements in exchange rates increased dramatically with the move to *floating* exchange rates early in the 1970s. In the 1950s and 1960s, most major foreign currencies were fixed or pegged to the U.S. dollar. Investors could profit from changes in parities, but such changes were infrequent at best. For example, between 1950 and 1970, the parity for the pounds sterling/dollar exchange rate was changed only once, from $2.80 = £1 to $2.40 = £1 in November, 1967.

Similarly, the parities for the German mark and the French franc were changed on only two occasions, while the parities for the Japanese yen and Italian lira remained unchanged. Even though the Canadian dollar floated during this period, the changes in price of the U.S. dollar in terms of the Canadian dollar were negligible. Inflation and the fall of the U.S. dollar brought an abrupt end to this age of apparent stability.

The contrast between the limited exchange rate movement of these years and the sharp movements in the 1970s raises two questions. What determines the exchange rate? Why has the range of movement in the last decade been so much greater than in the previous two decades?

An exchange rate is a price of one national currency in terms of another—the price at which the demand for foreign exchange equals the supply. Individuals—traders and investors—use the foreign exchange market to indirectly obtain foreign goods and securities denominated in the foreign currency. They buy foreign goods because they believe these goods are more attractive in terms of price and quality than domestically produced goods. Similarly, they buy foreign securities because they believe them to be more attractive than domestic securities in terms of risk and return.

Exchange rates moved in a different pattern during the 1970s because pegged exchange rates are only feasible when major countries achieve reasonable stability in their commodity price levels. Floating exchange rates, on the other hand, are inevitable when inflation rates among major countries differ significantly, or even if there are significant differences in the price level targets.

The most common belief is that changes in exchange rates reflect changes in the relationship between national price levels. Thus, if the commodity price level in Great Britain is rising more rapidly than the commodity price level in the United States, the man in the street believes that the sterling price of the U.S. dollar should increase—and by the amount necessary to match the growing difference between the national price levels. For example, if the British price level is increasing at 20 percent annually, and the U.S. price is increasing at 10 percent a year, the "prediction" is that the sterling price of the U.S. dollar should increase by 10 percent a year.

This point of view, however, seems inconsistent with patterns of exchange rate movements over the last decade, which have been much more volatile than changes in the relationship between national price levels. In 1978, 1979, and 1980, sterling appreciated by 25 percent relative to the U.S. dollar, even though British prices increased far more rapidly than U.S. prices. In terms of the U.S. dollar, the yen rose sharply and then depreciated sharply—much more so than appeared justified by changes in the price level relationship.

Behind Exchange Rate Shifts

Shifts in the exchange rates occur when investors seek to equalize the anticipated rates of return from holding dollar securities and comparable securities denominated in foreign currencies. For example, if sterling-denominated securities offer a 10 percent annual return and comparable U.S. dollar-denominated securities offer a 15 percent annual return, then investors— American, British, and residents of other countries—would be reluctant to acquire dollar-denominated securities until the anticipated returns are more nearly equal. Projected returns would be equalized only if investors anticipate that the sterling price of the U.S. dollar will increase five percent a year.

Sharp changes in exchange rates reflect either shifts in the relationship between domestic and foreign interest rates or adjustments in the anticipated spot exchange rates. Spot exchange rates *today* reflect spot exchange rates anticipated for various dates in the future, discounted to the present by the difference between domestic and foreign interest rates. Hence, whenever the anticipated exchange rates adjust sharply, today's spot exchange rates also change rapidly, and by about the same amount.

If domestic interest rates change radically while foreign interest rates remain stable, the spot exchange rates adjust sharply to equalize anticipated returns from holding foreign and comparable domestic securities.

Therefore, exchange rates shift much more rapidly than the relationship between national price levels because exchange rates adjust to equalize *anticipated* returns on domestic assets and on comparable assets denominated in foreign currencies. To the extent that anticipated exchange reflects the anticipated price level relationship, then the spot exchange rate shifts whenever the anticipated price level relationship shifts. Because exchange rates move to equalize returns on domestic and foreign securities, they may move away from values suggested by the relationship between domestic and foreign price levels.

The exchange rate is then subject to two different pressures: The relationship between the prices of domestic and competing foreign goods tends to move the exchange rate toward one value, while the anticipated spot exchange rates may move it toward another. Exchange rates move sluggishly and infrequently when these two values differ modestly; they may move sharply when they differ significantly.

Thus, changes in exchange rates reflect the views of market participants about future events and the impact of these events on future exchange rates. And the exchange rate moves as new information becomes available about changes in national prices levels, monetary policy, oil shocks, tax policies, coup d'etats, and other political events.

One paradox of the 1970s is that central bank intervention in the foreign currency market was much more extensive than in the previous decade. Usually, central banks have intervened to dampen or limit movements in the foreign exchange values of their currencies. In 1978, when the Japanese payment position was strong, the Bank of Japan bought billions of dollars to prevent the yen from appreciating too rapidly.

In 1979 and 1980, when the Japanese import bill soared due to the sharp increase in petroleum prices, the Bank of Japan sold U.S. dollars to slow the depreciation of the yen. Similar stories can be told about the intervention practices of other central banks. The consequence is that investors in foreign currency must pay special attention to the exchange market intervention activities of national central banks as well as to changes in their monetary policies.

Forward exchange rates represent the consensus view of future spot exchange rates for the dates when the forward contacts mature. If investors are to profit from shifts in exchange rates, they must be able to predict future spot exchange rates more effectively than the forward rates do. If an investor seeks to profit from anticipated changes in exchange rates and buys a currency in the forward market (or in the futures market), the investor will profit (or incur a loss) only if the forward exchange rate of that currency differs from the spot exchange rate upon maturity of the forward contract. If the forward rate accurately predicts the spot exchange rates at the time forward contracts reach maturity, then the investor will realize neither profit or a loss.

Numerous analytical studies have been undertaken to determine how well the forward exchange rates "predict" the future spot exchange rates. The general result is that there is no systematic errors, or at least, no significant errors. That is, on the average, forward exchange rates are "unbiased predictors" of future spot exchange rates. But the statement "on average" means that the forecast errors in one direction are offset or averaged out by forecast errors in the other.

In a period of sharp exchange rate adjustments, no forward exchange rate is likely to be an accurate predictor of the spot exchange rate at forward contract maturity. So there is considerable room for an individual investor to "beat the forward rate." How consistently anyone can do this, however, is an empirical issue.

In the last several years, more than 20 exchange rate forecasting services have been established to provide advice on the future movement of exchange rates. These services are sold by either large commercial banks, econometric forecasting services, or independent consultants. The fees charged range from about $3000 up to $25,000 per year or more. Cynical observers might note that because of the very large potential profit from successful exchange rate prediction, these services might be able to charge a much higher price.

Indeed, it might be argued, why would the owners of these services prefer to use their insight to advise rather than to seek profits? That these organizations have met the "market test" may indicate that their services are worthwhile. Various efforts to test the effectiveness of their predictions have shown that some forecasters beat the forward exchange rate more than others; however, no forecasting service appears capable of beating the forward rate consistently across a number of currencies for an extended period.

Buying and Selling Foreign Currencies

The easiest way for an investor to buy foreign currencies is to purchase a future's contract through any brokerage house. (For a detailed explanation of trade orders and the strategy in selling short for profit, see the chapter on commodities.)

An investor has three basic decisions to make when dealing in foreign currency futures: Which of the eight currencies to buy (or sell), which of the five or six futures contract months in each currency to buy, and how many contracts to buy. One related question is the maximum prices to pay for any particular purchase. Single contracts involve foreign currency equivalents ranging from approximately $40,000 to $80,000. The investor is obliged to provide an initial margin requirement (deposit) which is usually between two and three percent of the value of the contract.

As a rule of thumb, the more volatile the currency, the higher the margin. The margins set by individual brokerage firms exceed minimum margins set by the exchange. Commissions charged by brokers are relatively low—usually $75 per contract or by about one-tenth of one percent of the total contract value. Commissions may be reduced for regular clients who buy several contracts at a time. (In contrast, transaction costs in the interbank market are not explicitly recognized; the buyer pays a net price. These costs vary with the customer and are significantly smaller for large commercial accounts because banks want their deposit business.)

Orders from individual investors to buy and sell futures contracts are relayed from the retail brokerage offices to their representatives on the trading floor of the International Monetary Market in the Chicago Mercantile Exchange. There, the representatives of contract sellers meet the representatives of contract buyers, and contract prices are auctioned between them. (In contrast, the price of foreign currency is set on a bilateral basis in the interbank market.) At the exchange, brokerage firm representatives—floor brokers—deal with each other and with several other groups who may be present in the trading pits of particular currencies: *Speculators, scalpers, spreaders,* and *arbitragers*.

Speculators and *scalpers* deal for their own account, but with quite different time perspectives. The speculator, like the investor, seeks to profit from long-term swings in the exchange rates. Speculators purchase or rent seats (memberships) on the exchange, which allows them to trade without paying commissions. In fact, transaction costs may be as low as $2 per contract.

The scalper, by contrast, seeks to profit from short-term price swings—those that occur in the course of a day or even a few hours. Scalpers frequently end each trading day without having any position in particular currency. *Spreaders* seek to profit when the price differences between various contract months for the same currency seem unusually large; they buy one contract month and sell the other, and seek to profit from a decline in the spread. The *arbitragers* are representatives of major banks which deal in foreign exchange; they seek to

MONEY MAKER

profit from any unusual currency price differences between the futures market and the interbank market.

Calculating Daily Trades

On an average day, trading in the foreign exchange interbank market reaches $50 billion. Daily trading in futures contracts amounts to approximately $500 to $700 million. In addition, the transactions differ significantly in size; the average transactions in the interbank market is five to ten times larger than any in the futures market.

Price movements in futures contracts are calculated in decimal/dollar equivalents. (See Table 1 for exact relationships.) In dollar terms, changes in price for each contract are either in multiples of $10 or $12.50. In addition, there are daily limits to the maximum price movement allowed in each currency; when that limit is reached, further trading in that currency is prohibited. (Trading in the interbank market between banks and their commercial customers is not affected by these limits.) If the prices of foreign currency futures move parallel to exchange rates in the interbank market, futures currency trading may not occur for several days if interbank market exchange rates move very rapidly.

The rules of the International Monetary Market (IMM) require that investors maintain equity in their trading accounts equal to about two-thirds of the initial margin. In addition, the maintenance margins required by brokerage firms, like their initial margins, generally exceed those set by the IMM. (For examples of how initial and maintenance margin requirements are affected by various trading situations, see the chapter on commodities.)

At the end of each day's trading, every investor's net positions in foreign exchange are checked by clearing operations to see if there is any need, because of a margin call, to provide additional cash. These margin calls are one way of ensuring that the buyers of futures contracts will be paid by the sellers of these contracts—who incur losses as a results of the same price movement. If the seller cannot make payment, the burden falls on the brokerage firm; if the brokerage firm fails to make payment, the IMM must make the payment.

Investors rarely take delivery on future contracts. Rather, the positions are closed out before the settlement date. (A detailed explanation is in the offsetting delivery section of the commodities chapter.) Offsetting one's positions in futures contracts is less expensive than taking delivery. If investors have profited by selling out at a price above the cost, their accounts are credited with the profit; if a loss is incurred instead, their accounts are charged.

Because the futures market is such a small part of the total trading picture in foreign currencies, most commercial transactions—both hedging and speculative—occur in the interbank market. Transactions in forward exchange futures market are almost exclusively speculative; there are very few commercial hedging transactions. These speculative transactions in the futures market are arbitraged to the interbank market.

Participants in the foreign currency market are involved in a zero-sum game, unlike those who deal in the stock market. In the stock market, a majority of

TABLE 1: CHARACTERISTICS OF FUTURES CONTRACTS IN FOREIGN EXCHANGE

Currency	Contract Size Units of	U.S. Dollar Equivalent	Minimum Fluctuation	Daily Limit	IMM Margin Requirements: Initial	IMM Margin Requirements: Maintenance
British Sterling	25,000 BP	$46,925	$12.50 (.0005)	$1250 (.0500)	$1500	$1000
Canadian Dollar	100,000 CD	83,720	10.00 (.0001)	750 (.0075)	1500	1000
German Mark	125,000 DM	54,438	12.50 (.0001)	1250 (.0100)	1500	1000
Dutch Guilder	125,000 DG	53,425	12.50 (.0001)	1250 (.0100)	1500	1000
French Franc	250,000 FR	50,100	12.50 (.00005)	1250 (.00500)	1500	1000
Japanese Yen	12,500,000 JY	45,680	12.50 (.000001)	1250 (.000100)	1500	1000
Mexican Peso	1,000,000 MP	35,850	10.00 (.00001)	1500 (.00150)	4000	3000
Swiss Franc	125,000 SF	68,200	12.50 (.0001)	1875 (.0150)	2000	1500

As of March 10, 1981

Note: These IMM contract specifications are subject to change without notice and in no way are to be interpreted as being official permanent rules.

participants can achieve net gains over time, if the stock prices rise or if stocks pay dividends. There is a "real return" to distribute to the owners of stock on average. The question involves distribution of gains among participants. But in the foreign currency market, buyers and sellers exchange net positions. If the buyer of a sterling futures contract secures a profit, the seller necessarily incurs a loss. Various firms engaged in international trade and investment may be willing to pay investors to carry some of the exchange risk—the uncertainty associated with changes in exchange rates.

However, many large firms seek either to minimize the cost of avoiding exchange risks or to profit, as banks do, from the willingness of others to pay these costs. The foreign currency market is highly competitive, and individual investors, if they are to earn profits on a systematic basis, must recognize the nature of the game. Winners and losers in every transaction exist on a one-to-one basis with each other, and only the investor with insights that are not generally or even selectively available to other market participants will profit consistently.

Approaches to Currency Market Intervention

From our previous analysis regarding the major factors which tend to affect both current as well as future exchange rates, we can conclude that new information—such as changes in the rate of inflation or the price of crude petroleum—tends to be reflected immediately by changes in exchange rates.

The exchange rate forecasting services differ in their models of foreign currency markets and in the sets of variables they believe are likely to determine the exchange rate. Some rely on momentum models, which extrapolate the direction of past exchange rate movements to predict future movements. Such models do well when exchange rates move in one direction for an extended period, and they do poorly when the rates remain within a narrow band.

Some data-based models rely extensively on previous data covering a wide range of variables including prices, price levels, money supplies, interest rates, exports, and imports. Changes in exchange rates are analyzed as a function of changes in these variables. Other forecasting approaches simply involve seat-of-the-pants judgments by informed individuals.

Since some investors—either buyers or sellers—will profit on each transaction, the effective test of forecasting skills is whether the investor's returns in the long run outpace the modest transaction costs.

The factors explaining adjustments in the foreign exchange value of major currencies relative to the U.S. dollar differ. For example, in September, 1977, the value of the pound sterling was £1 = $1.55 U.S. at the end of 1976, the rate had been $1.70 and at the end of 1975, $2.02. In the summer of 1978, numerous observers had predicted that sterling would continue to depreciate until £1 = $1 U.S., because the British inflation rate was significantly higher than that of the United States and appeared likely to remain so. Yet by the end of 1980, sterling had appreciated to $2.39, even though the inflation rate in Great Britain remained above U.S. levels. At the end of 1981, the rate was £1 = $1.85.

Several factors explain why sterling appreciated sharply. For one, the Labour Government was able to gain the assent of the labor unions to limited wage increases. As expectations about increased inflation diminished, sterling strengthened. Second, the Labour Government—and then in 1979, the Conservative Government—showed a willingness to accept a higher rate of unemployment in the hope that such measures would reduce inflationary price pressures. A third was that Great Britain became nearly 100 percent self-sufficient in petroleum by the end of 1979, so the need to sell more exports in order to pay for increasingly costly oil imports was eliminated. Three years earlier, Great Britain had imported more than half of its petroleum. The fourth was the increase in the price of oil, which led to stepped-up British exports of goods, services, and securities to the OPEC countries—sterling was becoming a petro-currency.

Variations in the foreign exchange value of the Japanese yen relative to the U.S. dollar have been even more drastic than those of sterling. In late 1976, the rate was Y 295 = $1 U.S.; in November of 1978, after appreciating for 21 months, the yen reached Y 175 = $1 U.S. Thereafter, the yen began to depreciate, and in March of 1980, the rate was Y 250 = $1 U.S. One factor which might explain the appreciation of the yen was the U.S. economic boom and subsequent growth in U.S. imports from Japan.

By contrast, from 1976 until 1979, economic growth in Japan was sluggish by the country's own standards. Two consequences were that Japanese demand for imports increased slowly, and Japanese producers were eager to promote exports—especially since domestic demand was then significantly below their productive capacity. This combination of rapid export growth and only marginal demand for imports led to an increase in foreign exchange earnings and the appreciation of the yen.

The turnabout in the yen-dollar relationship was triggered by the "Defend the Dollar" policy adopted by President Carter in November, 1978; other currencies also weakened at the time. The subsequent depreciation of the yen by 40 percent reflects a sharp increase in the Japanese growth rate and the surge in oil prices, which led to a doubling in the Japanese oil import bill, from $30 billion in 1978, to $65 billion in 1980. Oil imports must be financed by exports which required an increase in price competitiveness brought about by the depreciation of the yen.

Whereas most major currencies had appreciated relative to the United States dollar in the latter half of the 1970s, the Canadian dollar depreciated from $1.03 Canadian = $1 U.S. to $1.19 Canadian = $1 U.S. In the past, the Canadian business cycle paralleled the U.S. business cycle. When the U.S. economy boomed—as in the late 1970s—the Canadian international payments position strengthened, mainly because of a surge in prices of Canadian raw material exports. Recently, however, such was not the case.

One factor which might explain the Canadian dollar's weakness was a belated adjustment to Canada's more rapid price level inflation. The delay reflected that high interest rates in Canada attracted a large influx of funds from the United States. However, as U.S. interest rates increased, this capital flow declined, and the Canadian dollar weakened.

The German mark is second only to the Swiss franc in showing the strongest secular tendency to appreciate. The usual explanation is that the Germany has been extremely concerned about inflation because of the two previous experiences with hyperinflation—one in the early 1920s and the other in the mid-1940s. Moreover, because Germany relied heavily on "guest workers" from Turkey, Greece, Italy, and Yugoslavia, unemployment has proven less of a problem in Germany than in any other major industrial country.

When commodity prices were increasing, the Germans moved quickly to raise interest rates; as interest rates on mark assets increased, foreigners acquired more mark assets, and the mark appreciated. Indeed, the greater success the Germans have had in limiting their commodity price levels may reflect their greater willingness to adopt contractive monetary policies; the stronger mark led to a reduction in the price of imported goods in Germany. The sharp swings of the mark-U.S. dollar rate appear to reflect changes in the phasing of contractive and expansive U.S. and German monetary policies. If Germany is relatively more contractive, the mark appreciates; if Germany is more expansive, the mark depreciates.

Therefore, while exchange rates in the long run—periods of four to five years or longer—may tend to correspond with changes in the relationship among national commodity levels, a number of other factors are likely to be more important in predicting exchange rate movements over the shorter run periods of interest to investors. These include changes in monetary policy and interest rate differentials, in the phasing of the business cycle, in the price of petroleum and other raw materials, and in the success of current government policies in light of the likelihood they will be reversed. The forward rate relects the market's view of these factors.

Shifts in exchange rate present investors with opportunities for profits and losses. At some distant future date, these opportunities may diminish if currencies once again become pegged. For the foreseeable future, however, as long as inflation rates in major countries differ significantly, major currencies will continue to float.

Chapter Fourteen

What You Can Bank On

There is a joke making the rounds in the banking industry that goes like this. Seems a little old lady was waiting in line at a teller's window, when a man approached another window and gave the teller a piece of paper. The teller scowled, pushed a button, and a guard appeared. The guard punched the man in the nose, threw him to the floor, kicked him, and finally took him by the coat collar and tossed him into the street. The little old lady gasped and said to her teller, "My goodness, I've never seen an attempted bank robbery before!" to which the teller replied, "That wasn't an attempted robbery—that was our substantial penalty for early withdrawal."

The story illustrates a point. Our banks, especially savings institutions, are desperate to keep deposits, especially low-interest savings accounts. If you've been reading their statements of condition, you'll know why. Many banks, especially savings institutions, have been losing money at prodigious rates.

Why? In the case of the thrift institutions, the reason is clear: Interest rates. First, for many years the government forced them to make most of their investments in the form of long-term first mortgages at relatively low rates of interest—savers, literally, were subsidizing mortgage borrowers. Second, banks were forced to raise the interest they paid to obtain funds via certificates of deposit in order to compete with the money market funds. And third, they were restricted by government regulation from raising the interest paid on passbook savings, making these low-yield accounts even less attractive as investments.

Commercial banks have fared a little better because their loans have been mostly short-term and thus have been able to reflect the high rate of inflation. But in either case, for the first time since the Depression, people have actually been asking, "Is my bank safe?"

The answer, in almost all cases, is "Yes—but." To find out, investigate.

Has your bank been showing a profit? If not, why not? Most important, has its net-worth position eroded to the point of danger? If so, how would you know this? The FDIC uses the ratio of assets to net worth (which includes surplus, undivided profits, and some reserves—the last items on a balance sheet). If the percentage of net worth to assets is less than 5 percent, the bank is deemed less than stable. The Federal Home Loan Bank, on the other hand, uses 3 percent or higher as a sign of stability. Opting for the higher figure is always safe, of course. You can get the figures for the calculation from a statement of condition available at any bank office.

In addition to doing your own figuring, you should realize that the government regulatory agencies are watching, too. Long before any bank could actually fail, those agencies—the FDIC, FSLIC, or whatever—would arrange a merger with a stronger bank, which would assume the assets and liabilities of the weaker one. Thus, to the depositor, all that would change is the name on the door—and the margin of safety on the balance sheet. Some experts estimate that between 400 and 1500 of the country's thrifts and mutual savings banks will experience such forced mergers within the next year or so. With fewer than 7000 such banks in existence, that means a sizable percentage are in trouble to some degree.

So where does that leave the average investor in the years ahead? Inflation is the key for 1982 and probably for many years to come. Being able to live with inflation boils down to a few economic basics: Paying less for what you get, getting the maximum earnings on your money, and keeping your income at least a little bit ahead of your outgo.

Using a Bank

Every investor, of course, must have some dealings with a bank. He or she must have a place to accumulate capital, from which to dispense payments, and from which to borrow as the need arises. However, in inflationary times, no one should think in terms of depositing money in a bank passbook account as an investment. Deposits earning 5½ percent interest, while inflation climbs from 10 to 20 percent annually, are simply losing money. Even those who are not following aggressive investment strategies can do better by placing the bulk of their savings in other vehicles, including some of the new high-yield bank CDs and money market funds.

Shopping for the bank that best suits your needs is essential during inflationary periods. You should investigate to learn:

1. Which bank pays the most interest on savings.

2. Which bank makes the lowest service charges on checking-type accounts, or offers the best deal on NOW accounts.

3. Which bank charges the lowest interest rates on borrowed money.

It is a balancing act to bring these factors into line, but an essential one in these days of high interest and tight dollars. What's more, the Depository Institutions Deregulation and Monetary Control Act of 1980 has made things even more complicated—and more competitive. Basically, it is a consumer-oriented law, but it is under constant fire from those with vested interests.

• Ceilings on savings interest rates are to be phased out over a six-year period. This sounds better in theory than it works in practice. Recently, the group charged with implementing the law, the Depository Institutions Deregulation Committee (DIDC) opted to ignore the intent of the law and to keep passbook rates at 5½ percent for at least six more months. Still, over the next five years, increases in interest rates will be allowed. But in the meantime, 2½-year "Small Savers" certificates of deposit (CDs) will have a rate cap of 12 percent and a floor of 9¼ percent at commercial banks and 9½ percent at thrifts. Six-month money market CDs will have a high based on the Treasury rates and will have a floor of 7¾ percent. The only real lifting of rate limits has been the introduction, effective January, 1982, of a flexible-rate CD with no set limits.

• Negotiable Order of Withdrawal (NOW) accounts started in New England in 1969. Basically, a NOW "check" is nothing more than a sight draft drawn on a nonbusiness savings account. It looks like a check and works like a check—but the account earns interest until the check is paid. As of January, 1981, NOW accounts were made legal everywhere in the United States.

• Automatic transfer accounts have also been legalized nationally. In this type of account, a depositor's funds remain in his or her savings account until a check drawn on a low or no-balance checking account clears, at which time a transfer is automatically made. These accounts have little consumer interest and can be expected to die out as NOW accounts catch on.

• Remote service units, both automatic teller machines and check-guarantee machines, have been legalized nationally and are great for banking at work or at such places as supermarkets.

• The Federal Deposit Insurance Corporation, the Federal Savings and Loan Deposit Insurance Corporation, and the National Credit Union Administration have increased their insurance coverage to $100,000 per account; and by opening individual, joint, and trustee accounts, this coverage limit can be increased many times over.

• State ceilings on mortgage interest rates have been set aside. States may legislate to re-establish limits, but it is doubtful that many will.

• Finally, new reserve requirements have little direct effect on consumers, but great indirect effect. By standardizing reserve requirements, banks' business costs will be more similar among types, thus making competition not only likely, but almost inevitable.

Two things have recently been allowed by the government that offer saving consumers a glimmer of hope. The smallest glimmer is from the All Savers Certificates, which have rates pegged at 70 percent of the T-Bill yield, and with which savers can earn up to $2000 tax-free interest for an individual, or $4000 for a married couple filing jointly. The idea sounds great, but the initial flurry soon died, and the public is ignoring them. The other new development is the new flexible-rate CD, available only since January 4, 1982. With this 18-month CD, banks can literally be competitive, setting rates as they wish. These rates may be fixed for the term of the CD, or, at some banks, may even fluctuate within the term. They will be extremely popular with anyone who believes in the inevitability of inflation and the wisdom of accumulating funds in a tax-deferred Keogh Plan or Individual Retirement Account.

Money Management

A new watchword among alert consumers, adapted from the practices of business, is money management. In basic and practical terms, this concept can be practiced in two simple ways: By having available funds earn the maximum amount, and, at the same time, by paying bills at the last possible moment commensurate with good credit practices.

A good example would be the payment of a life insurance premium. The notice will arrive over a month before the due date; however, life insurance premiums always have a grace period of 30 days. So the insured has three options:

1. To pay the premium when the notice is received;
2. To pay the premium when due; or
3. To pay the premium just before the expiration of the grace period.

Obviously, smart money management dictates that the premium be paid just before the expiration of the grace period. In addition, it requires that the funds used to make the payment be kept earning interest right up until the payment is made—ideally, until the check clears.

Using your bank for the optimum in money management requires a basic knowledge of banking services and their costs and benefits, and a willingness to utilize those services to your own best advantage.

In practical terms, getting these benefits varies according to the needs of each individual. Thus, an elderly widow who pays three or four bills a month may find that a savings account on which she can have bank checks issued offers all the convenience she requires—in addition, of course, to the presumed safety and availability of funds.

On the other hand, a young couple with the numerous expenses of a new home and a growing family would find such a bill-paying arrangement unwieldy. They would need the convenience of a checking account, which also offers the advantages of safety and availability.

The whole secret of getting the most from your bank is to know what services it offers, how much these services cost—both in terms of service charges and in terms of lost investment income—and how a combination of these services can best benefit you.

Tips on Checking

Checking accounts are the basic deposit service offered by commercial banks, though some thrift institutions are now also making them available. A checking account lets you disperse your own money whenever and wherever you want and in exact amounts. Your funds are totally safe because the money stays on deposit until your check actually clears; and, assuming that you have taken normal precautions, you are protected from loss. The disadvantage of a checking account is that money kept on deposit is not earning any investment income, so a minimum amount should be in your account.

NOW accounts, of course, offer an alternative. But while stated rates of interest may sound the same among banks, the fact is, charges made against the accounts vary widely. Thus, with interest at 5¼ percent, a New England bank may require no minimum balance on deposit and make no charge for drafts. And, in that area, banks that require a $300 or $500 minimum balance with no per-share charge are common. On the other hand, at least one Southern bank requires a minimum balance of $3000. Some banks even pay interest only on the balance above a set minimum—and so on.

Here's the way to get the maximum return or the minimum charge on any checking-type account:

1. Open a NOW account at the highest rate/lowest cost/lowest minimum balance, if possible.

2. Always keep a minimum balance in any checking account, including a NOW account.

3. Compare types of accounts available and choose the one with the lowest charges based on your probable account activity.

4. Realize that you are sometimes better off paying a service charge and maintaining a minimum balance, offsetting this with cash at interest in a savings account.

5. Use float to your best advantage. Float is the time it takes for a check issued by you to clear the payee's bank to your account. During this time, your bill is marked "paid," but the money is still in your account and earning interest. Float time varies widely, but a week or so is not uncommon. You can see how long it takes specific checks to have cleared in the past by looking at the deposit date on the endorsement on the back of the check and comparing it to the date that the check was credited to your account. Don't use float to deliberately write NSF (not sufficient funds) checks. Do use float to your advantage, possibly by selecting a smaller bank whose collection process is a bit slower or by using out-of-town suppliers.

6. Some banks offer automatic-transfer accounts, which keep a minimum of cash in a checking account with the bulk in savings. When a check clears, a transfer is automatically made from savings to checking. This allows the funds on deposit to earn interest up until a check clears. But these accounts will probably soon be replaced by NOW accounts because the bookkeeping involved is unwieldy for both the bank and the customer.

Tips on Savings

Savings accounts come in all shapes and sizes, ranging from the traditional Christmas Club to high-yield investment certificates. Here are the basic types:

Club accounts—Christmas, vacation, and tax—offer a method of forced savings for incurable spenders. For these people, they are a thrift incentive. Everyone else would do better to stick with an interest-bearing account.

Regular or passbook savings come in two basic varieties: no-notice accounts and 90-day-notice accounts. The latter pay a slightly higher rate of interest and have largely been replaced in consumer usage by the 30-month

CDs. All interest is regulated by the federal government, and thrift institutions are allowed to pay slightly more. Bear in mind that ½ of one percent interest per year on $1000, compounded daily, amounts to just $5.29. So switching to a bank that pays that differential may not even cover the extra cost in gasoline to get there.

Investment certificates fall into five basic types: minimum-deposit short-term certificates with a maturity of from one to two-and-a-half years; minimum-deposit medium-term certificates with maturities ranging from four to six years; long-term certificates that mature in six to eight years; the six-month money market certificates that have a minimum deposit of $10,000; and the all-new flexible-rate certificates that have no legal minimum and that mature in 18 months.

It used to be true that the higher rates went with the longer term and larger deposit, but with deregulation proceeding so slowly and clumsily, the best deals are usually the 18-month flexible-rate and 26-month CDs. The rates on these may, because of the minimum set by law, actually range above those paid on the six-month money market CDs. In February, 1982, they were paying approximately 2 percent higher rates than the money market funds.

Repurchase agreements, or repos, are offered by banks to improve their own liquidity positions. Technically, they are bonds issued by banks with the guarantee that they will repurchase them after an agreed upon short term and at an agreed rate of interest. They are especially valuable to businesses with short-term funds to invest. Typically, the minimum repo ranges from $5000 to $25,000; the term ranges from three days to three months; and the rate is usually about three points below the six-month money market rate. Repurchase agreements are not insured by the FDIC or FSLIC, but because the investments are made in government-guaranteed mortgage markets, they are quite safe. For the average investor, they work like short-term, high-yield CDs.

Here are some tips to maximize your savings:

1. Use a regular savings account only as an accumulator account. When the funds in it reach $1000, switch them to a CD.

2. Realize that after a point—depending on your net worth and income, but for most people, say, $25,000 in savings certificates—you should look into other investment areas. Build on savings first, then expand.

3. Don't use life insurance as a savings tool. You'll get low dividends and pay sales commissions on your savings dollars. Stick to term insurance and put your savings in a bank.

4. Shop for rates, but realize that a fraction of a point isn't worth excess travel costs or losing a credit advantage for future borrowing.

5. Check how interest is calculated. For example, 6 percent interest for one year on $1000 compounded annually amounts to $60; 6 percent interest for one year compounded daily amounts to $61.83. If you're a regular saver, this can add up.

6. As you know from the required phrase used in advertising CDs, there are "substantial penalties for early withdrawal." If you have a CD issued before July 1, 1979, and redeem it before maturity, you may lose three months' interest and have the balance of the interest calculated at the regular passbook savings rate. Or, with your consent, the bank may apply the new penalty, which means:

If you have a term certificate issued on or after July 1, 1979, and redeem it before maturity, you lose six months' interest. If you haven't earned six months' interest, the charge will be applied against the principal.

These penalties sound scary, but they aren't. If you have an older, low-rate CD, it is usually best to cash it in for a newer higher-rate one. Ask your bank to calculate the penalty and possible profit or loss to you.

Other Services

Banks offer many other services that can be of real financial benefit to the consumer. Among them are:

Safe deposit boxes, which offer invaluable security for important papers and valuables for pennies a day in rent. They are fireproof, virtually theft-proof, and, of importance to most people, they prevent papers from being misplaced or seen by prying eyes. Safe deposit boxes are only accessible with your key. Contrary to popular opinion, they are not a way to avoid inheritance taxes, since cash or valuables kept in them are subject to inclusion in an estate, and are often audited on the death of the renter. However, the rent is tax-deductible.

Traveler's checks, which are the best travel bargain available—and many banks even give them away with no issuance fee under special circumstances.

Trust services, which should be investigated by anyone with an estate of $100,000 or more. A bank as an executor under a will charges no more than an individual, but a bank never gets sick or dies, never goes on vacation, and does offer a huge pool of expert administrators.

Investment Opportunities

Generally speaking, banks are not investment houses. But for many people, banks are the place to begin. Some of the common investment opportunities available at most banks are:

Certificates of deposit may be purchased at any office of your bank, on the spot.

Keogh Plan accounts allow self-employed persons an opportunity to put aside tax-free dollars for retirement. Under the Economic Recovery Act, this same privilege has been extended to all employed persons and their spouses with an across-the-board extension of Individual Retirement Accounts. Most banks administer IRS-approved plans, using their own certificates of deposit as the investment vehicle. A self-employed person may put into an approved Keogh Plan up to 15 percent of his or her earnings to a maximum of $15,000, or a minimum of $750, or all of his or her self-employment earnings, whichever is less.

Any employed person may put up to $2000 per year, or $4000 for a couple with both parties working and who file jointly, into a tax-deferred IRA. For a couple filing jointly where only one party is employed, the maximum is $2250. Though you cannot withdraw the money without substantial tax penalties until age 59½, it makes sense in terms of today's inflation to invest in relatively short-term certificates and renew them as needed. The new flexible-rate certificates are ideal.

U.S. Treasury obligations may be ordered through many banks at the market price plus a commission or service charge. The advantage they offer over bank CDs is that they are marketable, thus there is no penalty for early withdrawal as there is with a CD. Check with your banker for details on Treasury bonds.

Investment opportunities offered by banks vary widely, depending on the type and size of the banking institution. Find out what the bank offers, what the current rates are, when the rates will change, what those changes are likely to be, and if there are any restrictions. Usually all that is required is a trip to the nearest bank office, where you sign a form and hand over the cash.

Recent Developments

R ecent banking developments fall into two categories—technical and consumer.

Technical developments are primarily the result of computer technology. Outstanding examples are:

● Automatic teller machines or ATMs. These are convenient services built right into the outside bank wall or even at a remote location. With a plastic "debit card" and a secret "personal identification number," or PIN, the customer can transact most banking business.

● Check-guarantee machines, usually called "point-of-sale" or POS terminals, enable a shopper with an ID card and a PIN to have any check guaranteed in a cooperating retail market. A usual exception is the third-person personal check, which most banks won't accept into this system. The individual's personal check is fine, however. The system relies on a hookup with a central computer that has a record of the customer's credit background.

● New in-bank devices, including teller's cash-dispensing and transaction machines, are being planned. These will help increase accuracy, speed up transactions, and, above all, are hoped to make bank robberies virtually impossible.

Consumer developments are the result of three factors:

1. **Consumer demand.** More and more, people know what they want, and they're going to banks that provide it. A good example is the NOW or interest-bearing checking account; people want a monetary return for making a cash inventory available to banks.

2. **Technology.** Technology, which has made ATMs, POS terminals, and other devices available, will free tellers from routine transactions and make them available for personal-service needs. In fact, some banks can call tellers "customer service representatives" or "personal bankers."

3. **Profits and competition.** Banks are increasingly aware of which services and functions are profitable and which are not. Thus, they are paying premium dollars and competing extensively for profitable accounts while they reject marginal ones. Several banks have even stopped accepting credit-card applications because the cards are not profitable for them.

The Future

In the short term, banking will be in a state of flux, changing in emphasis from the old style to the new. Increased experimentation with automation and electronic transfer systems will take place. Most important in the short term will be an increased emphasis on wooing the profitable consumer—which means he will be able to get more for his banking dollar.

In the long term, forecasters are predicting a "cashless society" in which the consumer will present a debit card or even use a voice-activated point-of-sale terminal to make an instant transfer of his funds to pay for his purchases. Although this may be a computer expert's dream, it is an unlikely probability. Consumer surveys repeatedly show that:

● People want checks in hand. Most Social Security recipients, for example, have rejected the direct deposit of funds to their accounts.

● People play the float and do not want instant payment of their obligations.

● Banks are predicting the widespread use of truncation, that is, using a checking-account statement for which cancelled checks are not returned to the depositor. Some banks in fact, have already implemented this system, and their customers reluctantly accept it, and then only if it is tied to an incentive such as an interest-bearing account. So, while this may someday become widespread, it will certainly not be in the near future.

● Although ATMs can function 24 hours a day, few customers use them on this basis. People will, however, find them increasingly convenient for saving time when it comes to making a quick deposit, withdrawal, or payment transaction.

● Savings Bank Life Insurance has worked so well in the few states in which banks offer it that some form of over-the-counter bank-based insurance eventually may come about. This would be very beneficial for consumers.

Strategies to Explore

"Bank investments offer an inadequate hedge against inflation." Have you heard that statement? But with a projected inflation rate of 10-plus percent, an adequate hedge is hard to find. In spite of the economy, here are some possibilities to explore:

1. Take advantage of a Keogh Plan or an IRA account. Some experts estimate that only 15 percent of those eligible do so. But realize that if your taxable earnings are, for example, $30,000 a year, and you put $4500 into Keogh in an 11 percent CD, you save over $1300 in taxes, while your investment earns $523.17 during the first year alone. And with an IRA, you can invest $2000 a year—that's $38 a week—and have a tax shelter plus a great retirement fund.

2. Some states exempt a portion of interest paid by in-state banks on CDs; check your state tax laws.

3. Consider setting up an educational fund for your children. To set up such a plan, ask your bank officer for details about a custodial account under the Uniform Gifts to Minors Act.

4. For many consumers, buying a home is the most viable tax shelter

available. Even with a mortgage rate of 13 percent, with a 30-year loan of $50,000, during the first year, $6,491.53 of the total payments of $6,637.20 is interest and deductible on Schedule A of Form 1040. Of course, the ratio of interest versus principle in the annual paydown decreases as the years go by; but, at the same time, if the trend toward rising real estate values holds, this will more than take care of the lessened tax break.

Here are a few points to keep in mind when you deal with a bank:

1. Use a NOW account if at all possible. Everyone needs a checking-type account, so why not have one that earns money rather than one that costs money?

2. Use a regular savings account only to accumulate funds for short-term goals. As soon as you have enough of a balance to go a step higher on the investment ladder and to cover possible emergencies, invest in high-rate CDs. For most investors, this means 30-month certificates.

3. Pay cash unless you can borrow at very favorable rates. Paying with an installment loan or with a credit card often costs in two ways—you may lose the possible discount that a cash sale can bring, and, more important, you pay 18 to 22 percent or more in interest charges. However, paying a credit card bill within the no-interest period—if you still have this option—is a good deal.

4. Realize that the tendency in housing is for prices to drop somewhat when mortgage interest rates are high. So, surprisingly, the best time to buy may be when these rates are up. Thus, you pay less for the house. If rates drop, you can refinance your mortgage, unless you have a rollover mortgage, in which case the drop will be automatic. And if rates don't drop, you are passing off a portion of the increased cost as a tax deduction, which you could not do with the purchase price of the house.

5. Use the float. Pay bills as late as is consistent with maintaining a good credit record. Paying bills at the last minute when due can save a single consumer with average expenses $200 or more a year if the funds are kept earning even modest interest. Add this to the $100 or more that can be earned both as interest and reduced charges by using a NOW account, and you have a $300-per-year raise!

6. To help plan your anti-inflation strategy, apply the "Rule of 72." Here's the way it works: Simply divide any given annual interest rate into 72. The answer you get is the approximate number of years it will take your investment to double at that rate with interest compounded. Thus, at 6 percent, money will double in 12 years; at 7 percent, in about 10 years; at 12 percent, in six years; at 14 percent, in five years.

The conclusions are simple. Pay as little as you can in extra costs, such as loan interest. Earn as much as you can on your dollars—all of them—invested or not. Remember, every penny you earn in interest is at least a penny you won't have to earn to offset inflation, or a penny you won't have to do without because of rising costs.

So, put all of your dollars to work, beginning right at your bank. Use your bank as a base—knowing that it is more a convenient place to hold some of your money for day-to-day use—and expand from there.

Chapter Fifteen

Collectibles: Profiting from Old Things

I t was not too long ago when collectibles were the darlings of the investment arena. Disenchanted investors, desperately panning for gold in the form of new investment ideas, were prospecting heavily in the past. Many became financial winners dealing in old porcelain, Persian rugs, rare coins, and even comic books. But today, these would-be collectors would be prospecting up the wrong creek.

The interest in collectibles has waned considerably, with a number of factors contributing to their decline. For one, inflation has dropped from around 18 percent to a more livable 8 percent; then, the U.S. dollar has shown more strength on the international monetary markets; and finally gold and silver prices have virtually vanished from sight.

Another blow to collectible investing has been Congress's recent ruling against their inclusion in Individual Retirement Accounts (IRA) or Keogh plans.

So if you're planning to build a new fortune on old things, the word is "proceed with caution." There are a lot of sellers around, but very few buyers. The main pitfall with buying collectibles for investments nowadays is disposing of them later. No buyers - no sales.

Collectibles became popular during the 1970s when investors were concerned about the perils of putting their cash into stocks, bonds, commodities, and the like. They felt that tangible objects - art, antique jewelry, vintage furniture, commemorative plates - were safer and offered more long-term potential. At the time, they were right - but times have changed. Today, the experts warn that you better buy for love and not for money.

While collectibles no longer share the glamour of stocks or even money market funds, these tangible assets nonetheless have retained great appeal. An investment in antiques, if properly selected, still can benefit the owners in a number of ways. And if inflation starts whittling away at the economy again, collectibles will once more become better than stocks or money in the bank.

What are Collectibles

C ollectibles (another example of modern-day simplicity in labeling) are old items worth collecting. Antiques are frequently lumped into a broad category with collectibles ,but there is a definite difference.While an antique is a collectible, not all collectibles are antiques. For example, a collectible may be a comic book or a beer can, and while these are valuable to some people, it would be hard to compare such items directly with the master craftsmanship and esthetic appeal of aged, finely hand-worked wood furniture.

What is more, collectibles and antiques are sometimes found among "previously owned" merchandise, too often fallaciously pushed as fine antiques, but more properly known as *junque*.

To appreciate the investment strategies of the antique and collectibles market, you first have to understand what these objects actually are. Although the definition of an antique varies, it is somewhat easier to pin down than that of collectibles. Some experts define antiques as anything pre-1930, since that year supposedly marked the end of the handcrafting era. The United States Customs Service maintains that antiques are anything more than 100 years old. Two broader definitions which millions of collectors find useful are: 1) An antique is anything no longer in original production which someone, somewhere, collects; or 2) An antique is a surviving relic of a past generation.

Although some collectibles are antiques according to these definitions, that is not the whole story. A collectible, in fact, is one of those things better defined by what it isn't than by what it is. For instance, a collectible is not "timeless." To the contrary, it specifically evokes some by gone era and tells us something concrete about the lifestyle and values of another day.

Furthermore, a collectible is not junk. If it were, it would have been "collected" by the garbage collector long ago, and forever relegated to obscurity. Every collectible once meant something to someone, which explains why it has been salvaged from the garbage heap time and time again. It had value to begin with—whether obvious economic value or purely sentimental or utilitarian value.

Finally, a collectible may or may not be an antique. Old, yes—but "Superman" comics and the original Mickey Mouse watches fall way short of the standard 100-year-old criterion for antiques.

An intriguing and diverse class of items, antiques and collectibles can also be lucrative for investors. Particularly since the dollar started to lose face in the Seventies and since inflation has brought into question the value of plain old money, real things such as fine old furniture and handcrafted glassware have enjoyed a virtual boom among investors.

It's not surprising when you recognize the appreciation that has brought some investors great profits. For example, a 1957 Pontiac Bonneville convertible that could have been purchased for under $400 in 1973, now sells for about $14,000. An antique music box recently sold for over $22,000 when the previous high sale had been under $5000. An Art Nouveau glass vase which brought $1000 in 1973 fetched $6750 in 1979. An Eighteenth Century snuffbox which sold for $80 in 1941 was resold in 1979 for $12,500.

While these represent outstanding examples, they are by no means isolated situations, and they illustrate just what has been going on in the antique and collectible markets recently.

Investment Angles

E xactly what is it about these items that investors are finding so interesting and remunerative? The first appeal is the inherent value in the fine craftsmanship and rarity of most collectibles. Obviously, if Tiffany lamp shades could have been cheaply but exquisitely mass-produced for the last 80 years, they wouldn't command the prices as antiques that they do now.

This means collectibles hold their value in an inflationary period, unlike money in the bank. Europeans in post-war periods, have long recognized that antiques are a viable hedge against inflation. Americans began recognizing this fact in the late '70s.

Therefore, the future demand for antiques will probably increase since more people will start collecting (investing in) them. In Europe, there are even investment trusts (similar to mutual funds) which invest in art and antiques. If these are initiated in the United States, it would increase demand in the art and antique market even more.

Another advantage of antiques as investments is that demand is usually increasing while the supply is usually decreasing. Fires, tornadoes, and other catastrophes destroy some antiques, and still others are forever removed from the marketplace when they are acquired by museums. Thus, the law of supply and demand is on the side of the antique investor. Since the supply does not increase, but the demand does, the recent upward trend in antique prices is likely to continue.

It is also appealing to investors that, although antique prices may seem to move slowly, they rarely move downward. Occasionally, there is even a chance for a quick return, although collectibles and antiques should, like gems, be viewed as a long-term investment. In addition, the antique market is open to the small investor as well as the large one—there is no minimum amount that must be invested in antiques.

There are also several tax advantages available to the investor dealing in antiques. Unlike interest and dividends, the annual increase in value of the investment is not immediately taxable. It is only when the antique is sold that income taxes must be paid. Then, the profits are taxed at a capital gain rate which can be less than one-half of the regular income tax. The postponement of taxes and the lower rates mean that an investment in antiques does not have to bring as high a rate of return as other investments in order to be profitable.

Most antique collectors feel that the biggest advantage of antiques as investments is esthetic since the investor can use the items while they are being held. You can furnish your house with them. In fact, it may be possible to furnish a house with antiques at less cost than new furniture. And new furniture will lose value while antique furniture will probably increase in value.

Investment Drawbacks

As with other types of investments, antiques are not always perfect. For one thing, there are few overnight profits in the antique business. In most cases, antiques are investments for the long term. The quick profits are usually the result of an imperfect market rather than knowledgeable investing. And, of course, antique investments do not pay dividends or interest. There is no way to live off the increased value of the investment without actually selling the item.

One of the biggest disadvantages of antiques is they are not liquid—they cannot be converted into cash easily. This means an investor is likely to suffer a loss if an item has to be sold in a hurry.

You must find a buyer for your items. This means searching out other collectors at auctions and antique shows, or advertising in periodicals that serve as trading posts for collectors.

Another disadvantage (usually minor) is that investments in antiques and collectibles need to be insured. Savings accounts are insured by an agency of the Federal Government. Insurance premiums on antiques, however, must be paid for by the investor. By the same token, though, this means you need not worry about losing your principal when you invest in antiques and collectibles.

Getting Your Start

Let's assume the investment possibilities have convinced you to go into collecting. What do you need to know and how do you get started? As a newcomer recently attracted to this boom, your first question may be "Can I build an investment collection of collectibles today?" The answer is definitely yes. Can it be done with a modest investment? Yes, again. You probably should be prepared to set aside two to three thousand dollars a year in a three-to-five year program.

The first step will be to decide what to collect. What appeals to you and will offer the most satisfaction during the search? And what seems likely to appreciate? It is definitely necessary to specialize in collecting, limiting your interest to one or two categories such as glass, porcelain, bronze sculptures, silver objects, clocks, or dolls. Remember that by narrowing your field you'll be able to learn it more thoroughly and become an expert sooner.

In antiques, which is in itself a very broad category, it is best to specialize in one or two types of items at first, but evenutally to diversify your collection in order to protect yourself against the whims of the marketplace. It's also a good idea to include both high-priced and low-priced items, which is another means of diversifying your investment. Low-priced items are often much easier to dispose of if the need for cash arises—although the higher quality, higher-priced items will be the gems of your collection and see the most appreciation.

For the beginning collector with modest funds, it's worth considering getting into one of the "just discovered" objects such as Nineteenth Century American silver, and particularly hollowware objects such as tea sets, coffee pots, and the like. Also attracting interest are bronze medals of topical subjects such as expositions and fairs, and automobile, aviation, and railroading items. Such medals, which can still be purchased at from $25 to $100 each, are beautiful examples of miniature bronze art.

Art and studio pottery, both American and European, of the late Nineteenth and early Twentieth Centuries, are two other good collectible areas. They are now beginning to be appreciated as a distinct art form, whereas the high-priced glass of the same period has been collected extensively for some time.

For investors with more funds available, it would be advisable to collect objects which are already-considered highly desirable, such as Nineteenth Century American cast-iron mechanical banks, French cameo glass lamps, Nineteenth Century Russian bronzes, or American weather vanes. Such items, many in the category of $1000 and up, fall within the realm of investment quality items. Their higher cost is balanced by the confidence of market acceptability, recognition, and accelerating price trends.

The list of what to collect is long and unending. Among other considerations, what you choose will depend on whether you're mainly a collector at heart or an investor. Collecting, as opposed to investing, requires courage and insight, and often a little luck! The investor, on the other hand, rides the coattails of a rising market and should be surer of long-term value. As long as the collector remembers the key criteria of collecting, namely quality and workmanship, he or she will generally be on safe ground.

You should not look on dealers as adversaries, but rather as friends who want to help you build a collection. Most dealers do not seek a one-shot sale, but rather look forward to helping collectors with their wants over a long period. Remember, while you may only be able to spend a few hours a week antiquing, a dealer is at it seven days a week, and can be a great source for material and information. Solicit the friendship of one or more dealers who specialize in your category, and you will be well rewarded. A good dealer will represent the condition and known authenticity of a piece he or she sells to you, and will be prepared to back it up.

Auction galleries can also be excellent places to buy because of the convenience. In one sitting, a collector sometimes can acquire a substantial number of objects by the flick of a finger. However, an auction gallery can also be dangerous in two respects. For one thing, collectors sometimes get carried away and pay much more for objects at an auction than they probably would pay for similar pieces from a dealer. Secondly, when you buy at auction, you buy "as is." You are on your own as to condition and authenticity. Most auction galleries will make an effort to identify a piece, but they make no guarantees.

An auction may not be the place to start a collection, but it is a good place to get an education. When you have established a beginning collection and are ready to buy additional items at auctions, you should always examine a piece prior to the start of bidding and be sure to decide what you're willing to pay so that you won't get swept away during the bidding. Also, do not forget that items purchased at an auction must be paid for promptly. There is no layaway plan purchasing at auction houses, as some dealers will allow.

Once you have established some familiarity with your collectible area, another good method of acquiring objects is through mail-order buying. A number of good publications, such as *Hobbies* (1006 S. Michigan Avenue, Chicago, IL 60605) and *The Antique Trader* (P.O. Box 1050, Dubuque, IA 52001), carry advertisements by collectors and dealers.

Such publications are an excellent source of material and should not be overlooked. In addition, perusing the ads will bring you up to date on the pricing of antiques and collectibles and keep you abreast of which items are in demand by other collectors. Also, some dealers solicit "want lists" through the magazines. In other words, you just write to them, listing what you collect, and they will notify you whenever they find items of possible interest to you. Collector's clubs, such as the National Association of Watch and Clock Collectors, can similarly provide help and keep you well informed.

Finally, some collectors have discovered real "finds" at flea markets, but this is generally a matter of potluck. Flea markets in the past have been good sources of material, but in recent years and in most areas, poor quality has been the rule, unfortunately. Depending on what you collect, you may want to check out a few flea markets—but you shouldn't count on them for the prime pieces of your collection.

The Question of Price

B oth as a beginner and, later, as an experienced collector, a recurring question that you will have to face is that of price. In this regard, you should know about the "greater fool theory," which is especially popular among those sellers who feel a need to comfort a buyer who has just paid an extremely high price for an item. The greater fool theory says that, no matter what price you have paid for a piece, some greater "fool" will come along and pay you more for it. Although this theory may make sense when "junque" is being traded, one must wonder who the fool really is when the theory is applied to fine collectibles.

What about using published price guides in assembling a collection? They can be useful, especially when you're first getting started, but don't be overly influenced by them. Published price guides are often outdated by the time they reach your hands. In addition, such price guides can at best be of a general nature, recording advertised prices and a few auction sale results.

Unfortunately, there are collectors who have become so hung up on price guides that they will pass up a desirable piece just because it does not conform to the price indicated in a guide. In building a collection, the aim is to acquire the best examples you can find, not to beat a price guide. In an expanding market, having the item is more important than the fact that you had to pay a small percentage more than what was listed in some price guide.

In building a collection, there is another situation involving price that is bound to arise at some point. A fine specimen will be made available to you which you feel you just cannot afford. What is "affordable" is relative and depends on what you have paid for other items and on your funds at the time. If it is an outstanding example, and unlikely to turn up again, you should close your eyes and buy it. Make an arrangement with the dealer to pay it off, but do not let it pass you by.

As you build your collection, you will be concerned about insuring it for loss by theft and fire. Rather then relying on your homeowners insurance policy, you probably will want to secure specific coverage for the collection. Your insurance agent will be able to supply you with specific details.

You also should keep records of actual prices paid and expenses incurred in forming the collection since upon selling your collection you may be subject to a capital gains tax under the hobby section of the IRS tax code.

Selling a Collection

The day may arise when you wish to sell your collection—but a warning is in order. Many collectors and investors, having started collections with money considerations in mind, find that after a time they have become attached to their collections and are reluctant to sell.

But, if the decision is made to sell, how do you go about it? The original three sources of acquisitions—dealers, mail order, and auctions—represent possible routes for selling. Your choice will depend in large part on your time frame for disposing of the collection.

Dealers generally will be prepared to purchase a collection intact, paying you cash promptly. Naturally, you should expect to sell to a dealer at a price less than the retail market in order to make it worthwhile for the dealer to handle your items. Dealers often are in an excellent position to resell your collectibles, as they may know numerous collectors who would be anxious to purchase your items.

Your second option is to sell your collection yourself by placing ads in the mail-order publications dealing with antiques, collectibles, and hobbies. You should prepare a detailed listing and photographs of your collection and be able to make them available to the dealers and collectors who respond to your ads.

Last, but not to be overlooked, is the option of having an auction gallery sell the collection for you. While this might be a good way, it is not without its difficulties. Selecting an auction gallery can be a problem as there is no assurance that the collection will bring the amount estimated. It may also take several months before a specialized auction suitable for offering your collection is scheduled. As a rule, though, specialized auctions will bring a higher price than a general auction.

You must realize that in any auction you have no control over the actual selling price other than a modest reserve, below which your items will not be sold. Still, for a quality collection, an auction is probably the best means of dispersal, with few unsold items expected and probably some spectacular prices for your outstanding pieces.

If you go this route, you should expect to pay an auction commission of 10 to 20 percent and you will probably have to pay a reduced commission on any unsold items. Payment to you usually will be made within 30 to 45 days after the auction.

The Marketplace: Where To Buy

After you've made the commitment to begin a collection and decided what category to focus on, the problem remains of where to start. Do you go to a local museum to learn about collectibles? No: While a visit to a museum is always enjoyable and instructive, what you seek are objects that have not yet appeared in museum collections.

The marketplace that deals in antiques and collectibles is diverse, but defined. One of the best places to start is at the various indoor antique shows.

Collecting is not a get-rich-quick scheme. But if you can be patient, time will work for you by increasing the demand and depleting the available supply. Briefly, the investment advantages of antiques and collectibles can be summarized as follows:

1. Antiques provide a hedge against inflation and dollar devaluation.
2. Demand for antiques increases while supply decreases.
3. There is little risk of losing your principal (if you purchase wisely).
4. There is no minimum investment required.
5. Antique investments enjoy favorable tax treatment.

The investment disadvantages include the following:

1. There is little chance for quick profits.
2. No dividends or interest payments are made to the investor.
3. Antiques are not highly liquid.
4. You must find a buyer.
5. Antiques need to be insured.

Antiques have been good investments in recent years, and while the present picture is not too bright, the future still holds promise. If you enter the arena with an understanding of just what makes a collectible or antique an investment, with a good feel for the area in which you specialize, and with patience (since time is on your side), you will find yourself in an excellent position to realize impressive profits on your collection.

As you build your collection and bide your time, there are benefits that no savings bank or broker can duplicate. One day, as you peruse the authoritative books in your field, you just may discover that the pieces illustrated do not impress you greatly. This is because not all the best pieces are in books —rather, they are likely in your collection!

COLLECTIBLE STRATEGIES

The basic strategies for investing in collectibles and antiques have already been described in the preceding sections of this chapter. However, for any area of specialization that you might go into, there is a need for special knowledge and special tactics. The following provides a sampling of these unique areas and approaches.

Antique Automobiles

With Cadillacs and Duesenbergs of the late 1920s and early 1930s selling in the price range of $175,000 to $200,000, it is hard to understand how antique car collecting can fit into the pocketbook of the average person. The primary reason that old car collecting is such a growing hobby is because antique autos no longer have to be very old to be a valuable collector's item.

Until the early 1970s, a car had to be of pre-World War II vintage to be considered an antique. In order to encourage more car collectors, the Antique Auto Club of America changed the definition of an antique auto. Currently, any car from 1952 or earlier is categorized as an antique. A year newer model car is admitted for membership every other year. Thus, in two more years, 1953 cars will be classed as antiques.

Post-World War II cars with the best investment potential are those with innovations in styling, that experienced limited production, or were marketing fiascos. An example is the Chrysler Town and Country sedan of the late 1940s and early 1950s. These wooden-sided cars sold for about $700 in 1970. Today, they will bring $15,000 or more. The design of the Studebakers from the late 1950s also makes them an excellent fodder for investors.

An example of a limited production vehicle is the 1957 Pontiac Bonneville (630 were produced, all of them white convertibles). The best example of a marketing fiasco is the Edsel. Nine-year-old Edsels sold for as low as $400 in 1968 before they became a popular collectible. Today an Edsel, even in poor condition, would bring at least $2000.

Overall, pre-1955 cars have been increasing in value at the rate of about 20 percent per year. Although this rate of return sounds high, it does not take into consideration the cost of insuring or storing antique autos. These costs can take a big bite out of an otherwise lucrative return.

Art

A rt investors need to have a broad, sophisticated knowledge of the market; yet, that in itself is no guarantee of profit. A work of art normally has to be held for many years before an investor can hope to make a profit.

It is possible for investors to make no money at all due to the lack of expertise in buying good quality art. However, a collector who buys art purely for esthetic reasons often makes money because future collectors find the piece equally pleasing.

The most popular types of art sold in the past decade have been American and modern European. This is not to say that every reader should run out and buy an American or modern European canvas. In fact, a major reason that many art investors lose money is because they are drawn to fashionable or fad art only after prices have already been run up.

Since most investors cannot afford the works of famous artists, it is necessary to find a promising young artist who has the potential of becoming famous. For example, the watercolors of Mississippi artist Emmett Thames currently sell for $900 to more than $1200—depending upon the size. Since Thames is recognized as one of the outstanding young realists in the United States, his works predictably have investment potential.

Liquidity is a major problem for art investors. Although antique shops exist in virtually every community, such is not the case for art stores. The lack of dealers to which art can be sold is not a major problem, however, since most sophisticated art collectors do not sell their collections to dealers. Dealers generally cannot pay as much as can be obtained from selling at art auctions. But an investor who wants the best price may have to wait several months before his money comes in. The auction house commission consumes anywhere from 10 to 25 percent of the price.

Comic Books

Did your mother throw out your comic books because they were just accumulating dust? If so, she may have thrown away a fortune. Comic books originated in the late 1930s and at that time they cost only a dime. Some now sell for a thousand dollars.

The most valuable comics are the early editions of *Action Comics* (1938) and *Superman* (1939) which sell for over $2000 each. *Superboy* (1949) comics bring over $100. *Donald Duck* and *Walt Disney Comics* from the 1940s are also quite valuable and some issues command a price of over $1000.

Anyone interested in comic book investments should study the *Official Guide to Comic Books* (by Michael Resnick) which is available at most book stores.

Generally, the comics with the best investment potential are first editions in mint condition. Other early volumes would normally have the next best potential. Comic books can be acquired at dealers in major cities and at flea markets and garage sales everywhere.

Stamps

Stamp collecting, a long-time hobby, emerged as one of the hottest investment areas of the 1970s. During the past decade, many stamp values increased at a rate of about 15 to 20 percent annually. The more popular issues skyrocketed even more. A portion of the increase in value is attributable to the fact that many speculators entered the market. Investors feel that stamps have excellent potential. Part of the reason for the optimism is that, historically, stamp prices have never declined, even during depressions.

Additionally, the small size of stamps makes it easy to store them safely in a vault or safe deposit box; a fact that is not true of antique furniture and art. Stamp investments can be made with only a few dollars. The rarer specimens, however, may bring a quarter of a million dollars. Generally, during the past decade, the higher-priced stamps have increased at a greater percentage than low-priced stamps.

The broad market for stamps is also a reason to be optimistic. Estimates place the number of collectors in the United States at over 20 million. Europeans are equally avid collectors. Since all of these collectors are going to be trying to enlarge their collections, the investor only has to buy today what those millions of collectors are going to want tomorrow.

Modern stamps of any country are produced in great quantities. Thus older stamps (at least pre-World War II) are generally the only ones with real investment potential.

Chapter Sixteen

There's Money In Coins

When a California coin collector found an uncirculated (new) 1927-S (San Francisco Mint) nickel that he immediately sold for $65, he told the *Oakland Tribune*: "Numismatics is a fascinating hobby." This remark prompted a *Tribune* editorial writer to comment: "This is an understatement. Anything that pays a 129,000 percent profit in 26 years isn't a hobby. It's a business, like operating gold mines."

Since 1953, when those words appeared on the *Tribune's* pages, the number of coin buffs in the United States, capitalizing on that "gold mine," has skyrocketed from several hundred thousand to several million. If all the "fringe" collectors in the United States and Canada were counted with the active numismatists, the estimated number would run higher than 20 million.

Most of today's numismatists—persons who study, collect, deal, and invest in coins—are fanatics about their hobby. And justifiably so. They have learned that coins not only are beautiful and have fascinating histories, but that coin investments, ranging from 25 cents to two million dollars, yield annual returns of 10 to 200 percent and more. These profits, of course, are much higher than those from most other types of investments.

In the past few years, coin profits for some investors have been fantastic. A mechanic in New York City bought a bag of uncirculated (new) cents from a local bank at face (cash) value. When he discovered the cents were a unique variety, he sold the $50 bag several months later for about $10,000.

Most of your coin investments will not net that much so quickly, but you could experience any of these typical cases:

● A physician from Texas bought $4000 worth of uncirculated rolls and netted a profit of $2150 within two days.

● In Washington, a farmer bought a desk and some coins for $40. He sold the desk for $45. But he kept the coins—uncirculated Indian Head cents. They are now worth about $10,000.

● A Louisiana coed is financing 70 percent of her way through five years of college by liquidating her coin investments. Her father formed her fund for her by investing $750 a year in coins for seven years.

These are just several of the thousands of persons from all walks of life who have profited from the hobby because they took the time to learn about the unlimited investment potential of coins. You, too, can join them. Here's how:

● Subscribe to a coin newspaper. Two leading weekly newspapers are: *Coin World*, POB 150, Sidney, OH 45367; $18 per year, and *Numismatic News*, 700 E. State Street, Iola, WI 54945; $15 per year.

● Subscribe to a coin investment newsletter. *The COINfidential Report*, published and edited by Don Bale, Jr., since 1963, $25 per year (10 issues). Order from Bale Publications, POB 2727, New Orleans, LA 70176.

● Contact a reputable coin dealer and/or broker. Check the telephone yellow pages or contact *Numismatic News* (Iola, WI 54945) for the name of a reliable dealer in or near your hometown. Most dealers will answer all your questions about coin collecting and investing.

● Join a coin club; it's one of the best places to trade coins and to learn which coins collectors need. *Coin World* (Sidney, OH 45367) will tell you which coin club is nearest you.

● Join the American Numismatic Association (ANA). Membership entitles you to the ANA's monthly magazine, *The Numismatist*, and library privileges by mail or visitation. Contact: ANA, 818 N. Cascade Avenue, Colorado Springs, CO 80903.

● Attend coin conventions and auctions, held nearly every weekend somewhere in the United States. The weekly coin newspapers publish dates and places.

How To Start Coin Collecting

Years ago, you could find most post-1900 coins you needed in circulation, but today the odds probably are about 1000 times greater against that happening. The quickest and best way to get coins today is to buy them from dealers, even though it may be necessary to buy scarce coins ahead of the market because today's demand is so heavy.

Sometimes you can buy coins at or near wholesale (bluebook) prices from noncollectors—friends, members of senior citizens' clubs, churches, YMCA, YWCA, or other groups. You also can run coin-wanted ads and notices in the coin and local newspapers (cheaper ad rates usually are offered by shopper's guides) and in club bulletins.

Banks sometimes are a good source for coins, especially new issues. It will pay you to cultivate contacts with tellers and to display your coins at banks and other places with a sign stating that you will appraise coins.

Many premium coins, however, never reach a bank. Consequently, resourceful numismatists turn to other sources—antique dealers, pawn shops, and jewelry stores. Many valuable coins have been found in sugar bowls, cigar boxes, trunks, attics, piggy banks, and other nooks and crannies where people have put them away and forgotten about them.

You will need R.S. Yeoman's *Handbook Of United States Coins,* listing prices dealers pay for all United States coins. The book can be purchased for $4.50 postpaid from Bale Books, POB 2727, New Orleans, LA 70176.

A coin's grade—an abbreviated description that is easier to use than a long expression of words to describe a coin's condition—is a value factor about as important as the coin's supply and demand. For instance, a choice uncirculated (MS 65) 1914-D (Denver) cent retails for at least $2975 but immediately drops to $595 when it gets into circulation; it then becomes an almost uncirculated (AU-50) coin. A 1914-D Lincoln cent that is heavily worn, with design visible but faint in areas is graded good and retails for at least $90.

Factors Affecting Value

S upply and demand is probably the most important coin value factor because the supply of coins readily available or the demand by collectors and investors can change rapidly; thus, raise or depress the values of coins, sometimes considerably. The demand for a coin often is temporary—a matter of whim, passing taste, local pride, personal regard, or a get-rich impulse. The supply, of course, usually is determined by the number of coins minted.

You can best see the coin supply-demand principle in action by attending large coin auctions where a coin's true value often is determined by the final bid. You also can estimate the true value of a coin by observing the swapping, buying, and selling of coins between collectors and/or investors, as well as analyzing the buying and selling advertisements in the coin periodicals. Coin values are determined by nearly the same methods as stock values. If everyone wants to buy, the prices go up; if they are all selling, the prices go down.

The supply-demand factor also is closely related to these value factors:

Denomination: The "King of American coins" is the cent. It is the most-sought-after coin because the lower the denomination—the monetary unit of the coin—the greater the demand. You can get a greater number of coins for your money. But silver dollars and other high-denomination silver and gold coins became more popular as the silver and gold bullion markets soared. If you think about it, the high-denomination coins actually are the best bargains at about ten times over their face value than many of the low-denomination coins that are priced at 25 times their face value.

Mint Mark: This is a letter placed on a coin to show which mint made the coin. Mint marks are important because these letters sometimes mean hundreds of dollars difference in the value of a coin. A choice uncirculated (MS-65) 1921-S (San Francisco) nickel is worth about $2800 but the 1921 (Philadelphia) in the same condition is worth only $650. Most mint marks are found on the reverse (back) of the coin. The various published guidebooks will show you exactly where to find them. Mints, mint marks, and dates of existence include:

C-Charlotte, NC (gold coins only). 1838-1861.

CC-Carson City, NV. 1870-1893.

D-Dahlonega, GA (gold coins only). 1838-1861.

D-Denver, CO. 1906 to date.

O-New Orleans, LA. 1838-1909.

P-Philadelphia, PA. 1793 to date.

S-San Francisco, CA. 1864 to date.

Date: Surprisingly, a newer coin of greater abundance may command a higher price than a scarce, old coin with a low mintage. The main reason for the intense interest in recent-date coins is that they are easier to find in circulation and to secure from banks and other sources. That partially explains why many Greek and Roman coins sell for lower prices than recent-date material, even though the Ancients are about 2000 years old and less plentiful. This trend has been reversing, however, since more investors are becoming aware of the investment potential of the reasonably-priced Roman and Greek and other pre-1900 coins.

Mintage: Mintage figures for most coins are available but they do not necessarily tell the actual supply of each year's coins that are available. Throughout the nation there are many coins isolated in bank vaults, and some gold and silver pieces have been melted, reminted, or exported, and sometimes millions of mutilated and worn out coins are withdrawn by the banks from circulation each year.

However, mintage figures still are important and reliable indices of the investment potential of coins. The 1844-P dime dramatically proves this; it has been selling for about $2000 in uncirculated (MS-60) condition while the uncirculated 1843-P and 1845-P Liberty Seated dimes are worth only about $485 each since about a million of each were minted. Only about 72,500 1844-P dimes were produced. But many late-date coins with high mintages have a high demand, and thus a high price, because few were saved and many low-mintage coins still sell for nominal prices. That's because the other value factors already mentioned are at work.

Limited Supply/Unlimited Potential

Intelligent coin investors make money; naive ones usually lose, although during coin booms most everyone prospers. But to stay on top, you should analyze coin auction result sheets, prices and price trends, and study articles and books by the coin experts.

Collectors still dominate and control the coin market, fortunately for investors, because the ultimate buyer must be a genuine collector. Both the collectors and investors primarily are trying to buy United States, Canadian, and other foreign coins, and paper money no longer in circulation. The supply is limited; consequently, the investment potential can be unlimited.

Coin prices generally have climbed since 1952 when many investors and speculators entered the hobby. Some of the highly speculative issues such as rolls of coins and varieties have dropped because their fantastic price advances were out of proportion to their actual rarity or value. Many common gold and silver coins fluctuate with the gold and silver bullion markets, but many continue to climb despite bullion market drops because of their numismatic value—collectors need the limited supply to complete their collections. Key (scarce) coins even reached a new high in early 1961 despite a recession.

Nearly all U.S. coin series have enviable track records; price increases have been outpacing the rate of inflation by a substantial margin. Many choice uncirculated gold coins and silver dollars have increased in value by 70-100 percent and more each year since 1975. However, many gold and silver coin prices started to level or fall slightly as the bullion markets dropped, but they should rebound if and when the bullion markets start soaring again.

One of the best United States gold performers during the past 25 years and the past five years is the 1913-S uncirculated Indian Head $10 gold piece, according to James M. Bieler, NLG, author of the second edition of *Value Trends of Rare United States Coins*.

Bieler points out that the 1913-S uncirculated Indian Head $10 gold piece could have been purchased in 1957 for $37.50, in 1977 for $750, or in 1981 for $13,500. Today, it would cost at least $22,500. Its annual compound growth over the last 25 years is about 30 percent, and about 93 percent compounded annually over the last five years. In the last year alone, it increased about 50 percent.

Of 254 rare coins analyzed by Bieler, not one has shown a decrease over the last 25 years, and only one in the past year. The average change for the 25-year period is more than 63 times. Forty-nine of the 254 coins have increased to 100 or more times their value 25 years ago.

Bieler reports that during the past five years there has been an increasing demand for higher quality uncirculated and proof coins. The trend towards higher quality coins, as well as towards certain dates or types, is common knowledge among those who invest in U.S. coins, according to Bieler, who also says:

"Many people are becoming aware of the profit possibilities of investing in U.S. coins because of recent articles in business and investment publications. Some are becoming disenchanted with the better known investment forms because of losses or small returns on their investments, the amount of time and effort necessary to remain in touch with the market, and the constant buy/sell decisions necessary due to changing market conditions.

"As with many other forms of investing," Bieler continues, "there is no guarantee of future profits. But, the past history of rising values and the increased demand and reduced supply resulting from the growing awareness of their potential, indicate that investing in United States coins will continue to be a profitable investment alternative."

The outlook for Canadian coin investments also looks rosy. Many Canadian issues have jumped at least 50 percent per year during the past two years, according to Jack Veffer, past president of the Canadian Paper Money Society. "Of course, this gain was at the retail level," Veffer points out. "It assumes the investor bought at retail and would be able to sell at retail. This is a fallacy in Canada as it is in other areas.

"It is seldom possible to buy wholesale and sell at retail. That would require a business operation far removed from the investment field. However, it is quite possible to buy below retail and sell close to retail. That is where personal involvement or the assistance of professional advice is imperative.

"Even allowing for the difference between the 'buy' and 'sell' price," Veffer says, "the price changes over a number of years quickly overcome this initial hurdle. It is wise to consider coin investments in that light."

One of the hottest Canadian series during the past several years has been uncirculated (new) Canadian silver dollars; they should continue to rise since there has been a strong dealer demand for them. Table I illustrates their recent price performance record.

Table I: Uncirculated Canadian Silver Dollars				
Date	Mintage	1975	1978 Retail Prices	1981
1935	428,707	$50	$40	$65
1936	306,100	50	45	75
1937	241,002	45	45	70
1938	90,304	85	130	160
1939	1,363,816	25	18	30
1946	93,055	50	80	150
1947 B7	65,595	110	125	150
1947 P7	for both	260	325	550
1947 ML	21,135	270	300	450
1948	18,780	600	650	1100
1949	672,218	35	30	40
1950	261,002	25	25	35
1950 Arn	for both	85	65	100
1951	416,395	16	15	30
1951 Arn	for both	75	215	150
1952 WL	406,148	16	15	30
1952 MWL	for both	22	28	35
1953 WE	1,074,578	9	8	28
1953 FB	for both	9	8	28
1954	246,606	18	18	30
1955	268,105	18	18	30
1955 Arn	for both	125	150	175
1956	209,092	21	22	30
1957	496,389	8	10	28
1957 1-WL	for both	20	35	36
1958	3,039,630	9	8	10

All of the Canadian silver dollars listed in Table I have produced profits since 1978. The 1953 Wire Edge and Flat Border issues more than *tripled* since 1978, the 1957 about *tripled,* the 1951 and the 1952 with Water Lines *doubled,* and the 1946 and 1948 nearly doubled. History may repeat itself, so consider investing in them.

The rest of the Canadian silver dollars also should advance, even the 1959-1967 issues, as the silver bullion market and dealer demand increase. Circulated Canadian silver dollars should fare well, too, if the silver bullion market soars.

Lagging interest and low silver bullion prices produced a mixed uncirculated Canadian silver dollar market between 1975 and 1978 (see Table I). But the 1981 retail prices indicate good profits have been made since 1978. Check ads of Canadian dealers in the coin publications for latest BUY-SELL quotations to help you determine market trends.

If you feel flush, you might try to acquire "The Emperor of Canadian Coins"—the 1911 pattern silver dollar purchased by Carlton Numismatics of Birmingham, Michigan, for more than $325,000, reputedly the highest price paid for a single Canadian coin. The pattern 1911 silver dollar is one of two known to exist. Carlton Numismatics has been asking about $650,000, and touting it as the most expensive 20th Century coin, which may top $2 million in several years.

Table II: Very Fine (VF-20) Scarce and Rare U.S. Silver Dollars

Date	Mintage	'76 Retail	'79 Prices	1982
MORGAN TYPE				
1878-CC	2,212,000	$10	$12	$37
1879-CC	756,000	38	47	85
1881-CC	296,000	52	60	100
1882-CC	1,133,000	16	16	40
1883-CC	1,204,000	16	16	40
1884-CC	1,136,000	17	17	49
1885-CC	228,000	50	55	210
1886-S	750,000	20	20	38
1888-S	657,000	23	25	47
1889-S	700,000	23	22	50
1889-CC	350,000	135	165	415
1890-CC	2,309,041	14	15	38
1891-CC	1,618,000	15	16	38
1892-CC	1,352,000	37	38	45
1893	389,792	26	28	70
1893-O	300,000	40	42	145
1893-S	100,000	365	650	2700
1893-CC	677,000	55	65	185
1894	110,972	100	125	535
1895-O	450,000	40	50	165
1895-S	400,000	70	100	175
1899	330,846	22	25	65
1902-S	1,530,000	40	42	75
1903-O	4,450,000	35	45	330
PEACE TYPE				
1921	1,006,473	$22	$23	$44
1927	848,000	19	20	30
1928	360,649	92	100	175
1934	954,057	16	16	32
1934-S	1,011,000	22	25	55

The United States silver dollar market should take off again if and when the silver bullion market starts soaring again. Table II lists some silver dollar issues that have and should continue to perform well as the growing collector demand depletes the supply of these LOW-MINTAGE issues, which have had an "ALL GAINS; NO LOSSES" track record since 1979:

Greatest silver dollar gainer since 1979 is the 1903-0; it nearly eightfolded. Other star performers include the 1885-CC; 1893-S, and 1894; they nearly or did *quadruple*.

All of the other silver dollars listed nearly *doubled* or *tripled* in value since 1979; the only loser between 1976 and 1979 was the 1889-S—off $1.

Long-term gains are likely for all of the silver dollars listed as the growing demand by collectors and investors depletes the limited supply. Dealer demand is also strong and dealers' buying prices run about 70-75 percent of retail.

United States Liberty Seated silver dollars should also continue to be a money maker. Table III indicates the track record for FINE issues.

All of the Liberty Seated silver dollars listed in Table III have advanced since mid-1980; the 1854 more than sevenfolded. Since all of the dollars have

Table III: "Top 24" Fine Liberty Seated Silver Dollars					
Date	Mintage	Retail Prices			
		1975	1980	1981	1982
1840	61,005	$75	$110	$180	$230
1841	173,000	65	90	155	215
1842	184,618	65	90	155	215
1843	165,100	65	90	155	215
1844	20,000	95	150	180	285
1845	24,500	95	150	180	260
1846-0	59,000	75	160	162	300
1848	15,000	90	135	195	465
1850	7,500	125	150	300	565
1850-0	40,000	75	115	200	575
1853	46,110	85	110	125	250
1854	33,140	140	140	225	1000
1855	26,000	165	150	350	900
1859-S	20,000	90	150	200	385
1862	12,090	85	175	375	500
1864	31,170	80	120	225	230
1865	47,000	80	120	225	230
1866	49,625	75	100	200	215
1867	47,525	75	100	180	215
1870-CC	12,462	130	145	225	465
1871-CC	1,376	650	700	750	2000
1872-CC	3,150	335	350	425	1500
1872-S	9,000	125	150	250	465
1873	293,600	65	90	155	180

advanced since 1975 as well, you should fare well regardless of which listed dates you buy. Investments in higher-grade Liberty Seated silver dollars may net you higher yields since affluent collectors want the best. But the majority of numismatists can only afford to collect the average circulated issues—fine or lower grades.

You might cash in, too, on gold bullion coins. The best time to buy, of course, is when you think the gold bullion market is near its bottom. But if you buy above the low you should make money anyway if the gold bullion market hits $2000-$3000 per ounce in the '80s, as many of the leading gold bugs such as Howard J. Ruff, author of the best-selling *How To Prosper During The Coming Bad Years,* predict. So, you might consider buying any of the more popular Gold Bullion coins listed in Table IV.

Table IV: Gold

Coin	Country	Fine Gold Content
Krugerrand	South Africa	1.0000 oz
2 Rand	South Africa	.2345 oz.
Maple Leaf	Canada	1.0000 oz
50 Peso	Mexico	1.2056 oz
20 Peso	Mexico	.4822 oz
10 Peso	Mexico	.2411 oz
2 Peso	Mexico	.0482 oz
100 Corona	Austria	.9802 oz
4 Ducat	Austria	.4439 oz
1 Ducat	Austria	.1110 oz
20 Dollar (Double Eagle)	U.S.	.9675 oz
Sovereign	U.K.	.2354 oz

The silver bullion market may also start soaring soon if the limited supply continues to dwindle and/or rampant inflation or deadly deflation sets in. Some silver insiders look for silver to soar as high as $20 an ounce within 18 months. The silver bullion market would take off immediately if the government started converting its silver into commemorative coins, as proposed by Senator James A. McClure (R-Idaho).

Now may be the best time to buy silver bullion since it's doubtful that it will dip much below $8 (at the time of this writing). Many investors favor silver for new buying and are swapping gold into silver because the gold and silver price ratio has been running about 47 to 1 (at this writing) and silver production is down 6.2 million ounces per month (January/September, 1981, over the same period in 1980).

You also may make a fast profit in United States proof sets—sets of coins that contain a cent, nickel, dime, quarter, half dollar,and dollar for the year in which they are produced. Investors sometimes double their money within a year on U.S. proof set investments.

Chapter Seventeen

Diamonds Are Forever

Diamond. It is nature's hardest substance and has intrigued mankind for thousands of years. As one of the most beautiful of nature's creations, it has many times been the cause of assassinations, revolutions, and wars. Diamonds have been the symbol of power and wealth throughout history, prized because there are consistent and reliable stores of value impervious to currency debasement. Whether diamonds are purchased for adornment or investment, the mystique has persisted down through the ages and is as strong today as it was back in ancient India when rich, rare alluvial stones—diamonds, were cut and worn as talismans and magical symbols.

Diamond is essentially pure crystallized carbon which possesses the unparalleled ability to reflect light and break it up into the colors of the spectrum. It was created during the formation of the earth 240 miles below the surface at approximately 5000°F and a pressure of 1,500,000 pounds per square inch. Diamonds were later carried to the surface of the earth by subsequent volcanic activity. Diamond gets its name from the word adamas, meaning "invincible" in Greek. The hardness of diamonds refers to its resistance to scratching, as nothing can scratch a diamond except another diamond. But while the resistance to breaking (toughness) for a diamond is considered good compared to other gem materials, it still may be fractured or chipped by a hard blow.

Why Invest In Diamonds

In general, diamonds possess the same sound qualifications for investment as colored stones. They have a long history of appreciation, are a proven inflation hedge, portable, and internationally liquid. But diamond, often called the King of Gems, is the best known gem and thus, the most liquid. In addition, diamonds have a much wider trading base than any other gem. Another element unique to diamond is a price support system enforced by a benevolent monopoly which benefits both producers and consumers. Lastly, diamonds are the only gems with an *internationally* recognized grading system.

The most important aspect to master for investing in diamonds is an understanding of how diamonds are graded. Only two percent or less of all diamonds mined and fashioned have the necessary cut, color, clarity, and size to be suitable for investment. Most dealers and sophisticated investors have set strict requirements for investment stones.

The term "four Cs" refers to the four factors of diamond grading: cut, color, clarity, and carat.

Cut refers to the accuracy to which a diamond has been finished to "ideal proportions." The term "cut" is also used to describe the shape of a diamond and the style of the cutting (marquise or round brilliant, for example). To distinguish between the two definitions, the term "make" will be referred to when speaking of proportions.

Diamond makes vary considerably and, under certain circumstances, it is often possible to identify the origin of some brilliant cuts by their make. While Gemological Institute of America standards for color and clarity are internationally recognized, their standards for make are not accepted on a worldwide basis. Essentially, some influential jewelers and manufacturers in the United States have favored the "American" cut or make, which has a smaller table (under 60 percent) than diamonds preferred by most Europeans and Asians. The recent trend in the United States has been toward a larger table. (The table is the large flat facet at the top of the diamond.) There seems to be much needless argument over which is the best table size. But between a 53 and 65 percent table percentage, it is strictly a matter of taste preference.

Although exactly what constitutes ideal proportions is in dispute within the trade; a diamond must be proportioned adequately so as not to detract noticeably from beauty in order to be considered of high quality. This, of course, is a realm subject to vast differences in interpretation.

All measurements of a round brilliant cut diamond are expressed as a percentage of the stone's diameter, and these measurements may fall within a range of percentages. A stone's make can be any of the possible combinations, *except combinations of extremes*. Deciding exactly what is the best make is better left to the academicians, as there are no real discounts in trade prices for stones having makes within the acceptable ranges.

Variations from the acceptable range of makes are usually caused by the cutter in order to obtain the maximum weight for the finished stone at the expense of brilliancy. Usually, a compromise between weight and brilliancy is sought in order to maximize profit. A beautiful make in a diamond is indicated by the overall brilliancy of the stone. This is most easily judged by measuring visually the quantity of light returned to the eye. A diamond which is cut to good proportions will always return a larger amount of light than a stone of poor proportions. This is because it conforms more completely to the mathematically produced formula of relationships between angles and percentages for maximum brilliancy.

A diamond's make is properly determined by using a millimeter gauge and a proportion reticle or proportionscope. This, of course, must be done by an expert. After measurements are taken, they are then noted in the grading report. A formula is then applied and variations from ideal proportions may be noted. An investor in diamonds should be aware that a make outside the acceptable range reduces the stone's value. If there is an extreme make, the difference in price from a well-made stone can be considerable.

The Critical Criteria of Color

Color is probably the most misunderstood, and yet the most critical, of all the four diamond grading criteria. Color refers to the interior body color of a diamond, which ranges from transparent colorless to deepening tinges of yellow or brown. It does not refer to the desirable multi-colored flashes of light which are caused by the breaking up of white light (brilliancy) into the colors of the spectrum (dispersion or fire). Absolute top quality is total absence of color with limpid, icy pure transparency. This extremely rare color is known in GIA terminology as "D" color. By GIA definition, colors "E" and "F" are also colorless, but possess a lesser degree of transparency. Colors "G" through "J" are considered "near colorless" by the GIA and colors "K" through "M" are termed faint yellow.

While it is true that the value of a diamond decreases as the more common yellow tinge deepens, there are rare diamonds which have enough body color to be attractive, such as canary yellow, coffee brown, blue, and pink. These desirable colors, known in the trade as "fancy colors," are priced higher than a colorless diamond with similar clarity. The term "blue-white" is so abused that it is not used much anymore, as many apply it to any stone that appears white in a mounting. A diamond must have a definite blue tinge to it to be called "blue-white" and when this occurs, it is more often just termed "light blue."

It is difficult for the untrained eye to detect any difference in the first six GIA color grades in normal light. The amount of color in any particular diamond is properly judged:

1. With the diamond table (top) down.
2. On a white background.
3. In a controlled, diffused lighting environment.
4. Compared side-by-side with master color comparison diamonds of known colors determined for this purpose by the GIA.

The investor should be aware that the more colorless diamonds have appreciated in value at a faster rate than stones with a lower color grade. Because they are much more rare, colorless diamonds are in greater demand and bear higher prices. When mounted in jewelry, a diamond's true color is often masked by the mounting, particularly if it is yellow gold.

Clarity grade describes the degree to which a diamond is free of flaws (inclusions in the interior of a stone) or blemishes (surface defects). As far as beauty is concerned, such flaws and blemishes become significant only if visible to the naked eye or interfere with the passage of light through the stone. Even though a high clarity diamond and a low clarity diamond may look the same to the naked eye, the stone of higher clarity is more rare and is consequently higher in price.

There are many clarity grading systems employed in the market today, but the most widely used and respected system is that created by the Gemological Institute of America. The GIA system is as follows:

Grade	Description
Flawless	Having no internal or external flaws under ten-power binocular microscope magnification utilizing darkfield illumination, except an extra facet on the pavillion (bottom) not visible from the crown (top), a *natural* confined to the girdle (edge) not visible from the crown or breaking symmetry, or internal twinning lines that do not break the surface or are not colored or cloudy.
Internally Flawless	Same as flawless, except that they may have *surface* blemishes, such as pits, scratches, wheel marks, extra facets naturals, and so on.
VVS	A VVS stone is very, very slightly imperfect, with inclusions that are extremely difficult to difficult to locate under ten-power.
VS	A VS stone is very slightly imperfect, with inclusions that are difficult to somewhat easy to locate under ten-power.
SI	An SI stone is slightly imperfect, having inclusions that are easy to very easy to see under ten-power.
I	An I stone is imperfect, with inclusions that are difficult to very easy to locate *with the unaided eye*.

All of the preceding grades (except Flawless and Internally Flawless) are further divisible into subgrades 1 and 2, subgrade 1 being of higher clarity than subgrade 2.

When analyzing the grade of clarity for a particular diamond, a gemologist must determine five factors:

1. Size of inclusions.
2. Type of inclusions.
3. Number of inclusions.
4. Location of inclusions.
5. Degree of difficulty in locating the inclusions.

Clarity grading is preferably done using a binocular microscope with darkfield illumination. While inclusions may be studied and discovered under a higher power, they must still be visible and oriented to size at ten-power for proper grading.

Carat Weight is the last of the "Four Cs" and the easiest of the factors to determine. It simply involves weighing the diamond on a precise diamond balance or electronic scale, with no human interpretation involved. There are

141¾ metric carats to an ounce. A carat is subdivided into hundredths or "points," so that a ¾ carat diamond weighs 75 points or ¾ of a carat. In conversation within the trade, it is often called a "75-pointer."

Because most gem laboratories use electric scales, accurate measurements are possible beyond the hundredth place, for example, .9999 carat, which for all practical purposes should be considered one carat. However, the Gemological Institute of America follows a ruling by the World Federation of Diamond Bourses which states that all numbers in a weight past the first two decimal places are *always* rounded *down*. So, a .9999 carat diamond is considered .99 carat, *not* one carat. If the stone does not make the point, it does not get it.

The Fifth "C"—Certification

The greatest protection a gem investor can have against misrepresentation of diamond quality is a quality analysis from an independent gemological laboratory. It is this certification which determines the price of a stone. Most investors cannot judge the quality of a diamond, so analysis by professional gemologists is mandatory. The recommended certification for a diamond is one put out by the Gemological Institute of America in Los Angeles and New York. The GIA standard is recognized and used worldwide. Other accepted certifications come from the International Gemological Institute and European Gemological Laboratories, both of New York, although certificates from these labs carry less clout in the marketplace.

It is extremely important for investors to realize that diamond grading is subjective and that any diamond may be graded slightly different each time it is resubmitted for certification. Therefore, it is mandatory for amateurs to obtain the services of an expert to verfiy the laboratory certification to avoid buying lab "mistakes."

For maximum investment potential, diamond grading specifications should fall within the following GIA parameters:

1. **Shape and cut:** Round brilliant.
2. **Measurements:** Less than 1.5 percent out of round.
3. **Weight:** .50 to .59 carat, .75 to .79 carat, and 1.01 to 1.09 carat are the most popular sizes but a good case can be made for diamonds down to .20 carats.
4. **Depth percent:** 58 to 62 percent, no double depth percentages.
5. **Table percent:** 53 to 65 percent.
6. **Girdle:** No extremely thin, very thick, or extremely thick.
7. **Culet size:** No large, none, chipped, or abraded.
8. **Polish:** "Good" or better.
9. **Symmetry:** "Good" or better.
10. **Clarity:** At least "VS₂" clarity.
11. **Graining:** None.
12. **Color:** At least "H" color.
13. **Florencence:** No strong.
14. **Comments:** Crown angles must be between 30 and 35 degrees.

Poorly cut diamonds sell at discounts and should not be purchased for investment.

Where To Buy Diamonds

Diamonds can be purchased from retail jewelers, auctions, pawn shops, private parties, or telephone hustlers. But these options carry either a high price or high risk or both. The best way to buy investment diamonds is from a firm which specializes in selling to the public at as close to a wholesale price as possible. There are many such firms and their names can be obtained from any of the gem investment publications.

Current Condition of Diamond Market

The investment diamond market is facing some serious challenges at present and can only be described as extremely illiquid with little or no trading. The current asking prices for investment diamonds are merely that—*asking* prices. They simply represent a level below which most sellers refuse to go. Those who must sell find that they are forced to offer diamonds far below average dealer asking prices in order to find a cash buyer. It seems that there are at least a hundred sellers for every buyer today, and it is only the one seller with the lowest sacrifice price which makes the sale. The asking price for a one carat "F" VVS$_2$ diamond may be $8000 per carat to the public, but actual sales are being made for as much as 40 percent below this figure. Most diamond dealers are unusually quiet at present. Since the market is obviously in a serious depression.

A round brilliant cut one carat "D" color flawless diamond of good proportions has fallen from $70,000 per carat ($16,000 in early 1978) to the public in early 1980, to approximately $30,000 per carat in early 1982, a drop of 57 percent. A one carat "F" color, VVS$_2$ clarity stone fell from $20,000 ($16,500 in early 1978) to about $8000 per carat over the same period. Diamonds that were subject to lower degrees of speculation, however, did not drop as much. An "H" VS$_2$ quality diamond, much lower on the Gemological Institute of America grading scale, has fallen only 38 percent, from $8000 ($3500 in early 1978) to $5000 per carat. It should also be noted that jewelry grade diamonds of less that H VS$_2$ quality which did not participate in the speculative run-ups in price have remained relatively stable during the last two years.

Why Diamond Prices Dropped

Investment diamond prices have dropped for several reasons. But by far the most important reason was the general belief among investors that the rate of inflation might be reduced dramatically by the new Reagan Administration's economic policy. When the inflation rate did begin to fall, investors lost interest in inflation hedges and began to liquidate to shift assets into potentially more profitable investments. Not only were investment funds attracted away from diamonds to high interest bearing money market instruments, but the financing of diamond inventories became increasingly expensive as the interest rate began to soar. The simultaneous recession and reduction of discretionary income available for investing further depressed prices as diamond sellers found it increasingly difficult to locate willing cash buyers.

Another factor in the weakening of the investment diamond market has been the negative publicity by the news media. The reports of softening diamond prices naturally has increased the desire for liquidation by holders of diamonds. Some news articles have cast doubt on the validity of diamonds at *any* time, and others question the strength of the DeBeers diamond monopoly which controls the supply of rough diamonds. Still other articles trumpet the recent Australian diamond finds as potentially the most significant in the world and blithely predict a glut of diamonds on the market in the near future.

DeBeers—Still A Force

DeBeers Consolidated Mines, the contract distributor for 80 percent of the world production of diamonds, has been sorely tested during the last two years. Before this period, DeBeers, or the "Syndicate," has been able to stabilize prices in the polished diamond market through adjustments in the supply and price of rough stones. But since 1976, and the advent of serious diamond investing on the part of Americans, Europeans, and Japanese, control of prices in the polished diamond market began to shift to the private investor. As with all commodities, those who control a majority of the supply control the price. And in the last several years, the private investor has controlled more diamonds than has DeBeers.

While suffering under sales which dropped 46 percent in 1981 over the previous year, DeBeers is still an active and powerful force in the diamond market. DeBeers moved to sharply reduce the supply of diamonds in 1981, by virtually eliminating the sale of investment quality diamond rough to cutters. They also cut the supply of lower quality diamonds by about half to stabilize the jewelry diamond market. But DeBeer's most significant action has been the heavy buying of surplus diamond inventories at the major cutting centers of the world. The diamond market would be in far worse condition today were it not for the massive stockpiling capability of DeBeers.

Diamond Forecast For '82/83

Because diamonds are used primarily as an inflation hedge, diamond prices probably will not begin to rise until the rate of inflation begins to increase. While they seem to have stabilized, the price may continue to drop further.

Diamond prices have tended to shadow the price of gold, so picking a bottom for diamond prices is difficult. As projected by many economists, further slowing of the inflation rate may cause weaker prices for hard assets in 1982. A deepening worldwide recession would only compound the problem. Other economists, however, predict that our massive budget deficit will force us into inflating our currency once again so that protective inflation hedges will come back into vogue by the spring of 1983.

Whether we have a deflation or more inflation, diamonds still add a degree of stability to any portfolio. With the myriad of strikes, revolutions, brush-fire wars, and economic instability around the world, the supremely profitable and universally accepted diamond may again be recognized as a critically important crisis hedge as it has for thousands of years.

Chapter Eighteen

Glittering World of Gemstones

Gems have been treasured since the beginning of recorded history for alluring beauty and extreme rarity. The archeological record is a testament of man's desire to own and collect objects of beauty and shows that gemstones were considered to be of supreme worth to ancient civilizations. Man's innate desires have not changed through the centuries and a fiery gem, that rarest of all nature's creations, continues to instill awe and wonder in the eyes of mankind. Although gems have been used for different and various purposes throughout the course of history, they have been highly valued at all times. This fact is as true today as it ever was.

In the last few centuries, man seems to have been more interested in the value of gems and maintenance of purchasing power than in the beauty of gems. This interest gave rise to the concept of "investing" in precious stones. Today, investment in gems for maximum return requires close attention to detail and world economics. Fast changing situations mean that profits are not guaranteed.

The current economic situation in the United States is one of confusion. Gems, as hedges against inflation, soared in price during the rampant double digit inflation in the late Seventies. But since early 1980, gem prices have flattened or fallen in a lackluster market due to high interest rates and the belief on the part of investors that the rate of inflation could be reduced by the Reagan Administration.

What, you may ask, will happen to the gem market? When will gem prices start moving up again? Will inflation hedges ever be popular again? Are we going to have a deflation or more inflation? These questions are asked daily by concerned investors and they are tough questions which nobody can answer with complete certainty.

Many economists support a strong case for deflation now with inflation rates heating up in several years. Others feel that all indications point to further increases in government spending, a major cause of inflation, and that monetization of government debt is inevitable. Because of conflicting views regarding which way the U.S. economy is headed in the near future, right now is definitely not the time to be liquidating gems.

The deflationists have everybody running scared from inflation hedges, and gems are being sacrificed by desperate sellers at low prices. But you must not lose sight of the long-term fundamentals now. The economic downturns in 1969-70 and in 1975-76, and 1981-82 were just giant replays. Recent history tells us that we should be preparing for the bull market that always follows every tight money, "Let's balance the budget," period.

Consumers now realize that there will be no budget cutting and have serious doubts about the real possibilities of long-term tax cuts. The deflationists have seriously underestimated the problems which will be caused by our mounting budget deficit. Only a few months ago, the Office of Management and Budget projected budget deficits of 43.1 billion for fiscal 1982, 22.9 billion for fiscal 1983, and zero deficits for 1984. But recently, with billions of dollars lost from shrinking tax revenues and higher jobless benefits, estimated budget deficits have been revised to 109.1 billion in 1982, 152.3 billion in 1983, and 162 billion for fiscal 1984!

Taxpayer's Choices

So who has to pay this debt? The taxpayers do. And how are taxpayers going to pay? They have four choices:

1. **Taxpayers can pay higher taxes.** Not likely. Reagan will not repudiate this campaign promise and the public wouldn't let him even if he wanted to.

2. **Taxpayers can borrow the money.** The government borrows money through debt offerings in the financial markets. This action is not inflationary but runs interest rates sky-high and destroys normal business activity.

3. **Taxpayers can default on the payments.** Simply refuse to pay. This would cause a massive depression.

4. **The government can monetize the debt, print more "money."** Just create it out of thin air like the government has been doing for years. This is most likely how the politicians will handle the debt in the future so they can get re-elected. Taxpayers will let them so they can get "benefits" (which they will only have to pay for later instead of now). This action, of course, would create a mind-boggling hyperinflation.

Now, *if we can rely on centuries of recorded history throughout the world, then the hyperinflation scenario is the one which will occur.* If those in power want to be re-elected, they must begin to reinflate the economy soon. If they don't, it will be too late to avoid a crunching depression and a wipe-out of gem prices. If inflation does occur, gem prices should start moving upwards again.

Gems are a hedge against inflation, not a deflation hedge. If you feel the United States is headed for a depression then sell all of your gems and get into cash. You will be able to buy the gems back much cheaper later.

You may think that you can get completely liquid now and wait to see what happens. For gems, this is an inadequate strategy. Not only will you be selling at a huge discount, but you will be buying back later at a substantial premium. Once the public realizes the imminent reality of a hyperinflation, the prices of gems will explode upwards so fast it will be difficult to get back in at advantageous prices.

However, holders of hard assets will continue to see paper losses for a few more months—possibly until the congressional election in the fall of 1982. But the end of declining prices for gems is truly near. Those with the fortitude to hold or "buy while there is blood running in the streets" will profit handsomely in the hyperinflationary era which is sure to come.

What Are Investment Gems?

There is much talk about "investment quality" gemstones today and all the advantages they offer to the confused investor. But just what criteria must a gem possess in order to be considered as an investment? If one were to ask ten different dealers, ten different answers may result. It is no wonder neophyte investors often become bewildered.

Initially, the term "gemstone" should be defined. For a mineral to be considered "gem" material it must possess beauty, rarity, durability, and be in demand. The term "investment gem" theoretically takes this definition a step further by requiring a stone to be *very* beautiful and *very* rare. It also must have a high degree of liquidity, consumer recognition, an adequate trading base, and a high supply/demand ratio.

Defining what is *very* rare, beautiful, liquid, etc., is where the controversy begins. Many diamond dealers, for instance, say that only diamonds are suitable for investments, and look upon colored stone dealers as unorganized used car salesmen. Compared to the diamond market, the colored stone market is very unorganized and thinly threaded. But colored stones, defined as any gem but a diamond, do offer the savvy investor fantastic appreciation potential.

Most fine colored stones appreciated on average at least 20 percent per annum from 1970 until 1978. In late 1978, because of galloping inflation, high media attention, and the advent of independent laboratory certification for colored stones, prices exploded. A good example is ruby which, depending on quality, gained 20-60 percent in 1978, 40-100 percent in 1979, and over 100 percent in the first part of 1980. Other gems like sapphire, topaz, aquamarine, tourmaline, and tsavorite rode the coat-tails of ruby as speculators sought diversification.

Why Invest In Gems?

The reasons for investing in gems today are the same as they were ten years ago. No other investment fully meets the criteria singular to gems. Fine gemstones are:

1. Rare, beautiful, and durable. One can even derive pleasure from wearing them.

2. Supremely portable, easily concealed, and stored. As a crisis hedge,

they are unparalleled. Many politically uprooted persons have started new lives in other countries with a stash of gems.

3. Internationally liquid. Unlike stocks, bonds, and other "paper" assets, gems have universal value. You can sell them in nearly every country of the world.

4. Maintain purchasing power in inflationary economies. In 1960, a top quality one carat ruby could have been traded for a Cadillac. The same claim can be made today.

5. Are not subject to government regulations, control, or overhanging supply. Gems are the last truly unregulated commodity.

6. Have a multi-thousand year track record of appreciation. They have been a legitimate store of value and have been held in high esteem by nobility and other wealthy individuals since the beginning of recorded history.

7. Are anonymous and private. Gem investing requires no paperwork or owner identification.

8. Subject to diminishing supply in the face of increasing demand. Gem supplies are finite and new finds are becoming exceedingly rare.

9. Geological flukes. The combination of factors necessary to produce gemstones is so rare that deposits are usually very small and scattered widely.

10. Usually subject to primitive hand tool mining so that production cannot be increased to meet increasing demand. Most deposits are too small to exploit with machinery.

11. Are mostly found in the politically and economically unstable countries of Thailand, Sri Lanka, East Africa, and Brazil which accounts for frequent supply interruptions.

There are some drawbacks to investing in gems. No interest is earned on gems so they must go up in value at least the average yearly interest rate every year for you to break even. During slow markets they are highly illiquid. Because of this, gems should be bought with at least a three year "hold" in mind and the realization that they may take months to sell at a fair price. They do occasionally go down in price for short periods of time.

How To Buy

Like diamonds, colored stones are quality graded as to cut, color, clarity, and carat. But grading colored stones is much more complex and less universally understood than grading diamonds. There are several good independent grading laboratories whose certificates are accepted in the trade for colored stones. American Gemological Laboratories and International Gemological Institute in New York, Asian Institute of Gemological Sciences, and United States Gemological Services in Los Angeles are all respected—with the AGL being the certificate of choice.

The Gemological Institute of America, the most respected name in diamond grading, does not yet offer a quality analysis for colored stones. But recent developments at the GIA suggest that this situation may not be far off. A quality analysis for colored stones by the internationally renowned GIA would revolutionize the precious stone market and drive prices up due to increased investor confidence. It should be noted that certificates issued by organizations which sell gems are totally disregarded in the gem industry and are generally useless.

With the same grading systems being used by most legitimate companies, comparing values over the telephone is relatively easy. Be sure to shop around for the best deal with at least three or four companies. Not only will you weed out the high-priced firms but the low-priced ones may cut their prices a little if they know they are competing for a deal.

Not all gems are graded accurately so it is important to have your purchases checked by an expert before the deal is made final. Also, be sure to compare *all* of the factors on a grading certificate because all are significant. It is important to remember that a gem must have the proper purity of color, clarity, and well finished proportions to be considered a suitable investment stone.

Buy the best quality you can afford and always buy unmounted stones. It is recommended that no more than 15 percent of your assets be invested in gemstones. Do not borrow money to buy gems and do not gamble with money needed for basic necessities. Avoid buying at retail and disregard any retail appraisal which may be supplied with a purchase. Appraisals are usually over-inflated and are used to unfairly impress the neophyte investor. Avoid any source of gems that does not come with impeccable personal recommendation. Unless you are an expert in gems, it is imperative that you deal with someone who is. Your source must not only be expert, but someone you have a good reason to trust.

Where To Buy

Where to purchase is the single most important dilemma facing the prospective gem investor. Many who invest in gems never make any money, not because they make incorrect market predictions, but because they deal with totally unreliable companies. Some firms are so weak financially that they must close their doors under the slightest pressure. Others know little about gems and even less about investing in them. Some companies harbor no illusions about their abilities and are outright frauds.

Unlike diamonds which are controlled by the DeBeers Diamond Syndicate, it is much easier to buy close to the source with colored stones. The stones flow from the miner, to the prime-source distributor, to the importer, and then to the wholesalers, retailers, and investment companies. Most gem investment companies will tell you they are importers when, in fact, few truly are. Also, "wholesale" is a much abused term which should not be used by firms selling directly to the public.

The key for profitable investing is to buy stones that have gone through as few hands as possible. For the layman this means buying from importers who sell to the public at low prices. You will be more successful at gem investing by becoming knowledgeable yourself, rather than depending solely on some expert. But consulting with an expert is mandatory for the amateur.

When shopping for a supplier of investment gems it is important to look for the following criteria:

A. Strong resources and financial backing.

Get references, (bankers, attorneys, accountants) and check them out. Remember that references are sometimes friends, and their reports are often glossed over.

B. Work history of company principals and salesman with whom you are dealing.

Interview them and make them be specific about their pasts. Undoubtedly you are much better off with a person who has been in the gem business ten years than one who was a shoe salesman last year.

C. Good track record in business.

Longevity is no guarantee of a good company but it is a good indication. Ask for a list of published recommendations they have made and a list of stones they have sold and what they are worth now.

D. Prompt delivery.

Do not do business with anyone who cannot deliver stones within ten days of receiving funds. Slow delivery indicates weak finances and no inventory.

E. Satisfaction Guarantee.

Every legitimate company allows a certain period of time after you receive a stone to check it out with an independent expert, usually ten to 30 days.

F. Trained gemologist on staff.

This is not a guarantee of honesty or accuracy, but a good sign.

G. Remarketing services.

Ask the company for a list of all stones they have liquidated for clients and ask their accountant to verify it. Most companies tend to ignore this low profit side of the transaction.

H. Selling technique.

Avoid suppliers who use heavy sales pressure and be wary of those who promise instant liquidity or exaggerate price performance. Do not use salesmen as investment advisers as many are more concerned about their commission than your success. The best salesmen first determine your suitability for gems before they attempt to sell.

What To Buy

Gems are esoteric investments and, as such, require the investor to possess specialized knowledge to be successful. Not all gems are good investments, however. In fact, less than 5 percent of all gems on the market have the necessary rarity, beauty, durability, and consumer recognition to be candidates for significant price increases.

Of all the stones suitable for investment, at least a few are inadvisable at any given time due to buying trends and cyclical price action for different varieties. A good example is ruby which has posted, on average, no significant price gains for the last two years. Because the fundamentals are unchanged, at some point in the near future rubies will become an excellent opportunity again. But at present other relatively unknown gems are the profit makers. Unknown to most speculators, little known gems such as red spinel and Tsavorite, have appreciated more than 100 percent during 1981.

The prices of different colored stones do not rise and fall in unison but run in separate cycles. This is another reason to invest long-term—to assure catching at least one major uptrend for a particular stone. At any given time, at least two or three stones are in favor among gem collectors and are increasing in price. As popular stones begin to be thought of as overpriced relative to the rest of the market, they level off for awhile until they are considered undervalued again at the start of the next uptrend. While all fine gems have proven to be excellent long-term investments, why not buy into the ones in the initial or middle stages of an uptrend?

Currently there are several colored stones which are accelerating in price: Fine red, orange, and pink spinel from Burma should continue to post significant price gains for 1982-83. The finest red stones are actually more rare than the ruby which they mimic and are still far less expensive.

Tsavorite, the beautiful green garnet from East Africa, is still highly sought by collectors. Since the demand does not seem to be letting up for this rare stone it should also be a highly profitable investment this year.

Pink, golden, and violet sapphire prices were left far behind during the ruby and blue sapphire boom of two years ago. But now their time has come again and they are poised at the beginning of a considerable upward price move. As more investors become comfortable with these lesser known colors of sapphire they should rise in price due to increased demand.

There are plenty of beautiful amethysts on the market, but top quality stones are actually hard to find. The market may take some time to develop but those who buy only the finest quality now will profit handsomely when prices take off from the low prices of today.

Colombian emerald is relatively expensive in its finest qualities but is a real sleeper among the investment stones. At present, insist on stones without obvious inclusions for maximum potential.

Ruby and blue sapphire can currently still be a good investment if it is bought at sacrifice prices in the best qualities. Ten years from now, ruby will probably be the most profitable precious stone.

Tourmaline in all colors, but especially the finest colors of red, pink, green, and blue, have great potential for near term price appreciation. Fine reds are rare and expensive while greens are relatively plentiful and low-priced.

Colored stones, with their special beauty and complex market structure, are an acquired taste. They are not easy to invest in and investors must study the market intensively to be successful. It is worth noting that those who have made the most money in gems have been those who truly appreciate their gems. A true appreciation tends to cultivate a special awareness which results in more advantageous trading.

The only real protection for the gem investor is to get to know the market intimately. Read books, magazines, and newsletters. Ask questions. Go to gem shows and museums. Learn all you can. If you don't you are likely to be just another sucker who gets taken. But if you do your homework before you invest, you will be a prosperous participant in one of the most exciting, interesting, and profitable investments available today.

Chapter Nineteen

The State of Real Estate Investing

I f you're into real estate investments in 1982, you'll find it's a whole new ballgame. Even the rules have been changed and you'll need a scorecard to separate the winners from the losers. Just a few years ago, before inflation began to ravage the American standard of living, it was wiser to put your money into real estate than to bury it in a bank where it could only depreciate. In 1982, however, the smart investor is putting his cash into Treasury bills, money market funds, CDs, and the like, while real estate investments have fallen into disfavor.

In 1981, housing production hit a post-World War II low of 1,086,000, but despite the incipient deflation in housing, owning your own home remained a sound investment. However, it is no longer the "open sesame" to a fast buck. Raw land, as well, is not the panacea it once was for speculators, unless the buyer has "inside" information that some builder has plans to develop a shopping center, housing project, or condominium complex on the site.

Office buildings are still considered to be profitable ventures, providing the tenants are committed to a long lease, with escalating clauses that make allowances for increases in operating costs.

Nonetheless, the gloom and doom engulfing the real estate industry notwithstanding, there is some room for optimism. Prices will rise again, since real estate, like most investment vehicles, moves in cycles. So, if you're already in real estate or raw land, the advice is to hang in there—a better time to sell is inevitable.

The culprits causing the real estate woes are inflation and high interest rates, which have now been joined by economic recession to further reduce housing starts sending real estate sales to record lows.

That's the bad news. The good news is that new home prices have levelled off despite soaring construction costs, because there are few buyers even at stabilized prices. The average value of existing houses is also no longer leaping ahead each year. In most areas, they have stopped increasing completely, while in other sections of the country prices are even on the downgrade. The statistics in Table I graphically illustrate the current bleak real estate picture:

TABLE I		
Year	Housing Starts (in millions)	Average Price
1973	2.1	$40,000
1975	1.2	45,000
1977	2.0	55,000
1979	1.8	73,000
1981	1.1	88,000

Increasing unemployment, a main ingredient of recession, has also contributed to limited real estate demand. Many farmers are in trouble financially because of low prices of farm products coupled with high interest rates. Furthermore, many savings and loan banks and other money lenders, which helped to fuel the real estate boom since World War II, are in financial trouble and are no longer active in the mortgage market.

The real estate market is a long range market. Not only does the investor in real estate have to know what real estate to buy in a depressed market, but he must also be aware of which real estate properties will "turn-around" in value, in order to make big profits when economic pressures ease. Demographic trends, where and what kind of people are no longer the buyers today, and who will be the buyers tomorrow, are all vital considerations. Most important, the real estate investor has to know how to finance bargain properties for leverage and profit in "tight money" times.

It's a buyer's market today and there are several basic real estate questions prudent real estate investors must resolve if they want to stay informed and operate with good, practical common sense:

1. Projections. What's going to happen? How are short-range and long-range factors going to affect real estate, particularly in local areas?

2. Financing. In these volatile economic times, how do you finance give-away properties?

3. What to Buy. For big profits later, in better times, how do you know which properties to pass up and which to buy now, during these bad times?

Projections in Real Estate

In 1982, housing construction and real estate will continue at a low level and real estate values will not go up. In fact, they'll probably go down. For the long run, real estate values should rise steadily, if intermittently.

Many factors, not just the present economic strife, will affect housing and real estate sales, and cause a broad value increase later in the decade. Increasing population pressures will continue to push against recurrent high financing and construction costs, and cyclical recession factors. The home-buying 35- to 44-year-old age group will increase by 45 percent between 1982 and 1990, while more than 40 million people will reach age 30, the largest such group in our nation's history to attain household-forming age in one period. Also, the major population movement from the city and inner-ring metropolitan suburbs (30-mile ring) to the outer-ring countryside (40- to 60-mile ring), which began in the 1970s, will accelerate during the 1980s.

These accelerating factors will be counter-balanced and even overridden irregularly by intermittent, high financing costs and recession, similar to what is happening now. However, the decade-long trend will be upward both in housing and in real estate values. And there will be recurrent, cyclical real estate booms because of the underlying, pent-up demand whenever a "window" of lower interest financing opens up.

The nature and type of housing will change dramatically, in the coming decade. Just as the types of households have changed—close to 60 percent of all American households will be composed of only one or two people, (married, single, divorced and not remarried), rather than the traditional family of two parents and two or more children. Latest census figures show that one of every two Americans is now over 30 years old and that average household size has dropped from 3.11 to 2.75 persons.

So the inspiring colonial house, with its many bedrooms, will no longer be the darling of real estate sales. There will be a great demand for smaller homes, condominiums, and cooperatives to satisfy a tremendously increased demand —from a tremendously expanding, changed group—for reasonable, smaller housing. In addition, many larger one-family houses will be converted legally (and sometimes quasi-legally) to one- to four-family dwellings, because of prevalent economic and population pressures. There will also be extensive rehabilitation of our existing housing. Many fine, old, sometimes historic homes, will be saved from demolition and will be rehabilitated for coming generations because of high new construction costs and other economic and population factors.

Land, vacant lots and tracts, well-located, with utilities, which could be subdivided into large acreage parcels in rural areas for residences and for associated services, will, in the long run escalate in value as the cities continue to spread out to rural countrysides. There will be brisk sales of large lots, one to five acres, for moderate to better homes, in the exurban areas.

Look for widespread increases in mobile homes and in land for mobile home sales and values in the 1980s, since they are a reasonable alternative for a majority of people who can no longer afford conventional housing.

New, Creative Ways to Finance

All the properties for sale now at "giveaway" prices, whether defaulted tax or mortgage foreclosure properties, farms, and raw land tracts are not feasible to purchase unless they can be bought at the right price—and with the right financing for proper "leverage" for later profits.

Inflation has forced banks and other mortgage lenders to find new pricing methods that prevent losses. Until recently, lenders set interest rates on mortgages at a few percentage points above savings account interest rates and there was generally a stable, uniform mortgage rate everywhere.

Now, everything has changed. You have to know financing to make profits in real estate. The same high and "tight money" financing which slowed down the real estate sales market, and in fact caused this slowdown, can be the same financing tool—in its changed forms—that you must use to finance your real estate investments and know what's going on in your local area. Table II is a chart of selected current typical mortgage rates and terms:

TABLE II	Some Current Typical Mortgage Rates and Terms			
Banks	Percent Down	Percent Rate	Points*	Term
A	25	17.75	3.5	25
B	20	16.5	2.5	30
C	25	17.75	4	3/25**
D	15	18	3	25
E	25	16.75	5	5/30
F	25	15.75	5	3/30
G	25	18	0	5/20
VA & FHA		15.5	4-8	30

A point is paid one time and is equal to one percent of the mortgage.
**In 3/25, for example, the first number (3) is the number of years the interest rate is fixed and the second number (25), the length of the mortgage.*

To buy or sell your home or property today, you can't depend on your "friendly" banker to provide a traditional, conventional, low-interest, fixed-rate mortgage. You probably cannot get such a mortgage in 1982, or next year, or possibly ever again!

Current mortgage interest rates averaging 17 to 18 percent are turning more and more buyers and sellers away from the real estate marketplace. Nonetheless, there are important reasons for buying and selling homes and other property today, and in the future. A host of new financing techniques have been created to make a market possible in real estate, our nation's single, greatest source of wealth.

Aside from personal needs to buy or sell property in today's tight money times, there is another compelling reason—*profits*. Such profits could be large for astute buyers, who know where to look for the real estate bargains which always occur during recession and when money is tight. In addition, extra profits can be achieved by sellers of property who are perceptive enough to sell for a higher price by capitalizing on the fact that their properties are subject to existing, old, *lower-interest* mortgages than can be secured today.

How do you get into this real estate action in homes and property when financing is so tight and expensive? How do you sell your home? How do you buy? Following are some of the new methods generally called creative financing:

"Due On Sale" Mortgage Clauses

Is the old, low-interest mortgage assumable on your home or the one you want to buy? If you're a seller, read your mortgage carefully, particularly the clause which states whether the full mortgage amount is "due on sale." In the absence of such a clause, then the buyer can assume the mortgage. If it's an FHA or VA guaranteed mortgage, then it is assumable by the buyer after the government agency approves the buyer's credit.

There is another important reason for sellers and buyers to check out existing mortgages on properties up for sale. It may have been sold to FNMA or FHLMC, private, federally subsidized, secondary lender agencies which buy mortgages from banks. Often the bank, which sells the mortgage to FNMA or FHLMC, continues to collect the mortgage payments from the owner who might not know that the mortgage has been sold. As the owner, you should ask the bank for this information—and they have to tell you.

This may be quite important to making a sale. Even if the mortgage does have a "due on sale" clause, it may not be enforced by the bank, because the bank has already sold it to FNMA or FHLMC. And the FNMA or FHLMC may permit the existing mortgage to be assumed or revised with comparatively favorable terms, conditions, and rates under the current market, making the transaction feasible.

Second Mortgages

Another alternative for those who want to take over an existing low-interest mortgage is to combine it with a second mortgage (usually for a short number of years; often with a "balloon" clause) from the seller. Approximately 60 percent of all current residential sales involve an additional loan from the seller to the buyer in the form of a second mortgage. Sellers are now taking back second mortgages in order to make their sales possible, but many don't know how to "service" such second mortgages.

At comparatively nominal servicing fees, some banks, real estate agencies, and credit bureaus are now offering to check out and service hundreds of thousands of second mortgages created by the needs of our economic times. They check buyers credit, collect on and handle the bookkeeping for second mortgages for sellers who don't know how to do it themselves.

Alternative Mortgage Instruments

In addition to the conventional, fixed-rate mortgages, there are now other types of mortgage instruments which banks are offering, generally labeled

Alternative Mortgage Instruments (AMIs). If you're told by your bank that they are not making conventional fixed-interest rate mortgages, ask about AMIs. Following are some Alternative Mortgage Instruments:

● **Shared Appreciation Mortgage** (SAM). The buyer of the property receives a lower-than-market interest rate in return for sharing some portion of the home's appreciation in value with the lender when the house is sold.

● **Graduated Payment Adjustable Mortgages** (GPAM). The borrower's initial monthly payments are low, but the lender is allowed to vary the loan's interest rate.

● **Variable Rate Mortgage** (VPM). This type of Alternative Mortgage Instrument is tied to reference indexes, and the interest on the mortgage can go up or down periodically as the index moves.

● **Graduated Payment Mortgages** (GPMs). GPMs are usually offered to younger buyers since the monthly payment on the mortgage starts off low in the beginning years, then moves up as the buyer's income presumably increases. The monthly payments usually level off after about five years.

● **Renegotiable Rate Mortgage** (RRM). Maximum interest swing of a number of percentage points is involved with RRMs.

● **Rollover Mortgages** (ROMs). This type of AMI also involves a changing interest rate. They are renegotiated every five years and are adjusted in accordance with current interest rates.

In general, it is true that the foregoing variable rate mortgages will cost you more than a conventional mortgage in the long run if rates continue to increase in the future, as they have in the past few years. However, at least you can now get a mortgage with these loans. Also, people usually sell their homes on the average, about every seven years, and since new mortgages will be created in the interim, the potential rate changes of the Alternative Mortgage Instruments becomes academic.

Conventional and Little-Known Mortgages

U sing other people's money has always been the method for amassing real estate fortunes. Real estate investors and property purchasers who bought during previous credit crunches and real estate recessions became the wealthy property owners when values boomed up again. The long range trend of real estate values is always up.

However, where can you borrow money during a credit crunch such as we are currently experiencing? Following is a list of the conventional, as well as little-known, sources of money and methods of financing:

● **Your Local Bank.** Even in today's tight-money times, there are still local banks that give mortgages to depositors. Other conventional mortgage sources, which should be checked, are local commercial banks, savings and loan associations, building and loan associations, and title and trust companies.

● **Mortgage Banker Companies.** Mortgage Bankers have become a major force in lending money because of current tight money conditions.

● **Government Guaranteed or Insured Mortgages.** Veterans Administration (VA) and Federal Housing Administration (FHA) housing loans are actually made by lending institutions as government guaranteed or insured loans. They are not loans made directly by the VA or FHA.

- **Direct Government Mortgages.** In addition, the VA and FHA offer direct government mortgages to buyers who purchase properties these agencies have foreclosed for non-payment and are re-selling. *You don't have to be a veteran to* get these loans.
- **The Small Business Administration** (SBA), Washington, D.C., still gives business loans, often for real estate purchases by expanding businesses. This agency also has lists of foreclosed properties that are for sale.
- **The Farmers Home Administration** (FmHA). The FmHA has offices in most county seats and makes housing and other loans in rural and small town areas.
- **Farm Credit System.** The main lender is the Farm Credit System, a network of hundreds of cooperative land and credit banks in rural and small town areas supervised by the Farm Credit Administration, an independent Federal Agency which specializes in loans for farmers and others who own farmland for investment.

An Array of New Products

In addition to the assumption of existing lower-interest mortgages which can be used if there is no due-on-sale mortgage clause, or if the clause is not enforced—and in addition to conventional bank loans and Alternative Mortgage Instruments now being offered—there are other creative financing ways which should be explored. Consult your attorney for specific legal advice.

- **Buy "Subject to" the Mortgage.** Many existing mortgages do not permit assumption, but rather require the seller to remain obligated, should mortgage payments ever be defaulted by the first buyer. As a subsequent buyer, you may still be able to take over such a mortgage. If the seller really wants to sell and is willing to be held responsible by the bank if you fail to make the payments, (particularly if there is good equity in the property), then you can buy "subject to" the mortgage. Again, be sure to consult your attorney before entering into such a mortgage.
- **Wraparound Mortgage.** There are even more sophisticated mortgage variations, such as in California, where sellers create "wraparound" deeds of trust by taking back the deeds (mortgages) at higher interest than the existing mortgages, but for the total amount needed above the down payment.
- **Contract or Installment Sale.** This is another little-known method of buying property. The buyer does not get a deed immediately; he does not own the property until he has paid in a certain agreed-upon percentage of the purchase price. Still, this is another alternative way to take advantage of the good deals which usually become available during periods of "tight-money."
- **Purchase Money Mortgage.** This is where the seller of a property, not a bank, finances the sale for the buyer, usually because there is little or no existing mortgage on the property.

● **Option-Purchase.** This is a variation of the contract or installment method. The difference is that there is a clause whereby the seller gives the buyer an option to buy the property within a specified period. Thus, the buyer can tie up the deal and take title later when financing is available. The seller gets money, usually an option payment for making a pending deal in a slow market.

Default Properties Good Buys

The current recession is creating a host of defaulting properties, but what is one man's loss could be another man's gain. Statistics show that during bleak economic times, numerous opportunities are waiting for alert, informed investors to cash in on high profits simply by picking up defaulted tax and mortgage properties at bargain prices. Following is what you need to know and do in order to get into this "hot," profitable market in defaults:

● Know *where* the supply of defaults originate.
● Know *how* to find them.
● Know *what* to do to use this information.
● Know *how* to follow the *procedures* for default investment.

Where Defaults Come From

Most important to successful investment in default properties is knowledge of the supply—particularly where these properties originate, so that you know as soon as they are available. Depressed economic periods increase the rate of tax and foreclosure sales of real estate.

There are many reasons why properties are forced into sale. People lose their jobs, or go into debt because of easy credit. They wind up buying so much on credit there is often no money left over for taxes and/or the mortgage. Modern life styles and divorce trends are also forcing an ever-increasing number of real estate properties onto the market. The death of the property owner is another reason for foreclosure. Marginal small farms, which decrease in productivity or where children don't want to continue to farm, are often thrown into foreclosure.

Still other causes for defaults occur when creditors sell off debtors' properties to collect on judgments; commercial properties go out of business; industrial buildings lose their tenants, and on and on. The following Default Statistical Table III dramatically illustrates the current economic pressures which are rapidly creating a vast pool of countless defaulted properties for investment and profit:

TABLE III	Default (and other) Statistical Chart	
Item	Current	Year Ago
Defaults	More than 1%	Less than 1%
Housing Starts	871,000	1,550,000
Unemployment	9,400,000	7,946,000

How To Find Defaults

The unfortunately assured, bountiful supply of default properties is usually a well-kept secret. However, this secret world of tax and foreclosure sales legally must be open to the public at various times. When they are, knowledgeable, informed investors can jump in. First, you have to find out where to look for such properties. The following source list identifies many places to acquire tax, foreclosure, and government surplus properties:

Default Source List

● **Your Own Bank.** One good source for finding out about default properties, is your own bank. Let the mortgage department know that you may be interested in purchasing properties they are foreclosing and ask to be notified when these are going to be auctioned.

● **Other Banks.** Savings and loans deal mainly in mortgages (and foreclosures). However, savings banks, commercial banks, and mortgage companies can also be contracted.

● **Newspaper Legal Notices.** Legal notices of defaults are required and they usually run several times on each property being foreclosed. They appear on the back pages of local newspapers and should be required reading for investors.

● **Real Estate and Property Management Brokers.** Government agencies, like the Veterans Administration and the Federal Housing Administration, designate local brokers to help manage and sell their foreclosed properties. They maintain lists available of VA and FHA foreclosures.

● **Attorneys.** Local attorneys who specialize in real estate often have information on pending foreclosures.

● **County Clerks Offices.** Offices of county clerks can also provide lists of default properties.

● **Newspaper Ads.** Many city, state, and federal government agencies insert paid regular news ads to announce regular or special auctions of groups of tax and/or mortgage foreclosures.

● **Title Companies.** Local offices of title companies also provide such data.

● **Federal Government Agencies.** For government surplus and foreclosed properties, check the following agencies: The *U.S. Department of Interior, Bureau of Land Management,* Washington, D.C., has local offices where you can get information on public land for sale. The *General Services Administration,* through local offices in many major cities, disposes of federal real estate. The U.S. *Department of Housing and Urban Development* (HUD) and the FHA, through regional offices, sell properties they have foreclosed. The Department of Agriculture, *Farmers Home Administration* (FmHA), has offices in most county seats which help sell foreclosed rural properties. *The Veterans Administration* also sells foreclosed properties through local brokers.

How To Buy Defaulted Properties

As a result of increasing defaults, the Farmers Home Administration, which has more than 400,000 loans, is now advising many debt-ridden farmers to possibly get out of farming rather than continue to operate their marginal farms in today's depressed economy. Before you rush out to the FmHA offices, or to any other sources for default properties, there are certain inspection and valuation procedures you must follow, but you may have to move fast. Because of the timing, it's important to touch every value and construction base beforehand. The following construction and valuation checklist (Table IV) is particularly pertinent to tax and foreclosure sales.

TABLE IV Default Investment Procedures Inspection Checklist
____ **Community facilities.** Shopping, schools, services, etc.?
____ **Access.** Public, maintained, paved access roads to property?
____ **Revitalization.** Turnaround area; buildings being upgraded?
____ **Block and lot drainage.** No flooding?
____ **Adverse influences.** No adverse neighbors like junkyards; odors?
____ **Utilities.** Public water, sewer, or properly operating wells, septic?
____ **Zoning.** Does zoning permit the current or contemplated usage?
____ **Exterior condition.** Roof, windows, doors, siding, and so on, okay?
____ **Interior condition.** Interior safe, sanitary, structurally sound?

Default Investment Procedures

In foreclosure investments, the price must be right. Also, when you invest in defaults, the cost of repairs may be the deciding factor. You can hire professional appraisers and inspectors but your decisions on the price you bid must be yours. You need your own estimate on the amount of money which will be the absolute bottom line below which you can lose money.

Market Approach. This valuation procedure is the best way to appraise tax and foreclosure properties for current market value. In such default appraisals, you need to know *as-is* and *as-rehabilitated* values. The best way is to compare the subject property to two sets of comparable sold properties—one set of *as-is* sales and one set of *rehabilitated* sales. If these as-is sales cannot be found and the subject property is in rundown condition, then deduct the cost of repairs, overhead, and anticipated profit from the rehabilitated value. Also deduct a contingency-valuation factor of at least 50 percent more (of the total repairs amount) to come up with your maximum bid price.

Income Approach. This approach should be restricted to commercial properties and then only when comparable sales for a market approach cannot be found. You estimate net income and capitalize it to arrive at market value (or hire an appraiser to do it for you). The cost approach to value should not be used on tax and foreclosure properties.

Good Land Buys Now

There is always a market and demand for good land. Economic swings, like the current recession, cause price fluctuations, but the long-range trend in land values is always up. Despite today's depressed economy, good land buys can be found in well-located commercial land, in residential tracts with public water and sewer, and in land suitable for subdivision into one- to five-acre lots in the fast-growing rural areas of exurban metropolitan localities.

Ten Principles of Land Investment

Here are ten land investment rules which you can use to make money on vacant land suitable for future homes or commercial use:

- Invest only *"excess" funds;* be ready to hold for two to three years.
- Check out *every detail* of a deal.
- Know *everything* about the land. Uninformed investment always loses.
- Have *reliable sources* of information.
- Invest *locally.*
- Know your local *area of investment* thoroughly.
- Learn to spot *turnaround* and *growth* trends.
- Know *value.*
- Get to deals *early* or first.
- Know how to *finance* and work with other people's cash.

Soft market times are the best periods to jump into the market for raw, undeveloped land. This is when you find good buys because there are people who cannot afford to hold onto their land. However, you would be ahead of the game if you look for land that will be needed for future development, when conditions improve and financing becomes available, rather than buying poorly located land because it is cheaper. The spread-city pattern of growth will continue and there will be great demand for one- to five-year lots and the tracts which can be subdivided. Closer-in land tracts for smaller lots with public water and sewer will also be at a premium when demand returns and financing is available for small homes and condominiums. If you can locate land zoned for mobile homes, there will be big profits in this aspect as well as in the exurban areas.

No matter whether it is commercial or residential, whether good times or bad, it is important to scrutinize each possible land purchase carefully, *before* you buy. Following is a Land Checklist:

Checklist For Land Buys
Commercial Sites

- **Get a car traffic count** from your local State Highway Department.
- **Check out curb cut regulations** to be certain you can get a permit.
- **Check out sign laws** to be certain sign regulations won't interfere.
- **Review zoning laws** to be sure that commercial use is allowed.
- **Are utilities available,** water, sewer for the proposed commercial?
- **Walk the site.** Don't just speed by. Examine every part.
- **Topography okay?** Is major cut or fill required? Rock? Gradients okay?
- **Drainage okay?** Does water drain off positively?
- **Drive by the plot slowly.** Would signs and buildings be visible both ways?
- **Check out recent comparable sales.** Come to your opinion of value.

Checklist For Land Buys
Residential Sites

● **Community facilities.** Schools, jobs, shopping, parks, churches, and so on.

● **The site.** Is it accessible? Views pleasant? Traffic okay? Air quality good? No flooding? Soil okay for bearing, no landslides or subsidence (land settling)? Noisy air traffic over site?

● **Public service and restrictions in area.** Is there public water, fire protection, electricity, telephone, street lighting, garbage removal, police protection, storm sewers, paved streets, public transportation, zoning for residential use? Is it a growth area? Master plan for development in area?

Financing Land Purchase

Most purchases of raw land are financed by the seller in the form of *purchase money mortgages*. The seller "lends" the buyer a percentage of the selling price so that the deal can be consummated. No mortgage money actually changes hands, as it does when a bank lends you money to give to the seller when you buy the property. Instead, the land-owner-seller holds the purchase money mortgage to secure the loan he makes to the buyer. This is the built-in mechanism of land financing. It allows you to find good deals at low prices in bad financing times and still be able to use little of your own money.

Options are another useful land speculation tool if you have information about the property and if you want to hold it for a while, until conditions improve. With an option, you can put down a sum of money to hold the land for a period of time, after which you are the only one that can sell that property.

Converting 1-Family to 2- or 4-Family Dwellings

Still another example of using recession to profit from real estate, there are 51,000,000 owner-occupied dwellings now in America, the vast majority of them one-family. Twenty-one million one-family dwelling owners are now over fifty-five. Forty million people will move into the over-30 age group and the 35- to 44-year-old group will increase by 45 percent during the 1980s. All these old and young, fast expanding age groups will need, in increasing numbers, more reasonable, smaller, less expensive shelter units.

To fulfill the need, one-family dwellings are beginning to be converted to one- to four-family, *mainly two-family* shelter units throughout the United States. It is a rapidly increasing fact of current and future real estate life.

Whether you do it to your own one-family dwelling, to keep up with inflation and reduced needs for living space, or whether you buy one or more such dwellings for conversion, this is one excellent way to go for real estate profits in a changing society with changing shelter needs.

Rehabilitating Rundown Houses

Another good real estate investment plan is rehabilitation of rundown properties. Projections show that because of increasingly high construction costs and land values, there will be a big market for retro-fitting existing housing stock to satisfy the pent-up demand for comparatively reasonable, smaller shelter units. Many people are making fortunes recycling, renovating, upgrading, renting, and selling older houses. You can too. Following is how to go about it:

• **The Turnaround Principle.** Like many great principles, this one is simple: buy run-down, distressed property and fix it up with as much of your own "sweat" as possible. Then sell it. You plow that "sweat equity" into the next two houses and so on. Equity is the best kind of net worth to have because it is tax-free until you sell the house. You can borrow money on the increased value of your property with a second mortgage and you best inflation since your property's value will rise because of what you have done, and because of the demand for upgraded houses in turnaround areas.

Avoid buildings that are not structurally sound and require new foundations, complete mechanicals, and so on. These are necessities and you can't raise rents or get higher sale prices sufficient to cover the cost. If the house or building is empty, start with roof repairs, obviously to protect any interior changes and then go on to the exterior and add paint or siding where needed. Fix doors or windows as needed. Next, get inside the house and start cleaning it up, upgrading kitchens and baths where necessary, and decorating. The expert's last secret is selling quickly. The more houses you turn over quickly, the more money you make.

Summary

There is always risk in real estate investment. Whether you invest now in bargains in defaults, land, condos, one-family conversions, rehabilitation, even commercial/industrial at sacrifice recession prices, you too can get stuck with property during hard real estate times if you can't hold out until turnaround times. You can also get great buys now from those who must sell if you analyze and project what's happening in your local area—set up the real estate deal now at bargain price and terms so you can cash-in later from the coming demand. It's all in how you go about doing it and what type of real estate you invest in—carefully, but aware that the best times for real estate buys are the worst times—like 1982.

Chapter Twenty

Money Market Funds

Most gamblers are intimately familiar with the old axiom, "Nobody gives anything away for nothing." All the ads in the sports pages about the "guaranteed system," the "system that can't lose," or "winning pro football analysis—20 years of profits" are, simply, advertisements: Just so much lurid come-ons. If the actual results were in any way equal to the ad copy, these services (or *touts*) would *never* be giving their information away, even for a hefty fee. The same trap exists with financial investments.

Have you ever wondered why all those people who start with nothing and make a million dollars in six months with a "system" write books explaining their secret? If you had a sure way to make a million, would you share it with anyone who plunked down $15 for your book? Really now.

Unless, maybe, you could make even more money that way—without screwing up the system, of course. There are, in fact, systems, and then there are systems. Aside from such crucial details as whether they work or not, some systems can be disseminated to the public without self-destructing.

Take some of the popular systems for leveraged real estate investment, for instance. If you followed the rules and pyramided your equity, and every other reader of the books did the same thing, there would still be plenty of investment opportunities around for everyone. The universe of real estate investment—that is, the number of possible investments—is so large that the effect of everyone's following the same investment pattern would distort the overall dollar-and-cents results very little.

Then consider a horse race. Now, I'm not recommending handicapping systems to anyone. Far from it. It's just that betting at a track is a perfect example of a small universe that could easily be distorted by the system—if such a system could ever be developed. Since the odds on a horse race are a product of the betting pattern, if there were a system, and if it worked, and if someone wrote a book about it, and if more people at the track used the system, why, then everyone would lose. The odds would drop to less than even, that is, you would get less than one dollar winnings for every dollar you wagered, even if your horse won. The track and the government would take their cut, and you would win—but with a return that could be as little as five cents for each dollar bet. As every horseplayer knows, this is the quickest and surest road to the poorhouse.

Use the SLY System

The SLY system is going to make you money, more money than you're making now. And it will let you sleep at night while doing it. The SLY system won't turn you into a millionaire in six months, unless, of course, you start with at least $950,000. But it will make your money work as hard as you do. It will consistently yield more than you'll earn by simply putting your money in the bank, or in Treasury bills.

The system works in one of the largest statistical universes created by man—that of the dollar. Here is a universe so huge—and it's expanding all the time—that even if everyone followed the SLY system, the consequent distortion would be minimal.

Again, most readers won't act. So the system's influence will be less than minimal, except to those who do follow it. They will be that much better off because of it. So be SLY. Put your money into high-interest gear.

What's So Sly About SLY? The words behind the initials stand for what you really want for your money. First of all is safety, as I've remarked before. In today's turbulent and uncertain world, there is no absolute safety. But with all the rip-offs, pyramid schemes, scams, government-sponsored inflation, and other devious deprivations to separate you from your money, you at least want to make sure you have the best possible chance of getting your capital back. A 50 percent return on your investment really isn't that great if you don't get the investment itself back. As Will Rogers allegedly said, "I am not so much concerned with the return on my money as with the return of my money."

Then there's liquidity. Liquidity is a crucial investment component in these fast-turning times. An investment without liquidity is like sitting on a priceless family heirloom you cannot sell to make your mortgage payments. You may save the heirloom, but at the cost of losing your house.

Additionally a truly safe and liquid investment whose yield is less than the rate of inflation leaves you safe, liquid—and broke. You need all three ingredients: safety, liquidity, and yield.

Fine, you say, I'll buy that. But where do I get those three good things?

Well, you get your three factors with about ten minutes reading a week. And yes, there's much more to the system than simply safety, liquidity, and yield, because in the economic turmoil of our now-you-see-it, now-you-don't politicized world, there no longer is a "best" investment. There is only a best investment for the moment, even though the money market deals in fixed-income investments, ones that guarantee a specific rate for a specific term.

Whichever way interest rates head—up or down, there will be no more quiet years when interest rates hold steady. And you need to know where to put your money with each shift in interest rates so that it earns the best return while remaining safe and liquid.

Tracking Interest Rate Trends

How to predict interest rates is the key question. Yet is is almost impossible for an individual to forecast interest rates. Some pundits have been able to do it for a while—even, in the case of the current major-domo of interest prediction, Henry Kaufman of Salomon Brothers, for a few years. But overall, one of the major problems in attempting to control the economy has always been an inability to accurately foretell interest rate trends. If the government can't do it at all, and the Wall Street wizards only for a little while, then you may well ask how you're supposed to do it.

The answer is simple, and to figure it out, all you have to do is be able to read a figure that you can find in the financial section of many major newspapers, including *The New York Times, Washington Post, Chicago Tribune, Los Angeles Times, San Francisco Chronicle, San Francisco Examiner, Baltimore Sun, Dallas Morning News, Milwaukee Journal, Boston Globe, Detroit News, Miami News,* and *Tallahasse Democrat.* This figure is called the average maturity index of money funds,and it will give you the most accurate prediction available regarding what interest rates are going to do in the near future.

The average maturity index of money funds is essentially a figure that represents the consensus on the future direction of interest rates from some of the smartest and most high-powered money fund managers in the country.

This average maturity of money funds figure has been an amazing precursor of interest rates to come. Since the fund managers who are responsible for it are putting over $120 billion of their money where their mouths are, you can feel confident in using this figure as a guide in how to invest money in a money fund. Or, looking at it another way, why not put their hard work to work for your money?

To do this, look in any of the previously-mentioned newspapers that carry a table of money fund yields. In the same table, you should find listed the average maturity of the money funds. This figure represents the money fund industry average. The average maturity for all funds can also be found weekly in *Donoghue's Money Fund Report* and biweekly in *Donoghue's Moneyletter*.

How the Average Maturity Index Works

In the money market, it's easy to remember relationships: everything is backwards. If interest rates fall, principal values of negotiable fixed-income investments rise; if the interest rates rise, values fall. It's the same with the money fund average maturity. If interest rates are expected to rise, the average maturity is shortened so the portfolio manager can renew his investments sooner since interest rates will be rising. On the other hand, if interest rates are expected to fall, the portfolio manager will extend (lengthen) his average maturity to lock in today's high interest rates longer and to avoid having to reinvest at lower rates as long as possible.

The most important factor to watch about the money fund average maturity is the direction in which it is moving, not where it is. For example, if money fund average maturities were at 40 days and the next week they were at, say, 37 days, you could conclude that money fund investment managers expected interest rates to rise. The same would be true if the average maturities were at 100 days and the next week they moved to 95 days.

Because of the size of many money funds—33 currently total over $1 billion dollars each—it is difficult for many money funds to change their average maturity moves are much more gradual than they used to be. So, a move of 3 days in any one direction followed by another move in the same direction could be considered significant. You can, of course, watch these moves in all the newspapers each week.

You should be aware that all statistics on our money market fund tables are collected on Wednesday nights, no matter when they are published. So don't be confused by thinking that Friday's and Sunday's *New York Times* tables were, indeed, separate compilations of data.

Use the AMI to Predict Rate Trends

Keep a running log of the money fund average maturity figures shown in the newspapers each week, noting the date on the table (not the date of the newspaper). That way you will be able to see the direction in which the average maturities are moving. Direction is everything because it reflects which way the money fund managers expect interest rates to move. The trend of interest rates is the most important information you can get in the money markets because if interest rates are rising, you definitely do not want to invest in a fixed or guaranteed rate investment, such as a money market certificate, since you will only get a guarantee that your investment's interest rate will not rise.

On the other hand, if you know that interest rates will be falling for some time then you would rather buy something that helps you lock in the current high interest rates as long as possible at the lowest cost (commission) in some investment that you can sell at a profit in a lower interest rate environment. That works with a Corporate Income Fund unit ($1000 each) or a Treasury bill ($10,000 minimum).

It does not work, of course, for a money market or small saver's certificate where getting out early will cost you a penalty not a profit. Profits are obviously better than penalties. If you follow the average maturities and use them as a guide for investing you will earn more in the money market. More is better than less.

Let's run through a real life example. Suppose you had watched the average maturity index and for the last few weeks it had been 25, 26, 27, 27, 27, 28, 27, and 27 and then it quickly went to 24 days. You could expect interest rates to move upward. If the next week that index was 23 days, you would have a confirming signal and could move into money funds safely knowing that interest rates, including yours, would be rising. If a month or so later the average maturity was at 24 and then it moved to 26 the next week and then to 29 and then to 31, you could safely expect interest rates to continue to fall. The important question is for how long will they fall?

If you follow the SLY principles, your investments will always be liquid so you will be able to get your money back without any significant penalty any time you want. You simply ride the interest rate roller coaster, shifting your investments to suit the interest rate trends.

For us, the proof of the pudding is that the Federal Reserve Board calls us each Thursday afternoon to find out the average maturity index (among other things). We think they are using it as a barometer of what the money market's best investors really believe about interest rate trends.

To give an example using the average maturity index, in November 1979, with the prime at 15.75 percent, the general press was saying, "All right, this is it. Interest rates have peaked and will soon decline." For the following ten weeks, however, the index fluctuated between 40 and 36 days. Then it dropped even lower.

At the time, the funds, with some $50 billion of their money on the line, said interest rates would not decline. They didn't. Instead, the prime crept up a full point to 16.75 percent a few months later, pulling all other interest rates with it. And the average maturity index remained on the increasing-interest-rate side of the scale even after that lofty prime was reached. This was at a time when people were again saying, "No, it can't go on." So it went until the prime nudged the unimaginable—20 percent.

Following the popular news commentators, you would have locked yourself into long-term money market investments when the prime reached 15.75 percent. Following the index, you would have waited, increasing your yield by around 4 percent. The pros know.

Using the SLY System

You'll want to start by parking your money in a safe, liquid, yet high-yielding money fund while you look over some of the preferred strategies for the future, using the index to guide you. The interest rates in the examples used here may not correspond to the interest rates behind the strategy, but they are just as valid, and just as profitable, no matter what the current interest levels are—and profit is, after all, the name of the game.

When Rates Are on the Rise, Stay Short and Liquid. Let's assume the average maturity index is declining two to three days each week—which means that interest rates are going to rise. Let's also assume the going investment rate is 12 percent (it would be reflected in the discount rate on Treasury bills, which you will find listed in the financial section of your newspaper every week). What should you do?

Well, if interest rates are rising, money funds are probably yielding about the same as Treasury bills. Actually, money fund yields may be a little lower, since money fund yields tend to lag, or follow, T-bill yields. As the rates rise, the yeild of both the T-bills and the money funds will rise too. So you have a choice of investing in a liquid money fund currently yielding 12 percent, a more restrictive money market certificate yielding the same, or a six-month T-bill yielding 13.1 percent.

Yet another alternative would be the Corporate Income Fund, which at this time would probably be yielding about 13.5 percent for six months, since these vehicles invest in more aggressive portfolios than Treasury bills.

Which do you choose, then? Well, comparing the Treasury bill with either the money fund or the money market certificate, clearly the Treasury bill is more profitable at the moment. However, comparing it with the Corporate Income Fund the Treasury bill's yield is lower. So if you're willing to accept a bit more risk, you should go with the Corporate Income Fund. After all, comparing it with the money fund, you find you would have approximately 13.5 percent coming for the next six months on the Corporate Income Fund, while the money funds are yielding only 12—12.5 percent.

But remember, you think interest rates are rising. So you put your money in the money fund after all. It has a slightly lower initial rate. But its rate will rise with the increasing rate of return for the marketplace. The money market certificate, T-bill, and Corporate Income Fund rates won't do that. Thus, you are better off putting your money into a money fund and waiting. Next week's Corporate Income Fund, Treasury bills, and money market certificates will all be yielding higher rates. That will be true for each subsequent week until interest rates peak. So there's no reason to lock in those rates yet.

Waiting for the Peak. You'll keep your cash in a money fund until you see that interest rates have leveled off. Then you'll decide how much of your money you can lock up, and you'll buy T-bills or Corporate Income Fund units. In the special case where T-bill interest rates are hovering at nine percent or below, however, an argument can be made for buying money market certificates. The extra half of a percent paid on money market certificates—purchased through a thrift institution, not a commercial bank, however—makes them attractive in that particular instance.

The $49 Billion Blunder. In July, 1979, the choice of investors was between a nine percent money market certificate and a 5.5 percent savings account. Obviously, the money market certificates looked good. To a lot of people, people with a combined $49 billion in savings, in fact, it looked as if the money market certificates were definitely the way to go, and that's where they put their money. People locked themselves at nine percent for six months, sat back—and watched interest rates rise while their return didn't.

When they redeemed their certificates in January, 1980, interest rates were already at 13 percent. Had they invested in a money fund, they would have averaged 11 percent instead of nine percent, and they could now have bought Treasury bills yielding 13.1 percent.

By accepting the current yield in a rising market and allowing the money fund rate to take your money along for a ride on the interest curve, then buying Treasury bills at or near the peak, you receive a much more substantial return. True, in the example given, the nine percent return seemed to be a high yield at the outset. But as soon as three months later, it certainly was not. Don't be fooled by high numbers. What counts is how an investment stacks up against current return. Interest rates change very rapidly these days.

At the Peak—Spreading Your Risk. On the other hand, don't expect to always be able to make your investment at the peak. As interest rates fall, however, you'll get another shot at those high yields you saw on the way up. Remember, they have to come down from a peak, even if the overall cycle is up. Let's say, for example, you've been watching a 13 percent yield go to 13.5 percent, and you begin to think, well, maybe I should invest now, but I'll wait a little longer. And the yields go back down to 13 percent. You can still pick up that 13 percent as it goes past you again. That's the time to lock up interest.

The trick in money market investment is being right 90 percent of the time. Nobody is right 100 percent of the time. You can't buy the curve. You can't have it all. What you want to do is to get most of it.

Keeping Your Options Open. Okay, but let's say, as a further example, that you were wrong, that 13.5 percent turned out not to be the top, and interest rates continued to rise. Had you stayed in a money fund, your yield would automatically have risen. And you could have liquidated without a penalty any time you wanted to. If you had wanted to get out of something like a unit investment trust, on the other hand, your $1000 share would have been worth less than you paid for it. You might have gotten out at $990 per share. As for a money market certificate, you couldn't have gotten out of that at all, because you'd have ended up taking a really substantial interest penalty—and some banks simply do not allow early withdrawal. Even a Treasury bill would have sold for less, because of the interest rates going up.

Conversely, suppose you were wrong, and you got into a money fund, and interest rates fell instead of rising. Then you could have changed your mind immediately and said, interest rates have fallen; I'll buy the unit investment trust or the Treasury bill now, before interest rates fall further.

When Rates Are Declining, Go Long. What do you do when interest rates are going down? Let's suppose the money fund average maturity index plus everything you read in the financial news indicates that interest rates are about to decline. At a certain point, you become convinced that the decline is going to be a long one rather than just a dip in an otherwise rising yield curve. The choices for investment, then, are the same. But the strategy is different.

First let's look at the money funds. As interest rates fall, their yields will tend to fall more slowly than those of direct investments in the money market. Remember, in the case of a money fund you're buying part of an already existing portfolio, one that has locked in higher than-market rates for months to come.

If you buy a unit investment trust, on the other hand, and interest rates fall, your shares will appreciate.

Money market certificates are really not a viable investment unless the market rate is below nine percent. Even then, you're trading that extra half of a percent for liquidity, so be sure you don't need the liquidity. Rarely should money market certificates exceed half of your total money market investment, even under the best of conditions.

Treasury bills offer some unique profit potentials as interest rates decline. They're also very flexible. You don't have to buy the six-month Treasury bill.

If you're not really convinced interest rates are going to decline over a full six-month period, there are three-month Treasury bills to be considered. And if you're convinced that a long, steady decline lies ahead, there are one-year Treasury bills to fit the decline.

Riding the Yield Curve

The real beauty of T-bills in a declining interest environment is their adaptability to the very profitable technique that large institutional investors developed to ride the yield curve.

Riding the yield curve for fun and profit, that wonderful way to increase your take, is an essential part of your operations when the market is in a declining interest mode. So let's review it. The greatest appreciation in the value of your securities in a declining interest period occurs about three to four months through to maturity—not at their actual maturity. This is because, while the value of your investment appreciated to match the current yield, it must return to par when it matures.

The strategy of riding the yield curve, then, is quite simple. Buy a one-year Treasury bill and sell it after six months. Or buy a six-month Treasury bill and sell it after three months. In each case, purchase a newly issued T-bill as the old one is sold. The securities are continuously replaced on a three- or six-month basis.

The $1000 Yield Curve Ride. Unit investment trusts also lend themselves to riding the yield curve. Their yield will be higher than that of T-bills, their safety fractionally less.

But what if your expectations prove wrong, and interest rates don't fall, but continue to rise. Well, with a money fund investment, the yield will rise along with the general level of interest rates. The Treasury bill will decline in value for a while and then rise back up to par. As it is simply held to maturity, no capital is lost. The interest earned is the original discounted rate for the whole period of retention. By holding it to maturity, you eliminate market risk at the cost of slightly lower interest.

Basically, as long as you are not forced to sell out because of a liquidity problem, the interest loss—the difference between the T-bill's fixed yield and its current yield—is twice as great for a one-year Treasury bill as for a six-month bill. Conversely, if you've guessed right, the additional gain on a year bill will be twice that of a six-month bill.

MONEY MARKET STRATEGIES

The key to being wrong safely is protecting yourself. This is where diversification in a conservative approach comes in.

• Put part of your money market investment in safety, with a capital S. That means either Treasury bills or money market certificates, the option beging exercised by that crucial 9 percent yield threshold. Below 9 percent, it's money market certificates from a thrift institution paying the quarter of a percent differential. Above 9 percent, it's T-bills.

● Put another part of your investment in money fund for liquidity. That's liquidity with a capital L.

● Put the last part of your money into the higher-yielding Corporate Income Fund, if available at the time of your initial investment. If not, add this amount to your money fund until a new Corporate Income Fund series makes its way down Wall Street.

TABLE I: CONSERVATIVE INVESTOR

What to Do When Interest Rates Are on the Rise:
1. Invest in money funds.
2. Never invest in anything else—you'll lose higher yields tomorrow.
3. Borrow at fixed rates to invest at higher rates. Make sure there are no prepayment penalties in the loans.

What to Do When You Think Rates Are About to Peak:
1. Put up to 50 percent of your portfolio into Corporate Income Fund, Short-Term Series units, if available. If not, use T-bills.
2. Keep 50 percent in money funds with short (under 20 days) maturities.
3. Wait for the peak.

What to Do When Interest Rates Peak:
Move another 25 percent of your portfolio from your money funds into Corporate Income Fund units.

What to Do When Interest Rates Are Falling:
1. Move into money funds with longer maturities (check Donoghue's Money Fund Report).
2. Add to unit investment trust holdings.
3. Sell unit investment trust holdings three months after buying them if they can be sold at a profit.
4. Reinvest in Corporate Income Fund units, if still available. If not, move back into money funds with long maturities.

What to Do When Interest Rates Begin to Climb:
1. Move back into a 100 percent money fund position.
2. Move into money funds with short maturities.

The Money Market Certificates and T-bills can be avoided entirely when general rates are over 9 percent. The confident investor should substitute Corporate Income Fund units.

Such a money portfolio maximizes your field while eliminating any substantial credit risk. It won't make you rich overnight. But it will let you get poorer more slowly than the rest of the population. And don't forget, for every story about millionaires made in the stock market, real estate, or precious metals, there are tens of thousands of untold stories about the people who took the same route—to poverty. So don't be sorry—by SLY.

Applying the SLY System—A Case Study in Strategies. In order to see how to apply the SLY system to your finances, let's first make some assumptions about what financial alternatives you have available and how they will be affected by fluctuating interest rates. We will use the money fund average maturity index to predict interest rate trends.

To keep the example simple, let's assume interest rates rise to a peak and then fall off at the same rate as they increased. In the real world, the change would be more erratic. However, the principle is the same and the results will show the effect of this interest rate fluctuation on your return for five different basic investment strategies.

TABLE II: MORE CONFIDENT INVESTOR
(When the Choices Are Clear)

How Your Money Market Portfolio Should Look

	Unit Investment Trust*	Money Funds * Percent	Money Fund Average Maturity Index
Rising rates	100	—	Shortening (decreasing)
Approaching peak	75	25	Shortens faster
At peak	50	50	Begins to lengthen (increase)
Falling rates	25	75	Continues to lengthen
At bottom	75	25	Starts to shorten
Rising rates	100	—	Continues to shorten

* The ultraconservative investor should substitute T-bills if desired. If UITs are not available, then use T-bills.

Fixed Income Investments Throughout the Interest Rate Cycle. Again to simplify the example and show you the basics, let's limit our investments to four instruments: money funds, unit investment trusts, and three- and six-month Treasury bills. (The reason I'm leaving out money market certificates—MMCs—is that you would always choose the higher-yielding unit investment trust over a money market certificate whenever interest rates are above 10%. Small saver certificates have been omitted because under most circumstances, you would not enjoy the required liquidity if you locked up your money for such an extended period.)

Four Investment Strategies to Improve Your Return. As you can see in

Table II all the money market investment strategies are the same when interest rates are rising. When interest rates rise, you should invest all your available money in money funds, because their yields, though lower at the time of purchase than other money market investments, increase each day, while the others remain fixed.

For example, if you invested in a unit investment trust when money funds were yielding 11.5%, the former would remain at 11.5% while the money fund yield would be free to climb to 11%, 12%, 13%, and on up. The monthly average yield for a money fund over a period of rising interest rates, then, is higher.

Additional Observations

A few things more can be said about the money fund field, although anyone following Donoghue's advice will do well. In their ten-year history, money market funds had absolutely their best year in 1981. The average return from the nation's 172 money funds was 16.8 percent—an increase from the 14 percent average enjoyed in 1980.

The effect of daily compounding brought the average overall yield to 18.2 percent for those investors who elected to reinvest their dividends. As of the beginning of March, 1982, returns had tailed off somewhat (averaging 13.3 percent), but they were still running well ahead of inflation, which was at eight percent and falling.

For those investors who are particularly concerned with safety, government income funds invest only in government-backed securities. If even more protection is desired, you can always consider six-month certificates of deposit. You will still earn high interest, but remember, you're sacrificing liquidity for the illusory protection of the FDIC.

Frank Zuckerman, president of Unified Securities, has this to say about money funds: "For the small or average investor, they are an excellent investment choice because they are a hedge against these days of wildly fluctuating interest rates—which directly affect the average investor's standard of living. However, for the investor with a great deal of money in hand, they are not as good. These investments do not affect his standard of living, and he pays a greater percentage of taxes on his interest. He would be better off diversifying into long-term investments (like AAA corporate bonds when interest rates are high) so he is not subject to the day-to-day fluctuations in the interest rates."

Some money market funds invest heavily in foreign CDs and Eurodollars; this might be dangerous. Read the financial statements and prospectuses. Whenever there is any doubt in your mind, reconsider—ask questions and shop around carefully.

But by all means, never select a fund that charges a sales fee or brokerage commission. You run the risk of negating in large part (if not entirely) any earnings advantage a money market fund might have over another type of investment. The interest paid by no-load (no sales charge) and load (commission paid) funds is remarkably similar, and it makes no sense whatsoever to pay the commission.

Chapter Twenty-One

Strategic Metal Investment Strategies

Back in 1980, when precious metals prices were descending from the Himalayan heights of $850 gold and $50 silver, many goldbugs latched on to another area of investment involving strategic metals. Taking a cue from the United States National Strategic and Critical Stockpile—and its accompanying act—the goldbugs found an eager public ready and willing to take risks in a relatively illiquid market—a market formerly the bailiwick of user companies rather than investors.

Heralding strategic metals as "the gold of the 1980s," leaders of the new investment wave appeared at hard money seminars to spread the "gospel." Indeed, at the annual National Committee for Monetary Reform New Orleans conference in November, 1980, it seemed every other display booth reflected some form of metals sales material. But, at the monetary Reform Conference the following November, there was not a single display anent investing or hoarding these metals, including cobalt, germanium, tantalum, and titanium.

What happened during the 12 months between November, 1980, and November, 1981? Why the sudden desertion of almost every investment adviser from recommending that people buy and hoard strategics?

What Are Strategic Metals?

Before tackling the answers to these questions, it is advisable to touch briefly upon what the leading strategic metals are and how they came to be attractive in 1980-1981.

The definition of strategic metals involves those items considered strategic and critical under the terms of the stockpiling act, which dictates that the United States store at least a three-year supply of these metals to insure an adequate available stockpile in the event of a "conventional war." However, this should also include such base metals as lead, zinc, and copper—and precious metals such as platinum and palladium. The promoters of the strategic metals concept, nonetheless, avoided the prosaic items and instead concentrated on cobalt, columbium (also known as niobium), germanium, gallium, europium, tantalum, titanium, and so on. Oddly enough, these metals have been traded for almost a century in London, and on the continent, under the rubric "minor metals." But who would be tempted to take risks in a minor metal?

This is one of the reasons that the category of minor metals suddenly came to be known—in the United States, anyway—as strategic metals. Moreover, since there is no federal agency regulating the sale of physical metals, predatory firms that capitalized on the gullibility of an unsuspecting public have opened boiler-room-like sales offices all over the country to hawk these metals at highly inflated prices. Thus, if the producer price of cobalt was $20 an ounce, if purchased from the agency marketing the metal from Zaire, people could pay $40 and $50 an ounce—without even being sure they were purchasing relatively pure metal, or knowing that metal was actually bought and stored for their account as per the sales pitch.

Proliferation of marginal firms marketing these metals caused alarm among the state fraud agencies, and it was only a question of time before many of them were closed down and their principals indicted.

While there were—and still are—some firms that prey on a gullible investing public, there were—and still are—others who are legitimate—companies like Bache Halsey Stuart and James Sinclair's Strategic and Critical Materials Corporation—who actively market some of these metals in a declining market. Thus, while sincerely servicing their clients, these firms market metal during a period of falling prices.

As a result, it is a safe speculation that no investor who bought any strategic metals during 1980 and 1981 will be sitting with a profit in 1982.

Beware of the Risks

Biggest example of a tremendous loss in a strategic metal is the United States Government—and lest we forget, that's us. During the spring of 1981, President Reagan spoke forthrightly for the need to purchase those materials and metals that might be hard to get because of our dependency upon other nations for the bulk of our supply.

Cobalt, for example, had priority over the purchase of all other metals because that element came primarily from ore mined in Zaire. Indeed, Zaire made the producer price, which was the price that users paid for long-term contracts with the primary source: Zaire. At one time, cobalt had soared to more than $60 a pound , when dissension and unrest occurred in Zaire, but the price of the metal had modestly declined to $20 to $25 in the marketplaces of the world.

Cobalt is a hard metal, resembling iron, but when alloyed with iron, nickel, and other metals, cobalt forms an alloy of unusual magnetic strength. The principal strategic use of cobalt is in super-steels needed for manufacture of aircraft, missiles, and space applications.

Despite an approaching recession that depressed the steel industry inside the United States, President Reagan authorized the purchase of 5.2 million pounds of cobalt from Zaire in the summer of 1981, at $15 a pound. At first, this was heralded as quite a coup, since the producer price at the time of purchase stood at $20 (a price, of course, made by Zaire), and our country managed to get a bargain at $15.

But shortly after the sale was effected, the market price of cobalt hit the skids. Down, down, down it went until it reached a nadir of $8.50 a pound in Europe as 1981 neared its final days. At this level, the U.S. Government overpaid Zaire by almost $35 million on a purchase involving $78 million, out of the $100 million alloted to the government to spend for strategic materials that fiscal year.

Interestingly enough, the priority materials the government was supposed to purchase during the fiscal year ending September 30, 1981, included: Aluminum oxide, bauxite, cobalt, columbium, manganese dioxide, nickel, platinum group metals, tantalum, titanium, and vanadium.

But sad to report, the purchase of cobalt precluded any sizable purchases of the other strategic metals and materials. And because of the recession in the United States during 1981, which has already spread to other industrial countries in 1982, there is little likelihood that prices will rebound in the foreseeable future.

20/20 Hindsight

Of course, the vendors and advisers who advocated purchase of strategic metals back in 1980 and 1981, had some highly lucrative track records to display. Here is the appreciation of the ten leading minor metals during 1972 to 1980 (by "leading" I mean 80 percent of the volume in the industry involved these metals):

TABLE 1: Price Appreciation of Leading Minor Metals (1972 to 1980)

Strategic Metal	Percent Price Increase: 1972 to 1980
Chromium	385%
Cobalt	1250%
Columbium	1300%
Indium	1215%
Magnesium	421%
Molybdenum	970%
Rhodium	400%
Silicon	370%
Tantalum	1480%
Tungsten	420%

In 1980, for example, indium traded actively above $20 an ounce. But from that summit the metal began dropping to trade, in early 1982, at $5.75 an ounce. Similar declines have occurred in many of the strategics—with rare, if any, price improvement during the past two years. Table 2 is a listing of the rather illiquid metals classified as "strategic" by the vendors.

TABLE 2: Minor and Rare Earth Strategic Metals

Metal	Major Uses
Antimony	batteries, flameproofing
Barium	medicine
Berylium	alloying application in aerospace, nonsparking tools, springs
Cadmium	plating
Cerium	misch metal
Cesium	ion propulsion systems, electronics
Chromium	plating, alloying with steel
Cobalt	alloying with steels and nonferrous metals
Columbium	alloying with steels
Europium	TV tubes and laser applications
Gallium	photovoltaics, electronics
Germanium	infra-red applications and electronics
Hafnium	nuclear reactor control rods
Indium	electronics and photovoltaics
Iridium	alloying with nonferrous metals
Magnesium	incendiary bombs, aircraft alloys
Manganese	alloying with steels
Mercury	medicinal and electronics
Molybdenum	steel alloys
Osmium	alloying with nonferrous metals
Rhenium	petroleum catalyst; alloying
Rhodium	plating
Rubidium	electronics and space applications
Ruthenium	alloying with nonferrous metals
Selenium	electronics and photocopy
Silicon	steel alloys
Tantalum	electronics and aircraft alloys
Tellurium	steel alloying
Titanium	jet engines and airframes
Tungsten	alloys for hard cutting tools, etc.
Vanadium	steel alloys
Zirconium	nuclear applications

Most of the above minor and rare earth metals were quite expensive at one time or another because of escalating demand and unavailable supply. For example, titanium, a metal used extensively in jet aircraft and bombers, first went into commercial production in 1948, when three tons were produced. By 1952, production had risen to 5250 tons. As demand soared for this metal, and as commercial methods of creating titanium sponge were perfected, a flood of titanium inundated the marketplaces of the world.

Today, the demand for titanium is much greater, of course, than it was in 1952. But this metal, made from rutile—one of the most abundant materials on the earth's crust—can be had at discounts from Japan, China, and continental marketplaces. Even though the United States contemplates building a massive fleet of B-1 bombers, there will still be much more titanium than is needed.

Strategics Outlook

Having touched upon the bad news side of strategic metals: i.e., an over-supply and a declining demand because of a worsening recession, is there any really good news in the future for owners or prospective purchasers of strategics?

One area of promise involved the flotation of massive mutual funds, which would bring a huge investment presence into the picture. One fund actually filed with the SEC during 1981, hoped to raise $50 million that would be invested in these metals. Since the fund was to be managed by an investment adviser who pioneered the vending of strategic metals, and since the fund had the sponsorship of a global brokerage firm, it was anticipated that there would be no problems in floating the fund when it came out of the SEC. But the fund never came out of registration; and in early 1982, the filing was withdrawn.

Other brokerage houses had been watching what would happen with this strategic metals fund and might have followed suit. But the declining prices of strategic and minor metals in the world dealer markets evidently discouraged the other firms, and at this writing no strategic "partnerships" are being filed for eventual distribution to the American investor.

This is not to infer that if America rouses itself out of its recession, if the steel business recovers, if we continue to spend massive sums for defense, missiles, aircraft, and space exploration, that some of these strategics will not improve in price. But, for that matter, if interest rates decline so that America can rouse itself from the slough of despondency into which it was cast by more than 14 months of double-digit prime rates, will not copper, lead, and zinc rise in value too?

Naturally, if investors become attracted to strategic metals in a rising market, and ownership for investment becomes widespread, these metals may shed their current illiquidity. But such an event cannot occur while prices are declining.

So when will prices rise? And which metals are the most favorable ones for a price recovery?

Best Strategics for 1982

Certain areas of the steel business will be favored by the defense efforts of the current administration. In this regard the price of molybdenum could improve markedly from its lows of last year. Another metal that could have a real runup is vanadium. The great growth in the size and the power of heavy machinery has presented the foundryman with the task of producing sound castings, not only of great size, but also of massive complexity, accompanied by the ability to sustain tremendous static and dynamic loads. The incorporation of vanadium into steel castings greatly improves their metallurgical properties. Because of superior distribution of microconstituents, vanadium steel alloys are able to sustain great stress, rather than rupture under sudden overloads.

In addition to vanadium, chromium and manganese are often added to the steel to give these alloys certain desirable qualities. Vanadium is also used in the manufacture of spring steels, cast steels, cast iron, and high-grade steel tools.

So three strategic metals that could improve greatly in price from last year are: 1. molybdenum; 2. chromium; and 3. vanadium.

Much ado has been made about certain rare earth metals like germanium, which ran up to about $1500 a kilo in 1980-1981, only to fall back in price in late 1981. Germanium, a metal not listed in the national strategic stockpile requirements, is increasingly used in infra-red technology and in electronics, including photovoltaics.

In this regard, gallium has been the subject of much experimentation along with indium, in connection with the feasibility of turning sunlight directly into energy. As solar energy catches on in years to come, the demand for these metals could exceed supply.

So three additional growth candidates that could be positioned for long-term appreciation are gallium, germanium, and indium. Of all these metals, indium may be best. This versatile metal has a plethora of other uses, including substitution for silver in some applications. Moreover, indium is selling for about a quarter of its 1980 price, and chances are the going price (under $6 an ounce) is actually below the cost of manufacture.

Finally, the best near- and long-term investments in strategic metals involve platinum and palladium. Platinum at $365 an ounce is at a bizarre discount from its producer price of $475. You might ask why General Motors will still buy platinum at $475 an ounce from Rustenburg mines when the metal is going in the marketplace at $365. And the answer is that GM has a long-term contract that enabled it to buy platinum at the producer price (then $420) when the metal traded in the market at over $1150 an ounce.

In similar manner, the going producer price for palladium was $110 an ounce, yet the metal sold for under $70 in the dealer markets of the world.

Both platinum and palladium trade on futures exchanges so that purchasers can exercise the leverage inherent in such transactions. Platinum trades in 50-ounce contracts on the New York Mercantile Exchange (now called NY Mex), and palladium trades in 100-ounce contracts on the same exchange.

Platinum and palladium are mainly used in antipollution applications on the exhaust gases of autos and trucks. Naturally, we have had a doleful year of poor auto sales and production so that the physical markets in platinum and palladium have become besieged by recycled metal, which accounts in part for the low going prices of both. But should any recovery occur on the American auto industry, then the prices or both metals will advance markedly.

Many professionals favor palladium over platinum, not only because it is trading at a more undervalued price. Palladium is a remarkable metal that the world is still learning to use. It is the softest of the platinum group metals and has slightly different metallurgical qualities. Palladium, unlike platinum, can be beaten and formed into very thin sheets and wire. As a catalyst—in a finely divided state—palladium has been proven an effective trap for carcinogens in a cigarette filter.

Profits From Losses in Strategies

U nlike securities, there is no wash sale in commodities. Thus, investors who overpaid last year or the year before for strategics can sell their holdings and switch to some other metal (a strategic, precious, or base metal) at currently depressed prices. In so doing the investor establishes 1. a real tax loss; 2. has reduced real taxes to pay on income or gains; and 3. may wind up with a metal that has more promise than the one being held in portfolio at a loss.

Hopefully, those who have invested in strategics at legitimate firms will be able to dispose of their holdings and switch to a more promising candidate. People who were defrauded in strategic metals schemes, of course, do not have their metals, and they probably already have their tax losses established, anyway. The thing to remember is that when sitting with metal at a paper loss it does not make sense to wait for a comeback. It does make sense to establish a tax loss and look elsewhere for a rebound so that taxes can be paid in 1983—or whenever the much-belabored recovery sets in.

Profiting from Loss

T his brings us to the final message on how to profit from losses in strategic metals. Instead of switching from metal held in your portfolio at a loss, to another metal that could result in a further loss if the recession continues into 1983, it makes sense to sell the metal and switch to companies who produce the strategics. The shares of these companies are deeply depressed at present and could be comeback candidates. If not, they certainly will offer a return via dividends while waiting for a price revival.

Here are some favorites for switching from losing portfolios of strategic metals into shares of companies creating the metals themselves: Amax, Asarco, Noranda, and Rustenburg.

Amax and Asarco are listed on the NYSE. At one time in 1981, a company bid $78 a share for Amax—an offer the company refused. It perhaps represents a real bargain at current prices. Asarco could be a prime takeover candidate, and its presently depressed price is a gift. In similar light, Noranda, which is traded on the Toronto Stock Exchange, reflects genuine value. And, Rustenburg Platinum Holdings at under $4 a share offers ownership in the free world's largest reserves of platinum group metals.

Chapter Twenty-Two

The Silver
Lining

S herlock Holmes believed that once the impossible was removed from any case, whatever remained—however improbable or incomprehensible—had to be the truth. In the case of the boom/bust, rise and fall of the roller coaster riding silver price—a gut-wrenching ride that has lasted from the summer of 1979 through March, 1982, and ran from about $9 an ounce up to $50 and back down to $8—the truth is that this "incorruptible" strategic metal will soon rise again. Like the legendary phoenix, silver is primed to rise from the ashes of recession, aimed at new highs in the coming years.

Of course, this may seem overly optimistic—silver has slashed through a ravaged market in the past year. January, 1981, saw the metal's high for the year, $16.45 per ounce. At the time, this compared very poorly to gold: About 35 ounces of silver were required to buy one ounce of gold. Way back when, in times of hard currency, the silver/gold ratio was fixed at 16/1, and it seemed that substantial upward pressure might influence silver's future.

However, when Ronald Reagan took office, the General Services Administration (GSA) again announced its intention to sell off the national silver stockpile—139.5 million ounces. For a change, the announcement had the Administration's blessing, and when news that both the GSA and the White House wanted to dump the silver stockpile in order to buy other so-called strategic metals, liquidation of both silver physicals and silver futures began in earnest.

In a classic bureaucratic miscalculation, the GSA had estimated that the silver stockpile would be liquidated at an average of $15 per ounce—for some reason, it eluded them that their own announcement to introduce over 139 million ounces to the market would quickly drive the price down to $12, then $10 per ounce, which it did. In the interim, the silver/gold ratio jumped to 40/1, then soared to 50/1.

For the first time in history, it took over 45 ounces of silver to buy a single ounce of gold for the period of an entire year. There have been occasions when over 80 ounces of silver were needed, and once the ratio hit 100/1, but the precious metals markets have never seen the silver/gold ratio above 45/1 for such a long period of time.

Interest Rates Affect Silver Prices

Naturally, much of the damper placed on hoarding or investing in physical silver in 1981 was provided by the extremely high interest rates prevalent in the United States through most of the year. Simply, why should investors hold or accumulate a metal that was steadily losing value, when they could receive yields in excess of 15 percent from money market funds or other low-risk investments? In addition, purchasers at firms using silver were understandably reluctant to stockpile the metal. First, there appeared to be no significant upside pressure on silver in the market, and second, the cost of carrying a silver inventory was absurd in the light of a very high prime rate.

In other words, investor disinterest and user neglect combined to decimate the physicals market in silver worldwide. As if this weren't enough, official rulings, geared to stop speculation of every kind in silver, virtually assured that no price recovery would occur. This was the case on both the COMEX and the Chicago Board of Trade—the nation's leading silver markets—and the anti-speculation campaign had a substantial influence on the world markets.

For example, position limits had been enacted by COMEX in January, 1980, (for good reason at the time) but they were never removed, even though the conditions that prompted the limitation had long since ceased to exist. Position limits discouraged participation by big players—whose large speculative positions would have given the metal's price a boost—and drove them into the gold pits. Speculators were also goaded from silver to the gold arenas by what amounted to blatant favoritism on the part of COMEX on the part of gold, particularly in margins.

Every time margins were raised or lowered, the margin requirement for silver futures turned out to be relatively higher (in terms of percentages) for silver, than for gold. In short, an implaccable attitude in the exchange itself to discourage silver speculation drove away the normal support for speculators who might go long. Only the hedgers (producers and bullion dealers) were left, and they had to short the metal in the absence of public buyers, which continued to depress the price.

As a result, gold futures were the reigning king of COMEX in 1981, partially by default—playing silver futures was no longer attractive to big investors. The subsequent decline in gold prices, of course, added to the downward pressure on the silver price. After all, both metals have been linked in the marketplace since Biblical times.

Thus 1981 ended with a maimed silver market, priced at $8.25 against gold's over-$400, and a silver/gold ratio of almost 50/1.

The average daily price for silver in 1981 was $10.52 per ounce. In 1980, the average daily price was $20.63. Why the collapse? Different people offer different reasons.

When Supply Exceeds Demand

The Silver Users Association, whose major *raison d'etre* is to lobby for lower silver prices for its user-members, claims that the 50 percent price drop was a result of fundamentals. By this they mean there's simply more silver available than is required by industry—supply exceeds demand, and the price must fall accordingly. In support of this contention, Silver Users states that while the demand for silver rose slightly in 1981, it was "the lowest since 1964" in 1980. Therefore, the decline in demand is attributed to the explosive jump in silver price during 1979 and 1980. Of course, it is safe to assume that the price of silver is still too high, as far as the silver users are concerned.

Yet the costs of creating an ounce of silver from ore to finished metal have skyrocketed since 1979. New labor agreements made with silver producers and with mining companies that produce base metal ores (which contain silver as a secondary metal) have spurred tremendous cost increases. Power costs, transportation, and financial costs have also soared, so that the estimated price of silver to primary producing companies—such as Hecla, Sunshine Mining, and Coeur d'Alene—has risen to about eight dollars per ounce.

All signs indicate that the same thing that happened to the copper industry—when the market price fell below the producer cost—will happen in the silver industry. Under such circumstances, the mines have only two alternatives: They can curtail production, or they can stop production altogether.

Production Vs. Consumption

Interestingly, an enormous gap remains between the amount of silver produced in the United States and what it actually consumes each year. Estimates for 1981 place new silver production from United States mines at about 36 million ounces. But about 132 million ounces were used. Where was the 96 million ounce deficit made up? In its "U.S. Silver Summary—1981" (available free from Walter Frankland, Silver Users Association, 1717 K St., NW, Washington, D.C. 20006), Silver Users reports that 60 million ounces came from scrap recovery (including coin melt), and another 60 million ounces were imported.

In other words, about 156 million ounces of silver were available to users and investors in the United States in 1981. But if only 132 million ounces were used, an obvious surplus of 24 million ounces should exist.

Along with this apparent expansion of supply over demand, something strange has happened to the refined silver stocks stored in exchange warehouses. In 1980, these stocks swelled—year-end saw 155.9 million ounces stored and acceptable for exchange deliveries. But in 1981, these stocks mysteriously began to shrink, even when they should have grown by the surplus. COMEX lost 10 million ounces, which probably wound up behind the Iron Curtain. The Chicago Board of Trade lost 27 million ounces, which rumor places in a Delaware bank on behalf of the Hunts. And the London Metal Exchange gained almost six million ounces, as large speculators transferred their holdings and market machinations outside the reach of the Commodity Futures Trading Commission (CFTC).

Despite an apparent oversupply of 24 million ounces, 1981 ended with only 124.6 million ounces of silver warehoused for exchanges in America and London. There is nothing obviously fishy about this: What is important is the implications of smaller reserves. If there is any return to industrial and speculator demand in the physical silver markets, the price could explode.

During the summer of 1981, the GSA obtained approval to dispose of 105 million ounces of silver from the national stockpile, to be auctioned over a three-year period. The first auction was held last October. Over the course of six auctions, some two million ounces were sold for about nine dollars apiece.

However, near the end of the year, Senators McClure and Symms of Idaho (the so-called "Silver State") managed to effect legislation halting any silver auctions until at least July, 1982. Their effort to protect their constituency also required President Reagan, through the Federal Emergency Management Agency (FEMA), to report to Congress as to whether or not the nation's silver was indeed surplus. In other words, FEMA was asked to justify the auctions.

This has created a double-edged situation. On the one hand, dumping the nation's giant strategic stockpile when demand is low further depresses silver prices by increasing supply. On the other, the ever-present possibility of such a jump in supply also serves to hold prices down. The GSA's wasted effort to dispose of the hoard caused a severe depression in silver's price. Yet holding onto the silver, when speculators and users expect it to be sold at any time, also depresses the price.

In the end, the short-term outlook for silver is not wildly bullish. Failing any international event which would cause a flight from dollars into gold, it is also difficult to envision any industrial calamities that would boost the currently depressed silver price back toward the $50 per ounce level in 1982.

Chinese Demand for Silver

In 1981, massive amounts of silver moved from the various world markets to the Soviet Union. And for the first time in years, China attempted to reverse the flow of its ancient trade dollars through Hong Kong. Enterprising junk captains have been smuggling old Chinese coins from China to Hong Kong for many years. The contraband has been exchanged for western goods, including radios and tape recorders. To regain some of its lost silver, the Peking government opened an agency in Hong Kong; during 1981, they managed to regain over 169 *tons* of silver in coin form for recycling.

It is no secret that China hungers for westernization, both in terms of strategic alliances and in consumer benefits, such as apartment houses, golf courses, and televisions, as well as in terms of technology, especially computers. If this trend continues, China should develop a silver demand comparable to the current needs of the U.S.S.R. by the late 1980s. The best estimates place Soviet demand for silver at ½ ounce per capita per year. In the

United States, annual consumption is placed at ¾ ounce per capita—but, of course, the high level of technology in the country contributes to the highest silver consumption level in the world.

Assuming that China's demand reaches current Soviet levels by, say, 1986, the silver requirements of just three nations would be staggering:

Country	Silver Demand
United States	180,000,000 ounces
U.S.S.R.	160,000,000
People's Republic of China	500,000,000

In other words, just three major users would require 840 million ounces of silver each year. In addition, other industrialized countries use their own share of the metal. (Bear in mind, though, that China's consumption may not reach the ½ ounce per capita level.)

The Silver Institute estimates that in 1986 the total world production of newly mined silver will be only about 425 million ounces. If China's need was only half of the projection, the shortfall would exceed 100 million ounces. If China's consumption rises to ½ ounces per capita, then the shortfall will be in the neighborhood of 415 million ounces! If this is the case, where will the silver come from? The Hunts? Investors? Government hoards?

It seems likely that the late 1980s will see a visible (or perhaps invisible) trade war for silver. In fact, demand could increase to such an extent that projections of $50 to $100 per ounce for silver might turn out to be highly conservative.

In such an event, of course, people would once again rush to stores and fly-by-night motel rooms to sell their grandmother's candlesticks, family service sets, and other sterling heirlooms. When silver hit $50 per ounce in January, 1980, about 166 million ounces of silver were refined. Estimates for 1981 run from 60 to 80 million ounces of "scrap" sold by the dollar-hungry public. Hold onto your sterling silver fruit bowl a while longer—eight or nine dollars per ounce will have you gnashing your teeth when silver bursts up, if it bursts up, of course.

Silver in 1982

Given that silver will probably do little in 1982, why should you tie any of your money to it? It's a good question, of course, but it can be answered. Since nobody knows exactly when the top or bottom of a price cycle will occur, it makes sense to start accumulating a precious metal when the price drops below the cost of production. This applies equally to all precious metals. To an extent, it also applies to base metals, but since most investors pursue precious metals with their intrinsic value in mind, any time it costs the mines more to produce silver, gold, or platinum than what you are paying for an ounce of the metal, you should buy it.

Silver is currently trading in the physicals and futures marketplace at below producer cost to primary mining companies, at least in the United States. This points to long-term appreciation. And, if you decide to accumulate this desirable metal over a fairly long period of time, it is amazingly easy to do so. You can dollar average by participating in accumulation plans.

Of course, you can also invest in shares in silver mining companies. Bear in mind that you should try to buy the mining shares when silver seems to be at or near its bottom. When the producer cost is below the spot price for the metal, the mining companies are operating, obviously, at a loss, and their shares should become progressively less expensive. The major companies involved in American silver mining are listed on the New York Stock Exchange as follows: ASARCO, CALLAHAN, HECLA-DAY, and SUNSHINE. In addition, many silver stocks are traded over the counter (OTC).

Silver futures, of course, are not investments: Silver futures are speculations. Perhaps they are sensible, but they aren't for the faint-hearted. If you want to buy silver futures contracts as investments, the thing to do is to simply buy a 1000-ounce futures contract on the Chicago Board of Trade or a 5000-ounce COMEX contract and *pay for it in full*. You'll never get a margin call, and you can, like the Hunts, roll over your future when it approaches the spot delivery month, to a more distant contract date. This, of course, requires a fair amount of money, but you can put it to good use. For example, you can put the money into T-bills in the interim, earning double-digit interest on money that would otherwise be placed in a sterile metal bar or in coins.

The ultimate point is this: Silver has value, both for its industrial applications and for its time-honored status as a precious metal. This year, 1982, may well be one of the great silver buying opportunities of all time.

How Other Experts View Silver

Vincent J. Conway, the senior metals analyst at Merrill Lynch, recently issued his forecast for silver for the next year. "The silver market could experience transition during the next four to eight months," he said. "During this period, the negative factors evidenced for much of the past two years could become fully discounted, and the market might begin to focus on future influences. During much of 1982, the bulk of price activity should develop between $6.50-$9.00 area. Thereafter, a more sustained price advance to better than $10.00 by mid or late 1983 should develop."

Conway anticipates lingering price weakness, with occasional rallies of modest proportion for at least the first half of 1982. High interest rates, which increase the costs of holding silver and create other investment opportunities, and the recession, should remain the overriding influences. He is not totally negative on silver despite certain price depressive considerations. Firstly, recent price declines could have nearly discounted lower inflation rates, the recession and overall lack of interest in silver. Unless the economic situation becomes decidedly worse, or there is an unexpected increase in supplies, he doubts that heavy additional selling pressure will develop, although the market could be searching for a bottom. The net result is that he anticipates only moderate additional silver price weakness during the first half of 1982. He expects the market to find reasonably good buyer interest and support around the $6.50-$7.00 area.

Price stability followed by a more sustained price improvement should develop during late 1982, according to Conway. "Prospects for an economic upturn and lower interest rates could mean rising silver values via increased demand from both the commercial and investor sectors," he told MONEY MAKER. "The projected huge fiscal 1983 budget deficit situation clouds the interest rate outlook, however. Additional potential influences include the November, 1982, elections, a major test of the Reagan Administration's economic policies. A significant shift in the makeup of Congress could send some shocks through the silver market.

"World political considerations are also capable of sudden price impact. The Mid-East, Eastern Europe, and the more recent problems in El Salvador could cause price increases should events in one or more of these areas create an environment that causes a flight from paper into tangibles. Another consideration is a possible reduction in the world oil glut if the level of economic activity increases. This could be accompanied by a threat of OPEC price increases. Just as lower oil prices contributed to the collapse of gold and silver prices, rising oil prices could trigger a big advance," Conway concluded.

Conway sees 1982 as a turning point for the silver market in the sense that the two-year bear market could be coming to an end. If the economy improves as anticipated, a strong advance could commence late in the year and continue during 1983. In summary, a tight monetary policy, recession and reduced inflation could inhibit rally attempts especially during the first half of 1982, but, he believes that the bulk of these and other negative influences has already been discounted by the silver market.

Vincent Valk, senior vice-president of the Unified Securities Corporation, is another recognized expert in commodities trading, and he views the silver market somewhat differently from others in the industry. During 1982, especially at present low levels, he is advising investors to accumulate silver physicals—especially U.S. silver dollars in the best condition one can afford, preferably in mint condition or uncirculated coins. As an alternative, Valk suggests coins minted before July 23, 1965, that contain a high silver content (dimes, quarters and half dollars); and 10-ounce bars or smaller from reputable firms such as Engelhardt, Handy and Harman, and Deak-Perera. One must remember, though, that the smaller the bar (or wafer as they are called), the higher the premium paid for purchase. Valk's rationale for accumulation of silver physicals is based on three salient points:

1. In these recessionary times, silver physicals will give the investor added insurance against further bad times or uncertain economic conditions. Remember, no matter what happens to the silver market, a silver dollar will *always* be worth a dollar in value (because it is legal tender). A silver futures contract or stock in a silver company can always go down below what you paid for it. A coin can *never* decline below its intrinsic worth. From a "survival" point of view, hard assets are always better than soft ones, and they are immediately convertible into cash.

2. By accumulating coins, one never has to worry about the purity (or fineness) of the metal, the costs for certification, insurance, storage handling and other related costs, and one needs to have a relatively small space for storage (like a safety deposit box or some secure place in your home).

3. Silver coins in mint condition and wafers make ideal gifts for birthdays, holidays like Christmas, graduation presents, wedding presents and the like.

Martin Orenzoff, market strategist for Unified Securities, sees the silver market for the remainder of 1982 fluctuating between a low range of $5.50-$6.00 to a high range of $10.50-$11.00.

Steven Jerro, senior technical analyst for Deak-Perera, the international banking firm, sees the intermediate term for silver as a trader's market. "Traders will be buying and short-covering on excessive sell-offs, or the $6.50-$6.85 area (for the spot, or current, month), and selling when the metal hits the $7.80-8.00 area," Jerro predicts. He believes the present dumping (silver is selling at approximately $7) is a result of bad publicity and the fact that the price of gold is dropping. Jerro says that at present (3/10/82) he would only be about 10 percent vested in the market because of its uncertainty and the whiplash back-and-forth movements that are likely to characterize the next few months.

The Outlook for 1982

Stocks of silver in the hands of investors and speculators throughout the world continued to increase during 1981. It is estimated that the accumulation now exceeds 350,000,000 ounces of refined bullion. In addition to this very large supply, there are a number of other significant sources of secondary silver potentially available. The largest of these is the old United States 90% silver coins which have virtually disappeared from circulation. It is estimated that as much as 655,000,000 ounces of silver are still available from this source, depending on price inducement.

These stocks are not the only source over and above new production from which silver can be obtained in the years to come. During the last 15 years, some 500,000,000 ounces came out of India, and silver is continuing to flow into the market from that part of the world. Also, the U.S. Government may resume sales of silver from the strategic stockpile.

Regardless of the exact figures, the existence of these massive stocks, even though not pressed for sale, can be expected to exert a restraining influence on any upward price trend. On the other hand, industrial consumers of silver will look to speculative accumulations as a necessary source of silver, and future price levels are going to depend to a considerable extent on the degree of inducement needed to bring about their liquidation.

In summary, there will continue to be ample supplies of silver in the future as in the past for industrial needs, and while another year of price fluctuations is expected, they will probably not be as violent as in the past two years. The speculator and investor has been a major market factor for a number of years and still holds the key to the future course of silver prices.

Chapter Twenty-Three

Golden Opportunities

Gold has taken a steady, violent hammering since it peaked early in 1980 at $875 per ounce—diving over 60 percent in just two years. One apparent bottom after another has been shattered, and those who bought the metal at its high (often as a hedge against inflation) have seen it perform precisely opposite its intended goals. Even the loudest of the strident "gold bugs" are now hurrying to jump from the metal's crashing bandwagon, and various advisers are predicting a continued decline to below $200 per ounce.

Does all this indicate that gold is a terrible investment? On the surface, definitely, and if gold does indeed sink to, say, $150 per ounce, the surface indications will have proved correct. However, United States citizens are still facing the dual possibilities of hyper-inflation (or at least, a renewed inflationary spiral) and depression.

Gold is internationally liquid, and even those who have watched their bullion lose more than half its value still own the bullion—it is the best available insurance against disaster, and it will continue to serve that role. Of course, this still doesn't justify *investing* in gold, however much it may justify *owning* some of the metal.

But when even the strongest proponents of an investment abandon it, it is time to study it carefully for an "oversold" situation—a time when too many investors have dumped too many holdings, and large hoarders begin to inhale the metal at bargain prices, driving the price straight back up. In short, gold may now be fulfilling the old investment maxim, "Buy when everyone else is selling, and sell when everyone else is buying."

Gold has followed a wave pattern of "ascending bottoms" over the past decade. In 1974, when gold had run from $35 to $200 per ounce, countless people bought in. The metal then slid from $200 back to about $120 per ounce.

The next rise began in 1977 and 1978, when gold was completely out of favor—and it rose to $875. Now, the metal has been battered for some 18 months. Given the percentage changes of the turnarounds for gold over the past decade, a rise to $1500 is certainly possible. Thus, the downside risk from $300 per ounce must be weighed against an upside potential of perhaps $1200 in profits.

In the end, investors who get into gold now, whether it has further bottoms to test or not, may still be those who "Bought straw hats in winter, when nobody wanted them, and sold the hats in the summer, when everybody needed them."

Why Precious Metals?

For 6000 years, gold has been the most prized portable asset for all peoples. One theory about its ancient discovery is that Egyptian farmers noticed unusual yellow stones near the edge of the Nile around 4000 B.C., and its fascination caught on quickly. Simultaneously, New World civilizations coveted the metal, as did people in the Orient. Gold does not tarnish; it can be pounded into almost every conceivable configuration; and it is virtually indestructible—gleaming brightly after centuries underwater, its lustre unchanged after millenia in Egyptian tombs.

These remarkable qualities have earned gold (and its sibling silver) the moniker "incorruptible," which, of course, is deliciously ironic considering the vast numbers of people who have been corrupted by these "incorruptible" metals.

By virtue of their widespread use in jewelry or mintage, three metals are generally designated as "precious": Gold, silver, and platinum. Of these, gold is the unquestioned overlord (except in Japan, where platinum is more greatly coveted in jewelry)—silver and platinum are generally more greatly valued for industrial applications than as precious stores of wealth, these days. (See the chapters on silver and strategic metals for more detailed discussions of silver and platinum.)

Obviously, the human urge to own and hoard gold is not unique to this century (or to the past few years, regardless of appearances). The hard money of most countries in ancient times involved gold coins for the expensive portions of the mintage and silver for the inexpensive portion. (Platinum was only attempted once, in Czarist Russia, and was so poorly received that many of the platinum coins were plated with gold to make them acceptable to the populace!)

In the United States, the gold/silver ratio of 16/1 was fixed by federal law in 1896. However, when the government passed the Silver Act in 1934, the 1896 law was completely disregarded as silver was confiscated at 50 cents an ounce. Of course, the government had confiscated the citizens' gold a year before at $20.67 an ounce. So even though the gold/silver ratio stood at 16/1, the United States Government appropriated its citizens' silver at a ratio of 40/1.

The point is, if during times of depression and weak currency governments become hoarders of precious metals, how can people be blamed for doing the same thing?

For over 500 years, political upheavals, wars, and revolutions have ingrained a "gold mentality" in the people of Europe and Asia. Many families attempted to have a gold reserve in some handy form that could be readily transported across borders or handed down to heirs. With inflation currently afflicting economies on a global scale, and while the United States Government has progressively emptied its gold reserves while increasing the production of paper money, it is understandable that intelligent investors in America have now turned toward such a "chaos hedge" while paper currency continues to become increasingly worthless. And, once again, the possibility of confiscation is being bandied about by financial advisers.

Gold is almost universally found throughout the world. In its natural state, gold occurs in dust, flakes, nuggets, and ores. It is actively retrieved from rivers and creeks as well as the depths of the earth. In terms of annual new mine production, South Africa and the Soviet Union are the world's leading gold producers. After it is mined (or recycled), it is cast into a standard shape and purity. Thus, gold fit for delivery to the London Gold Market arrives in standard 400-troy-ounce bars of minimum 99.5 percent purity. As supply and demand continued to spiral upward, the cash market for precious metals evolved into forward markets in England and futures markets in the U.S.

Gold Trading

The London Gold Market, consisting of five major bullion dealers, has been functioning—with some interruptions—since the 19th Century. Twice each trading day, representatives of the five firms meet in the offices of N.M. Rothschild & Sons to set a mutually agreeable price at which to buy and sell gold bullion. This price, or "fixing," normally occurs at 10 a.m. and 3 p.m. (Eastern Standard Time), and the prices fixed at these meeting are used as a reference for gold traders around the world.

In the late 1960s, three enterprising banks in Zurich accumulated a massive pool of bullion to form a basis for the Zurich Gold market. In addition, daily prices for gold are established in Paris, Frankfurt, Hong Kong, Bombay, Sydney, and elsewhere.

Until the 20th Century, the international gold standard (25.8 grains of 90 percent gold equals $1 U.S. in paper) provided for the free circulation of standardized gold coins between trading nations. In time, this meant that the currency of each nation was tied to a fixed legal price for gold. Naturally, variations in the value of national currencies were determined by their relationships to this gold standard, and each country called a different amount of gold by its own name: 7.32 grams of gold were called a "pound" by the British; 0.29 grams of gold were called a "franc" by the French and the same amount was called a "lire" in Italy; 1.5 grams of gold were called a "dollar" in America, and so on.

The stabilizing effects of this international gold standard broke down in the aftermath of World War I, both in the resulting world depression and the new-found proclivity of governments to print more paper money than could be backed by their gold against this standard. This led to the creation of the gold-exchange standard, where nations fixed the values of their currencies to a foreign currency—the U.S. dollar—which in turn was supposedly fixed to gold.

However, as American commitments abroad siphoned gold reserves from the nation, confidence in the dollar weakened, and the Nixon Administration finally scrapped the gold standard in 1971—possibly forever—in an attempt to preserve the dollar as the world's reserve currency, without its gold backing. (OPEC's reaction to this is well known.)

Subsequent administrations have spared no effort in attempting to sever gold from its role as a monetary metal. This is for the simple reason that if the United States were presently forced to redeem every one of its outstanding dollars with 1.5 grams of gold, an ounce of gold would cost approximately $3300 dollars. However, the rest of the world is somewhat disinclined to de-monetize gold, and from the time the artificial $35 per ounce ceiling was removed from the metal, its price has skyrocketed.

Using 20/20 hindsight, it is easy to see what happened to the value of precious metals since the United States elected to divorce them from the reserve behind our currency. Gold went to $875 an ounce on paper. What this really means, though, is that the U.S. currency shot downward—today, an ounce of gold will buy you a fine suit of clothes; 100 years ago, an ounce of gold would have bought you a fine suit of clothes.

Toward the end of 1979, the American public finally came to realize that in wildly inflationary times and periods of internal and international instability everybody needs a little gold, a little silver, a little land, and so on. So the stage was set for the entrance of the private United States investor on a large scale into the precious metal demand scene. But much of the current demand is coming from institutional investors as well.

In this light, it now makes sense to examine different kinds of gold investments and see what the advantages and disadvantages of each type are to the investor or speculator. The types of investments available in precious metals are:

1. The metals themselves
2. Bullion coins
3. Collector coins (numismatic coins)
4. Medals and medallions
5. Jewelry
6. Shares in companies mining or refining the metals
7. Precious metal funds
8. Precious metal futures
9. Precious metal options
10. Precious metal leverage contracts

Leverage Contracts

While this is a common angle for investing in strategic metals (which are not offered in futures or commodity markets—see the chapter on strategic metals), the best advice regarding gold leverage or limited-risk fixed maturity contracts is, simply avoid them. These are option substitutes, unnecessary when dealing with regulated commodities, and are vended by firms under the scrutiny of the Commodity Futures Trading Commission, which wanted to ban the activity on January 1, 1980, but was persuaded by Congress to hold off. These are clearly on the way out.

Gold Options

Precious metals options are currently vended in the United States by authorized dealers of Mocatta Metals and Metals Quality Corporation, a Mocatta affiliate. Calls—options to buy 100 ounces of gold at a set price for a fixed period of time—are issued and guaranteed by Mocatta through their agents. The buyers pay a money premium to purchase the gold call and can either resell it to Mocatta, if successful, or actually take possession of the optioned gold, if desired. If the option is held until the last day of its "life," and gold is trading at a level lower than the contract or strike price of the gold call, it will expire worthless.

Thus, a speculator can attempt to make money on a Mocatta call if the gold price rises. On the other hand, the speculator is insured of a limited loss in the event gold drops drastically during the life of the option.

The costs of Mocatta gold options are directly related to the volatility of gold prices and the length of time for which the option is issued. Understandably, with the extreme volatility of the precious metals market over the last year or two, option premiums run at a fairly high level. Any authorized Mocatta agent can provide daily option quotes upon request.

Gold Futures

Trading in metals futures was once extremely attractive because the leverage was almost beyond belief. In early 1979, when gold was trading for about $300 an ounce, the margin (deposit) required to buy a $30,000 futures contract was only about $750! However, price volatility in the metal drove margin requirements up, to a high of $20,000 on COMEX and $12,000 on the International Monetary Market of the Chicago Mercantile Exchange. Now, the margin requirements are somewhat lower, as the price of gold has fallen, but they are still fairly high.

Any commodity subject to rapid short-term price changes, like gold, offers gutsy speculators the opportunity to profit from price declines as well as from the upside. However, shorting gold can be a very risky investment, since any kind of international upheaval can send the metal soaring, if only temporarily. (For complete information on futures trading, see the chapter on commodities.)

Despite the great risk of futures trading, though, trading in precious metals futures offers tremendous liquidity. During trading hours—and under normal market circumstances—the owner of a futures contract can liquidate with a phone call and receive the funds the following day. This is clearly part of the appeal in this arena, but the main drawing card is the gargantuan profits that can be gathered in an extremely short time. Of course, this is offset to a degree by the staggering risks of futures trading.

Gold Funds

An investment method which offers far less risk than trading in futures (but which also offers far less in returns) is to participate as a shareholder in one of several mutual funds emphasizing gold investments. Such funds have outstanding long-term records, but their fortunes have declined recently —which could be a clear signal that now is the time to buy into them.

The value of any metal-oriented fund, of course, will rise and fall according to the movement of precious metals prices. For example, in 1980, investors in gold funds would have received gains ranging from 40 to 60 percent. In 1981, though, they would have lost between 15 and 30 percent. But in the long run, the gold-based mutual funds have paid off handsomely.

Such funds have developed as a method for investors without large amounts of capital to participate in gold. Each of the funds has a different investment strategy, but all are involved to differing degrees with South African mining shares, gold exploration, and gold bullion. Among the primary funds are International Investors, Inc, Golconda Investors Ltd., Strategic Investments Fund, Inc., United Services Fund, and Goldfund, Inc.

Table I: GOLD FUNDS

Sales Fund	Minimum Charge	Investment Investment	Percentage Strategy	Changes 1976-81	1981
International Investors	8.5%	$1000	diversified mining and mining finance	+434.55%	−17.86%
United Services Fund	no load	$ 500	gold mining shares, primarily South Africa	+464.06	−27.99
Strategic Investments Fund	8.5%	$ 500	South African mining shares	+493.12	−27.64
Golconda Investors	no load	$ 500	bullion and diversified mining	+222.98	−17.86
Goldfund Inc.	no load	$ 500	bullion, South African and Canadian mining Shares	NA	−32.10

In the period from 1961 to 1981, International Investors was second in the top 25 mutual funds in the country, with an overall gain of slightly over *1340 percent*. International Investors was the top fund for the ten-year period from1971 through 1981, with gains of 884 percent. And for the five-year period from 1976 through 1981, the top three mutual funds in the country were gold funds (respectively, Strategic Investments, United Services, and International Investors), and Golconda also made it onto the top-25 list.

However, 1981 was a bad year for gold, and consequently for the gold funds. 1982 may be sluggish as well, but any rise in the price of gold will place these funds back among the top performers in the nation. Table I shows a cross-section of each fund's operation, along with its recent history. (See chapter on mutual funds for additional information.)

Gold Mining Shares

Much excitement has been generated by the fortunes made through investment in South African gold mining companies. Lately, Australian mines are becoming another focus for mining shares. In either case, the easiest way to participate is through American Depository Receipts (ADRs), which are discussed below.

Approximately 80 percent of the free world's supply of gold comes from South African mining shares. Individual companies obtain long-term leases from the South African government. The companies characteristically returned dividends in the neighborhood of 18 or 20 percent, even when gold prices were falling, and the performance of the bulk of the mines has been outstanding. Table II lists representative South African stocks, their cost at the beginning of 1979, their price at the height of the gold stampede in 1980, and their current prices. At today's radically depressed prices, the South African gold stocks represent exceptional buys.

In addition to the South African mines, investors may participate in Homestake (a United States company), Redlake and Dome in Canada, and in any of several Australian companies, such as MIM Holdings, Queen Margaret Gold Mines, Newmont Mining, Broken Hill Proprietary, or Gold Mines of Kalgoorlie. These are most conveniently purchased in ADRs, like the South African holdings.

Buying American Depository Receipts. Participating in a foreign mine is not much different from buying common stock in a United States company when ADRs are used.

An ADR is the written evidence you receive when you buy shares in a foreign company. In the case of South African mines, for example, the actual share is held either in Johannesburg or London. If you wish, you may obtain the actual share, although this is a time-consuming process both coming and going—you wait three or four months to receive the share, and you spend the same amount of time selling it, because of exchange rates, handling, transfer of title, and on and on.

Any one of four major banks—Morgan Guaranty Trust Company, First National City Bank, Irving Trust Company, or Chemical Bank of New

Table II:
PERFORMANCE OF SOUTH AFRICAN MINING SHARES

	Price Per Share		
South African Mines (ADRs)	3/26/80	3/30/81	3/19/82
Blyvoorizicht	$12	$16⅛	$ 8¼
Buffelsfontein	29	44	29
Doornfontein	12	21	10¾
Driefontein Consolidated	21	28¼	19½
Durban Deep Levels	25	25½	10¼
East Rand Proprietary	21	20¼	7¾
Free State Geduld	49	75	21⅝
Harmony	18	19½	10¼
Hartebeestfontein	51	65½	34½
Kinross	11	15¼	8⅝
Kloof	27	33½	22⅜
Leslie	3	3⅜	1¾
Libanon	19	19½	11½
Loraine	6	5³/₁₆	1¹³/₁₆
President Brand	33	45	27¾
President Steyn	33	42	22⅜
Randfontein	62	64	36½
St. Helena	35	39	22½
Southvaal	19	30¼	21⅛
Stilfontein	19	21½	11½
Vaal Reefs	52	73	41¾
Welkom	13	16⅝	7¼
Western Areas	7	6⅝	2½
Western Deep Levels	33	51¼	23
Western Holdings	55	76	31¾
Winkelhaak	25	35½	21⅜

York—can issue an ADR as evidence of your purchase of a gold stock.

Each of the banks charges a fee for the service, just as a broker would if you were buying American stock. The charge covers the transfer and registration of the ADRs as well as dividend payments to you. The dividends are paid semi-annually, and a 15 percent withholding tax is first taken out by the mining company (in South Africa).

In one sense, the purchase of South African gold mining ADRs is similar to the purchase of an annuity offering a varying rate of return from year to year. This is due to the *finite* life of the mine—South African mining companies maintain their lease holdings for a specific number of years, and are expected to go out of business at the end of the period of time. Generally speaking, when less than ten years are left in the corporate life of a South African gold company, the value of its shares may decrease year by year—if there are no dramatic increases in the price of gold.

If a mine has a life of over 15 years ahead of it, the present value will increase, even if there is only a modest escalation in the price of gold. In the case of a new mine that has not yet started paying dividends (or is paying only nominal dividends), the value of the shares will increase year by year for at least several years.

What the ADR does is it essentially lets the purchaser avoid having to go to the foreign country for quotes and avoid having to convert dollars into another currency to buy. The ADR certificate is as fully guaranteed by the issuing bank as is the stock of any U.S. company. Upon purchasing the stock, the proper number of shares is transferred into your name as the registered shareholder just as quickly as if you were buying AT&T.

Selling the shares is equally simple and speedy, and monitoring them is no problem, either—the South African gold stocks are listed daily in *The Wall Street Journal* and weekly in *Barron's,* quoted in dollars.

For additional information, the *Mining Journal,* a quarterly review published in London, contains the most objective, factual information obtainable. And, of course, there are stockbrokers who specialize in analyzing South African gold shares and vending them to the public.

Jewelry

This is another form of investing in precious metals, although gems and collector value also comprise part of this area. In Japan, *the* precious metal for jewelry is platinum, but in Europe and the United States gold holds sway.

In addition to intrinsic value, jewelry represents both creativity and innovation. Some jewelry, because of its craftsmanship, is priceless and is generally not coveted for its monetary value alone. Liquidation of jewelry is singularly poor, as well.

Investors who are interested in jewelry for its precious metal content should also be aware that gold in jewelry is rarely "pure" gold. In this regard, gold jewelry is labeled acording to its karat content as follows:

Karat Count	Purity
24	100 percent gold
22	91 percent gold
18	75 percent gold
14	58 percent gold
10	41 percent gold

A karat is a unit of gold fineness equal to $1/24$ proportion of pure gold. Pure gold jewelry (24K) is rarely found simply because it is too soft for normal wear. In Europe, gold is synonymous with 18K. In America, gold jewelry is mostly formed from 14K and 10K metal; any metal containing less than 41 percent gold cannot be called "gold" in the United States.

Traditionally, precious metals have been weighted according to the troy system of measurement:

- 1 troy pound equals 12 ounces, or 240 pennyweights, or 5760 grains

- 1 troy ounce equals 20 pennyweights, or 480 grains
- 1 pennyweight equals 24 grains, or .05 ounce
- 1 grain equals .041 pennyweight or .002285 ounce

Thus, when submitting old jewelry for recycling, it should be born in mind that there are 20 pennyweights of fine gold per troy ounce. If the jeweler offers $20 a pennyweight for the gold in an 18K item, he or she is offering $400 an ounce for 75 percent pure gold. A person can arrive at what a proper price for a pennyweight of pure gold should be by simply dividing the day's gold fix by twenty.

Medals and Medallions

Investment in medals and medallions containing gold is not recommended for those seeking sale in the short term. Quite often, the price expended for new medallions alleged to have collector value will never be redeemed in the collector's lifetime. These items bear sentiment and are artifacts of history, but as investments they are questionable at best.

Collector Coins and Bullion Coins

This is not the case with collector coins. Any uncirculated coins containing precious metal have been increasing in value year after year. The prime reason for such annual appreciation is simply the growing number of collectors—each seeking the same limited supply of collector coins. The institutional entrance into the rare coin field has also fueled price rises. Most important in this area is the advice of an expert; most people do not have the necessary familiarity with this market to make educated decisions on their own.

Bullion coins, on the other hand, are valued strictly for their gold content based on the current price of gold in the marketplace. In effect, bullion coins are simply substitutes for the noble metals themselves, issued mainly to earn a premium on the gold for the nation striking them. On the other hand, if numismatic value of the coins can be demonstrated, you may be considered a collector rather than a hoarder and thus be safe from confiscation. In any case, the premium on South African Krugerrands, for example, has ranged from seven to 10 percent above the London gold fix.

It is usually better for smaller quantity gold buyers to purchase bullion coins rather than bullion itself. A major consideration is liquidity; an investor can sell from 10 to 1000 buillion coins and receive funds from the sale promptly. This assuredly is not the case when selling to a bullion dealer. This type of sale is subject to examination—destructive or otherwise—because bullion dealers trust nobody and they invariably cut the bars to check for authenticity.

The most popular bullion coins are those that contain precisely one ounce of fine gold in each coin: the South African Krugerrand and the Canadian Maple Leaf. The Austrian 100 Kronen contains slightly less than one ounce of fine gold (33.8753 grams of 90 percent gold) and is quite acceptable for purchase as a gold substitute. The Mexican 500 Peso gold coin is also a beautiful coin, but it trades at too high a premium for investors interested solely in a gold substitute.

Bullion

Purchase of gold bullion has traditionally required either considerable capital or ready credit in large amounts—often a combination of both. For example, an investor contemplating purchase of a single gold bar, good for London market delivery, would require $200,000 if the price of gold were as low as $500 per ounce. Buyers of less than five bars would probably have to pay a premium since only orders of 2000 ounces (five bars) or more would go at the fixing price. Thus an order for five gold bars at $500 an ounce would come to one million dollars worth of bullion. If the buyer had excellent credit, this could be financed for only 10 percent down. However, 10 percent is $100,000.

The minimum amount sold by bullion dealers is generally one kilogram—slightly less than 33 ounces. Some reliable sources also vend one to ten ounce "bars," which are stampings.

Lately, banks are offering gold and silver "passbook" accounts in precious metals. An example is the First National Bank of Chicago, which offers such a plan. The minimum amount of gold that may be purchased initially is five ounces, and this balance must be maintained. Thereafter, the investor may add to the account in one ounce increments. The bank charges one-eighth of one percent of the U.S. dollar value per quarter (or one-half percent per year) for storage and insurance. The option to receive the gold itself is also open to investors, and they are charged $25 for the transfer of title. The commissions are scheduled, with the maximum being two percent of the cash value of any transaction up to 25 ounces.

A corollary to this program has been around somewhat longer, which is also offered by banks, and is also called a "passbook" account. The investor initially deposits $1000 and can purchase gold bullion in multiples of $100 as often as desired. This investment is pooled with money from other investors, and gold purchases are made for the account slightly above the London fix.

PRECIOUS METALS INVESTMENT STRATEGIES

Once you have become aware of the different methods available for investing in precious metals, the next step is to decide which metal(s) and what form(s), of it—funds, options, futures, coins, bullion, or mining shares—offers you the best current investment opportunity. After this decision has been made, immediately forget all the other alternatives for the time being and concentrate on the chosen target. Learn all you can about the fundamental supply/demand situation in the metal of your choice to help guide your decisions.

If futures happen to be your choice, you can obtain free reports from any commodity commission merchant who is a member of major exchanges and handles orders for the public. The Futures Industry Association located in Washington, D.C., the COMEX in New York, the Chicago Board of Trade, and the Chicago Mercantile Exchange (IMM division) can send you literature listing names of their members. Any of these sources can provide you with information about gold and silver futures. If platinum is selected, the New York Mercantile Exchange can supply appropriate literature.

Obtain charts showing past price performances of the metal futures you're interested in. The charts are offered free from almost any exchange member. There are also many businesses offering chart services. One of the best is Commodity Research Bureau, 1 Liberty Plaza, New York City. This source, like all the charting services, charges for its information.

After you have selected which metal future to trade in, you should consider your financial situation, the limits of financial exposure desired, the points at which trades will be made, and so on. Having formulated your "trading plan," it is time for action.

Paper trade for at least three months. This means putting your plan of action on paper, as if it were actually carried out at a commodity brokerage firm. Paper trading will season you to calculate your equity on a daily basis and make any necessary adjustments or alterations to the plan, based upon market movements. It will also teach you to keep accurate daily records of each paper transaction, and this habit will be useful when your plan is actually put into operation later.

At the end of three months, analyze the results and see for yourself if it pays to take the risks involved in trading metal futures.

If the risks seem too great, or you haven't the capital to trade futures actively, explore the other possibilities. Mining shares in gold can be as expensive as bullion and futures, but they return dividends. The same is true for silver. (See the chapter on silver for a discussion of silver mining shares.)

In addition, a valid approach for the small investor is modest but regular investments in coins—silver or gold, bullion or collectibles. When the gold price exploded in 1979 and early 1980, purchasing Krugerrands in excess of $850 became, to say the least, burdensome. When the price dropped to the neighborhood of $500, such purchases became more realistic, but still prohibitively expensive for many investors. So investors turned to silver coins of the past, in large part—American silver dollars to be specific.

However, there are also gold bullion coins today that will function as well. The Soviet Union, for example, offered the Chevronetz in 1979, a ¼-ounce gold coin which retailed for slightly more than one quarter of the price of an ounce of gold. Canada has also offered half-ounce coins; and many Mexican coins (ranging from the two-peso to the 20-peso pieces) offer a chance to accumulate bullion in small increments. Probably the most popular among these smaller gold coins are the Krugerrands in ½, ¼, and ¹/₁₀ ounce sizes. With the ¹/₁₀ ounce Krugerrand, the investor can accumulate gold very inexpensively, when compared to the larger coins.

A bit of research indicates that certain countries still circulate coins containing silver, which are trading at artificially low values because of governmental fiat. Thus, until mid-February, 1980, it was possible to gather silver-containing French 10, 20, and 50 franc pieces at bargain prices. But in mid-February, the French government suddenly "demonetized" those coins and local shops were mobbed as the citizenry turned them in for French paper currency at eight to 10 times their face value. The point is, any coin that actually contains a precious metal is worth far more than its denomination.

Since 1975, various large New York Stock Exchange member firms have entered the coin business—notably Merrill Lynch, Bache, and Thomson McKinnon. Deak Perera and Manfred, Tortella and Brooks are among the larger coin dealers who cater to the investing public. Potential gold and silver coin investors should cautiously deal only with large, reputable firms. Dealing with local coin stores or with telephone or mail solicitors offering bargains increases market risk, and coin investing is an area that requires either trust or a great deal of expertise on the part of the investor.

Check Information Sources

People who invest in precious metals, of course, have more than just a passing interest in daily market activity. The *American Metal Market*, a daily trade paper published by Fairchild in New York City, is probably the best single source to follow. Another good reference is the daily *Journal of Commerce* which has covered all markets for over 150 years. Daily reporting on metals can also be found in *The Wall Street Journal*. For those following the market in coins, there are several reliable magazines and newsletters, including *Coin Collecting*, published by Krauss Publications in Iola, Wisconsin, and *The COINfidential Report*, published by Bale Publishing in New Orleans. There are several others as well.

At some point, precious metals investors may want to liquidate their holdings, or some portion of their holdings. In stocks, this is easily conducted through your broker, of course. As regards bullion or collector coins, it is always best to consult with the same type of reliable firms as previously mentioned. Bullion firms such as J. Aron or Mocatta normally do not deal directly with the retail public. They are wholesalers who will not handle orders for less than, say, 100 Krugers or 100 Kroners. Chances are, however, that one or more of their agents will handle lots as small as 10 coins or 10 ounces of gold. A query to Mocatta or J. Aron would probably produce a list of authorized agents in your vicinity to contact about sale information.

Whenever possible, avoid selling bullion coins or coins below collector grade at an auction. The fee for doing this can slash into the proceeds. Charges as high as 40 percent can be levied—especially when the dollar value of the auction is relatively small.

The Future of Precious Metals

Where will metals go in 1982 and beyond? While it seems fair to assume that the past performance of the metals cannot guarantee equal success in the future, the facts involved in trading dynamics and hoarding (and supply/demand verities) would suggest that a price collapse is unlikely.

History has indicated that gold, silver, and platinum (to say nothing of the base metals and strategic metals) have only one long-term trend to follow—and that is up. Each fall from the peaks lands in a higher valley. The following chart shows what happened to the metals in the past decade, and current prices (which are substantially down from their highs):

		Price per troy ounce		
Metal	1970	High: 1980	3/30/81	3/19/82
Gold	$40	$ 875	$539	$327
Silver	1.40	50	13	7
Platinum	$80	1025	475	475

In the meantime, there is little doubt that the world is running out of precious metals. Gold is the most abundantly found; between stocks above ground and reserves still in the ground, there is estimated to be more than a 100-year supply of visible and unrecovered metal. However, industry depends upon gold least among the three metals.

Silver, on the other hand, is absolutely essential to many facets of industry, and is much less prevalent than gold—estimates of free world supply, indicate that less than 25 years worth of silver remains in the world, should demand continue to increase annually (which it is likely to do). Platinum is the rarest of the three major precious metals, and experts feel that less than 15 years remain before all known supplies are exhausted, should demand continue at present rates.

Obviously, precious metals can be recovered from finished materials. Coins can be melted, heirlooms converted back into their basic metals from alloyed conditions. But although recycling aids tremendously in filling annual supply shortfalls, the world is still running out of metal.

However, waiting in the winds is the development of atomic fusion. Should scientists eventually be able to control the heat of fusion, which immediately returns recycled materials into their natural components, and apply it safely and properly, the world's metal problems could be solved. But while progress has been steadily made in this area, we are still years away from converting fusion research to fusion technology. And in the meantime, precious metals are almost sure to remain on a steadily rising curve—at least as long as the United States and the world are plagued by cost-push inflation. And the constantly increasing cost of power will also do its part to keep the prices of metals high.

Gold's Dependence on Oil

To mine precious metals, refine them, cast them in salable forms, ship, store, and guard them takes plenty of power—and the prime source for this power at present is oil.

Since oil and gold are both universally vended in dollars, there can be little doubt that if the price of oil keeps rising, the value of gold and other precious metals will respond accordingly. Conversely, in the event that oil prices decline (as they have for several months), the price of gold and other precious metals would probably likewise decline, which it has.

And while it is relatively safe to assume that precious metal prices will continue to rise over the long term, there are situations in which prices can undergo short, but drastic, declines. This could happen any time major stockpilers suddenly stop investing and liquidate their holdings. For example, any sale from the United States Strategic Stockpile of silver will push the price of that metal down.

At the present time, there are two major categories of holders and hoarders of precious metals: OPEC members and their citizenry and central banks of countries around the world. In both categories there is little likelihood of any significant precious metal sales in the near future, simply because such sales would only produce more depreciating dollars as United States inflation accelerates.

One consequence of this trend is that OPEC nations have begun demanding that oil payments be made in a "basket of currencies" rather than American dollars. However, OPEC's power has declined with the world oil glut.

The probability of future gold sales by central banks is also one that defies reality—although the United States has a vested interest in the continued demonetization of gold. For many years it has been the thrust of cautious central banks, such as in West Germany and Switzerland, to partially remonetize gold and re-establish its rightful place as backing for paper money. The formation of the European Monetary System during 1979, when nine countries pooled reserves to back a new money supported by a 1 to 2 gold-to-paper ratio, is proof of this desire. Of course, the United States printing presses have been churning out dollars in the meantime, and any remonetization of gold would be devastating to the U.S. currency.

But the International Monetary Fund has also been conducting gold auctions for years in order to provide gold for third-world countries and thus "strengthen" their currencies.

In any case, since there were no significant sales of gold by either central banks or large OPEC investors when gold prices exceeded $850 per ounce, the chances of future sales at lower prices seem slim.

Gold in a Depression

But what would happen to precious metals in an industrial depression? What would happen to precious metal prices in hyperinflation? Reagan's policies could easily give us either unpleasant alternative.

In either case, small holders might be inclined to liquidate; but that would be rather ill-advised. In a recession (or hyperinflation)—and the worsening depression that generally follows either—business performance deteriorates: Corporate failures and defaults increase, bonds are not redeemed on schedule, indebted companies go into receivership, and common stock holders historically have been wiped out by any corporate reorganization in favor of debt holders.

Essentially, investment in non-financial assets like precious metals are superior during times of recession and depression. In hyperinflation, paper currency becomes worthless, yet precious metals retain or reassert their ancient monetary values. Of course, precious metal values would decline in instances of national deflation, but only in relation to quantities of paper currency, not in a sense of true value. Although a deflationary collapse is certainly possible in the United States, the first stage of that scenario seems likely to be increased inflation. In either condition, ownership of precious metals stands in a favorable light.

The United States inflation rate is primed to rise to 25 percent or 30 percent, possibly higher—and the government cannot be trusted to do anything significant to stop it. (Although inflation is currently declining, the Federal Reserve may be forced to reinflate in order to prevent a depression.) This obvious goad to shift money into inflation hedges and hard assets will simply create ever-greater demands at all levels of American life for precious metals. And prices for the metals will have only one direction to go—up.

Even if wage/price controls were placed upon everything salable in the United States, precious metal prices abroad would probably continue to rise, because large exporters overseas would have nowhere else to go with dollars except real property, equity investment in operating companies, or precious metals.

Since investments in real estate and operating companies require time-consuming management, it is quite understandable that precious metals appeal to many investors who are seeking an easy-to-maintain, portable, and liquid storehouse of wealth.

Of course, there is one additional possibility that can cause the prices of precious metals to collapse, which was mentioned at the beginning of this chapter—governmental confiscation. Can it happen again? Of course. For this reason, many investors in precious metals make their purchases in the United States and conduct financing and storge operations elsewhere—preferably in London or Switzerland—while they hold enough gold to escape the country, if necessary.

Chapter Twenty-Four

Turning Penny Stock Into Dollars

For the cost of a package of peanut M&Ms, you could have bought two or even three shares in a brand new oil exploration company. For what you might pay for a package of cigarettes, a gallon of gasoline, or a beer in your local bar, you could have bought five or ten shares of the same stock. And for the price of a brake job on your car, you could have had 2500 shares of oil exploration!

What would you have received for letting your car sit for a while? If the shares had been in Loch Exploration at 10 cents apiece, you would have sold it less than a year later for almost $1.80—$250 would have turned into $4500!

What is this miraculous, wild investment? Penny stocks, of course—that much-maligned realm considered suitable for either old women or wild-eyed gamblers with limited funds. The more lenient in the investment community consider penny stocks an entertaining pastime to be conducted in the lulls between ''serious'' investments, and anyone holding any of these views is absolutely wrong.

Penny stocks are loosely defined as those issues selling for less than one dollar per share, although a more liberal view includes stocks priced up to five dollars per share. (However, this becomes a gray area quite quickly—if the five dollar criterion is used, then International Harvester should be considered a penny stock, even though it is listed in the Dow Jones Industrial Average.) Basically, pennies are those stocks not listed on the large exchanges and selling for very low prices, when compared to the ''blue chip'' issues.

Are they risky? Of course—many are issued by untested companies that have just begun offering shares on the over-the-counter (OTC) market for the first time, and their prices can move with blinding speed. Jerome Wenger, publisher of the *Penny Stock Newsletter*, watched his ten-cent shares of Chipola Gas & Oil shoot to a dollar per share in a few weeks and then drop even more quickly back down to six cents. However, he has also seen a $2000 investment in Applied Medical Devices grow to $44,000 in just one year, and his $1000 investment in Premier Energy earn him $15,000 in 11 months! Such are the risks and rewards of penny stocks.

However, the risk is actually somewhat limited. You can often acquire 5000 shares in a new company for as little as $500—although you can lose the $500, that is the most you can lose.

In short, no other investment offers such astronomical returns in such a short period of time. Of course, the low-priced shares are in no way as secure as T-bills or CDs, but the payoff—when it comes—is vastly better. In fact, the gains are so spectacular that a strange thing happens to penny stock speculators— they begin to consider profits of 400 or 500 percent mundane, and concentrate on gaining 1200 to 1700 percent!

To be sure, there are many, many losers as well as the dramatic winners. After several years of strong growth, the penny stock market fell into some disfavor in 1981 (although it is still threatening to bypass the New York Stock Exchange) after a banner year in 1980. This was probably because the high-flying oil exploration and high-technology area lost their swarms of misguided but enchanted investors.

But penny stocks are still hot, and absolutely *anyone* can participate in them, from the smallest of small investors with only $400 at hand to giant corporations with millions to risk. While the pennies have remained the realm of the small investor (and probably will), the tremendous profits available won't be denied.

Why Penny Stocks?

There are plenty of good reasons, not the least of which is the low cost. But many disillusioned investors are turning away from the major exchanges and toward the OTC market for another, equally compelling reason—they feel the NYSE and American Stock Exchange are controlled 80 percent by institutions. For these people, investing in the conventional market became a frustrating, unrewarding, costly experience. Instead, they have found their oasis in penny stocks, where mutual funds, banks, and insurance companies— which can call the shots on the NYSE and the Amex—wouldn't dare to risk their huge blocks of cash.

Unlike the major exchanges, where specialists function as institutionalized market makers, the market makers for penny stocks can create a free trading environment—when you put your money into the OTC market, you have as much chance as anyone else to profit from your decision, regardless of the sums involved.

As was mentioned above, penny stocks are loosely defined as those issues selling for below $5 per share. Most such stocks are traded over-the-counter (OTC). In the OTC market, there is no central location (exchange) where the shares are traded. Such stocks have not yet met the listing requirements (minimum assets, capital, number of shareholders owning given amounts of the stock, and on and on) of the New York or American Stock Exchange. And this can give the investor more room to bargain for the best price, since any given stock is bought and sold through several dealers rather than through a single specialist, as is the case on the major exchanges.

Investing in Penny Stocks

Before 1971, investors shopped for OTC stocks like they shopped for cars. Market makers, like car dealers, could offer widely varying prices for the exact same stock, and such gouging was certainly common. The only way the investor could communicate with a market maker was via the telephone, and the only way they could determine whether or not they were getting the best price was to call several different market makers—who were often scattered across the country.

Then enter the NASDAQ (the National Association of Securities Dealers Automated Quotations system)—a computerized quotation system which displays the highest bid and lowest offer of all the market makers handling a particular stock. In addition to legitimizing the entire OTC stock system, this assures investors of receiving pretty much the best available price for an issue.

However, OTC stocks which have not yet met the listing requirements of NASDAQ are still traded in the old mode—and investors must call cautiously around to various market makers in order to establish the best prices.

In a way, though, you will still receive the best prices from the disparate market makers. To buy an OTC stock, you must usually call a brokerage house—who can buy the stock whether or not they are the market makers. The brokerage house buys the stock you want from the market maker, adding their commission to the commission already being charged by the market maker. In other words, you can pay eight percent extra for the stock, on top of the five to ten percent already being charged by the market maker—sometimes it's best to contact the market maker directly, which is always the case with OTC stocks not included in the NASDAQ.

To find a market maker, check with your broker or look in a publication devoted to penny stocks.

Of course, pennies are also listed on the NYSE, Amex, the other major exchanges (Philadelphia, Midwest, and Pacific), and on the regional exchanges, such as those in Salt Lake City, Spokane, Denver, and Vancouver. To purchase low-priced stocks listed on the regional exchanges, you must work through a broker who is a member of the exchange, or have your own broker do so. Once your broker is acting as an additional middleman, you may again end up paying extra commissions. Finding the regional brokers isn't easy, either, but it can be done—look through the yellow pages for the city you want, or check the listings in the penny stock periodicals.

New Issues

All companies offering stock to the public for the first time will initially sell those shares in the OTC market. Consequently, these so-called "new issues" are viewed as "ground-floor" opportunities by many investors. Most of the stocks, though, are highly speculative in nature; but when you choose the genuine winners destined for a long life and probable movement from the OTC market to the NYSE or Amex, the payoff is tremendous. The trick, therefore, is to minimize risk.

During the 1979-80 penny stock boom, speculators couldn't get enough of the raging new issues—anything and everything seemed to go up. This, in turn, validated the "bigger sucker" theory and prompted some underwriters to ignore the quality of the companies they brought public. And this led to a temporary waning in public interest.

Suddenly, there was a glut on the OTC market, especially in oil issues. This combined with a general market downturn and a worldwide oil surplus to force investors to become more selective about new issue purchases. Marginal companies that had been swept along by the emotional furor of the boom were suddenly forced to rest on their own merits, and many collapsed in the aftermarket (public OTC trading).

People's blood begins to boil when they see stocks like Loch Exploration turning $1000 into $17,800 in one year, and it makes little or no difference whether a company has sound prospects or not. Once the public catches the fancy of a stock, its shares shoot up in percentage leaps that are simply astounding. But most penny stocks tumble just as quickly as they rise—when mining claims prove worthless, or escalating prices have discounted even real future profits into the next century.

Many disenchanted speculators who get in on "hot issues" at their peaks claim that the companies promoting such stocks never expect the equities to make money—they just want to cash in on new or newly promoted issues. Such claims are not without justification, but if some promoters are uninterested in real values, so are many of the speculators—who rely on the "bigger sucker" theory.

Such traders don't really expect a company to become profitable (or care if it does) but buy low-priced new issues anyway, planning to sell them to bigger suckers who always seem to come along later and buy the stock at inflated prices. While such a strategy may work for a time in a booming market, it has the same flaw as a Ponzi Scheme—it has to fall apart eventually, which is precisely what it did in 1981.

Better to seek companies which rise and stay up—the ones that actually have something going for them. Remember, most junior exploration companies *do* hope to make the next big find; most new technology companies *do* expect to become the future's IBM; and although the percentage of those who succeed is small, numerically there are many.

However, investors should take a lesson from this boom/bust cycle—do your homework before leaping into the new issue market.

Analyze the Prospectus

Many new issues are "concept" companies with no tangible assets, no prior operating history, no management expertise, and a questionable business plan. In other words, their risk is high. Conventional trading strategies would dictate that potential investors investigate past performance of the stock from both a trading aspect and an earnings/growth view, but most new issues have no trading history and a non-existent operating background.

So, given that conventional analyses are difficult at best and impossible at worst, what can you do? The only real key is through the company's prospectus—the offering circular which the Securities and Exchange Commission (SEC) requires be provided to potential investors.

Unfortunately, no two prospectuses are identical. A general format is followed, of course, because the SEC requires it, but the language, illustrations, and disclosures vary a great deal.

The SEC mandates a full disclosure of all facts and data before a company can make an initial or secondary offering of securities to the investing public. Most companies use 40 or 50 pages to do so, and all comply with the letter of the law. However, anyone who has taken a close look at advertising certainly knows that words can be artfully used to give a good impression, even while delivering a ''full disclosure'' of very negative facts.

But with nothing else to go on, a careful reading of the company's prospectus is absolutely necessary. Since the prospectus relates the complete story of a company planning to go public, it can serve very well as a guide prior to making an investment decision. Just remember that while the company must disclose important facts regarding its history (if any), management, current operation, and so on, it is still giving its very best effort to convince the reader that an investment in its venture would be wise—after all, a prospectus is a selling document. Both the underwriter and the issuing company will present themselves in the best conceivable light, so you have to be discerning.

The cover page of a prospectus generally reads like a billboard or a ''get rich quick'' advertisement, only more lurid, if that is possible. The company name will blaze proudly from the top of the page. Below it will be a bold (as required by law) warning: ''These securities have not been approved or disapproved by the SEC, nor has it passed on the accuracy or adequacy of the prospectus.'' This warning also forbids the underwriter from making any comments on the securities other than information contained in the prospectus.

The underwriter is the firm or individual engaged in the sale or distribution of the security. Often, when a stock is being sold to the public, the underwriter will invite other security dealers to participate, creating a selling group. However, there will still be a lead underwriter who is responsible for disposing of the largest quantity of the stock. Frequently, a close relationship exists between the underwriter and the issuing company.

Back to the prospectus. The front page, in addition to the company name and the SEC disclaimer, will also contain the price per share of the stock (as of the offering date), the commission siphoned off to the underwriter (you didn't really think they did it because they believed in the company's goals, did you?) and the proceeds of each stock sale that will go to the company. The usual fee for the underwriter is about 20 percent of the selling price. If the underwriter's fee exceeds that amount, be very careful—high underwriter commissions can be an indication that the underwriter believes the issue will be difficult to sell. It could mean that the underwriter intends to take profits from the issue quickly, on a high commission, and it should be considered a danger flag in the prospectus.

In addition, the degree of risk is listed on the front page of the prospectus. Don't be automatically dismayed by the words "high degree of risk" or "only for the speculative investor," since almost all new issues must say this. It's perfectly true, of course, but it doesn't give any real indication that one company is any riskier than another. However, those which *do not* include this warning, rare though they are, can be considered secure investments.

The front cover also lists the number of shares being offered. This is alternately known as the size of the issue, and there is generally a correlation between this figure and the price of the stock—the lower the price, the greater the number of shares being offered. After all, most new companies need to raise roughly the same amount of capital, and they can either offer 100 shares at $10,000 apiece or 10 million shares at ten cents apiece to accumulate a million dollars.

Last, but not least, the cover page includes the name of the chief underwriter and the date of the prospectus. In short, a lot of information is included on the prospectus cover, all of it presented factually and in full compliance with SEC requirements.

Inside the prospectus, the story is somewhat different. Since any prospectus is essentially designed to promote sales, the company brochure may include photographs of new, "revolutionary" equipment being developed by the company or the beaming countenances of the company principals, all having at least a vague conneciton to the major function of the company. New organizations engaged in scientific work are famous for displaying photographs of their new water treatment devices, or the enthusiastic grin of a scientist in a lab smock testing a complicated piece of equipment designed to isolate a marketable microbe, and on and on and on. True or not, in a phrase, don't be overwhelmed by photographs. Just because an intensely active and excited drilling rig is pictured (although if anyone has the audacity to picture the gusher of movie romance, chuckle all the way to the SEC with your lawsuit—it just doesn't happen that way), it doesn't necessarily mean it is *their* rig, or that they own more than one. A picture may be worth a thousand words, but when those words are specifically designed to misrepresent the facts, a picture is a perfect way to lie without actually stating untruths (for which one can be prosecuted) in a prospectus.

With little more to go on, however, a prospectus may assist you in making an investment decision. In other words, always ask for it in advance. Generally speaking, if you don't find any thinly veiled lies in it, the company deserves further scrutiny. If you invest, you will receive a prospectus, in most cases, but by then, you have already turned over your cash—ask your broker to obtain a prospectus *before* you buy.

The first few pages will contain a detailed history (if any) of the company, what it does, and how long it has been doing whatever it does. This will be followed by a selected financial statement. At all times bear in mind that this is a sales document, and you will have to glean the hard information from between the lines of the glowing prose—it is like watching a television advertisement for a giant oil company: For all their sincere talk of concern for America's energy needs, it is best to remember that their annual profits run in the billions and that they sold crude to both sides in World War II.

In the end, financial statements from young companies have little real value. Read such information, but then move quickly on to the section entitled "Risk Factors"—these can depress even a recent lottery winner. If you can get through this section without bursting into tears, the company may be worthwhile. The area of paramount importance in the risk section is a review of the company's development. One tip: If the company grew out of a previously bankrupt firm but retained many of the same directors as the Chapter XI company, use the prospectus to line your garbage can—most are printed on paper that absorbs grease.

Examine Management and the Underwriter

This leads naturally to two other very important areas of the prospectus— management and the underwriter. If these areas contain flaws, as you perceive them, the company is doomed—they could have the best idea in the history of the world and you're still practically guaranteed of a loss, in the long run.

Many experts agree that a company is only as good as its management—that management is the key to a company's success or failure. This is most certainly true in the early stages of a company's development, although good arguments can be made against this premise when talking about older, established firms. Carefully read the description of the experience and education of the company's managing officers, particularly as regards the company's field. If it is an oil and gas exploration company, make sure the company's principals have experience in petroleum geology, for example. If an officer has knowledge of the business area and experience in the field, don't worry about formal education. However, if the principals don't have business experience in oil and gas drilling, for example, or past jobs with petro-chemical companies, then formal education in petroleum geophysics can compensate. For example, a company might have a chief engineer with no business expertise or a previous career with a biotechnical company, but if he or she just completed a Ph.D. program in genetic engineering at Harvard, you can be reasonably sure that officer knows the field.

If all three areas are lacking, though, why on earth should you pay for on-the-job-training? In addition, if the company's principal officers hold other jobs—meaning they will be giving your potential investment part-time effort—dump it. There are so many related issues entering the market all the time that there is absolutely no reason to select any but those which satisfy all your requirements.

Be especially wary of nepotism in the prospectus. If all or many of the company's executives are related to one another, take it as a strong danger sign—when the Director, Associate Director, Executive Director, Executive Assistant , and Fulfillment Manager all have the the the same last name, leave the company to stew in its family juices. You know the situation: Nephew Joe flunked out of the fourth college in as many years and no one knows what to do with him, and now he is employed as director of training. Aunt Betsy always had an inkling that she was temperamentally suited to executive work, and she got sick of soaps and the crosswords, so now she's the chief of operations and makes the best cheese blintzes in the executive pyramid. If you see signs of nepotism in the prospectus and feel exceptionally generous, send a check to the family fund. But don't invest your money in the company's stock. Of course, this isn't true in every case—but why take chances?

Salaries doled out to corporate management can also be an informal signal of whether you should buy or avoid. Although there isn't a clear guideline, astronomical salaries for the company's principals can often be taken as a sign that the company's executives are using the new issue to get rich as fast as they can. Apply the "prudent person principle."

You want to determine whether or not the salaries are excessive for the role played by the executives in the company's organization. To use an exaggerated example, you should not invest in a company where the president—who sits on the boards of six companies and is retired, giving four hours a month to the new prospect—is drawing a salary of $50,000 per year in lieu of assuming his actual duties in 1995. It would be safe to assume that this person's salary is somewhat excessive, and that the promoters must want his name more than his abilities.

A related indicator of a company's potential is the number of employees. If the company has been operating for several years, and its staff has steadily increased during that time, take it as a good sign for the future.

Assess the Underwriter

Rating the underwriter can be valuable, although this is sometimes overrated as an indicator of company strength. Many Wall Street followers will swear that a good underwriter will move a stock up, so they recommend taking a close look at this aspect of a new issue. However, this "rule-of-thumb" has not proved itself valid over the years.

Certain underwriters seem to do a better job than others when it comes to screening companies before deciding to bring them onto the market. But basing your investment decision is like betting the jockeys at a racetrack—even the best rider draws a nag every now and again. At the same time, you would do well to review the performance of the issues sold by an underwriter over the past two years. This sounds more complex than it is, because the list is generally not long. An investment firm will usually underwrite a maximum of four or five new issues a year, so it is a relatively easy process to compare initial offering prices with current levels—just ask your broker for the names of the companies. If the underwriter has a good record, it always helps.

Of course, the prospectus isn't the only consideration. The penny stock market does not operate in a vacuum, after all. The same economic and political environment that affects the major exchanges shapes the performance of the penny stock market. For example, if high technology/computer stocks are in vogue on the NYSE, the same industry group can be expected to be hot on the OTC markets. This is especially true of new issues.

Bear in mind, though, that the initial upward performance of a new issue in the current "hot" group is often temporary, and new prices will usually settle back until the company proves itself. Of course, you could profit by buying the new issue and selling at the top of the initial climb. If you felt the company was solid, you could always buy it again after the price had dropped.

We've talked mainly about what investors can do to help themselves. What about experts who offer advice? While Wall Street analysts teem as thickly as mosquitoes, there is a definite shortage of good advice available on the pennies. In other words, while this financial community's growth will probably spawn an increase in sophisticated advisory services, for the time being, you're on your own. However, your own wits are your greatest weapon in any securities market—careful analysis could gather profits for you in the penny stocks.

Penny Stock Movement

There is an enormous attraction in the possibility of making a killing with a small outlay of capital—and there is certainly nothing new in that. Money gambled on the long shot pays off big when it hits.

This fever for quick and easy riches is often touched off by a succession of "finds" in natural gas, oil, silver, uranium, iron, cobalt, and other minerals too numerous to list—and from claims of revolutionary discoveries in solar power, windpower, geothermal applications, and other energy techniques.

In the past few years, there have been dozens of moves such as these: Consolidated Rambler, 71 cents to $7.50; Discovery Mines, 40 cents to $6.38; New Delore, eight cents to $1.80; Wilroy Mines, 90 cents to $16; Wright-Hargreaves, 76 cents to $11.

But for every stock that continues to rise, hundreds plummet. Many companies become dormant or die out altogether. Others plod along, holding leases on property they cannot explore for lack of capital. At the same time, fraudulent promoters, who always flourish in a speculative climate, are bound to make fortunes from imprudent investors.

Now that millions of speculative dollars are finding their way into hundreds (even thousands) of new or small ventures, we can expect a continuing surge of titillating rumors, a handful of breathtaking discoveries, and a multitude of stocks reaching for the sky.

You can get information about U.S. penny stocks from most brokers, through the NASDAQ system (see the chapter on the stock market). You can also follow many of them in the OTC and regional listings in your local newspaper, *The Wall Street Journal*, and *Barron's*.

Canadian penny stocks can be followed in *The Northern Miner*. This publication thoroughly covers the mining field, with up-to-the-minute mining news and prices of oil and mining stocks traded on the Canadian exchanges and over-the-counter. *The Northern Miner* also publishes an annual, the *Canadian Mines Handbook*. This valuable directory reveals vital information about every Canadian mining company and provides price ranges for the last eight years.

As has been said before, you can either trade penny stocks, looking for profits from price swings, or you can seek long-term investments in companies that have latched onto something worthwhile. If the latter is your goal, the *Penny Stock Newsletter* is priceless—its detailed analyses of new issues and viable concerns can help you isolate those companies which will eventually be returning strong dividends.

PENNY STOCK STRATEGIES

There is a method for the average investor to make healthy profits from penny stocks. These profits can be based upon 1) the psychology that causes even worthless securities to soar temporarily, and 2) the fact that substantial percentage moves are common, and not necessarily always based on sheer fantasy.

At certain times and at *certain prices*, real values *are* available in penny stocks. Premier Energy is an outstanding case in point—it is a strong, actively producing oil and natural gas company, and at $2 per share, or even $10 per share, it was a bargain. The wide trading ranges resulting from alternating moods of optimism and pessimism on the part of the investing public, though, offer anyone who has given sufficient study to the problem an opportunity to make big profits with little risk.

Many energy stocks will never become valuable producers of the minerals they hope to find or already own and can't afford to mine economically, although some will. But past history indicates that whenever overall speculative booms develop, most penny stocks multiply rapidly in price with little regard to their actual or even potentially real values.

Given this aspect of the penny stock arena, the surest and safest way to profit is the following:

1. Determine the price level at which each security that interests you has an upside potential far in excess of the downside risk.

2. Buy shares in as many different stocks as possible—only at your predetermined prices.

3. Whenever possible, buy stocks in companies that have existed for at least five years and have a price pattern you can use to establish buying practices. This is a safeguard for guaranteed profits, so far as it can be guaranteed, and will not usually lead to the stellar percentage gains so familiar to the penny stocks.

If a stock has a consistent up-and-down record, you can sometimes increase profits by buying shares of a dropping stock at planned intervals. (This procedure is only applicable to penny stocks because the cash outlay is relatively small—it would not be a good idea with higher-priced securities, since it can become a quick way to lose a fortune.)

Conversely, when the stock rises, you can do one of three obvious things.

1. You can sell everything at your original own sell price, or objective.

2. You can start taking profits every time your specific purchase price doubles (selling the stock you bought for 15 cents when it reaches 30.)

3. Or you can sell half your stock as soon as it will return your original investment and ride the rest up in hopes of a killing. For example, you would sell half the stock you bought for 20 cents as soon as it reached 40, and you would hold the other half and see how high the stock intended to climb.

Whatever else, never buy and hold *all* your stock! The key to consistently making money in penny stocks is trading them often.

Another strategy that may prove useful is designed to combat the fact that penny stocks can make major moves (up or down) in days or even hours. To trade them successfully, many people find that using Open Orders (instructing their brokers in *advance* to buy the number of shares they want at the price they want to pay, and telling the brokers to leave the order in until it is executed or they tell him or her to cancel) simplifies their trading machinations.

Open orders can sit for months; stocks may advance so far above your "Buy" price that you forget all about them, then something causes the stock's price to collapse, and the result is that you suddenly own shares bought at prices that haven't been seen for months. The key to this, of course, is that your "Buy" order be at a level you can reasonably expect the stock to drop to, then climb from. In the case of Aurus again, if your "Buy" order was placed at 15 cents, for example, it is possible that the order would never be executed.

Successful Areas

If you prefer to hold stock for the long pull, either looking for the IBM or Getty Oil of tomorrow, or seeking a killing by selling at a stock's absolute peak, the best strategy is to select an industry you think has strong potential, buy shares in many different companies, and sit back and wait. This system garnered fortunes for people with gold and silver stocks in recent years.

Obviously, oil and gas remains outstanding, although it is possible that many of the petroleum-related penny stocks are quickly over-priced. Virtually any new offering that includes the word "petroleum" in its corporate name is sure to rise substantially from its offering price.

Solar energy may be an area to consider now. The combination of massive publicity, increased governmental aid (either from grants or tax breaks), and the great number of new companies that have entered the field may indicate that this area will yield the next great energy breakthrough. Some of the smaller companies that are totally in solar experimentation and development have an inside track and are already showing profits.

Silver mining may also become one of the hot areas in the penny category (see the chapter on silver), medical industries are consistently strong (although without the dramatic price rises of the oil and gas stocks—ranging only around 100 to 300 percent), and many of the so-called "high tech" stocks remain on an upward track. The *Penny Stock Newsletter* provides detailed analyses of new stocks and broad areas of industry.

In addition, the new issue market for penny stocks is growing rapidly, especially throughout Canada and the Rocky Mountain region of the United States. In fact, Denver has emerged as the leading exchange for penny stocks and new issues.

New issues, according to Glen Parker, publisher of the investment newsletter *New Issues*, is "one of the few areas you can still invest one dollar and get back $100." But, he cautions, "obviously you can lose it as well . . . New issues are very volatile. We believe you have to be able to diversify."

Parker's service, however, does not recommend penny stocks; it is more concerned with higher quality technology growth stocks. But except for the fact that his companies are more seasoned (and have higher per share prices), the principle of investing small amounts of money for potential big winners is the same. New penny stock issues are making their appearance by the dozens.

If you trade consistently active stocks and can follow them every day, you will probably find it more fun and potentially more profitable to watch them without entering open orders. But you must be able to act fast to buy or sell when the stocks you want reach the prices you want.

When you watch a stock, keep an eye on the trading volume. That enables the alert investor to hold on longer, buy lower, and sell higher than if you trade automatically at predetermined prices. When volume is heavy during a price rise, or slacks off heavily during a price drop, you have no reason to be alarmed. This is usually normal profit-taking. However, if the stock swings wildly in both directions on heavy volume, it is time to get out. Otherwise, you may watch your stock double, triple, quadruple—then plunge, almost before you know it, back to where it started, or below.

But no matter what, gambling with penny stocks is far more enjoyable (and generally more lucrative) than betting on ball games or the horses. It can provide more thrills over a longer period of time, and with some research and intelligent planning, your odds can be very good. If nothing else, the long shot that doesn't come in right away can be watched indefinitely—provided you follow a careful diversification strategy to gradually regain your initial investment while you wait for the big gains. There is always tomorrow, and with tomorrow, more hope.

Chapter Twenty-Five

Tax Shelters for Small Investors

One thing can definitely be said for 1982, recessionary year or not—it is the best year for individual taxpayers in decades. And contrary to popular belief, the new tax laws don't favor the rich alone; if you know where and how to look, you can easily find tax breaks for yourself as well as any giant corporation.

The rules are changed, thanks to President Reagan, and as of April, 1982, his scheduled tax cuts (ten percent off this July, and another ten percent a year later) are still in the works. This could change, of course, but the alterations in the tax code won't.

However, with the abundance of arguments for and against the Economic Recovery Tax Act of 1981 (ERTA) that have stormed in and out of the media for the past six months, it is natural to conclude that there is no way for a taxpayer to obtain three, four, or five dollars worth of deductions for just one dollar invested this year. Wrong! The act reduced but by no means eliminated the opportunities for affluent Americans to participate in tax shelters. In fact, the marketplace is flooded with public and private offerings.

What Are Tax Shelters

Unfortunately, tax shelters are traditionally seen as the sole province of the rich—everyone has read infuriating articles about multi-millionaires avoiding taxes entirely for years. Now, though, even modestly successful investors are swamped with solicitations: Earn fantastic returns on money that would otherwise go to Uncle Sam in oil and gas ventures, coal mining, gold, movies, Broadway shows, lithographs, records, timber, farming, and on and on.

Generally, tax shelters have been recommended only for those in a 50 percent or higher tax bracket. While inflation and progressive tax rates (taxflation) have increased the number of people suffering in this category, these are still fairly well-heeled taxpayers. Are these the only tax victims who can benefit from sheltering their incomes? Not in the least.

At the same time, there is a certain amount of truth in the traditional view. Anyone whose tax bracket is below 20 percent has no use for a shelter. For one thing, excess cash for investment purposes is unlikely in today's economy when the income is limited. For another, the risks associated with tax shelter investments are not appropriate to anyone whose tax rate will not benefit substantially from taking the risk.

In short, tax shelters are useful only to those with a fair amount of extra money at the end of the year. But if you *do* have some extra money left, it is also likely that the government has conveniently placed you in a higher tax bracket that will siphon off the excess. A shelter of some kind may definitely apply to you.

Tax-Deferred Retirement Plans

On the most basic level, a family with limited investment funds might protect some of it in an Individual Retirement Account (IRA) or Keogh Plan. Each has its advantages and disadvantages, and each will provide an extra tax deduction. However, neither is a tax shelter *per se*—neither provides an Investment Tax Credit (ITC), which is the fundamental goal of a true tax shelter.

A Keogh (or HR10) is designed for the self-employed, and an IRA can be exploited by everyone else. A "Mom and Pop" retail store, for example, would qualify for either; a salaried individual may use an IRA only, but beginning in 1982, one may be used regardless of company pension plan.

Under a Keogh Plan, a self-employed individual puts a tax-deductible portion of total earnings into a special retirement account which can accumulate interest tax free. Under ERTA, an individual is allowed to deduct 15 percent of income up to a total of $7500. After January 1, 1982, the maximum was increased to $15,000 per year.

An IRA is similar but with lower maximums—15 percent of income up to $1500 until January 1, 1982, and up to $2000 thereafter. These figures can double for married couples filing joint returns. The catch is this: Interest earned in either retirement plan is tax-free until the money is removed. If the money is removed prior to retirement, relatively stiff penalties ensue—these are intended as retirement vehicles.

Just the same, an applicable plan allows for a direct deduction from taxable income, whether you itemize or not, which can help people below the 35 percent tax bracket as well as those above. (See the chapter on IRAs for a more detailed analysis.)

Tax-Deferred Annuities

Another means of conserving assets tax-free is called a tax-deferred annuity. This can be used with an IRA or Keogh, or by itself. Its purpose is exactly what its name suggests, to defer your tax obligation on the interest earned by the annuity. Such vehicles can be purchased only from a life insurance company.

Tax-deferred annuities are enjoying growing popularity mainly because they are so simple, and because they offer a wide range of eventual options. You purchase an annuity contract that is specifically designed to earn compounded interest on money you deposit with an insurance company until some point in the future. You pay no tax on the interest until you withdraw the money. (You can elect to take a lifetime annuity, cash in the policy, or withdraw, tax-free, part or all of the premiums you paid. In effect, it is a savings plan that isn't taxed until you withdraw the money, either in a lump sum or as an annuity.)

If you take the lump sum, you pay taxes on the total accrued amount minus the premiums you paid. If you take the money on a monthly basis, you must pay taxes as you receive the funds. However, you pay taxes only on the increase in value—the portion that would be considered principal or return of capital in a lump-sum arrangement is not taxable—only the "interest" portion.

A number of advisers equate such annuities to U.S. savings bonds. While there are some similarities, the annuities have some clear-cut advantages. For one thing, the annuities are more readily converted into cash. For another, such annuities are more accepted by banks as collateral, often to almost the face amount of the annuity, which is something that can rarely be said of a savings bond.

All-Savers Certificates

When a family's income reaches the 35 to 40 percent bracket plateau, it is time to study other methods. The main goal, of course, is to use the capital that would otherwise have been paid in taxes to expand your net worth instead.

If you are willing to tie up a large sum for a year, the new all-savers certificates are worth more than a second glance. Although these are generally available for as little as $500—and sometimes even less—they are probably most applicable to those with upper-middle incomes or better.

But no matter how small the amount you place in an all-savers certificate, the interest is tax-free up to $1000 for individuals and $2000 for couples filing joint returns. You can remove the interest as it is earned, but the principal is, for all practical purposes, out of your reach for a full year: If you withdraw the principal early, you lost three month's worth of interest and any tax exemption on the whole amount.

An easy way to determine whether an all-savers certificate will offer you advantages is to glance at Table 2—it shows the equivalent taxable yield you would have to receive to beat the all-savers' tax-free return, tax bracket.

Real Estate Partnerships

Traditionally (and accurately, up to a point), the most inflation-proof investment in the United States has been income real estate. Some real estate investments will yield a cash flow even while delivering more deductions than the investor spends on the project each year, thereby sheltering some

TABLE 1: GROWTH OF AN IRA

Age Begun	Total Deposit	8% Interest		11% Interest		14% Interest	
		Total Value	Monthly Payment	Total Value	Monthly Payment	Total Value	Monthly Payment
20	$90,000	$961,713	$7753	$2,845,142	$28,656	$8,958,466	$109,642
25	80,000	632,554	5099	1,621,049	16,327	4,398,527	53,833
30	70,000	413,125	3330	920,124	9267	2,155,727	26,383
35	60,000	266,845	2151	518,769	5225	1,052,610	12,882
40	50,000	169,330	1365	288,950	2910	510,043	6242
45	40,000	104,323	841	157,354	1584	243,182	2976
50	30,000	60,986	491	82,001	825	111,927	1369
55	20,000	32,097	258	38,853	391	47,369	579
60	10,000	12,838	103	14,147	142	15,617	191

The table shows how an Individual Retirement Account can pay off at age 65, based on three different interest rates. The assumptions are that the maximum amount ($2000) is placed in the account each year and that the interest is compounded daily. Monthly payment estimates are based on a 22 year lifespan after 65.

additional income. An example of such a venture would be a small shopping center, strip stores, or single-family home equity participation programs.

However, a small taxpayer wouldn't be able to consider a project involving millions of dollars, but with the right leverage, even small investors can enter limited partnerships involving hundreds of thousands of dollars for just a small amount down. In fact, the amount can be as little as $3000-5000.

This is what is known as investing in a syndication. If the deal is structured well, you may even be able to write off over twice the total amount of cash you invested in the first year. In other words, you would be paying for the investment with tax dollars, if your tax bracket is high enough. The traditional cut-off point for tax shelters is the 50 percent bracket, but that becomes something of a moot point when it is the absolute limit of taxation, as dictated by ERTA. In any case, that level is about $46,000 in taxable income for married taxpayers filing jointly, and about $35,000 for single taxpayers. Of course, these amounts changed in 1982, to $85,600 for married and $41,500 for single taxpayers.

If you were lucky enough to have everything fall into place on a syndication, you could receive a small cash flow that would in itself be tax-free. As long as the partnership exists, mortgages are generally amortized and the value of the property is appreciating, at least on paper. In the event that you simply break even—taking in enough to cover all your obligations associated with the income generated by the property—you benefit when the property is sold. You will receive all of the appreciation and principal that you paid, and you can usually consider these as long-term capital gains.

In addition, you can use your real estate investments to pyramid your wealth by engaging in tax-free exchanges. This involves a careful strategy of trading your property for properties of greater value, permitting you to accumulate larger properties and more debt, along with the attendant increases in income, more depreciation expenses, a greater store of equity built up, and more equity build-up with leverage. Obviously, the idea is to trade up, as dramatically as is feasible—so that you increase your mortgage debt after each transaction—to avoid paying taxes.

"Exotic" Shelters

In addition to real estate, of course, there are a wide variety of aggressively promoted tax shelters that apply, if you will believe the salespeople, to almost anybody. These are the so-called "exotic" tax shelters, and if ever the conventional view about who should be involved in tax shelters applied accurately, this is its natural realm. Exotic shelters are, generally, *so* speculative that no one without a great deal of money, whose genuine concern is more for the tax dodge than any possible gain, should blithely pursue such investments.

Exotic shelters offer enormous write-offs for a relatively miniature investment. ERTA has made it abundantly clear that any such shelter should be meticulously examined to determine economic viability. But their popularity is based on a good reason: If the deal *is* economically viable, the tax advantages are almost obscene, mainly because of enormous leverage.

Investors interested in such avenues must check first whether there is a viable means of paying back the debt incurred when the shelter is entered—if not, the investor is in for trouble. Examples of exotic shelters include equipment leasing, movies, television shows, playing the Broadway Angel, oil and natural gas ventures, timber development deals, cattle feeding or breeding, lithographs, and anything similar to such risky investments. Most exotics can usually be identified as those ventures which would, because of an almost outrageous degree of risk, never attract anyone, if not for the tax advantages.

The reason to avoid such schemes is simple: The tax advantages will not exceed the money the investor is likely to lose. Before investing in *any* exotic tax shelter, always have your tax adviser, CPA, tax attorney, or all of the above examine the program to determine its merits.

Charitable Contributions

Giving to charity is a traditional tax shelter that has an additional wrinkle in ERTA. Everyone may deduct $25 in charitable donations, whether they itemize or not. Obviously this provision will be subject to considerable abuse when it is available in 1982. In 1984, the maximum will be raised to $75; in 1985, half of all donations will be deductible; in 1986, total donations will be deductible. However, this provision will expire in 1987.

In the meantime, there is a variety of ways to use charity as a tax shelter. Donating appreciated long-term capital gain property results in a deduction of the full fair market value of the property, providing, of course, that the charity is fully qualified. You are limited to 30 percent of your adjusted gross income as an itemized deduction of the property, and you are not required to pay any tax on the appreciate value. In other words, such donations create a double tax saving.

Property held for only a year or less can also be donated, yielding deductions of up to 50 percent of your adjusted gross income, again providing that the recipient is qualified.

In either case, the deductions are generally limited to your cost basis and are not allowed to exceed the fair market value of the property at the time of the gift—it can skyrocket the day after you donate it, but your deduction is limited to price when the gift was made. Some property, such as clothing or automobiles, may not be worth the price you paid, although you may still deduct their current market value. However, a wide range of other donations, such as collectibles, antiques, artwork, or signed and numbered limited-edition lithographs,usually appreciate in value—the market value at the time of the gift will exceeed your cost, and the deduction improves accordingly.

In fact, for those in higher tax brackets, an amazingly simple method of escalating such a deduction is available. In such a situation, the taxpayer buys a piece of art, for example, at an established catalog price, paying about 20 percent in cash and giving the seller a non-negotiable nine percent note for the remaining 80 percent of the purchase price, payable in about 12 years. In other

TABLE 2: ALL-SAVERS vs. TAXABLE INVESTMENTS

| | Single | | | Married, filing jointly | |
Taxable Income	Tax Bracket	Yield Needed	Taxable Income	Tax Bracket	Yield Needed
$0-$2300	0%	12.14%	$0-$3400	0%	12.14%
2300-3400	12	13.80	3400-5500	12	13.80
3400-4400	14	14.12	5500-7600	14	14.12
4400-6500	16	14.45	7600-11,900	16	14.45
6500-8500	17	14.63	11,900-16,000	19	14.99
8500-10,800	19	14.99	16,000-20,200	22	15.56
10,800-12,900	22	15.56	20,200-24,600	25	16.19
12,900-15,000	23	15.77	24,600-29,900	29	17.10
15,000-18,200	27	16.63	29,900-35,200	33	18.12
18,200-23,500	31	17.59	35,200-45,800	39	19.90
23,500-28,800	35	18.68	45,800-60,000	44	21.68
28,800-34,100	40	20.23	60,000-85,600	49	23.60
34,100-41,500	44	21.68	85,600 and up	50	24.28
41,500 and up	50	24.28			

The table compares the yield of an all-savers certificate to what the equivalent yield would have to be, in order to show a greater profit, in various tax brackets. ("Yield Needed" lists the appropriate percentage.) The comparison is based upon 1982 tax tables, meaning the highest tax rate is 50 percent. The equivalent yield must be better than 70 percent of the current one-year Treasury bill rate. In this case, the amount is 12.14 percent. As can be seen, the all-savers certificates only begin to offer a competitive alternative at the 35 percent tax level.

MONEY MAKER

words, the items is purchased on installment.

The purchaser then donates the property to a qualified charity and obtains verification that the total amount of the property was donated for the actual catalog price. Such an outright gift provides the donor with deductions for the fair market value, and if the taxpayer makes the donation immediately upon purchase, the tax benefits are available in the same year.

For example, suppose a taxpayer purchases a selection of art with a catalog price of $35,000. The taxpayer puts up $7000 in cash and finances the $28,000 balance with 12-year, nine percent, full recourse promisory note. The taxpayer then gives the artwork to a qualified charity and is immediately entitled to a $35,000 deduction. The deduction may not exceed 50 percent of the taxpayer's adjusted gross income, but the unused amount can be carried forward as a deduction within the next five years.

Clearly, such a plan is most appropriate to those in high tax brackets who need an immediate deduction.

Consider a Second Business

ERTA also makes starting a second, part-time business an even better tax shelter than it was previously. For one thing, a second business can be used to spread income among family members, thereby shielding taxable income. In addition, the second business can be structured in such a way as to take full advantage of the Internal Revenue Code provisions for fringe benefits. Fringe benefits are generally concessions that are tax-deductible to the company and tax-free (or tax-deferred) to the business' employees. Many of these benefits are available only to corporate employees, however, so consult a tax attorney before attempting such a plan.

In any case, a well-constructed second business can employ family members and provide them with such deductible fringe benefits as medical reimbursement plans, group legal service plans, employer subsidized (or supplied) meals, and lodging for the benefit of the employer. An obvious example is when the owner of an income-producing apartment building supplies a resident manager with a free apartment.

Good Records Essential

Good record-keeping, of course, is absolutely essential. For individuals, this means careful accounts of auto expenses and mileage concerning the use of your personal automobile, both for business purposes and for trips to the doctor or other medical uses, even for doing volunteer work for a charity. With proper documentation, such expenses can be deducted as medical costs or charitable contributions.

Obviously, in order to deduct medical expenses, charitable gifts, interest paid, real estate taxes and local sales taxes, uninsured casualty losses, gasoline taxes, state income taxes, child care expenses, union dues, the cost of work clothing and their cleaning, tools used on the job, bad debts, and moving expenses, you must be able to document each expense. If you do, though, every single item on the long list is completely deductible. Some people even

REDUCING TAX SHELTER RISKS

Before entering into any tax shelter, be sure you, and an attorney, have satisfactorily answered each of the following questions. Investing in a tax shelter is a complex and sophisticated form of investment, often offering tremendous capital gains to offset the equally large risk.

  1. **What is the level of business risk?** What business are you really going into? Is it one you are willing to enter? A truck or barge is unlikely to become obsolete, but a computer will. A salmon hatchery may make money, but it isn't assured. Most shelters involve a basic business decision, such as, "Would I rent trucks to a major corporation?" The decision should be made independent of the tax implications of the deal, and will often involve a credit decision.

  2. **What is the level of tax risk?** Oil and gas drilling programs have been around for years, and the deduction for drilling costs is a pretty well-defined area of the tax law. Some other ventures may be breaking new ground in tax interpretation, and therefore carry a high degree of tax risk.

  3. **Who is promoting the deal and why?** If the deal in question is being promoted by one of the national brokerage houses or some other well-known organization with a good reputation, the chances are much better that it is a safe investment. While the national brokerages have, on occasion, promoted bad shelters, it is unlikely that they will deliberately push an illegitimate deal. However, some of the best shelters are promoted locally, and here you must make a careful judgment of the people involved.

  4. **Why you? Does it fit your needs?** There are all types of shelters. If you are a doctor who can expect a large taxable income for years to come, a shelter that provides an ongoing tax benefit over a period of years is highly suitable. For others, a totally different structure, with a large one-time write-off and little ongoing contribution is more appropriate.

  5. **Does it pass the "experts" test?** If you are going to make a substantial investment in a shelter deal, go out and get the advice of someone with expert qualifications in the area. You will probably have to pay for the advice, but it could be the best investment of all.

  6. **Does it pass the "nausea" test?** Perhaps this should be the first test. Read the promotional material—especially the risks section—of the deal's prospectus, and read the "Related Parties to This Transaction" section. If you can get through these two sections without any queasy feelings in your stomach, proceed with your investigation of the proposal's merits.

  7. **Does it pass the "Bottom Line Test?"** Where will you be when the program is complete? Unless the tax money you have saved has been invested at a return rate high enough to justify the entire exercise, it is a waste of time. You may have deferred taxes for a few years, but to make money the time will have to be well spent.

keep a box of sales receipts throughout the year, simply to document their deductions of local taxes.

If you are planning to move to another location, be sure you have a job before you go house hunting, since you can only deduct expenses occurred in moving for work.

If you wish to transfer money to family members (other than as gifts), interest-free loans offer fairly good flexibility. However, the new gift tax rules under ERTA make gift-giving an excellent way to reduce your tax burden.

Starting in 1982, there is no limit on any amount you may give to a spouse, whether during your lifetime or after your death. Also, the amount you may give anyone as a gift has been raised from $3000 to $10,000. If the gift is from both you and your spouse, the maximum you may pass along, tax-free to a child, for example, is $20,000. The child pays tax on the amount, but his or her tax rate will undoubtedly be lower than yours.

While ERTA reduced the number of available shelters, it did not eliminate them. A rule of thumb is that a tax shelter will offer potential gain in the future (with the exception of charitable donations), that you will strike oil, find a new vein of coal or gold, that the company leasing your equipment will stay in business long enough to pay out the lease and that you will, indeed, receive the salvage value for the equipment at the end of the lease. In the meantime, though, the legitimate shelter will protect you from the substantial ravages of Uncle Sam, leaving you to profit or lose on the merits of your own choices—not because inflation and increased taxation remove the decision.

Chapter Twenty-Six

Inflation-Proofing Your Insurance

L ife insurance" has become a dirty word. Part of the reason for this attitude is legitimate—people realized that the "whole life" policies they had purchased at great expense amounted to little more than granting an insurance company a three percent loan on their money, for example. But other reasons are founded simply in ignorance—ignorance of the fact that the life insurance industry has swept into the 1980s armed with a battery of new systems, most of which are genuinely geared toward helping the individual.

There are currently over 146 million life insurance policy holders in the United States, and most of them are paying too much money for their coverage. Ironically, most of them are also underinsured, and as more and more people become investors, the number of underinsured individuals is sure to grow.

In 1980 alone, 14 million new policy holders bought over $527 *billion* worth of life insurance. Life insurance companies receive more than $30 billion a year in premiums. Why, in spite of these awesome figures, do most people overpay for inadequate insurance coverage?

Because most people fail to understand what their life insurance is, how it works, how money can be saved, or that a cost revolution has occurred in the insurance industry. For example, few are aware that contrary to popular belief, rates have dropped as much as *50 percent* in the past year. Again, contrary to the common attitude, insurance policies are not created equal—the price difference for similar coverage can vary as much as *400 percent*.

Very simply, people are paying too much for life insurance because they won't stop, shop, and compare. Literally thousands of dollars can be saved through careful analysis of existing and new policies; substantial increases in coverage can be obtained at little extra cost, through a careful review of antiquated policies in relation to the new products available.

The insurance agent (or company) who sold you a policy four years ago may well have sold you the best product then available at the best current price. However, none of those previous advantages may still apply. It is incumbent upon every policyholder to review every nuance of his or her policies, just as he or she would review any other part of a financial portfolio—is it cost efficient? Does it continue to serve its original purpose? Can the same result be achieved at a lower cost? In other words, everything must be analyzed according to how it measures against newer vehicles, and the same applies to insurance.

For the first time in history, individual consumers (and insurance companies) have been able to receive 15 percent and more on certificates of deposit, Treasury bills, and other financial issues. For creative insurance companies, this factor—along with mortality tables indicating a longer lifespan in America—has prompted a competitive move: The advantage has been passed along to the customers in the form of lower-prices products. New creative forms of life insurance were hatched to the benefit of consumers (such as adjustable life, universal life, economatic, and extra life policies) that have rapidly relegated the traditional policies to the past.

Assess Companies

In the United States there are two principle types of life insurance companies: Mutual and stock. The key words to watch for are *par* (for "participating") and *non-par* (for "non-participating"). Mutual companies offer a "participating plan," which pays dividends to its policy holders. Stock companies offer "non-participating plans," which provide no dividends but guarantee that the premium on a permanent life insurance will remain unchanged.

This seems simple enough, except that the traditional differences between par and non-par companies are beginning to disappear—many of the non-par companies include participating, dividend-paying policies in their portfolios. Some of these new products include adjustable premiums (either up or down) according to investment results. Others tie death benefits to the company realizing the gains it predicts. However, changes in the traditional alignment of insurance companies won't be important if you understand the differences between the broad groups of insurers.

Mutual Life Insurance Companies. Theoretically, a par company allows the consumer to participate in the company's profits. In such a case, the government requires that part of the profits be used to create reserves and surpluses to maintain stability. Thus, any "dividend" received by the customer is in reality an overpayment of premium, and is therefore not taxable. In the end, this functions to lower the premium at year-end, although it has been criticized as a means by which par companies receive interest-free loans.

The dividends are not guaranteed, but they have been paid regularly since the 1840s by some companies. In general, the dividends have been increasing over the last three decades. Better still, the premiums—once much higher initially than the stock companies—have been falling dramatically.

Stock Companies. Non-participating companies gained a foothold in the market mainly because they had a lower initial expense for the policyholder, and because they guaranteed a lifetime premium level. However, the "dividends" remitted by the par companies have reduced the premium levels to a point that the par policies are a better buy over the lifetime of the policy.

Consumers must remember that a stock company's first obligation is to its stockholders, who will receive most of the company's profits. This holds true even of non-par companies offering "participating," dividend-paying policies. But most importantly, the net cost (long-term premium total) for par companies is generally lower.

For example, the premium for a par company might be $3100 annually, as opposed to a non-par premium of $2600. As dividends reduce the par premium, the yearly price is about the same in five or six years. Twenty years later, the non-par policy still costs $2600 per year, while the par policy, as a result of dividends, is considerably less, in total. Par policies have still another plus: Because of the higher premiums, the cash value is higher. In fact, the advantages of a mutual company over a stock company, for the individual, simply pile up, the claims of non-par salespeople notwithstanding.

Assess Policies

This can be a difficult task, if only because there are so many valid alternatives. There are no pat answers, and each situation must be carefully analyzed in terms of individual needs, first, and then in terms of saving as much money as possible for the coverage desired.

For example, a 29-year-old man was pleased to have avoided dealing with an insurance agent by securing an additional $100,000 of group term insurance at work for $350 per year. His reasons all sounded good: The trying experience of dealing with several insurance agents was completely avoided by the simplicity of his employer's group policy. In addition, an all encompassing financial book told him, in authoritative tones, that group term insurance is the cheapest method available. Unfortunately, if he had spoken to an agent, he would have found that the same $100,000 of yearly renewable term insurance could have been purchased for $135—or $215 less in the very first year.

In another example, a middle-aged woman says she can no longer afford her $50,000 life insurance policy on her husband, because the premium is $2000 per year. Her husband is 62-years-old and in excellent health. He is a non smoker, and his current policy has a cash value of $15,000. But she feels compelled to surrender the policy.

However, the new products available will allow her to buy a similar whole life policy for $35,000 with a $1500 annual premium. By surrendering her $15,000 cash value and using the money to buy, for instance, municipal bonds paying eight percent annually—$1200—her actual outlay in insurance premiums is only $300 ($1500 minus $1200.)

In the event of her husband's death, she will still receive $50,000 ($35,000 from the new policy plus $15,000 in bonds). In other words, instead of losing insurance protection at this late date, she is able to continue the same amount in death benefits at a savings of $1700 per year.

In one example, a term policy is used; in the other, one of the new Extralife policies is involved. Both demonstrate some of the creative approaches that can be utilized to substantially reduce today's price of life isurance.

Term Insurance

This may well be one of the greatest myths ever perpetuated on the American consumer. Proponents will insist that it is the only type of insurance to buy, but it is only truly useful for those with a limited cash flow or a short-term need.

Term insurance is simply insurance for a specific period. The least expensive variety is a yearly renewable term policy, for which the premiums increase continuously as you climb the mortality tables. In other words, as you become older (and therefore closer to death), term insurance becomes more and more expensive. Such policies are generally most useful to those who want to cover themselves for a given amount over a realitively short term.

For example a person who has recently purchased a house and wants to assure payment in the event of his or her death might make use of a term policy, simply because the lower premium will not be an additional burden.

However, if the cash flow is established, a convertible term insurance policy would probably be preferred. This enables the policy holder to switch from term to permanent insurance at any given time. Unfortunately, the longer you wait to switch, the higher the premiums for the permanent policy will be. Worse, every penny spent on the term policy is gone forever—no equity is built in a term policy.

If you require life insurance for the rest of your life, the best buy will be permanent insurance (providing you can afford the initial outlay). Term insurance has a lower premium at first, but in later years when you will probably want the insurance the most, the cost becomes exorbitant.

Permanent Insurance

Also known as "whole life," "ordinary life," "straight life," "level premium life," or "cash value insurance," these policies essentially maintain a stable premium level until the age 100. This is the predominant form of insurance sold in America, if only because the high cost of insurance in a person's later years is eased by averaging out premium costs. The policy develops cash value (equity) over the years, which can also be inventively used.

In some cases, it is advantageous to pay off the insurance policy, and there are permanent plans to enable this. However, in such a case the premiums are substantially higher. Such policies are called *limited pay whole life* and have the advantage of creating a higher cash value in a shorter period of time. Their advantages, overall, are questionable.

Extralife-Economatic Plans

Such new low-premium plans are revolutionizing the insurance industry. Essentially, Extralife-Economatic insurance greatly reduces the premium cost of insurance by paying less than the whole amount of the permanent policy. The balance of the amount is filled by a combination of additional insurance and one-year term insurance that is purchased from the dividends of the base policy—in all, providing the desired coverage. As more paid-up policies are added, the term insurance is eventually dropped, at which point the dividends are taken in cash, used to buy more insurance, or whatever.

This sounds complicated, but it isn't. What such a plan does is allow a consumer to lower the price of a permanent insurance policy. For example, if a new policy buyer wanted insurance coverage of $100,000, an Extralife-Economatic policy would allow him or her to pay only on $70,000. The balance would come from additional paid-up insurance policies and one-year term insurance purchased from the dividends on the $70,000 policy.

In 12 to 20 years, the paid-up policies would equal $30,000, and term insurance would be dropped. Throughout the life of the permanent plan, the insured would be covered for $10,000, while paying substantially less in intial premiums. The disadvantage, of course, is that the dividends that would be received by those who can afford the $100,000 policy outright would be used to buy the one-year renewable term insurance.

An Extralife-Economatic policy is even more effective in a minimum-deposit arrangement. In this case, the insured pays an absolute minimum by borrowing from the policy's cash value each year to pay the premiums. Similar programs exist for older policies, but since the premium for an Extralife-Economatic plan is so much less, the insured borrows much less. This is a good way to purchase large amounts of insurance for low amounts of cash, but the face amount of the policy deteriorates eventually.

A decent insurance agent can explain such programs in greater deail. One thing is clear, however: Extralife-Economatic policies are probably the most workable form of permanent insurance ever created, and consumers who do not investigate this alternative are doing themselves a great disservice.

In addition, such revolutionary concepts are prompting insurance companies to explore other new products. One is a combination of annuity and term products which marry cash value and death benefits, called Universal Life. A variation, called Adjustable Life, is also developing.

In any case, of the many variations now available, the worst is straight term insurance. Term insurance has its uses, but any agent who pushes this as the most viable alternative does not have your best interests in mind.

Resistance and Mythology

Without a strong frame of reference, consumers lack the understanding to make the proper decisions when confronted by the myriad products and insurance agents presenting themselves. Unfortunately, there is little comprehensible background information available that will guide individuals to the proper coverage (at the lowest prices) for family or business needs.

Add to this lack of basic information the classic, hard-selling life insurance agent and you have the source of grim comedy. Scenarios involving a fast-talking salesman who draws a heavy black "X" through the "Daddy" on a representative photo, or strident ad campaigns implying that the provider who has not arranged adequate coverage for his or her loved ones somehow doesn't love the survivors, have by no means left the industry.

However, the resistance to life insurance is more to the subject itself than to the agents. No one really wants to discuss their own mortality or the decisions that must be made relative to their family and the disposal of their goods. Quite understandably, most consider the subject gruesome and would prefer to avoid it, either consciously or unconsciously. This mental block appears as a great deal of anger toward insurance agents. The words "life insurance" themselves conjure many images, none of which are favorable. But logic would indicate that unscrupulous agents have long since learned to turn this antagonism to their advantage—if people are willing to shop around for insurance, it is possible to get a quick signature on the dotted line, even when the policy purchased is in no way to the buyer's advantage.

In fact, people rarely review policies they have already purchased. The inclination is to buy and forget—the policy is buried in the bottom of a drawer and never seen again, until it is discovered to be totally inadequate. Often, people don't even know what their yearly premiums are. But if you are to save substantial money while assuring the appropriateness of your policies (both in terms of today's economy and your objectives), this "hope-it-will-go-away" attitude must be overcome. Every single policy should be reviewed in the light of today's environment—surprising amounts of money can be saved through up-dating insurance plans.

Many myths and misconceptions surround life insurance, some perpetrated by the industry itself. One of the greatest of these is the notion that life insurance is an investment. Some say life insurance is a bad investment, others claim it's a good investment—it is neither, because it isn't an investment at all, it's a financial instrument, clear and simple.

Life insurance shouldn't be bought with the intent of retirement income or savings. While these are side effects of a whole life policy, they aren't a reason to buy one. First, savings accrue more interest in bank, and even more in other vehicles. Second, a whole life policy should be purchased because you want death benefits for the entirety of your life. Investments are investments; insurance is insurance—it provides survivors with money in the event of your death.

Insurance agents are often criticized for failing to mention the alternatives to life insurance. In a clear view of insurance, there simply isn't an alternative —you either want to be insured, or you don't. For example, it is often proposed that money spent on insurance would be better placed in stocks, real estate, or whatever. From an investor's point of view, this is certainly the case. However, insurance is not meant to function in this way.

If you invest $1000 in real estate, stocks, a money market fund, or even your local savings and loan, you do so in anticipation of a long-term return of some kind. If you should die a month later, your survivors will receive approximately $1000 from your investment. If the same $1000 is placed in a life insurance policy, and the policy is written, the same event a month later will return some $100,000 to your heirs. This is a hefty appreciation, but the only way to receive it is certainly not to be desired. In other words, the only way to perceive insurance as an investment is ghoulish—investing in one's own death.

If you want to be insured, then the question revolves mainly around whole life or term insurance, not around investment strategies. That decision should be based upon your personal objectives. Whole life might be bought because of its lower premiums over a lifetime, but never for its investment advantage—it simply is not an investment. Term insurance might be bought by a person who is heavily invested to provide death benefits while the investments are maturing—again, it is in no way an investment itself.

Another stunningly absurd myth, and one which the industry or its salespeople are definitely guilty of espousing, is "Never change an old policy." True, you shouldn't—unless, of course, it is to your advantage. At times, replacing a policy will be to your advantage, and to not do so would be absolutely ridiculous.

Actually, this myth developed in large part as a result of efforts by the life insurance industry to protect its customers. The industry watched too many whole life programs destroyed by poorly conceived "Buy term and invest the difference" plans that were not in the best interest of the clients. Such policies simply served the purposes of salespeople, and as a consequence the industry has become gun shy about the word "replacement." Nevertheless, there are many high-priced term policies that can easily be replaced by lower-priced terms policies, and there are many whole life policies that can be replaced, in the best interest of the insured, by new, lower-priced permanent policies.

In addition, there are many inadequate whole life policies that were written for people who couldn't afford the larger amount of life insurance they wanted or needed. This could have been avoided with a cheaper (for the time being) term policy, which would have produced adequate coverage until the proper whole life policy could be written. In short, any policy should now be thoroughly reviewed to determine, first, if the coverage required by your family or business is provided, and, second, that the price is the lowest available.

Creative Options

If a life insurance salesman a few years ago told a 49-year-old client that he could save the client more than $1700 per year on his premiums for an equivalent amount of coverage, and furthermore that in 28 years the client would have more than $300,000 in available cash for the same cash outlay, the salesman would probably have been dismissed as a charlatan.

But in today's world of inflation and intense competition among insurers, such a miracle can be accomplished. While few insurance brokers are hammering on executive doors, singing the praises of replacement, consumers are beginning to view the notion enthusiastically.

For example, our above 49-year-old has, say, a life insurance policy for $256,000. By replacing his current policy, he can save $1771 a year, reducing his premiums from $7244 to $5473. In 28 years, at age 77, the new total premium paid would be $101,913, compared to the total premium paid on the

GUIDELINES FOR BUYING INSURANCE

1. Compare. Call at least five agents, and suffer through a discussion with each. Ask for the agent's credentials. Determine whether the person is accustomed to selling to people in your income bracket or your business, and try to determine their knowledge and experience.

If any is ignorant of any of the programs discussed in this article, find someone else. Ask to see the person's lowest terms and whole life rates, and tell them you will be comparing their offers to at least four others. You may not get the best agent in your city, but you should be able to pick the best out of five.

2. Determine how much life insurance you will need. Use the formula described earlier as a background, then work with a professional insurance agent. The combination of formulas will help you assess your proper coverage.

3. Choose between term and whole life insurance. This should be based on whether your need is short- or long-term. Of course, take your cash flow into consideration. It is more important to have the correct amount of life insurance than the correct *type* of life insurance. If you can afford it, the optimum would be to have both. Remember, the new Extralife-Economatic and similar policies (Universal Life, Adjustable Life, Interest Assumption, and so on) are far lower in cost than you might expect.

4. Have your agent show you the best way to buy the policy. It is quite possible that it could be made tax-deductible and estate tax-free. Depending upon your tax bracket, this could be very important.

Forearmed with proper knowledge, and aware of a few ways to cut insurance costs, you should truly be able to save a fortune on your life insurance.

---

previous policy of $202,832. If the $101,919 difference is accumulated at eight percent net interest, he would have $261,701 more value for the same outlay.

In addition, the surrender value of his current policy when accumulated over the years would be worth an additional $47,854. So, for the same outlay, he would have an additional $309,555 in available cash (the total cash value of the new policy would be $166,414 as opposed to $164,864 for the old policy).

If the client does not use the compounded funds, the total money available at the person's death would be $565,555, compared to $256,000 on the replaced policy. Thus, the replacement could amount to an additional death benefit of $309,555.

Further, since increasing numbers of people are living to 85, rather than 77, the differential becomes even greater. At 85, the same client would have a total death benefit of $668,449!

Replacement may not be for everyone, but all policies should be reviewed and analyzed in an effort to find such deals. A policy should be retained only if it is clearly to the benefit of the client. In any case, show your replacement proposal to the previous insurance company, and let them tell you why it *wouldn't* be in your best interest to make the switch. In these cases, take all the advice you can get, and listen to it with discernment.

Insurance for Women

This subject has fast become most important. Obviously, women are the major breadwinners in many of today's families, especially in cases of divorce or death. They should be treated no differently than men who support families, and in this area insurance companies are finally beginning to catch up with the times. There are now more women who have established substantial businesses and need insurance for the usual business reasons (partnerships, stock redemptions, bank loans, and so on). Like men, women with substantial assets require insurance for the purpose of covering their estate taxes.

For example, men and women alike have built fortunes in real estate, which is probably the most illiquid of all assets. The ramifications of real estate liquidation can be severe, especially if your estate is forced to liquidate in a soft market. If your estate taxes are, say, $1 million, the estate may be forced to sell property with $1.5 million in net equity in order to realize the tax burden.

Of course, this assumes that the property would deliver a full million dollars. This applies equally to either sex. To carry the scenario a bit further, the loss of such property merely to pay off the government extends much further than the immediate loss, if you consider the appreciation and income the property would have produced for children and grandchildren.

Rating Your Insurance

How much insurance do you need? There are various formulas which will apply. One of the simplest is based upon replacing your current income. If you make $30,000 per year, you can be economically replaced by $300,000 earning 10 percent interest—which would yield the same $30,000 per year. Using that as a base formula, you can then assess how much less your survivors would need without your expenses. To carry it further, the lowered principal can be offset by any social security benefits your survivors might recieve as well as other liquid assets and your current life insurance.

All policies can be compared by this and other methods. The easiest method is simply to shop around. For example, write down the figures from the enticing television or Sunday supplement newspaper ads, and compare what other agents can offer you—with a little creative arranging, you will be surprised how cheaply you can be insured to whatever amount is required.

No matter what, you owe it to yourself to explore the revolution that is sweeping through the life insurance industry. The new products can be a source of tremendous savings, particularly when those savings are compounded over the course of a lifetime. Remember, no two programs are the same; each program should be tailored to the individual's objectives, needs, and pocketbook.

Other Types of Insurance

So much for the revolution in life insurance—other types of insurance are changing, too. One of the biggest reasons, of course, is inflation. Even with the inflation rate flattened out at about eight percent, it means that in 10 years today's dollar will be worth only 46 cents, and in 20 years the dollar will shrink to 21 cents. At a 10 percent rate of inflation, those values become 38 and 15 cents, respectively. At 14 percent it becomes painfully clear that you must keep all your insurance attuned to inflation or it will run away with your policies as well as your protection.

There's a bit more to it than simply buying more insurance (as some life agents suggest) or increasing property policies. You ought to know if new policies are being developed to fight inflation. You should keep an eye on how inflation weakens your insurers, and what you can do. You ought to be aware of the problems inflation is building for your pension or retirement fund.

In the past four years, no less than 30 property-casualty insurance companies have become insolvent. Even worse, more than 50 property-casualty compan-

---

WHAT TO DO WITH DIVIDENDS

Since dividends are the basic difference between par and non-par insurance policies, their various uses can demonstrate their value.

1. You can take the dividend in cash, and use it for a separate investment.

2. The dividend can be used to reduce the premium, eventually paying the premiums themselves so that less of your cash is used for insurance payments.

3. Some people allow the dividends to accumulate with interest at the insurance company. However, the interest rate is so low when compared to other investment avenues that this should not be seriously considered.

4. Use the dividends to buy additional insurance, called the "paid-up adds" approach. The dividend itself can purchase each year—at net cost, with no commission to the agent and no new examination for the client—a paid-up policy. The policy has a paid-up death benefit, its own cash value, and its own dividend. This option guarantees additional insurance and is best for people with health problems, who are thus allowed to buy insurance at standard rates despite any future health problems.

5. Purchase one-year term insurance each year with the dividend. Again, there is no agent commission or health examination. This term insurance is used to cover the cash value of the insured's policy. Thus, if the insured dies, the survivors collect not only the face amount of the original policy, but the cash value as well. This is very popular in "minimum deposit" plans.

---

ies now operating are actually insolvent, according to Richard M. Haverland, president of Progressive Casualty Insurance Co. One of the major reasons, he says, is that traditional industry practices lead many companies to overvalue their bond portfolios. Check, through your own research or that of your insurance adviser, to determine if your carrier is financially sound.

Life companies, too, should be checked, although there have been far fewer insolvencies among them than among property casualty carriers. When the Equitable—one of the nation's largest—fired several hundred of its home office executives, its president gloomily predicted belt-tightening for the entire life industry. Inflation, while not the primary cause, is nonetheless contributing greatly to the life industry's problems. The outlook is that the rate of policy lapses will increase somewhat while the rate of cash value loans will soar. Sales will be down a bit. A smaller percentage of sales will consist of high-profit cash value policies.

Home Coverages

Whether you're a tenant or owner, inflation is wreaking havoc on the values of what you have.

Building: If you think the general rate of inflation is bad, then be aware that the rate of inflation for construction materials is much worse. Lumber prices have been known to skyrocket 30 percent in one year, for example.

It's vital that you insure your dwelling to at least 80 percent of its replacement cost at the time of a loss; if insured for less than that, you will suffer penalties through markdowns for depreciation and co-insurance. Replacement cost at time of loss are key words. It's your obligation—not your insurer's or agent's—to keep your policy values current, and to keep coverage abreast of inflation.

Don't be lulled into a false sense of security by inflationguard riders which increase coverage by six to eight percent a year; even with such riders, your policy could fall far below the 80 percent-of-replacement cost mark in just one year.

Here's what to do:

1. Get a fairly accurate estimate of how many square feet your dwelling contains. If you don't have floor plans, draw a rough diagram and pace off each dimension. If multi-level, show each floor separately.

2. Label each section of the house by its construction, e.g., frame, brick, masonry, etc.

3. Identify the roof covering, e.g., tar paper and gravel, flat tile, barrel tile, etc.

4. From the above data, derive today's replacement cost. Your insurance agent or carrier may have current construction costs which would indicate, say, $35 to $40 per square foot in your locale. Whatever the figure, multiply it by the number of square feet in your home to produce today's replacement cost, roughly.

A better idea is that you insure your dwelling for its full replacement cost instead of the 80 percent many advisers have suggested. Not only will you be fully covered in case of total loss, but in event of partial loss (which is much more likely to occur) you won't be penalized by co-insurance penalties, nor will you lose the benefit of "new for old" replacement.

At least once a year, review policy values. With your policy, keep a record of your dwelling's area and construction data. Write your agent (and keep a copy with the policy) asking that he or your carrier advise, as often as they think necessary, what they recommend you carry. While this doesn't place a legal obligation on them, it does give you a strong moral argument if you're allegedly underinsured at claim time—if, of course, you followed their advice.

Contents: If you think inflation is shocking at the food market, check a furniture store!

Too many people are financially clobbered when they try to replace household goods with insurance proceeds. They're hit with a double blow: (1) most policies cover only the depreciated value of contents, and (2) because of inflation, replacement costs force large out-of-pocket expense, over and above insurance.

Here's what to do:

1. Make a room-by-room inventory, showing as accurately as possible each item's cost when new, its age, and its present replacement value. To get an idea of replacement values, you might use a big-store catalog. Include all movable items—furniture, rugs, drapes, clothing, etc.—but not items to be scheduled, as discussed below.

2. Calculate your contents' value two ways: (a) its replacement cost at today's prices, and (b) replacement cost minus depreciation.

3. Discuss with your insurance adviser what your options are. Several companies offer policies which will not reckon depreciation on a contents claim, in effect letting you profit from a loss by getting new contents to replace the old. To get that benefit, however, you're supposed to carry a high enough amount of coverage to reflect replacement costs.

Note that whether you opt for depreciated or new, in either case the current, inflated costs are a key figure. Don't feel that you can ignore coverage reviews because your contents are simply depreciating with age; rampaging inflation is a large offsetting factor, and replacement costs are always involved in any claim.

Inflation has another effect, unfortunately. As more people get caught in financial squeezes caused by inflation, crime will increase. Burglaries will hit more homes and your chances of having to make a claim will grow.

One of your guards against inflation, then, is to be more security-minded. Loss prevention, always important, is now vital.

Scheduled Items: Jewelry, furs, silverware, fine arts, cameras, sports equipment, and stamp or coin collections are some—but not all—of the types of items which call for careful thought. Two important factors: current value, and form of protection.

In view of the breathtaking rise in value of gold, silver, precious and semi-precious stones, any appraisals more than one year old should be considered obsolete. You should:

1. Get current appraisals. Some companies will accept wholesale jewelry valuations so marked.

2. Consider the options in jewelry coverage:

    a. Blanket (unscheduled) coverage in $100 increments above the usual $500 blanket coverage in the Homeowners policy;

    b. World-wide, all-risk coverage;

    c. Reduced-rate coverage for jewelry while in a bank vault;

    d. Reduced-rate coverage limited to U.S. only;

    e. Possible credits for home alarm systems, vaults, etc.

It is important that jewelry appraisals reveal a gem's good points, such as clarity, color, cut, lack of flaws, etc., because the insurer has the option to replace the item, as described in your appraisal, in lieu of making a cash settlement.

Similarly, appraisals should show current values of antiques, fine arts, collectibles, and other valuables, some of which have quadrupled in value in just a few years.

The broadest form of protection for such items is the all-risk floater which covers against most (but not all) perils. Discuss whether you qualify for protection credits, but also confirm that you're covered if you display your items at a show, or engage in some buying and selling for profit, or whatever other situations may apply.

Liability: Part of a Homeowners policy offers personal liability coverage for occurrences away from home as well as on your premises. Bodily injury and property damage liability are included, and both reflect the ravages of inflation.

If a neighbor's child is hurt and damages are claimed against you, the claim will be built in part on medical expenses, one of the fastest-rising items in the inflationary spiral.

If a neighbor's roof is burned due to your negligence, the claim will soar along with rising costs of construction.

Both examples—bodily injury and property damage—illustrate why comfortable policy limits of a few years ago are obsolete today. Inflation has hit court judgments: six-figure and million-dollar awards are common now. Yet many homeowners are carrying liability limits unchanged since they bought their houses. Some are careful to increase limits on their auto policies, but they overlook the danger of ruinous lawsuits in non-auto cases.

You should:

1. Review liability limits wherever exposure exists: home, auto, boat.

2. Consider carrying an Umbrella (or Catastrophe) Liability policy, usually costing less than $100 a year and providing limits of $1 million or more per claim. If you're already carrying a $1 million policy, investigate increasing the limit. Million dollar judgments are common with inflation and liberalizations of law. If you permanently disable a college student, for example, the court may find that his expected earnings might have come to $25,000 a year for a 40-year career (to age 65). If it's only that much, you're dealing with $1,000,000 in lost earnings alone; add medical expenses, compensation for pain and anguish, and you can see why some courts have awarded seven figure judgments in favor of persons who haven't yet earned a dime!

Now it may look as if we're answering inflation with recommendations to buy more insurance. Well, more insurance is part of the answer when there are more values to be protected, or when you're likely to be hit with a larger lawsuit.

But additional insurance may not cost as much, proportionately, as the additional items it covers. A recent 10-year period, for example, saw a 115 percent increase in construction costs, but only a 54 percent increase in property insurance rates.

Auto insurance rates, on the other hand, have moved in tandem with wages, medical and auto repair costs, and somewhat higher than the rate of increase for new car prices.

Auto Coverages

In some areas, companies are reducing premiums even while others are increasing theirs. Some ill winds blew a bit of good; gas shortages and high prices, along with the 55-mile-an-hour speed limit on highways, have lowered our accident and death rates on the road. Premiums are in a state of flux.

If you have a big gas-guzzler, you may know that its value has dropped disproportionately fast. Its replacement (or insurable) value may now be low enough for you to consider dropping collision insurance or increasing the collision deductible.

On the other hand, you should keep "inflatable" coverages under regular review, including liability, medical payments, and Uninsured Motorist coverages. The latter is an especially overlooked item, and it will be increasingly important as the inflationary squeeze induces more drivers to drop their liability insurance.

When reviewing your liability coverages, don't assume that the big claims occur only when people are hurt. Property damage can be huge, too. Consider the driver carrying $25,000 in P.D. liability who hits a fire hydrant, causing it to break and flood a nearby furniture store.

Uses of Deductibles

Inflation forces insurance-buyers to self-insure or non-insure on a sensible basis. You simply can't afford first-dollar coverage for everything, nor does it make sense. If you can be financially sound (although bruised) by paying certain losses out-of-pocket, you're dollars ahead in the long run by building your insurance program on that basis.

Deductibles permit you to be covered for serious or catastrophic losses while relieving your insurer of the burden of handling the small and frequent claims. Usually the premium savings are attractive.

Auto collision insurance is perhaps the best-known type of coverage involving deductibles, and it serves as a familiar example. $50 deductible was the usual rule just a few years ago; now many companies use $100 as the standard, and we see many with $250 and $500 collision deductibles. This illustrates not only the cheaper dollar accompanying inflation, but also the wider adoption of partial self-insurance.

The same principle can be used in many other forms of insurance. Check on introducing or increasing deductibles on the following coverages:

- Homeowners;
- scheduled articles, personal articles floaters;
- boats, airplanes, other property;
- medical payments, medical expense plans;
- disability income plans (the "elimination period," or number of days of disability which must pass before benefits begin, is in effect a deductible).

In some cases, deductibles may also be carried on liability policies but this category is least likely to be practical or attractive unless used on certain types of business policies.

Medical Expense Coverages

Medical costs have increased 429 percent since 1965, but many folks are still carrying obsolete policies which unlike fine wine definitely do not improve with age.

If your present policies haven't been reviewed within the past year, have it done now.

Many policies—group or individual—carry lifetime aggregate maximum benefit of $250,000. While a quarter million dollars seems ample for most typical situations, inflation raises an ugly possiblity, especially for people in their 20s and 30s. A long-term sickness or accident can hospitalize a person for year or two at present-day costs of over $10,000 per month, including doctors, nurses, etc. Even less drastic cases can gobble money: kidney dialysis machines are rented at $25,000 to $30,000 per year. Now if a person has one such claim at a comparatively early age—and people do, of course, have such huge claims—then for the rest of his life he may carry a medical expense policy with little or no benefit remaining of the $250,000 lifetime maximum. In effect, the policy may be exhausted as it pays for its owner's rejuvenation. And such a survivor may of course be vulnerable to other long-term disabilities, making insurance essential.

Solution: If a group policy, ask the employer to have maximum benefit increased to $1,000,000.

If a non-group policy, check with the agent or company about increasing its limit.

In either case, if higher limits are not available on the present policy, try to get a separate supplemental policy.

Disability Income Protection

Policy benefits have been broadened in the past few years, so that claims will cover a wider range of conditions and, in some cases, will pay for situations previously uninsured. But this coverage, which is probably the most neglected major form of protection, needs to be reviewed as often as any other. Consider increasing the amount of monthly income benefit you're carrying in order to keep up with what inflation demands. Companies have liberalized the amounts they'll issue, provided that your income justifies the increase. You needn't necessarily buy additional coverage from the company carrying your present coverage; it's a good idea to compare rates and benefits among several companies. Some individual agents are able to present policies of several leading companies, so you needn't be bothered shopping.

Some companies offer "cost-of-living" riders which offer increased benefits based on the Consumer Price Index or some other inflation measurement. Also available from some carriers is a "guaranteed issue option," which promises to let you buy certain increased coverages at intervals of a few years. Still others offer automatic increase in benefits if you pay your premiums on an annual basis rather than semi-annually or quarterly, so that in effect you'd improve your benefits by, say 10 percent in that way.

Inflation is insidious. It makes a mockery of figures and concepts we've gotten comfortable with. In insurance, you must keep an all-round watch at all times with yearly reviews.

Chapter Twenty-Seven

How To Manage Your Money

O f all possible reasons for entering any investment area, the first has to be the desire for wealth. Second is a desire for security and independence. Inflation, although on the downswing in 1982, is still hammering into everyone's concern for security, making the investment arenas matters of necessity rather than risk—risk has become necessity, and smart investing has become more an issue of survival than of speculation. Appalling though it is, survival now relies on speculation—things are becoming that bad.

Inflation has rewritten the rule books concerning realistic household budgeting. In one sense, it is more important than ever to be a smart spender, buying necessary items before their prices launch into a higher orbit. But, parodoxically, the classic virtues of thrift and living-within-your-means are absolutely essential. Our wild-card world has made life itself both confusing and nerve-racking.

And now that the rules have changed, the place to start is your own life, in your home. In order to aggressively take charge of your life and achieve some independence, you must fight inflation with every weapon available. And your ammunition is money and gold—and you must generate money in order to invest it. The place to begin creating money is in your daily life, your life's investments, from your home to your car to your groceries. Everything must be evaluated with the goal of increasing investment capital, for this is the only way to outrun inflation. But inflation itself is a tool by which you can assess your life investments.

Future Value and Present Value

H ow should you calculate the worth of household expenditures? By assessing them against their present and future values, by estimating the time value of money itself. We will use a hypothetical individual to demonstrate this procedure.

One day while driving to work in his eight-cylinder Oldsmobile Ninety-Eight, Don Campbell decided it was time to invest in a new economy car. Personally, Don preferred the room and convenience of his present car, and it was completely paid for. But he knew he was losing money in a big way every time he visited a gas station, since his machine drank gasoline at a rate of a gallon for every ten miles covered, compared to the 30 mpg possible in most small models.

Besides, he had been told (and he believed it, too) that it was his patriotic duty to conserve fuel, particularly with the oil fields of Iran and Iraq burning under the wings of the ravens of war and the rest of the OPEC nations flexing their muscles so mightily. Don was a little confused about how the oil company profits and patriotism had somehow become the same thing, and he wondered how on earth the gas prices could continue to increase while a surplus of petroleum built up in the country, but, for the most part, he was willing to assume that his duty to his nation included the purchase of a small car. And even though the American-made small cars weren't as cheap or efficient as the imports, he planned to buy an American car: Again, it was his patriotic duty.

But since Don Campbell was cursed with curiosity, he decided to investigate the cost factors involved. When he returned home that evening, he took out a piece of paper and did some quick calculations. First, he figured the cost of buying a new 1982 economy car and then the cost of operating it over a four-year period. Next, he compared this total to the cost of keeping his old car on the road for the same length of time (see Table I).

According to Don's calculations, the economy car he chose would cost him $11,350 to buy and operate for four years. The old luxury car would consume an estimated $12,000. That clinched it—Don made up his mind to purchase a new, American-made compact car.

The next day, however, Don mentioned the subject to his neighbor, who happened to be a financial adviser. The adviser listened to Don's rationale, which apparently proved that the economy car would be a good investment. The adviser had heard car salesmen use the same argument.

The adviser explained that in inflationary times, the U.S. dollar constantly loses its purchasing power. Don was well aware of that fact, but not of its full implications. At a 10 percent inflation rate, which the adviser used as a figure that the government was using as of March, 1982, one dollar becomes worth about 90 cents after one year. After four years, it is worth only about 65 cents. Therefore, the dollar spent today could be worth substantially more than the dollar that will be spent in the future. The adviser then showed Don a way to calculate the "present value" of his car expenses, or the amount of today's dollars that would be required. Table II shows the calculations with dollars converted to their present value.

Suddenly, the economy car didn't look so economical to Don, not at a purchase price of $7000 plus tax. In today's dollars, Don concluded that retaining his big car could actually be more economical in the long run.

TABLE I — Don Campbell's Auto Cost Comparison
(Without using present value)

	New Car	Old Car
Assumptions:		
Sticker price	$7000	—
Sales tax	350	—
Annual maintenance	500	1500
Miles per gallon	30	10
Annual miles driven	10,000	10,000
Gas price/gallon	1.50	1.50

Cost	Current	Year 1	Year 2	Year 3	Year 4
Option					
New Car/cost + maintenance	$7350*	$500	$500	$500	$500
New Car/gas	500*	500	500	500	
	$7850	$1000	$1000	$1000	$500
Old Car/cost + maintenance	0*	$1500	$1500	$1500	$1500
Old Car/gas	$1500*	$1500	$1500	$1500	$1500
	$1500	$3000	$3000	$3000	$3000

Total outlay in present dollars:	New car $11,350
	Old car $12,000

* Assumes that gas is purchased at start of year; maintenance is required at year end.

Of course, this fictional situation involves a highly simplified estimate of the costs. Don's calculations assume no resale value for either the old car or the new car after four years. It also assumes that Don would pay cash for the new compact car. However, the figures will not change much if Don buys the car "on installment," so long as the interest rate he pays is at, or above, the rate of inflation, and you can be sure the lending company will do its utmost to make sure that such is the case.

In any case, the fact is that in times of high inflation, the best economy may mean keeping a gas-guzzling big car that is paid for and postponing major outlays or commitments of cash as long as possible, so that you can make payments for other things you might buy with cheaper dollars. Better yet, the cash that would otherwise be swallowed by the major purchase could be better used to actively combat inflation through another investment—one that returns something more than, say, fuel economy. And the higher inflation climbs, the better this strategy becomes.

This may appear to be the antithesis of conventional wisdom, which advocates: "In times of inflation, own things, not dollars. Things are

TABLE II	Don Campbell's Auto Cost Comparison				
	(Using Present Value at 14%)				
Cost	Current	Year 1	Year 2	Year 3	Year 4
Present Value ratio	1	.878	.771	.677	.594
New car cost	$7850	$ 878	$ 771	$ 677	$ 297
Old car cost	$1500	$2634	$2313	$2031	$ 891

Total outlay in present dollars: New car: $10,473
                                          Old car: $ 9,369

Don Campbell's Auto Cost Comparison
(Using Present Value at 20%)

Cost	Current	Year 1	Year 2	Year 3	Year 4
Present Value ratio	1	.833	.694	.579	.482
New	$7850	$ 833	$ 694	$ 579	$ 241
Old	$1500	$2499	$2082	$1737	$ 723

Total outlay in present dollars: New car: $10,197
                                          Old car: $ 8,541

constantly appreciating in value, while dollars are constantly depreciating.''

However, this is not always true. Automobiles and many other goods (such as home appliances) generally depreciate over a period of time. Meanwhile, dollars can appreciate if they are invested wisely.

Obviously, inflation has affected all of our lifestyles. In the past, it was important to sit down with a pencil, paper, and a pocket calculator and compile some quick figures before making any major purchases. Now, when economic conditions are tight and getting tighter, you should calculate the impact almost every purchase (other than incidentals) will have upon your household budget. You must be especially wary of two types of purchases: 1. Those which gobble up large amounts of current cash. 2. Those which lock installment debt payments far into the future.

Again, this runs contrary to conventional wisdom. It is true that in inflationary times it is generally better to be a borrower than a lender; borrowers are constantly repaying lenders in deflated dollars. However, the best household budgets for times of high inflation must contain some flexibility, if only because high inflation has historically been accompanied or followed by genuine social, economic, and political disaster. You must be able to cope with the unexpected. If you pledge every penny you have (or hope to save) in your income to a creditor, your choices are eliminated—no flexibility exists.

Tables III and IV contain ratios for calculating present and future values of money. To see how they work, we'll follow the mythical Taylor family as they try to decide whether to buy or rent a home.

			Inflation Rate					
Years	6%	8%	10%	11%	12%	14%	16%	20%
1	.943	.926	.909	.901	.893	.878	.862	.833
2	.890	.857	.826	.812	.797	.771	.743	.694
3	.840	.794	.751	.731	.712	.677	.641	.579
4	.792	.735	.683	.659	.636	.594	.552	.482
5	.747	.681	.621	.593	.567	.522	.476	.402
10	.558	.463	.386	.352	.322	.272	.227	.162
15	.417	.315	.239	.209	.183	.142	.108	.065
20	.312	.215	.149	.124	.104	.074	.051	.026

TABLE III   **Ratios for Calculating Present Value**

			Investment Rate				
Years	6%	8%	10%	11%	12%	14%	16%
1	1.060	1.080	1.100	1.110	1.120	1.140	1.160
2	1.124	1.166	1.210	1.232	1.254	1.297	1.346
3	1.191	1.260	1.331	1.368	1.405	1.478	1.561
4	1.262	1.360	1.464	1.518	1.574	1.683	1.811
5	1.338	1.469	1.611	1.685	1.762	1.917	2.100
10	1.791	2.159	2.376	2.839	3.106	3.675	4.411
15	2.397	3.172	4.177	4.785	5.474	7.045	9.266
20	3.207	4.661	6.727	8.062	9.646	13.504	19.461

The Taylors are being transferred to a new city, where they expect to live for five years before being relocated somewhere else again. They have the option of either buying a new home or renting, and they only want to know which will be the most economical choice. If they rent, they can sign a five-year lease at a fixed rental price of $650 per month, or they can pay $500 a month through the first year and have their rent increased by the inflation rate (they also optimistically estimated an annual rate of 14 percent) each following year. (See Table V.)

Using the "future value" approach to calculating costs, the Taylors assumed that they had a housing fund of $50,000, upon which they are constantly earning interest. Again, to arrive at conservative figures, they only allowed 12 percent earnings on all the money in the fund. Money is regularly withdrawn from the fund to make mortgage or rental payments, and for simplicity they calculated these payments as a lump sum made at the end of the year rather than monthly, since the end result varies only slightly. Also for simplicity, they decided that whatever they would pay in maintenance or taxes on any home

TABLE V — Taylor Home Cost Analysis

Assumptions: Investment (future value) rate 12%
Home cost $80,000
Down payment $20,000
Mortgage terms 30-year, 11% (11.43% annual constant)
Comparable rent value $500 per month, increasing at 14% per year; or a fixed $650 per month for five years.

Calculation of Cost Without Future Value

Cost	Current	Year 1	Year 2	Year 3	Year 4	Year 5
Option						
Buy	$20,000	$6858	$6858	$6858	$6858	$6858
Rent variable lease		$6000	$6840	$7798	$8890	$10,135
Rent fixed lease		$7800	$7800	$7800	$7800	$7800

Total outlay:	Buy (not counting downpayment)	$34,290
	Rent variable	$39,663
	Rent fixed	39,000

Calculation of Cost With Future Value at 12%
(Assumes a $50,000 initial "Housing Fund")

Cost	Current	Year 1	Year 2	Year 3	Year 4	Year 5
Option						
Buy	$50,000	$33,600	$29,951	$25,864	$21,287	$16,160
	−20,000	−6,858	−6,858	−6,858	−6,858	−6,858
	$30,000	$26,742	$23,093	$19,006	$14,429	$ 9,302
Rent variable lease	$50,000	$56,000	$56,000	$55,059	$52,932	$49,327
		−6,000	−6,840	−7,798	−8,890	10,135
	$50,000	$49,160	$47,261	$44,042	$39,192	
Rent fixed lease	$50,000	$56,000	$53,984	$51,726	$49,197	$46,365
		−7,800	−7,800	−7,800	−7,800	−7,800
	$48,200	$46,184	$43,926	$41,397	$38,565	

Buy: Remaining fund plus downpayment plus equity build-up:	$31,566
Rent variable:	$39,192
Rent fixed:	$38,565

The Taylors must resell their house for $87,726 to beat the cost of renting (variable). They must resell for $86,999 to beat the cost of renting (fixed).

they owned would be offset by income tax savings.

Without calculating future value, purchasing a home was the clear winner. The total mortgage payments over five years are $34,290, and of this $2264 goes toward principal, leaving a net cost of $32,026. The comparable costs for renting are $39,000 under the fixed-rent and $39,663 under the variable-rent lease.

However, when future value is applied, the figures change dramatically. If the Taylors buy the home, their $50,000 hypothetical fund is reduced to $9302 (counting downpayment) after five years, compared to $29,263 with the fixed lease and $29,890 with the variable lease. Adding back in the downpayment and equity build-up, the Taylors found they would need to resell their home for $86,999 to beat the fixed lease, and $87,626 to beat the variable lease.

In short, calculating the "time value of money" has become extremely important. Let's try another hypothetical situation, again using Tables III and IV to draw some cost comparisons.

You are considering the construction of a swimming pool in your backyard for family recreation. By building the pool, you figure your family will save money each year, money you would have spent on vacations and travel. The swimming pool will cost a flat $15,000. The question is: How much would you have to spend on vacations for the pool to "pay for itself?"

First, you decide whether this problem involves present value or future value. Here is one rule of thumb: Use future value to analyze the true cost of a current expenditure. Use present value to analyze the true value of future income. The swimming pool obviously involves a current expenditure of some size. Therefore, you must use the future value table (Table IV).

Another way to determine which table to use is to ask yourself, "Must I build into this analysis an inflation rate (present value) or an investment rate (future value)?" The inflation rate determines how fast money loses its value over a period of time. The investment rate determines how fast it compounds in value. In the case of the swimming pool, you are obviously dealing with the investment rate at which the $15,000 you will spend would compound if it were left in a vacation account at your bank (or, hopefully, in some higher-yielding vehicle). Thus, it is a future value problem.

One note of caution, however. You can use whatever inflation or investment rate you choose in making these calculations. Tables III and IV give you some latitude, and your guess is probably as good as that of the bureaucrats in Washington who created inflation in the first place. Unfortunately, the average investor can rarely invest his money at guaranteed interest at a rate as high as the rate of inflation. Any investment rate at or above the inflation rate usually involves some risk. To be safe, therefore, it is prudent to select an investment rate at a percentage point or two below the inflation rate you select.

In the case of swimming pool versus vacations, let's use an investment rate of 11 percent. If you look in the future value table (Table IV), under 11 percent, you will note that after one year the ratio is 1.110. Multiply this by the $15,000 you would have spent on the swimming pool, and you will see that after one year your $15,000 would have grown to $16,650. You could withdraw $1650 to spend on vacations and still have your $15,000 investment intact.

Or, if you choose not to take a vacation in the first year, you could let the money accumulate until the second year, when the ratio (at 11 percent) would be 1.232. The total fund would then be $18,480, on your original investment ($15,000) plus $3480. In the second year, you could enjoy two vacations costing $1740 and still have your $15,000 intact.

Now, let's work the same problem in reverse. You have budgeted $2000 a year on vacations over the next five years. You want to build a swimming pool instead, using the vacation money to pay for it. The question is: "How much can you afford to spend on a swimming pool you build today?"

A quick answer is $2000 times five years, or $10,000. But that is an incorrect answer. Since you are dealing with a present value problem, the $2000 you plan to spend on vacations each year is obtained from future income. After one year, the present value of $2000 at a 12 percent rate of inflation is .893 times $2000, or $1786. In the second year, the $2000 you will spend is really worth only .797 times $2000, or $1594 in today's dollars. This exercise can be continued until you have a column that looks like the following:

Year	Ratio	Value
1	.893	$1786
2	.797	1594
3	.712	1424
4	.636	1272
5	.567	1134
		$7210

Of course, this is a highly simplified example which ignores such important factors as maintenance of the pool, the amount of value the pool might add to the home, or any interest cost that might be incurred in financing the pool. However, this example does demonstrate how to make use of present and future value in your budgetary calculations.

Spend Successfully

A gain, to invest money you must create capital. Accomplishing this requires an aggressive but carefully considered approach to all of your household budgeting.

To start, you should adhere to the following basic rules of successful spending:

1. Always use present value and future value (as previously described) in budgeting major outlays of cash. This, of course, will be most appropriate when you are considering the purchase of a home, a vehicle, appliances, or anything else that carries a hefty price tag.

2. Purchase items with the potential to appreciate. Delay the purchase of items with a high potential for depreciation. In an inflationary age, items with

appreciation potential are in high demand. Consequently, they rise in price faster than the Consumer Price Index (CPI).

Conversely, many items which depreciate rapidly are not in demand and will not rise in price as quickly. For example, clothing depreciates very rapidly, and it has also declined significantly as a percentage of total household expenditures. In 1960, 8.1 percent of all average expenditures disappeared into clothing. By 1977 that average figure had dropped to 6.8 percent.

Durable goods usually depreciate more slowly than nondurable household goods. From 1960 to 1981, the percent of household income spent on durables (refrigerators, televisions, stereos, and so on) remained fairly steady, while the percentage spent on nondurable items declined.

As a rule, items which depreciate rapidly are more cyclical in price than items which appreciate. By delaying purchases of non-essential depreciating assets, you may be able to buy them at a bargain. Today, the small, "inexpensive" automobiles tend to depreciate faster than most luxury cars, but mid-sized vehicles are most likely to be sold at discounts or with rebates.

3. Lock in recurring expenses for as long a term as possible. While the CPI has been racing upward at double-digit rates, the fact is that many Americans have escaped much of the CPI increase, simply because they own their own homes or purchased them at fixed rates far below the prevailing interest rates and substantially below the rate of inflation. They locked in the cost of housing when housing was much cheaper.

Because housing accounts for about 40 percent of the weighting in the CPI, these families have, in effect, experienced inflation of only eight to ten percent, while renters have been hit by a rate of 12 to 14 percent.

Of course, when a homebuyer moves or "trades up" to a new house, some of the pent-up wrath of the CPI will be felt. And, as has been said, the rules have changed for someone seeking to purchase a house now; these persons face new inflation-related obstacles, not the least of which is the simple fact that the old "fixed rate" mortgage may be a thing of the past.

There are several less significant ways to lock in long-term expenses which can nonetheless add up to big savings. In purchasing subscriptions or paying dues, customers are often offered special rates for paying three or four years ahead of time. These rates have often resulted in significant savings when subscription rates were later raised. In some cases, individuals have bought "lifetime" memberships or subscriptions at a rate only a few dollars above the current one-year rate!

You can also try other, more ingenious ways of locking in costs. For example, in times of tight credit, it is often a struggle for a young doctor to obtain the cash flow necessary to pay for his or her education, office, and equipment. Meanwhile, medical costs are one of the fastest-rising components of the CPI. (From 1970 to 1981, for instance, the average price of an office visit more than doubled). In this climate, it is not unusual to find relatives and friends making low-interest loans to new doctors in return for an agreement to provide low-cost medical care for many years.

If you enjoy vacationing in a particular area, you can lock in part of your costs by purchasing a "time-sharing" interest in a condominium. A larger freezer can almost pay for itself by allowing you to lock in the cost of meat and other expensive foods. Barter is still another way to preserve capital for investment purposes.

4. Don't, don't, don't let your money sit idle. Avoid tying up capital in a while-you-wait layaway or Christmas savings plan. This type of plan may have made great sense, once: You couldn't afford a particular item now, so you paid a deposit to hold it and then gradually paid it off. When inflation rested at two or three percent, the convenience benefits outweighed the "cost of money," but not any more. Even the $100 you have in a layaway account can be earning high interest in a money market fund; even less than $60 can buy you a little hard security in the form of a small gold coin. Banks are now offering NOW accounts, paying interest on checking account deposits, and some stock brokerage firms are paying interest on balances.

All of your money should be working for you, right now. If someone owes you money or a refund check, ask for prompt payment. The worst offender of all is the federal government, which collects millions of dollars each year in interest-free loans through overcollection of income tax payroll deductions. If you usually cash a refund check in the spring, check with your employer to see if you can legally claim more deductions, to reduce your participation in this interest-free loan privilege the government enjoys.

5. Check your life insurance cost against benefits. As a practical matter, most financial planners say that the easiest way to free up "cash flow" and investment money in a household budget is by rearranging the insurance coverage.

Insurance companies enjoy a situation second only to the government's overcollection of payroll deductions. Through the cash values of a typical whole life insurance policy, you are, in reality, making an extremely low-interest loan to an insurance company. In fact, a recent study by the Federal Trade Commission revealed that this loan generally yields interest at a rate of three to four percent or less. Weighed against annual inflation of 14 percent, each whole life insurance dollar is losing eight percent or more per year.

Many agents who sell term insurance will now perform a free analysis for you to determine how you can keep the same insurance coverage at a lower annual cost. In any case, it makes no sense to consider such vehicles "enforced savings" plans; even ordinary passbook accounts return better than three or four percent.

However, the worst offender in the life insurance racket is not whole life but a kind of policy called "industrial life" or "debit" insurance. Such policies usually contain a face value of $10,000 or *less* while requiring monthly or even weekly premiums. Studies done in the South, where this type of coverage is predominantly sold, have shown that some families have been sold 50 or more debit insurance policies and pay more in insurance premiums than they do for their home mortgages!

Generally, overlapping insurance coverages should be considered wasteful; there are much better ways to use your money.

6. Read all the fine print related to interest costs and credit. In times of tight credit, a new business arises. People who do not have the cash or credit to buy new televisions or other expensive appliances are approached by companies which will rent them the goods for two years. After 24 monthly payments, the renter will own the appliance free and clear. For a television, the payments are usually in the range of $60 per month, which does not seem overly burdensome in a month-by-month scenario. The only problem is that renters eventually pay more than $1400 to own a television set which would retail for $500 or less. They are victims of a credit crunch and are easy prey for unscrupulous promoters out for a fat deal. In short, don't let the credit squeeze and high inflation push you into a deal you would otherwise consider laughable.

7. Establish credit. Don't abuse it. One of the cardinal rules of small business success is: "You can never get credit when you need it most. You can always get it when you don't need it."

In difficult economic times (and our times are likely to become more difficult, rather than less), it is most important to establish your credit and create new credit sources in anticipation of even worse times ahead. Unfortunately, this message has often been translated to "buy all you can on credit."

This is dangerous for two obvious reasons. First, if inflation and interest rates should ease, people who have overextended their credit will find themselves stuck with a mountain of debt incurred at higher-than-prevailing rates. And bear in mind that in Great Britain, inflation has been combatted by massive unemployment. Second, if things get worse, those who have abused credit will be the first to find themselves "over their heads." An argument can be made that when everyone is in debt (in political terms), no one is in debt. However, this thinking applies only to a depression scenario with attendant government moratoriums on debt, and under such circumstances things will be bad no matter how you view it.

In times of high inflation, classic thrift and good judgment are at a premium, and good credit relations can provide a first-line safety net.

8. Consider making foreign travel or foreign investment decisions now. While inflation is a worldwide epidemic, it threatens more greatly to undermine the United States economy than the economies of several other industrial nations which do not indulge in as much wasteful government spending or high-level bungling in monetary policy. For example, the U.S. dollar has demonstrated long-term weakness against the Swiss franc and the German mark, where inflation is being held at rates lower than those in the U.S. (For a detailed discussion of foreign exchange rates, see the chapter on foreign currencies.)

As dollars become ever cheaper on the international market, foreign products can only become more expensive. In addition, foreign travel may again become the province of only the very wealthy.

There is a corollary to this rule: Consider holding some of your assets in a currency that is more stable than the U.S. dollar, perhaps in a Swiss bank, as a means of protecting your eroding assets.

9. Try to establish some income other than a straight salary. In 1979, as inflation sped along at a 14 percent annual rate, average personal income increased at only about eight percent, and that seems to be the trend of the future. After paying federal, state, and local taxes, typical salaried workers watched their standard of living decline by as much as eight percent in one year. Taxes certainly haven't been reduced, wage increases certainly haven't been accelerated, and inflation certainly hasn't been controlled; people's standards of living will certainly continue to decline.

10. Create a household budgeting process. This may seem obvious, but too few people adhere to this principle. Start each year at a "zero-base." Most household budgeting has been an informal affair, haphazardly created and soon forgotten, but it will increasingly become a science as pennies are pinched coming and going. Particular attention should be paid to such rapidly rising components of household expenditures as transportation and recreation, with emphasis on ways to eliminate expenses which do not create convenience or value. Just as companies have adopted "zero-based" budgeting techniques, households should start each year with a thorough evaluation of each "line item." Long-term budget goals (such as a college education fund for children, for example) should not be routinely sacrificed for short-term contingencies. Present value and future value, as mentioned earlier, should be calculated when considering all major expenditures.

Increase Your Capital

All of these procedures should be directed at a single goal: Creating money for investments to outpace inflation. Most people believe that to become financially independent, they must save and let their money grow. However, most people give their money's earning power to a bank or other savings institutions rather than investing it themselves. You must seek the highest possible return for all of your money; if some savings vehicle can do this, then it is appropriate to use it. However, this is unlikely.

People fail to achieve the goal of security for several reasons:
- Procrastination,
- Failure to establish goals,
- Ignorance of what money must do to accomplish the goals,
- Failure to understand and apply our convoluted tax laws, and
- Failure to buy the right kind of life insurance.

Quite simply (and depressingly), the future is bleak for the U.S. economy. The time to act is immediately, if not sooner; the years of carefree spending ended in the last decade. And, of course, individuals will suffer the most. The place to start is in your own home. You must either protect yourself now, and make a habit of concentrating your thought and energy toward combatting the continued mismanagement of our collapsing economy, or you will have to reconcile yourself to a continually declining standard of living.

Chapter Twenty-Eight

What To Do With Your IRA Dollars

To paraphrase the immortal Jimmy Durante, "Everyone wants to get in the IRA act," as a result of the new less-restrictive federal legislation that allows any working individual to participate. Americans by the millions are finding Individual Retirement Accounts to be highly attractive investments and, eager to capture their share of the market, almost every bank, thrift institution, brokerage firm, insurance company, and money market and mutual fund firm in the land is offering special inducements to get people to sign up for IRAs with them.

The competition for the IRA dollar has become fierce, even brutal. Consider:

● The Bank of America, the largest bank in the United States, offers a 15 percent interest rate on IRAs, in addition to chances on cash and other prizes in what they call the "IRA plus nest egg sweepstakes." Even employees of the bank who open accounts for customers get chances in the contest.

● Merrill Lynch, America's biggest brokerage house, opened 13,000 IRA accounts in one day—January 4, 1982, the first day they became universally available. Merrill now provides at least 20 different types of financial instruments for IRA investment.

● Merchants National Bank in Cedar Rapids, Iowa, in what must have been a dizzying wave of euphoria, briefly offered a 50 percent rate of interest for the first quarter—but cancelled the program when it was inundated with orders.

The IRA: What It Is

In case you've been so deluged with details on the accounts that you've lost track of their basic purpose, IRAs are a tax-sheltered way of saving money for retirement. The latest government rules on IRAs are liberal. You can set one up with almost any type of financial institution in virtually any type of money-making venture (except collectibles). And you have almost unlimited freedom to move your money from one investment, or institution, to another.

The maximum annual tax-sheltered deposit is $2000 per person, $4000 per working couple. If only one person earns an income, a couple can set up one IRA for the wage earner and a separate account for the non-working spouse. In such a case, the couple can shelter as much as $2250 of the gross income, but no more than $2000 can be deposited in one of the IRAs.

The Internal Revenue Service does not require any minimum deposit, or any deposit at all from year to year; the amount you deposit, when you deposit it, and where it is deposited is up to you. Obviously, though, the more you put into your IRA from year-to-year, the larger your nest egg will be on retirement.

Except in a spousal IRA, no one may deposit more than his or her total earned income (exclusive of interest, dividends, capital gains, or pension income) in any given year. Thus, if you earn $1500 from part-time employment in a calendar year, no more than $1500 can be deposited in your IRA for that particular year.

You cannot withdraw IRA money without penalty until you are 59½ years of age, unless you become disabled or die before that time (in which case, your heirs can make the withdrawal). The IRS penalty for any early withdrawal is ten percent of the amount withdrawn, plus payment of ordinary income tax on the withdrawn amount. Should you die prematurely, your beneficiary would receive the money with the right to use it immediately or spread out withdrawals throughout his or her life.

Another rule is that even after 59½, you must pay ordinary income tax on the amount withdrawn each year. Even if some of that amount represents a capital gain on a stock investment, you will not be eligible for the lower capital gains tax.

The attraction is that you will probably be in a lower tax bracket during your retirement. And the two tax breaks you will have received through your IRA in the meantime should more than make up for the retirement tax burden.

The tax break that has the most appeal is the deduction of the total amount you deposit in the account each year. But the second break—tax-free interest and dividends until the money is withdrawn—may prove more valuable, especially if you maintain the account for 10 or more years. The clearest way to show this works is through an example. Take someone who deposits $2000 a year in equal monthly installments in an IRA with a 16 percent annual return. If he contributes for 10 years before retirement, he will accumulate close to $50,000.

And that's only part of it. As he withdraws money in retirement, say for 15 years, the balance in the account continues to earn tax-sheltered interest. So, instead of withdrawing 1/15th of $50,000 or $3333, each year, he can withdraw close to $8600 a year.

Other IRA Pluses

Without an IRA, assuming the individual is in the 25 percent tax bracket, he would give one-fourth of the interest to Uncle Sam each year. The retirement nest egg would be less than $39,000 and annual retirement withdrawals would be a little more than $5500. And, if the wage earner is in the 50 percent bracket, the nest egg would be less than $31,000, and the retirement withdrawals below $3500 a year.

For the person who contributes to an IRA for 30 years before retirement, the difference the tax break offers is even greater. In an IRA returning 16 percent a year, he or she would accumulate close to $1.5 million and take out more than $20,000 a month (or $250,000 a year) for 15 years.

In an account with no tax shelter on interest, he or she would have close to $600,000 at retirement and withdraw almost $84,000 a year, if in the 25 percent tax bracket. In the 50 percent bracket, the individual could accumulate only $250,000 and withdraw less than $30,000 a year. For this person, the tax break on IRA interest means his or her retirement income would be more than eight times larger. (If the individual had contributed only $1000 a year to his or her IRA, all the preceding numbers would be halved; if only $200 had been contributed, all the numbers would be divided by 10).

Despite the two big tax breaks IRAs bring, they were not particularly popular investments before the start of 1982. Most experts attributed the lack of interest to the lower public awareness of IRAs and to the fact that people then eligible for them—those not covered by an IRS-qualified retirement plan—were mostly self-employed or part-time workers who could not afford to put away money they would not be able to use for decades.

Pre-1982 IRAs were also less attractive in that account holders could deposit and deduct only 15 percent of earned income up to $1500, (or $1750 if the account included a non-working spouse). The changes that made all workers eligible and raised deposit levels came in the Economic Recovery Tax Act of 1981.

Where To Put Your IRA

One attraction of Individual Retirement Accounts, apart from their tax-shelter features, is that you can invest your money for optimal returns almost anywhere, except in collectibles. But while that wide a choice can be wonderful in theory, it can be overwhelming in practice, because there are so many variations on this particular money-saving, money-making theme.

Many bank IRA accounts are similar to certificates of deposit. That is, you start a plan at, say 14 percent, for a two-and-one-half year period. At the end of that period, you can reinvest at whatever interest rate is available or roll it over into another bank or another plan. You can transfer your IRA funds into a new, and perhaps, higher-yield account at least once a year. There is no tax penalty on transfers, if you roll over the funds within 60 days. But you cannot take the money out.

You can set up an IRA at banks, savings and loans, credit unions, brokerage firms, mutual funds, or insurance companies. Interest rates vary, but if you invest your IRA in a mutual fund or some kind of security, the capital appreciation could be much more important. You may have a high return on your money in some years, and a low one in others. In a bank or savings and loan, your money will be federally insured, whereas mutual funds or other money instruments will not be, at least not under the present law.

Choosing Financial Institutes

A wise first step is to consider the type of financial institution that fits your individual situation and optimum investment potential. Banks, savings and loans (those with strong fiduciary condition), and well-established credit unions represent the more conservative possibilities, while stock and bond brokerages and mutual fund companies rank at the other end of the spectrum.

Perhaps the most conservative of all is the U.S. Government, where you can set up an IRA with U.S. Individual Retirement Bonds. These are sold in increments of $50, $75, $100, and $500, and they currently yield nine percent interest compounded semiannually; the rate is guaranteed for the life of the IRA, through age 70½, when the bonds must be redeemed. These bonds are available at the nearest Federal Reserve Bank or through the mail from the Securities and Transaction Branch, Bureau of Public Debt, Washington, DC 20226. The investor who chooses this route, of course, is likely to believe that interest rates eventually will come down and that inflation will average less than nine percent per year.

When you begin to explore the myriad possibilities among private institutions, matters become a bit more complicated. Fees are an important consideration here, and they do vary widely. But you will also want to know details on investment options in the IRA, rules on minimum deposits, and how often you may deposit money in your IRA account during each calendar year. Another important point: Be aware of any restrictions and fees involved in moving the IRA to another company.

If the interest at one institution is compounded daily and at another on a monthly basis, ask both how much your IRA would accumulate by the end of the year if you had $1000 on deposit on January 1. That way you can compare apples with apples.

Recently, much has been made of the fact that financial institutions have touted the "you can become a millionaire" theme in its various forms. The reaction from many CPAs has been that this is really creative bookkeeping. It is true that after 40 years or so you would have accumulated more than a million dollars, but these would be in the year 2020 dollars, rather than 1982 dollars. So, in terms of 1982 money, you might have only $100,000, depending on what rate of inflation you assign to the next 25 or 30 years.

There may be some drawbacks to investing in IRAs if you are young, say under 30 years of age, for example. The problem is that you will not be able to touch the money for more than 20 years without paying a high penalty. Additionally, the money cannot be used as collateral to take out a loan to buy a house, or car, or any other major purchase. You also are not allowed to use it to further your own education or for your children's college.

Selecting Your Investment

I f the institution offers a choice of investments, select the one that is best suited for you. This is largely a matter of personal taste, and whether you expect stock prices and interest rates to rise or fall. The stock price implications are clear—if you think the prices will rise, invest in a stock mutual fund or your own stock portfolio; if you think they will fall, stick with other investments. If you think interest rates will rise, go for money market funds, or variable-rate certificates of deposits; if you think they'll fall, invest in bonds, bond mutual funds, or fixed-rate CDs.

Because you'll be tying up the money for years—maybe even decades—you may want to consider a long-term investment. American National Bank of Chicago lets IRA customers choose the term of their IRA certificates, all the way up to 45 years for a 20-year-old who expects to retire at 65. At most other institutions the terms for IRA investments are much shorter, often five years or less, but you can find some in the 10 or 15 year range.

Remember that you could regret making a long-term investment if interest rates were to rise later or if some other type of investment were to become more attractive and you were unable to switch to it without penalty.

There will continue to be new wrinkles to this IRA business, now that the financial community has jumped into the fray at full gallop. Innovations will be limited solely by the extent of the imagination of their creators. One of the newest is called the "salary-reduction plan" or SRP. Under this concept, you can save as much as 10 percent of your pre-tax income every year. As with any IRA, earnings are tax-free until age 59½, but in this case, employees may also match contributions to a SRP offering a wide variety of investment choices.

You cannot get a direct income tax deduction like you do with an IRA, but your savings are not considered current taxable income. When you receive the money from your plan at retirement, it also has the advantage of lower taxation. One further wrinkle is that some of the cash may be withdrawn early without penalty in certain "hardship cases"—such as for higher education purposes. Participation in an SRP would not prevent you from having an IRA also, and some firms have already made provisions for adopting both through a payroll deduction program.

IRA QUESTIONS & ANSWERS

Because IRAs vary widely and because they involve large amounts of money, most potential IRA holders have questions they would like answered before they sign up. Following are some of the more frequently asked questions and their answers:

Q: Do I have to start withdrawing IRA money at 59½?

A: You do not have to start withdrawing until you are 70½ years old, even if you retire before then.

Q: Do I have to open an IRA by December 31st to get a deduction on my 1982 taxes?

A: No. You may open an account any time up until your next tax filing date, April 15, 1983, or even later if you get an extension.

Q: Does that mean I can open an IRA before April 15, 1982, and still get a break on my 1981 taxes?

A: *Not unless you were eligible for an IRA in 1981, which means you were not covered by an IRS-qualified pension plan. The vast majority of company pension plans are IRS-qualified, but if you think yours may not be, ask your employer.*

Q: How does an IRA keep pace with inflation? Wouldn't I be better off investing my money where it will keep up with inflation for sure?

A: *There probably isn't a better place to shelter your savings from inflation than in an IRA, unless you're prepared to put your retirement funds in a high-risk investment, like a joint venture. IRA money can be put in almost any relatively safe type of investment. And because of the IRA tax-exemption on interest and dividends, your investment has a better chance of beating inflation in an IRA than in an ordinary, taxable investment.*

Q: If I have so many deductions that I pay little or no federal income tax, should I still open an IRA?

A: *Clearly, the tax deduction would not be as beneficial since you would be in a low tax bracket. But you would still get the benefit of tax-exempt interest or dividends, which would enable your savings to grow faster.*

Q: How much money should I deposit in my IRA?

A: *Because of the early withdrawal penalty, you're probably better off not depositing more than you think you can do without until you retire. But don't be too conservative. The ten percent IRA penalty is not nearly as tough as, say, the all-savers certificate early withdrawal penalty.*

If you find you must withdraw some IRA money before you're 59½, but you've had money in the IRA account for more than a couple of years, you'll probably find the tax advantages of sheltering it for those years more than offset the penalty.

Q: Is there an advantage to depositing the full $2000 at the beginning of the calendar year?

A: *Yes, if you can afford to do it. The sooner you make your IRA deposit, the more tax-sheltered interest you will earn each year.*

Q: What happens if I deposit more than the maximum allowable amount in my IRA?

A: *Nothing, as long as you take out the excess before you file your tax return for that year and include in your taxable income all interest or dividends earned on that excess amount.*

But if you take the excess out even a day after filing your return, you must pay a penalty tax of six percent of the excess amount. That penalty continues for every year the excess is there. If, for instance, your allowable maximum is $2000, and you deposit $2200 one year, but only $1800 the next year, you would pay the penalty tax on the excess $200 plus earnings for one year only.

Q: May I have both an IRA and a Keogh retirement account?

A: Starting this year, yes, you may have both accounts, as long as you have the self-employment income necessary to set up a Keogh. With both accounts, you can contribute and deduct up to a total of $17,000 from your 1982 taxes.

Q: May I have more than one IRA?

A: You may have as many IRAs as you want, as long as your total deposits to all IRAs do not exceed your maximum—$2000 per person in most cases.

Generally, though, opening several IRAs is not a good idea, as you will probably have to pay more fees. But if you put your first-year IRA money in a three-year bank certificate and then decide you don't want to put your second-year contributions into the same bank, you can open an IRA elsewhere while holding the bank IRA until the three years are up.

Q: How do I report my IRA deduction on my federal income tax form?

A: If you have an IRA deduction, you must use the long, 1040 form, whether or not you itemize deductions. There's a special line for the IRA deduction on the front page of the 1040, and there's an optional separate form you may also file if you wish.

Q: Where can I get more information on IRAs?

A: The institutions offering them are giving away free brochures and answering questions by the thousands. You can also get quite a lot of information from some IRA advertisements.

Q: I have several brochures on IRAs, and each shows different results on how much I will have in retirement at the same interest rate. How come?

A: Total annual yields vary, depending on how often interest is compounded. For example, if you put $2000 a year into an IRA that pays 12 percent compounded daily, it will be worth over $400,000 more after 40 years than one paying 12 percent compounded yearly, according to Donoghue's "Moneyletter."

Also, different totals reflect different patterns of deposit—all at the beginning of the year, gradually throughout the year, or all at the end of the year.

Q: What happens if there's a divorce?

A: *Under the new rules, a divorced spouse is allowed to use alimony along with compensation as a basis for contribution to a "divorced spouse" IRA, if certain conditions are met. The new rules allow contributions if an IRA was established for the divorced spouse at lease five years before the divorce. Also, the former spouse must have made spousal contributions to the divorced spouse's IRA for at least three of the five years preceding the divorce.*

If these conditions are met, contributions can be made up to the lesser of $1125 or the total of the divorced spouse's compensation and alimony included in gross income. (If the divorced spouse has compensation of more than $1125, however, a regular IRA contribution can be made up to the higher limits as long as no alimony is counted.)

Q: If both spouses filing a joint return have compensation during the tax year, can they co-mingle funds in a jointly owned IRA or IRAs?

A: *No. Each must establish a separate IRA or IRAs up to the limit of $2000 in total annual contributions each, for a total of $4000.*

Q: Must working couples file a joint return if they both have IRAs?

A: *No. They may both file individual returns if they wish. (The requirement for a joint return applies only if a working spouse makes and wishes to deduct an IRA contribution for a non-working spouse).*

Q: For married couples, would an IRA affect the new marriage penalty deduction in the tax law?

A: *Yes. In 1982, a two-earner married couple filing a joint return may deduct from gross income up to 5 percent of the first $30,000 of income earned by the lower-earnings spouse. This deduction will increase to 10 percent after 1982.*

Q: What is compounding and what difference does it make on my IRA?

A: *When interest is compounded, the earnings (interest)-for a specified period of time are added to the principal (main sum) so that interest for the following period is computed on the principal plus accumulated interest. An account at a bank, savings and loan or money market fund may be compounded daily, weekly, monthly, quarterly, semi-annually, annually or it may just earn simple interest.*

For example, $2000 invested in a savings account that earned 14.75 percent interest would earn $322.54 if compounded daily (16.127 percent annual yield), $315.74 if compounded semi-annually (15.29 percent yield) and $295 at simple interest.

Q: Were any changes made in eligibility for spousal IRAs?

A: *No. They are available to any married couple who file a joint tax return and has one non-working spouse who earns no compensation during the year. You must be married at the end of the tax year and meet all other IRA requirements.*

Q: What happens if the unmarried spouse gets a job or earns other compensation during the year?

A: *In that case a spousal IRA contribution cannot be made. However, a regular IRA contribution could be made, governed by the more liberal rules for such a contribution.*

Q: Can a couple with a spousal IRA combine the money in a single account or investment?

A: *No. As before, each spouse must have his or her IRA. However, if they wish each can name the other as beneficiary.*

If the lower-earning spouse has an IRA, the IRA deduction must be taken first. This will reduce that spouse's earned income for purposes of the marriage penalty deduction. For instance, if the lower-earning spouse earned $10,000 in 1982, the deduction without an IRA would be 5 percent of that or $500. But if that spouse had contributed $2000 to an IRA, the $2000 would have to be subtracted from the $10,000 before calculating the marriage penalty deduction—in this case 5 percent of $8000 or $400, a difference of $100.

However, you'll always come out ahead with the IRA. The IRA deductions are not only much larger than the forfeited part of the marriage penalty deduction, but tax-sheltered money in an IRA may grow many-fold as well.

Q: Are fees for opening IRAs and annual custodial services deductible from my income tax and do they come out of the IRA or am I billed separately?

A: *Merrill Lynch says it has a letter from the Internal Revenue Service stating that the fees and charges on an IRA are deductible, but the IRS has refused to confirm this. We will have to wait for a further ruling. As for billing, you can handle the fees either way you desire, but the prudent investor would be billed separately so as not to reduce the amount of tax-free money working for you in the account.*

Q: What is an employer-sponsored IRA?

A: It is where an employer elects to contribute to some or all of its employees regular IRA's rather than establish a qualified retirement plan. The employer increases the salary of each employee to be covered and contributes the increment to that employee's IRA. The employee's W-2 wages show the regular salary plus the increase. The employee deducts the IRA contribution from his gross income on his tax return. The contribution limits and eligibility requirements are the same as for a regular IRA.

Q: Once an IRA is established, must you make a contribution each year?

A: No, you decide each year if you wish to contribute. You may skip one or more years and start contributing again.

Q: If you are eligible to make a contribution but put in nothing, or less than the maximum amount allowable for that year, can you make up the amount not contributed in later years?

A: No. If any contribution is less than the maximum allowable amount, the balance may not be contributed in subsequent years.

Q: If you die, will distributions from your IRA to your beneficiaries be included in your taxable estate?

A: Distributions to beneficiaries other than an executor will not be subject to the federal estate tax if they are made in regular payments for a period of at least 36 months. If these provisions are not complied with, the distributions will be part of your taxable estate. Inheritance taxes, which are imposed by the states, are another matter. You should check with your tax advisor regarding the law in your state. In addition, the beneficiary will be required to pay income taxes on the distribution as it is received.

Chapter Twenty-Nine

Suggested References

The current state of the economy and perpetual fears of worsening recession and inflation have spawned a proliferation of financial books. The following is a brief summary of selected books on investments and personal financial management culled from the staggering array of current issues. To obtain copies of the reviewed books, write directly to the publisher.

Collectibles

Collecting & Care of Fine Art, by Carl David (Crown, New York, NY $10). For the neophyte, this book provides specific examples ranging from the pitfalls to the potential rewards, including advice on tax strategies, avoiding fakes, and pricing.

Know Your Antiques, by Ralph & Terry Kovel (Crown, New York, NY $13.95). An in-depth guide to evaluating, buying, and caring for any antique, by foremost experts in the field.

Know Your Collectibles, by Ralph & Terry Kovel (Crown, New York, NY $16.95). Expert advice on how to preserve, protect, and sell your collectibles, covering a wide variety of objects both of established and anticipated value.

The Encyclopedia of Collectibles, edited by Andrea DiVoto (Time-Life Books, Alexandria, VA). A highly informative, well-organized, wide-ranging series of volumes, including cookbooks, furniture, photographs, quilts, sporting equipment, pottery, and more.

Diamonds & Other Gems

Grow Rich With Diamonds, by Bernhard Dohrmann (G.P. Putnam's Sons, Harbor Publishing, San Francisco, CA $12.95). The author, one of the U.S.

pioneers in diamond investing, tells why diamonds are a safe and profitable investment in today's market.

How To Buy & Sell Gems, by Benjamin Zucker (Time Books, New York, NY $12.95). A guide to the would-be investor in gems, with practical advice on rubies, sapphires, emeralds, and diamonds.

The World of Diamonds, by Timothy Green (William Morrow, New York, NY $12.95). The inside story of the miners, cutters, smugglers, and investors.

Commodities

Commodity Speculation for Beginners, by Charles Huff & Barbara Marinacci (Macmillan Publishing, New York, NY $11.95). Everything you need to know to get started in one of the most potentially rewarding games in town: commodity speculation.

The Dow-Jones-Irwin Guide to Commodity Trading, by Bruce G. Gould (Dow Jones-Irwin, Homewood, IL $13.95). A professional trader explains the commodities markets and demonstrates the logic and skills of successful trading.

The Fastest Game in Town: Commodities, by Mark Robert Perry (Prentice-Hall, Englewood Cliffs, NJ $9.95). A well-written, interesting dissertation describing the workings and pitfalls of commodity trading.

Winning In The Commodities Market, by George Angell (Doubleday & Co., Garden City, NY $12.95). In-depth analysis of the futures market, with 1001 questions from commodity traders.

Inflation

How To Use Inflation To Beat The IRS, by B. Ray Anderson (Harper & Row, New York, NY $14.95). A comprehensive guide to turning inflation to your advantage when battling the IRS. Every method explained is completely legal.

Inflation-Proof Your Investment, by Harry Browne & Terry Coxon (William Morrow & Co., New York, NY $14.95). How to protect yourself today by creating your own long-term, low-cost investment program that will keep you ahead of inflation, depression, and taxes.

99 Ways To Make Money In A Depression, by Gerald Appel (Arlington House, Westport, CT $14.95). Investment strategies to use during the economic turmoil in the 1980s, including selling short and buying puts in a bear market.

Protecting Profits During Inflation/Recession, by Bruce M. Bradway &

Robert E. Pritchard (Addison-Wesley, Reading, MA $7.95). A thorough primer to coping during inflationary times for owners of small businesses.

Insurance

How To Save A Fortune On Your Life Insurance, by Barry Kaye (Carol Press, Los Angeles, CA $12.95). Complete explanation of the intricate machinations of life insurance and ways to cut your costs while increasing your coverage.

Investing

Fail-Safe Investing: How To Make Money With Less Than $10,000, by Peter Nagan (Putnam's Sons, New York, NY $10.95). A conservative, how-to-invest book for neophyte investors that includes approaches to stocks, bonds, real estate, tax shelters, and other vehicles.

Fundamentals Of Investing, by Lawrence J. Gitman & Michael D. Joenk (Harper & Row, New York, NY $12.95). A general reference textbook for experienced and non-experienced investors.

Handbook Of Financial Markets: Securities, Options, Futures, edited by Frank J. Favozzi & Frank G. Zabb (Dow Jones-Irwin, Homewood, IL $37.50). A useful and informative, broad-based book running the gamut of investment topics—the markets, tax savings, etc.

How To Buy Money: Investing Wisely For Maximum Return, by Barry R. Steiner & David W. Kennedy (John Wiley & Sons, New York, NY $12.95). A questions-and-answers format that reveals a collection of legal tax dodges ranging from shelters to bad debts, and more.

How To Make Your Money Make Money, edited by Arthur Levitt, Jr. (Dow Jones-Irwin, Homewood, IL $11.95). A virtual cornucopia of investment advice ranging from stocks to movies to wine to oil to bonds, collectibles, stamps, art, etc.

The Psychology Of Successful Investing, by Jacob Bernstein (Wiley & Sons, New York, NY $11.95). A psychologic approach to investing geared toward improving the individual investor's "I.Q." (Investing Quotient).

Sophisticated Investor: How To Target Prime Investments, by Albert M. Church III (Prentice-Hall, Englewood Cliffs, NJ $15.95). Covers a broad range of investment media in a relatively short book: tax exempts, CDs, money market funds, commodity and financial futures, stocks, gems, bonds, and real estate.

Money Management/Financial Planning

Bankruptcy: Do-It-Yourself, by Attorney Janice Kosel (Addison-Wesley,

Reading, PA $11.95). A clear, concise, and sympathetic guide that provides access to legalities, explanation of the latest laws, advice regarding lawyers, and guidance through the bankruptcy process.

Book Of Incomes, by Gerald Krefetz & Philip Gittelman (Holt, Rinehart & Winston, New York, NY $6.95). An exploration of the work world, offering views of specific positions, unusual professions, job descriptions, and the going rate for various employment.

Getting Rich: A Smart Women's Guide To Successful Money Management, by Diane L. Ackerman (A&W Publishers, New York, NY $11.95). Not for women only, this is a clearly-written education in financial management and investing.

Magic Of Thinking Rich, by Ralph Charell (Simon & Schuster, New York, NY $12.95). Focuses on the psychology of wealth, that may not tell you how to make a fortune, but it will tell you what attitudes make millions.

Money Dynamics For The '80s, by Venita VanCaspel (Reston Publishing, Reston, VA $15.00). A comprehensive guide to personal finance including review questions at the end of each chapter and abundant appendixes and an impartial listing of each investment's advantages and disadvantages.

Personal Finance, by Lawrence J. Gitman (Dryden Press, Hinsdale, IL $18.95). All the fundamental bases of personal financial management.

Personal Financial Planning: How To Plan For Your Financial Freedom, by Victor Hallman & Jerry S. Rosenbloom (McGraw-Hill, New York, NY $5.95). A comprehensive guide to the individual's planning, explaining the important aspects of insurance, retirement, and offering the basics of investing.

Making It On Your Own, by Dr. Norman Finegold & Dr. Leonard Perlman (Acropolis Books, Washington, DC $12.50). What to know before you start your own business.

Money Market Funds
Complete Money Market Guide, by William E. Donoghue (Bantam Books, New York, NY $3.50 paperback). A self-help guide that gives you all the vital specifics to get the most out of money market funds.

Precious Metals
Gold: Where & How To Find It, by William Bleifuss (Bobbs-Merrill, New York, NY $7.95). Explanation of the process of gold formation, reclaiming techniques, and tools essential for any modern-day gold hunter.

Looking For Gold: A Modern Prospector's Handbook, by Bradford

Angier (Stackpole Books, Harrisburg, PA $8.95). Complete guide to gold prospecting, including "how to" and "where to" directions whether taking a vacation or prospecting for fun or for fortune.

Your Gold & Silver, by Henry A. Merton (Collier Books, New York, NY $5.95). Comprehensive handbook to appraising household goods, precious metals, coins, and jewelry, how to determine prices, how to get rating on old coins, how to rate gold quality.

Real Estate

How to Cash In On Little-Know Real Estate Opportunities, by Samuel T. Barash (Prentice-Hall, Englewood Cliffs, NJ $10.95). Tells how to locate secret deals, get there first to exploit opportunities with little or no cash of your own.

How To Get The Money To Buy Your New Home, by Dennis Jacobe & James N. Kendall (Dow Jones-Irwin, Homewood, IL $11.95). Old and new options available for prospective home buyers.

How To Go From Rags To Riches In Real Estate, by William Dooner (William Morrow, New York, NY $13.00). A step-by-step guide to putting "cheap" or neglected real estate to work for you, turning depressed property into millions in the 1980s.

Real Estate Investments & How To Make Them, by Milt Tanzer (Institute for Business Planning, Englewood Cliffs, NJ $18.95). Covering all aspects of real estate investment, how to establish investment goals, where to find money, how to operate, when and how to sell, how to exploit tax shelters.

Get Rich On Other People's Money, by William H. Pivar (Arco Publishing, New York, NY $6.95). Real estate investment secrets that deal with creative financing and imaginative investing that can lead to profits.

Getting Rich In Real Estate Partnerships, by Ruth Baker Bricker (Warner Books, New York, NY $12.95). Tells how to use the advantages of team investing to reap profits when individual real estate investments are beyond your means.

Retirement

Invest For Retirement, by David H. Rubinstein (Free Press, New York, NY $12.95). A guide to financial independence through common stocks, with instructions on how to choose the investment best for you.

Retirement Money Book, by Ferd Nauheim (Acropolis Books, Washington, DC $11.95). New way to achieve more income despite inflation through real estate, securities, insurance, barter, and new careers.

Stocks

How To Cash In On The Coming Stock Market Boom, by Myron Kandel (Bobbs-Merrill, Indianapolis, IN $12.95). A timely guide that gives the small investor information on picking up remarkable buys in stocks during present economic upheaval.

How To Make Big Money In Low-Priced Stocks In The Coming Bull Market, by Ralph Charell (William Morrow, New York, NY $9.95). Tells you how you can parlay successful trades into lasting financial security, how to get profitable "inside information" legally, how to tax shelter your profits, and how to avoid losses.

How To Make $1,000,000 In The Stock Market Automatically, by Robert Lichello (Signet, New American Library, New York, NY $2.25). Mathematical system of steady buying and selling of stock that seems to work effectively in hypothetical-numerical situations.

How To Profit From The Coming Bull Market, by Max Ansbacher (Prentice-Hall, Englewood Cliffs, NJ $12.95). Author predicts Dow-Jones Average to smash through 2000 barrier and demonstrates how investors can capitalize on the coming bonanza.

Stock Market Primer, by Claude N. Rosenburg, Jr. (Warner Books, New York, NY $14.95). Basic guide to security markets and investing.

Taxes

How To Survive A Tax Audit, by Mary Sprouse (Doubleday & Co., Garden City, NY $11.95). A comprehensive analysis of what to do before and after you hear from the IRS, written by former IRS auditor.

In This Corner, The IRS, by J.C. Price (Dell Publishing, New York, NY $2.95 paperback). A former IRS special agent gives you the inside story and all the strategies to come out a winner.

Perfectly Legal, by Barry Steiner & David W. Kennedy (John Wiley & Sons, New York, NY $12.95). A questions and answers format that reveals a collection of legal tax dodges ranging from shelters to gifts, from insurance to bad debts.

Sylvia Porter's 1982 Income Tax Book, by Sylvia Porter (Avon Books, New York, NY $3.95 paperback). Line-by-line guide through a tax form, with clear instructions for reducing your income tax.

Tax Havens: What They Are & What They Can Do, by Adam Starchild (Arlington House, Westport, CT $12.95). Explains the advantages and disadvantages of various havens and how to use them.

Chapter Thirty

Definitions of Investment Terms

Note: Terms are keyed at the end of each definition according to the investment area to which the definition applies. The key is as follows: mb—municipal bond market; s—securities market; g—gem industry; cu—currencies market; co—commodities market.

Accrued Interest—Interest accrued on a bond since the last interest payment was made. The buyer of the bond pays the market price plus accrued interest. Exceptions include bonds that are in default and income bonds. (See: *Flat Income Bond*) (s)

Arbitrage—The purchase of futures in one market for their immediate sale in another market in order to profit from a difference in price. (co)

Arbitrage—A technique employed to take advantage of differences in price. If, for example, ABC stock can be bought in New York for $10 a share and sold in London at $10.50, an arbitrageur may simultaneously purchase ABC stock here and sell the same amount in London, making a profit of 50 cents a share, less expenses. Arbitrage may also involve the purchase of

rights to subscribe to a security, or the purchase of a convertible security—and the sale at or about the same time of the security obtainable through exercise of the rights or of the security obtainable through conversion. (See: *Convertible; Rights*) (s)

Assets—Everything a corporation owns or due to it: Cash, investments, money due it, materials and inventories, which are current asets; buildings and machinery, which are known as fixed assets; and patents and goodwill, called intangible assets. (See: *Liabilities*) (s)

Auctions Market—The system of trading securities through brokers or agents on an exchange. Buyers compete with other buyers while sellers compete with other sellers for the most advantageous price. Most transactions are executed with public customers on both sides since the specialist buys or sells for his own account primarily to offset imbalances in public security and demand. (See: *Quotation*) (s)

Averaging—(See: *Dollar Cost Averaging*) (s)

Balance of Payments—Country's surplus or deficit resulting from total international transactions. (cu)

Balance Sheet—A condensed financial statement showing the nature and amount of a company's assets, liabilties, and capital on a given date. In dollar amounts the balance sheet shows what the company owned, what it owed, and the ownership interest in the company of its stockholders. (See: *Assets; Earnings Report*) (s)

Basis—The difference between the spot price and the price of futures. "Basis" can also refer to the difference between the cash-market price at a given local point as opposed to current delivery-point prices. In other words, statements of basis can apply to location as well as time. (co)

Basis Price—The price expressed in yield or net return on the investment. (mb)

Bear—Someone who believes the market will decline. (s)

Bearer Bond—A bond which does not have the owner's name registered on the books of the issuer and which is payable to the holder. (See: *Coupon Bond; Registered Bond*) (s)

Bid and Asked—Often referred to as a quotation or quote. The bid is the highest price anyone has declared that he wants to pay for a security at a given time; the asked is the lowest price anyone will take at the same time. (See: *Quotation*) (s)

Block—A large holding or transaction of stock—popularly considered to be 10,000 shares or more. (s)

Blue Chip—A company known nationally for the quality and wide acceptance of its products or service, and for its ability to make money and pay dividends. (s)

Bond—Basically an IOU or promissory note of a coporation, usually issued in multiples of $1000 or $5000, although $100 and $500 denominations are not unknown. A bond is evidence of a debt on which the issuing company usually promises to pay the bondholders a specified amount of interest for a specified length of time, and to repay the loan on the expiration date. In every case a bond represents debt—its holder is a creditor of the corporation and not a part owner as is the shareholder. In most cases, bonds are secured by a mortgage. (See: *Collateral Trust Bond; Convertible; Debenture; General Mortgage Bond; Income Bond*) (s)

Book Value—An accounting term. Book value of a stock is determined from a company's records, by adding all assets, then deducting all debts and other liabilities, plus the liquidation price of any preferred issues. The sum arrived at is divided by the number of common shares outstanding and the result is book value per common share. Book value of the assets of a company or a security may have little or no significant relationship to market value. (s)

Broker—An agent who handles the public's orders to buy and sell securities, commodities, or other property. For this service a commission is charged. (s)

Bull—One who believes the market will rise. (s)

Call—(See: *Option*) (s)

Callable—A bond issue, all or part of which may be redeemed by the issuing corporation, under definite conditions before maturity. The term also applies to preferred shares which may be redeemed by the issuing corporation. (s)

Capital Gain or Capital Loss—Profit or loss from the sale of a capital asset. A capital gain, under current Federal income tax law, may be either short-term (12 months or less) or long-term (more than 12 months). A short-term capital gain is taxed at the reporting individual's full income tax rate. A long-term capital gain is subject to a lower tax. The capital gains provisions of the tax law are complicated. You should consult your tax adviser for specific information. (s)

Capital Stock—All shares representing ownership of a business, including preferred and common. (See: *Common Stock; Preferred Stock)* (s)

Carat—⅕ of a gram; unit of weight (g)

Cash Flow—Reported net income of a corporation plus amounts charged off for depreciation, depletion, amortization, extraordinary charges to reserves, which are bookkeeping deductions and not paid out in actual dollars and cents. (See: *Amortization; Depreciation)* (s)

Cash Market—Market for immediate delivery of and payment for commodities. (co)

Central Bank—Official organization to issue national currency and regulate money and credit. At times, authorized to act as government's fiscal agent. (cu)

Certificate—The actual piece of paper which is evidence of ownership of stock in a corporation. Watermarked paper is finely engraved with delicate etchings to discourage forgery. Loss of a certificate may at the least cause a great deal of inconvenience—at the worst, financial loss. (s)

Closed-End Investment Company —(See: *Investment Company (s)*

Collateral—Securities or other property pledged by a borrower to secure repayment of a loan. (s)

Collateral Trust Bond—A bond secured by collateral deposited with a trustee. The collateral is often the stocks or bonds of companies controlled by the issuing company but may be other securities. (s)

Commission—The broker's basic fee for purchasing or selling securities or property as an agent. (s)

Common Stock—Securities which represent an ownership interest in a corporation. If the company has also issued preferred stock, both common and preferred have ownership rights. The preferred normally is limited to a fixed dividend but has prior claim on dividends and, in the event of liquidation, on assets. Claims of both common and preferred stockholders are junior to claims of bondholders or other creditors of the company. Common stockholders assume the greater risks, but generally exercise the greater control and may gain the greater reward in the form of dividends and capital appreciation. The terms common stock and capital stock are often used interchangeably when the company has no preferred stock. (s)

Contract—A term of reference describing a unit of trading for a commodity future. Also, an actual bilateral agreement between the buyer and seller of a futures transaction as defined by an exchange. (co)

Contract Month—The month in which futures contracts may be satisfied by making or accepting delivery. (co)

Convertible—A bond, debenture, or preferred share which may be exchanged by the owner for common stock or another security, usually of the same company, in accordance with the terms of the issue. (s)

Cost-of-Living Index—Reflects major changes in general price level. Upward movement means decline in purchasing power of the currency. (cu)

Coupon Bond—Bond with interest coupon attached. The coupons are clipped as they come due and are presented by the holder for payment or interest. (See: *Bearer Bond; Registered Bond*) (s)

Coverage—This is a term usually connected with revenue bonds. It indicates the margin of safety for payment of debt service, reflecting the number of times or percentage by which earnings for a period of time exceed debt service payable in such period. (mb)

Cumulative Preferred—A stock having a provision that if one or more dividends are omitted, the omitted dividends must be paid before dividends may be paid on the company's common stock. (s)

Current Assets—Those assets of a company which are reasonably expected to be realized in cash, or sold, or consumed during the normal operating cycle of the business. These include cash, U.S. Goverment bonds, receivables and money due usually within one year, and inventories. (s)

Current Liabilities—Money owed and payable by a company, usually within one year. (s)

Current Return—(See: *Yield*) (s)

Day Order—An order to buy or sell which, if not executed, expires at the end of the trading day on which is was entered. (s)

De Beers Syndicate—The so-called diamond syndicate. (g)

Debenture—A promissory note backed by the general credit of a company and usually not secured by a mortgage or lien on any specific property. (See: *Bond*) (s)

Debit Balance—In a customer's margin account, that portion of purchase price of stock, bonds, or commodities covered by credit extended by the broker to the margin customer. (s)

Debt Limit—The statutory or constitutional maximum debt-incurring power of a municipality. (mb)

Debt Ratio—The ratio of the issuer's debt to a measure of value, such as assessed valuation, real value, etc. (mb)

Debt Service—Required payments for interest on and retirement of principal amount of a debt. (mb)

Default—Failure to pay principal or interest promptly when due. (mb)

Deferred Futures—The futures, of those currently traded, that expire during the most distant months. (co)

Delivery—The tender and receipt of an actual commodity, or warehouse receipts covering such commodity, in settlement of a futures contract. (co)

Delivery Month—A specified month within which delivery may be made under the terms of the futures contract. (co)

Depreciation—Decline in value of a currency in terms of gold and/or purchasing power. (cu)

Depreciation—Normally, charges against earnings to write off the cost, less salvage value, of an asset over its estimated useful life. It is a bookkeeping entry and does not represent any cash outlay nor are any funds earmarked for the purpose. (s)

Diamond—Carbon arranged in an isometric way. (g)

Discount—The amount by which a preferred stock or bond may sell below its par value. Also used as a verb to mean "takes into account" as the price of the stock has discounted the expected dividend cut. (See: *Premium)* (s)

Discretionary Account—An account in which the customer gives the broker or someone else's discretion, which may be complete or within specific limits, either to handle the purchase or sale of securities or commodities, including selection, timing, amount, and price to be paid or received. (s)

Diversification—Spreading investments among different companies in different fields. Another type of diversification is also offered by the securities of many individual companies because of the wide range of their activities. (s)

Dividend—The payment designated by the Board of Directors to be distributed pro rata among the shares outstanding. On preferred shares, it is generally a fixed amount. On common shares, the dividend varies with the fortunes of the company and the amount of cash on hand, and may be omitted if business is poor or the directors determine to withhold earnings to invest in plant and equipment. Sometimes a company will pay a dividend out of past earnings even if it is not currently operating at a profit. (s)

Dollar Cost Averaging—A system of buying securities at regular intervals with a fixed dollar amount. Under this system the investor buys by the dollars' worth rather than by the number of shares. If each investment is of the same number of dollars, payments buy more when the price is low and fewer when it rises. Thus temporary downswings in price benefit the investor if he continues periodic purchases in both good

times and bad and the price at which the shares are sold is more than their average cost. (s)

Equipment Trust Certificate—A type of security, generally issued by a railroad, to pay for new equipment. Title to the equipment, such as a locomotive, is held by a trustee until the notes are paid off. An equipment trust certificate is usually secured by a first claim on the equipment. (s)

Equity—The ownership interest of common and preferred stockholders in a company. Also refers to excess of value of securities over the debit balance in a margin account. (s)

Ex-Dividend—A synonym for "without dividend." The buyer of a stock selling ex-dividend does not receive the recently declared dividend. Every dividend is payable on a fixed date to all shareholders recorded on the books of the company as of a previous date of record. When stocks go ex-dividend, the stock tables include the symbol "x" following the name. (See: *Net Change; Transfer)* (s)

Ex-Rights—Without the rights. Corporations raising additional money may do so by offering their stockholders the right to subscribe to new or additional stock, usually at a discount from the prevailing market price. The buyer of a stock selling ex-rights is not entitled to the rights. (See: *Ex-Dividend; Rights)* (s)

Extra—The short form of "extra dividend." A dividend in the form of stock or cash in addition to the regular or usual dividend the company has been paying. (s)

Face Value—The value of a bond that appears on the face of the bond, unless the value is otherwise specified by the issuing company. Face value is ordinarily the amount the issuing company promises to pay at maturity. Face value is not an indication of market value. Sometimes referred to as par value. (See: *Par*) (s)

Fiscal Year—A corporation's accounting year. Due to the nature of their particular business, some companies do not use the calendar year for their bookkeeping. Most companies, though, operate on a calendar year basis. (s)

Fixed Charges—A company's fixed expenses, such as bond interest, which it has agreed to pay whether or not earned, and which are deducted from income, before earnings on equity capital are computed. (s)

Flat Income Bond—This term means that the price at which a bond is traded includes consideration for all unpaid accruals of interest. Bonds which are in default of interest or principal are traded flat. Income bonds, which pay interest only to the extent earned are usually traded flat. All other bonds are usually dealt in "and interest," which means that the buyer pays to the seller the market price plus interest accrued since the last payment date. (s)

Flexible Exchange Rate—System whereby rate is subject to relatively frequent official adjustments. (cu)

Floating (Fluctuating) Exchange Rate—System whereby currency's value fluctuates freely against other currencies according to supply and demand. (cu)

Floor Broker—A member of the Stock Exchange who executes order on the floor of the Exchange to buy or sell any listed securities. (s)

Forward Exchange (Futures)—Purchase and/or sale of foreign exchange for delivery at future, pre-arranged date. (cu)

Free and Open Market—A market in which supply and demand are freely expressed in terms of price. Contrast with a controlled market in which supply, demand, and price may all be regulated. (s)

Fundamental Research—Analysis of industries and companies based on such factors as sales, assets, earnings, products, services, markets, and management. As applied to the economy, fundamental research includes consideration of gross national product, interest rates, unemployment, inventories, savings, etc. (See: *Technical Research*) (s)

Funded Debt—Usually interest-bearing bonds or debentures of a company. Could include long-term bank loans. Does not include short-term loans, preferred or common stock. (s)

Futures—A term used to designate all contracts covering the sale of commodities for future delivery on a commodity exchange. (co)

General Mortgage Bond—A bond which is secured by a blanket mortgage on the company's property, but which may be outranked by one or more other mortgages. (s)

General Obligation—A bond secured by pledge of the issuer's full faith and credit and taxing power. (mb)

G.I.A.—The Gemological Institute of America—a nonprofit, educational institute. (g)

Gold Exchange Standard—System whereby a currency, officially convertible into gold at a fixed price, temporarily serves as a gold substitute in another country's monetary reserves, with the currency's international value guaranteed through its convertibility on demand into gold at its Central Bank of issue. (cu)

Gold Standard—System whereby currency's international and domestic value is kept stable in terms of a fixed gold price and in terms of other currencies based on gold by means of its free redemption into gold and/or gold coins at the Central Bank. (cu)

Good 'Til Cancelled Order (GTC) Or Open Order—An order to buy or sell which remains in effect until it is either executed or cancelled. (s)

Government Bonds—Obligations of the U.S. Government, regarded as the highest grade issues in existence. (s)

Gross Debt—The sum total of a debtor's obligation. (mb)

Growth Stock—Stock of a company with a record of growth in earnings at a relatively rapid rate. (s)

Guaranteed Bond—A bond which has interest or principal, or both, guaranteed by a company other than the issuer. Usually found in the railroad industry when large roads, leasing sections of trackage owned by small railroads, may guarantee the bonds of the smaller road. (s)

Guaranteed Stock—Usually preferred stock on which dividends are guaranteed by another company; under much the same circumstances as a bond is guaranteed. (s)

Hedge—(See: *Arbitrage; Option; Short Sale*) (s)

Holding Company—A corporation which owns the securities of another, in most cases with voting control. (s)

Inactive Stock—An issue traded on an exchange or in the over-the-counter market in which there is a relatively low volume of transactions. Volume may be no more than a few hundred shares a week or even less. (s)

Income Bond—Generally income bonds promise to repay principal but to pay interest only when earned. In some cases unpaid

interest on an income bond may accumulate as a claim against the corporation when the bond becomes due. An income bond may also be issued in lieu of preferred stock. (s)

Indenture—A written agreement under which bonds and debentures are issued, setting forth maturity date, interest rate, and other terms. (s)

Inflation—Increase in volume of money and credit in relation to availability of goods, resulting in substantial and continuing rise in general price level. (cu)

Institutional Investor—An organization whose primary purpose is to invest its own assets in trust by it for others. Includes pension funds, investment companies, insurance companies, universities, and banks. (s)

Interest—Payments a borrower pays a lender for the use of his money. A corporation pays interest on its bonds to its bondholders. (See: *Bond; Dividend*) (s)

Interest Dates—The dates on which interest is payable to the holders of the bonds, usually set at semi-annual intervals on the first or the fifteenth of the month. (mb)

Interest Rate—The interest payable each year, expressed as a percentage of the principal. (mb)

Investment—The use of money for the purpose of making more money—to gain income or increase capital, or both. Safety of principal is an important consideration. (See: *Speculation*) (s)

Investment Banker—Also known as an underwriter. He is the middleman between a corporation issuing new securities and the public. The usual practice is for one or more investment bankers to buy outright from a corporation a new issue of stocks or bonds. The group forms a syndicate to sell the securities to individuals and institutions. Investment bankers also distribute very large blocks of stocks or bonds—perhaps held by an estate. Thereafter the market in the security may be over-the-counter on a stock exchange. (See: *Over-the-Counter; Primary Distribution; Syndicate*) (s)

Investment Company—A company or trust which uses its capital to invest in other companies. There are two principal types: the closed-end and the open-end, or mutual fund. Shares in closed-end investment companies are readily transferable in the open market and are bought and sold like other shares. Capitalization of these companies remains the same unless action is taken to change, which is seldom. Open-end funds sell their own new shares to investors, stand ready to buy back their old shares, and are not listed. Open-end funds are so called because their capitalization is not fixed; they issue more shares as people want them. (s)

Issue—Any of a company's securities, or the act of distributing such securities. (s)

Issuer—A municipal unit which borrows money through the sale of bonds. (mb)

Leverage—The effect on the per-share earnings of the common stock of a company when large sums must be paid for bond interest or preferred stock dividend, or both, before the common stock is entitled to share in earnings. Leverage may be advantageous for the common stock when earnings are good, but may work against the common when earnings decline. (s)

Liabilities—All the claims against a coporation. Liabilities include accounts and wages and salaries payable, dividends declared payable, accrued taxes payable, fixed or long-term liabilities such as mortgage bonds, debentures, and back loans. (See: *Assets; Balance Sheet*) (s)

Lien—A claim against property. A bond is usually secured by a lien against specified property of a company. (See: *Bond*) (s)

Limit, Limited Order, or Limited Price Order—An order to buy or sell a stated amount of a security at a specified price, or at a better price, if obtainable after the order is represented in the Trading Crowd. (s)

Liquidation—The process of converting securities or other property into cash. The dissolution of a company, with cash remaining after sale of its assets and payment of all indebtedness being distributed to the shareholders. (s)

Liquidation—Any transaction that offsets or closes out a long or short position. (co)

Liquidity—The ability of the market in a particular security to absorb a reasonable amount of buying or selling at reasonable price changes. Liquidity is one of the most important characteristics of a good market. (s)

Listed Stock—The stock of a company which is traded on a securities exchange, and for which a listing application and a registration statement, giving detailed information about the company and its operations, have been filed with the Securities & Exchange Commission, unless otherwise exempted, and the exchange itself. The various stock exchanges have different standards for listing. (s)

Load—The portion of the offering price of shares of open-end investment companies in excess of the value of the underlying assets which cover sales commissions and all other costs of distribution. The load is usually incurred only on purchase, there being, in most cases, no charge when the shares are sold (redeemed). (s)

Locked In—An investor is said to be locked in when he has a profit on a security he owns but does not sell because his profit would immediately become subject to the capital gains tax. (See: *Capital Gain*) (s)

Long—Signifies ownership of securities: "I am long 100 U.S. Steel" means the speaker owns 100 shares. (See: *Short Position; Short Sale*) (s)

Long—One who has bought a futures contract to establish a market position and who has not yet closed out this postion through an offsetting sale or by taking delivery. (co)

Manipulation—An illegal operation. Buying or selling a security for the purpose of creating false or misleading appearance of active trading or for the purpose of raising or depressing the price to induce purchase or sale by others. (s)

Margin—The amount paid by the customer when he uses his broker's credit to buy a security. Under Federal Reserve regulations, the initial margin required in past years has ranged from 50 percent of the purchase price all the way to 100 percent. (See: *Equity; Margin Call*) (s)

Margin—(See: *Security Deposit*) (co)

Margin Call—A demand upon a customer to put up money or securities with the broker. The call is made when a purchase is made; also if a customer's equity in a margin account declines below a minimum standard set the the Exchange or by the firm. (See: *Margin*) (s)

Marketability—The measure of the ease with which a bond can be sold in the secondary market. (mb)

Market Order—An order to buy or sell a stated amount of a security at the most advantageous price obtainable after the order is represented in the Trading Crowd. (See: *Good 'Til Cancelled Order; Limited Order; Stop Order*) (s)

Market Price—In the case of a security, market price is usually considered the last reported price at which the stock or bond sold. (s)

Matched and Lost—When two bids to buy the same stock are made on the trading floor simultaneously, and each bid is equal to or larger than the amount of stock offered, both bids are considered to be on an equal basis. So the two bidders flip a coin to decide who buys the stock. Also applies to offer to sell. (s)

Maturity—The date on which a loan or a bond or debenture comes due and is to be paid off. (s)

Melee—Tiny precious stones less than .5 carat in size. The bulk of diamonds and colored stones are "melee size." (g)

Monetary Reserve—Amount of gold and foreign exchange held by a country. (cu)

Mortgage Bond—A bond secured by a mortgage on a property. The value of the property may or may not equal the value of the so-called mortgage bonds issued against it. (See: *Bond; Debenture*) (s)

Municipal Bond—A bond issued by a state or a political subdivision, such as county, city, town or village. The term also designates bonds issued by state agencies and authorities. In general, interest paid on municipal bonds is exempt from Federal income taxes and state and local income taxes within the state of issue. (s)

Mutual Fund—(See: *Investment Company*) (s)

NASD—The National Association of Securities Dealers, Inc. An association of brokers and dealers in the over-the-counter securities business. The Association has the power to expel members who have been declared guilty of unethical practices. A primary objective of the NASD is to "adopt, administer and enforce rules of fair practice and rules to prevent fraudulent and manipulative acts and practices, and in general to promote just and equitable principles of trade for the protection of investors." (s)

NASDAQ—An automated information network which provides brokers and dealers with price quotations on securities traded over-the-counter. NASDAQ is an acronym for National Association of Securities dealers Automated Quotations. (s)

Negotiable—Refers to a security, the title to which is transferable by delivery. (s)

Net Asset Value—A term usually used in connection with investment companies, meaning net asset value per share. It is common practice for an investment company to compute its assets daily, or even twice daily, by totaling the market value of all securities owned. All liabilities are deduced, and the balance divided by the number of shares outstanding. The resulting figure is the net asset value per share. (See: *Assets; Investment Company*) (s)

Net Change—The change in the price of a security between the closing price on one day and the closing price on the following day on which the stock is traded. The net change is ordinarily the last figure on the stock price list. The mark + 1-⅛ means up $1.125 a share from the last sale on the previous day the stock traded. (s)

New Issue—A stock or bond sold by a corporation for the first time. Proceeds may be issued to retire outstanding securities of the company, for new plant or equipment, or for additional working capital. (s)

Noncumulative—A preferred stock on which unpaid dividends do not accrue. Omitted dividends are, as a rule, gone forever. (See: *Cumulative Preferred*) (s)

Odd Lot—An amount of stock less than the established 100-share unit or 10-share unit of trading: from 1 to 99 shares for the great majority of issues, 1 to 9 for so-called inactive stocks. (See: *Round Lot; Inactive stock*) (s)

Offer—The price at which a person is ready to sell. Opposed to bid, the price at which one is ready to buy. (See: *Bid and Asked*) (s)

Open-End Investment Company—(See: *Investment Company*) (s)

Open Interest—Number of open contracts. Refers to unliquidated purchases or sales but never to their combined total. (co)

Open Order—(See: *Good 'Til Cancelled Order*) (s)

Option—A right to buy (call) or sell (put) a fixed amount of a given stock at a specified price within a limited period of time. Individuals may write (sell) as well as purchase options and are thereby obliged to delivery or buy the stock at the specified price. (s)

Orders Good Until a Specified Time—A market or limited price order which is to be represented in the Trading Crowd until a specified time, after which such order or the portion thereof not executed is to be treated as cancelled. (s)

Overbought—An opinion as to price levels. May refer to a security which has had a sharp rise or to the market as a whole after a period of vigorous buying, which it may be argued, has left prices "too high." (s)

Oversold—An opinion—the reverse of overbought. A single security or a market which, it is believed, has declined to an unreasonable level. (s)

Over-the-Counter—A market for securities made up of securities dealers who may or may not be members of a securities exchange. Over-the-counter is mainly a market made over the telephone. Thousands of companies have insufficient shares outstanding, stockholders, or earnings to warrant application for listing on the New York Stock Exchange, Inc. Securities of these companies are traded in the over-the-counter market between dealers who act either as principals or as brokers for customers. The over-the-counter market is the principal market for U.S. Government and municipal bonds. (See: *NASD; NASDAQ*) (s)

Paper Profit—An unrealized profit on a security still held. Paper profits become realized profits only when the security is sold. (See: *Profit Taking*) (s)

Par—In the case of a common share, par means a dollar amount assigned to the share by the company's charter. Par value may also be used to compute the dollar amount of the common shares on the balance sheet. Par value has little significance so far as market value of common stock is concerned. Many companies today issue no-par stock but give a stated per share value on the balance sheet. In the case of preferred shares and bonds, however, par is important. It often signifies the dollar value upon which dividends on preferred stocks, and interest on bonds,

are figured. The issuer of a 6 percent bond promises to pay that percentage of the bond's par value annually. (s)

Participating Preferred—A preferred stock which is entitled to its stated dividend and, also, to additional dividends on a specified basis upon payment of dividends on the common stock. (s)

Penny Stocks—Low-priced issues often highly speculative, selling at less than $1 a share. Frequently used as a term of disparagement, although a few penny stocks have developed into investment-caliber issues. (s)

Percentage Order—A limited price order to buy (or sell) a stated amount of a specified stock after a fixed number of shares of such stock have traded. (s)

Petro-Dollar—U.S. dollar holdings of oil-exporting nations. (cu)

Point—In the case of shares of stock, a point means $1. If ABC shares rises 3 points, each share has risen $3. In the case of bonds a point means $10, since a bond is quoted as a percentage of $1000. A bond which rises 3 points gains 3 percent of $1000, or $30 in value. An advance from 87 to 90 would mean an advance in dollar value from $870 to $900 for each $1000 bond. In the case of market averages, the word point means merely that and no more. (s)

Portfolio—Holdings of securities by an individual or institution. A portfolio may contain bonds, preferred stocks, and common stocks or various types of enterprises. (s)

Position—An interest in the market, either long or short, in the form of open contracts. (co)

Preferred Stock—A class of stock with a claim on the company's earnings before payment may be made on the common stock and usually entitled to priority over common stock if the company liquidates. Usually entitled to dividends at a specified rate —when declared by the Board of Directors and before payment of a dividend on the common stock —depending upon the terms of the issue. (See: *Cumulative Preferred; Participating Preferred*) (s)

Premium—The amount by which a preferred stock, bond, or option may sell above its par value. In the case of a new issue of bonds or stocks, premium is the amount the market price rises over the original selling price. Also refers to a charge sometimes made when a stock is borrowed to make delivery on a short sale. May refer, also, to redemption price of a bond or preferred stock if it is higher than face value. (See: *Discount; Short Sale*) (s)

Price-Earnings Ratio—The price of a share of stock divided by earnings per share for a twelve-month period. For example, a stock selling for $50 a share and earning $5 a share is said to be selling at a price-earnings ratio of 10 to 1. (s)

Price Limit—The maximum price move for a given commodity allowed by Exchange rules for any one day's trading, up or down from the previous day's settling price. (co)

Primary Distribution—Also called primary offering. The original sale of a company's securities. (See: *Investment Banker; Secondary Distribution*) (s)

Principal—The person for whom a broker executes an order, or a dealer buying or selling for his own account. The term "principal" may also refer to a person's capital or to the face amount of a bond. (s)

Profit-Taking—Selling stock which has appreciated in value since purchase, in order to realize the profit which has been made possible. The term is often used to explain a downturn in the market following a period of rising prices. (See: *Paper Profit*) (s)

Prospectus—The official selling circular that must be given to purchasers of new securities registered with the Securities and Exchange Commission so investors can evaluate those securities before or at the time of purchase. It highlights the much longer Registration Statement filed with the Commission. It warns the issue has not been approved (or disapproved) by the Commission and discloses such material information as the issuer's property and business, the nature of the security offered, use of proceeds, issuer's competition and prospects, management's experience, history and remuneration, and certified financial statements. A preliminary version of the prospectus, used by brokers to obtain buying indications from investors, is called a red herring. This is because of a front-page notice (printed in red ink) that the preliminary prospectus is "subject to completion or amendment" and "shall not constitute an offer to sell . . ." (s)

Proxy—Written authorization given by a shareholder to someone else to represent him and vote his shares at a shareholders' meeting. (s)

Proxy Statement—Information required by SEC to be given stockholders as a prerequisite to solicitation of proxies for a security subject to the requirements of Securities Exchange Act. (s)

Puts and Calls—(See: *Option*) (s)

Quotation—Often shortened to "quote." The highest bid to buy and the lowest offer to sell a security in a given market at a given time. If you ask your broker for a "quote" on a stock, he may come back with something like "45-¼ to 45-½." This means that $45.25 is the highest price any buyer wanted to pay at the time the quote was given on the floor of the Exchange and that $45.50 was the lowest price which any seller would take at the same time. (See: *Bid and Asked*) (s)

Rally—A brisk rise following a decline in the general price level of the market, or in an individual stock. (s)

Ratings—Designations used by investors' services to give relative indications of quality. (mb)

Record Date—The date on which you must be registered as a shareholder on the stock book of a company in order to receive a declared dividend or, among other things, to vote on company affairs. (See: *Ex-Dividend; Transfer*) (s)

Redemption Price—The price at which a bond may be redeemed before maturity, at the option of the issuing company. Redemption value also applies to the price the company must pay to call in certain types of preferred stock. (See: *Callable*) (s)

Refinancing—Same as refunding. New securities are sold by a company and the money is used to retire existing securities. Object may be to save interest costs, extend the maturity of the loan, or both. (s)

Refunding—A system by which a bond issue is redeemed from the proceeds of a new bond issue at conditions generally more favorable to the issuer. (mb)

Registered Bond—A bond which is registered on the books of the issuing company in the name of the owner. It can be transferred only when endorsed by the registered owner. (See: *Bearer Bond; Coupon Bond*) (s)

Registered Representative—Present name for the older term "customer's man." Also known as an Account Executive or Customer's Broker. (s)

Regulation T—The Federal regulation governing the amount of credit which may be advanced by brokers to customers for the purchase of securities. (See: *Margin*) (s)

Regulation U—The Federal regulation governing the amount of credit which may be advanced by a bank to its customers for the purchase of listed stocks. (See: *Margin*) (s)

REIT—Real Estate Investment Trust, an organization similar to an investment company in some respects but concentrating its holdings in real estate investments. The yield is generally liberal since REIT's are required to distribute as much as 90 percent of their income. (See: *Investment Company*) (s)

Return—(See; *Yield*) (s)

Revaluation—Increase in value of currency resulting from official increase in gold content. (cu)

Rights—When a company wants to raise more funds by issuing additional securities, it may give its stockholders the opportunity, ahead of others, to buy the new securities in proportion to the number of shares each owns. The piece of paper evidencing this privilege is called a right. Because the additional stock is usually offered to stockholders below the current market price, the rights ordinarily have a market value of their own and are actively traded. In most cases they must be exercised within a relatively short period. Failure to exercise or sell rights may result in actual loss to the holder. (See: *Warrant*) (s)

ough—Uncut gem material; a cut and faceted rough becomes a gem. (g)

uby—Corundum that is red. (g)

apphire—Corundum that is blue or any color other than red. (g)

cale Order—An order to buy (or sell) a security which specifies the total amount to be bought (or sold) and the amount to be bought (or sold) at specified price variations. (s)

eat—A traditional figure-of-speech for a membership on an exchange. Price and admission requirements vary. (s)

EC—The Securities and Exchange Commission, established by Congress to help protect investors. The SEC administers the Securities Act of 1933, the Securities Exchange Act of 1934, the Securities Act Amendments of 1975, the Trust Indenture Act, the Investment Company Act, the Investment Advisers Act, and the Public Utility Holding Company Act. (s)

econdary Distribution—Also known as a secondary offering. The redistribution of a block of stock sometimes after it has been sold by the issuing company. The sale is handled off the NYSE by a securities firm or group of firms and the shares are usually offered at a fixed price which is related to the current market price of the stock. Usually the block is a large one, such as might be involved in the settlement of an estate. The security may be listed or unlisted. (See: *Investment Banker; Primary Distribution; Special Offering; Syndicate*) (s)

curity Deposit—A cash amount of funds which must be deposited with the broker for each contract as a guarantee of fulfillment of the futures contract. It is not considered as part payment of purchase. Also called margin. (co)

Serial Bond—An issue which matures in part at periodic stated intervals. (s)

Settlement—Conclusion of a securities transaction in which a customer pays a debit balance he owes a broker or receives from the broker the proceeds from a sale. Term also applies to continuous daily netting out of transactions among brokerage houses, usually through centralized securities clearing corporations. (s)

Short—One who has sold a future contract to establish a market position and who has not yet closed out this position through an offsetting purchase or by making delivery. Opposite of a long. (co)

Short Covering—Buying stock to return stock previously borrowed to make delivery on a short sale. (s)

Short Position—Stocks sold short and not covered as of a particular date. Short position also means the total amount of stock an individual has sold short and has not covered, as of a particular date. (s)

Short Sale—A person who believes a stock will decline and sells it though he does not own any has made a short sale. Stock exchange and Federal regulations govern and limit the conditions under which short sale may be made on a national securities exchange. Sometimes a person will sell short a stock he already owns in order to protect a paper profit. This is known as selling short against the box. (See: *Up Tick*) (s)

Sight—The parcel containing rough stones sent ten times a year by De Beers to two hundred fifty diamond dealers. (g)

Sinking Fund—Money regularly set aside by a company to redeem its bonds, debentures, or preferred stock from time to time as specified in the indenture or charter. (s)

SIPC—Securities Investor Protection Corporation, which provides funds for use, if necessary, to protect customers' cash and securities which may be on deposit with an SIPC member firm in the event the firm fails and is liquidated under the provision of the SIPC Act. SIPC is not a Government Agency, It is a non-profit membership corporation created, however, by an Act of Congress. (s)

Special Offering—Opposite of special bid. A notice is printed on the ticker tape announcing the stock sale at a fixed price usually based on the last transaction in the regular auction market. If there are more buyers than stock, allotments are made. Only the seller pays the commission. (See: *Secondary Distribution*) (s)

Speculation—The employment of funds by a speculator. Safety of principal is a secondary factor. (See: *Investment*) (s)

Speculator—One who is willing to assume a relatively large risk in the hope of gain. The speculator may buy and sell the same day or speculate in an enterprise which he does not expect to be profitable for years. (s)

Split—The division of the outstanding shares of a corporation into a larger number of shares. A 3-for-1 split by a company with 1 million shares outstanding results in 3 million shares outstanding. Each holder of 100 shares before the 3-for-1 split would have 300 shares, although his proportionate equity in the company would remain the same. Ordinarily, splits must be voted by directors and approve by shareholders. (See: *Stoc Dividends*) (s)

Spot Exchange—Sale or purcha of currency for immediate deli ery. (cu)

Spread—A market position that simultaneously long and sho equivalent amounts of the san or related commodities for deli ery in different months. In son markets the term "straddle" used synonymously. (co)

Stock Dividend—A dividend paid securities rather than cash. T dividend may be addition shares of the issuing company, in shares of another compa (usually a subsidiary) held by th company. (See: *Ex-Dividen Split*) (s)

Stockholder of Record—A stoc holder whose name is registere on the books of the issuing corp ration. (s)

Stop Limit Offer—A stop ord which becomes a limit order aft the specified stop price has bee reached. (See: *Limit Order; St Order*) (s)

Stop Order—An order to buy at price above, or sell at a pri below, the current market. St buy orders are generally used limit loss or protect unrealize profits on a short sale. Stop se orders are generally used to pr tect unrealized profits or lim loss on a holding. A stop ord becomes a market order when th stock sells at or beyond the spec fied price and, thus, may n necessarily be executed at th price. (s)

Street Name—Securities held the name of a broker instead his customer's name are said be carried in a "street name This occurs when the securiti have been bought on margin the customer wishes the securi to be held by the broker. (s)

Surcharge—Levy on already existing tax. (cu)

Switching—Selling one security and buying another. (s)

Switch Order—Contingent Order—An order for the purchase (sale) of one stock and the sale (purchase) of another stock at a stipulated price difference. (s)

Syndicate—A group of investment bankers who together underwrite and distribute a new issue of securities or a large block of an

Synthetic Stones—Having the same physcial and chemical proportions as gems, but man-made and of limited commercial value. (g)

Take-Over—The acquiring of one corporation by another—usually in a friendly merger but sometimes marked by a "proxy fight." In "unfriendly" take-over attempts, the potential buying company may offer a price well above current market values, new securities and inducements to stockholders. The management of the subject company might ask for a better price or fight the take-over or merger with another company. (See: *Proxy*) (s)

Tax Base—The total resources available for taxation. (mb)

Tender Offer—A public offer to buy shares from existing shareholders of one public corporation by another company or other organization under specified terms good for a certain time period. Stockholders are asked to "tender" (surrender) their holdings for stated value, usually at a premium above current market price, subject to the tendering of a minimum and maximum number of shares. (s)

Third Market—Trading of stock exchange listed securities in the over-the-counter market by non-exchange member brokers and all types of investors. (s)

Ticker—The instruments which display prices and volume of securities transactions worldwide within minutes after each trade. (s)

Time Order—An order which becomes a market or limited price order at a specified time. (s)

Trade Balance—Difference between value of a country's exports and imports. (cu)

Trader—One who buys and sells for his own account for short-term profit. (s)

Trading Market—The secondary market for issued bonds. (mb)

Transfer—This term may refer to two different operations. For one, the delivery of a stock certificate from the seller's broker to the buyer's broker and legal change of ownership, normally accomplished within a few days. For another, to record the change of ownership on the books of the corporation by the transfer agent. When the purchaser's name is recorded on the books of the company, dividends, notices of meetings, proxies, financial reports and all pertinent literature sent by the issuer to its securities holders are mailed direct to the new owner. (See: *Street Name*) (s)

Transfer Agent—A transfer agent keeps a record of the name of each registered shareowner, his or her address, the number of shares owned, and sees that certificates presented to his office for transfer are properly cancelled and new certificates issued in the name of the transferee. (See: *Transfer*) (s)

Treasury Stock—Stock issued by a company but later reacquired. It may be held in the company's treasury indefinitely, reissued to the public, or retired. Treasury stock receives no dividends and has no vote while held by the company. (s)

Trustee—A bank designated as the custodian of funds and official representative of bond holders. (mb)

Turnover Rate—The volume of shares traded in a year as a percentage of total shares listed on an Exchange, outstanding for an individual issue or held in an institutional portfolio. (s)

Underwriter—(See: *Investment Banker*) (s)

Unlisted—A security not listed on a stock exchange. (See: *Over-the-Counter*) (s)

Up Tick—A term used to designate a transaction made at a price higher than the preceding transaction. Also called a "plus-tick." A stock may be sold short only on an up tick, or on a "zero-plus" tick. A "zero-plus" tick is a term used for a transaction at the same price as the preceding trade by higher than the preceding different price. Conversely, a down tick, or "minus" tick, is a terms used to designate a transaction made at a price lower than the preceding trade. A "zero-minus" tick is a transaction made at the same price as the preceding sale but lower than the preceding different price. (See: *Short Sale*) (s)

Volume—The number of shares traded in a security or an entire market during a given period. Volume is usually considered on a daily basis and a daily average is computed for longer periods. (s)

Voting Right—The stockholder's right to vote his stock in the affairs of his company. Most common shares have one vote each. Preferred stock usually has the right to vote when preferred dividends are in default for a specified period. The right to vote may be delegated by the stockholder to another person. (See: *Proxy*) (s)

Warrant—A certificate giving the holder the right to purchase securities at a stipulated price within a specified time limit or perpetually. Sometimes a warrant is offered with securities as an inducement to buy. (See: *Rights*) (s)

Wire House—A member firm of an exchange maintaining a communications network linking either its own branch offices, offices of corespondent firms, or a combination of such offices. (s)

Working Control— Theoretically, ownership of 51 percent of a company's voting stock is necessary to exercise control. In practice—and this is particularly true in the case of a large corporation —effective control sometimes can be exerted through ownership, individually or by a group acting in concert, of less than 50 percent. (s)

Yield—Also known as return. The dividends or interest paid by a company expressed as a percentage of the current price. A stock with a current market value of $40 a share paying dividends at the rate of $2.00 is said to return 5 percent. The current return on a bond is figured the same way. (See: *Dividend; Interest*) (s)

Yield to Maturity—The yield of a bond to maturity takes into account the price discount from or premium over the face amount. It is greater than the current yield when the bond is selling at a discount and less than the current yield when the bond is selling at a premium. (s)

Chapter Thirty-One

Directory of Investment Services

The following is a selected source list of governmental and private agencies that can provide further information regarding the investment areas discussed in this book. These sources are accessible to everyone, and should be consulted for any supplemental or updated information that may be needed. When requesting information, it is advised that you consult local agency offices first, prior to contacting main offices.

U.S. Government Agencies And Information Sources

Chamber of Commerce U.S.
1615 H Street N.W.
Washington, DC 20062

Federal Reserve System
20th & Constitution, N.W.
Room B 2046
Washington, DC 20551

Tax Foundation, Inc.
1875 Connecticut Ave. N.W.
Washington, DC 20009

U.S. Dept. of the Interior
18th & C Streets, N.W.
Washington, DC 20240

Internal Revenue Service
Dept. of the Treasury
1111 Constitution Ave., N.W.

Room 3000
Washington, DC 20224

U.S. Dept. of Agriculture
14th & Independence, S.W.
Room 200-A
Washington, DC 20250

Superintendent of Documents
U.S. Govt. Printing Office
Washington, DC 20402

U.S. Dept. of Commerce
14th & Constitution, N.W.
Room 5851
Washington, DC 20230

Treasury Dept.—Consumer Affairs
15th St. & Pennsylvania Ave. N.W.
Washington, DC 20220

Federal Trade Commission
Pennsylvania & Sixth, N.W.

Room 440
Washington, DC 20580

General Services Administration
Consumer Information Center
18th & F St., N.W.
Room 6137
Washington, DC 20405

National Credit Union
Washington, DC 20456

Dept. of Justice
Constitution & 10th, N.W.
Room 5111
Washington, DC 20530

Securities and Exchange Commission (SEC)

Atlanta Regional Office
1375 Peach Tree St. N.E.
Atlanta, GA 30309
(404) 881-4768

Miami Regional Office
300 Biscayne Blvd.
Miami, FL 33131
(305) 359-5765

Boston Regional Office
150 Causeway St.
Boston, MA 02114
(617) 223-2721

Chicago Regional Office
219 S. Dearborn St.
Chicago, IL 60604
(312) 353-7390

Detroit Regional Office
1044 Federal Bldg.
Detroit, MI 48226
(313) 226-6070

Denver Regional Office
410 17th St.
Denver, CO 80202
(303) 837-2071

Salt Lake City Regional Office
9 Exchange Place

Salt Lake City, UT 84111
(801) 524-5796

Ft. Worth Regional Office
411 W. 7th St.
Ft. Worth, TX 76102
(817) 334-3821

Houston Regional Office
515 Rusk Ave.
Houston, TX 77002
(713) 226-4986

Los Angeles Regional Office
10960 Wilshire Blvd.
Los Angeles, CA 90024
(213) 473-4511

San Francisco Regional Office
450 Golden Gate Ave.
San Francisco, CA 94102
(415) 556-5264

New York Regional Office
26 Federal Plaza
New York, NY 10007
(212) 264-1636

Seattle Regional Office
915 2nd Ave.
Seattle, WA 98174
(206) 442-7990

Washington Regional Office
4015 Wilson Blvd.
Arlington, VA 22203
(703) 557-8201

Main Office
500 N. Capitol
Washington, DC 20549
(202) 272-2000

Commodity Futures Trading Commission (CFTC)

Eastern Regional Office
1 World Trade Center
Suite 4747
New York, NY 10048
(212) 466-2067

Midwest Regional Office
233 S. Wacker Dr.
Suite 4600
Chicago, IL 60606
(312) 353-5990

Southwestern Regional Office
4901 Main St.
Room 208
Kansas City, MO 64112
(816) 374-2994

Western Regional Office
2 Embarcadero Center
Suite 1660
San Francisco, CA 94111
(415) 556-7503

Midwest Regional Office
510 Grain Exchange Bldg.
Minneapolis, MN 55415
(612) 725-2025

Main Office
2033 "K" Street N.W.
Washington, DC 20581
(202) 254-6970

Federal Reserve Bank and Branch Locations

Atlanta, GA: Birmingham, AL; Jacksonville, FL; Miami, FL; Nashville, TN; New Orleans, LA
Boston, MA
New York, NY: Buffalo, NY
Cleveland, OH: Cincinnati, OH; Pittsburgh, PA
Richmond, VA: Baltimore, MD; Charlotte, NC
Chicago, IL: Detroit, MI
St. Louis, MO: Little Rock, AR; Louisville, KY; Memphis, TN
Minneapolis, MN: Helena, MT
Kansas City, MO: Denver, CO; Oklahoma City, OK; Omaha, NE
Dallas, TX: El Paso, TX; San Antonio, TX; Houston, TX
Philadelphia, PA
San Francisco, CA: Los Angeles, CA; Portland, OR; Salt Lake City, UT; Seattle, WA

NON-GOVERNMENT ASSOCIATIONS AND RESOURCES

American Bar Assn.
77 South Wacker Drive
Chicago, IL 60606

American Society of Certified Life Underwriters
270 Bryn Mawr Avenue
Bryn Mawr, PA 19010

Direct Mail/Marketing Assn.
6 East 43rd Street
New York, NY 10017

National Association of Realtors
430 N. Michigan Avenue
Chicago, IL 60611

National Retail Merchants Association
100 West 31st Street
New York, NY 10001

Investment Company Institute
1775 K Street, N.W.
Washington, DC 20006

National Foundation for Consumer Credit
Suite 510, 1819 H Street N.W.
Washington, DC 20006

Official Commodity Futures Exchanges:*

Chicago Board of Trade
141 W. Jackson Blvd.
Chicago, IL 60604
(312) 435-3500

Chicago Mercantile Exchange and International Monetary Market (IMM)
444 W. Jackson Blvd.
Chicago, IL 60606
(312) 648-1000

Mid America Commodity Exchange
175 W. Jackson Blvd.

Chicago, IL 60604
(312) 435-0606

Kansas City Board of Trade
4800 Main St.
Kansas City, MO 64112
(816) 753-7363

Minneapolis Grain Exchange
150 Grain Exchange Blvd.
Minneapolis, MN 55415
(612) 338-6212

Commodity Exchange Inc.
4 World Trade Center
New York, NY 10048
(212) 938-2900

AMEX Commodities Exchange
86 Trinity Place
New York, NY 10006
(212) 938-6291

New York Cocoa Exchange
127 John St.
New York, NY 10038

Coffee, Sugar Exchange
4 World Trade Center
New York, NY 10048
(212) 938-2800

New York Cotton Exchange and Associates
4 World Trade Center
New York, NY 10048
(212) 938-2650

New York Mercantile Exchange
4 World Trade Center
New York, NY 10048
(212) 938-2222

Proposed Commodity Futures Exchanges**
New Orleans Cotton and
    Commodity Exchange
New York Futures Exchange

*There are many smaller regional and local exchanges; however, they are not currently recognized

by the C.F.T.C.
**No active trading at time of printing.

PUBLICATIONS & PERIODICALS

Barron's
Dow Jones & Co., Inc.
22 Cortland St.
New York, NY 10007

Business Week
McGraw-Hill Publishing Co.
1221 Avenues of Americas
New York, NY 10020

Dun's Review
Dun & Bradstreet Publ. Corp.
666 Fifth Ave.
New York, NY 10019

Money Maker Magazine
Consumers Digest, Inc.
5705 N. Lincoln Ave.
Chicago, IL 60659

Standard & Poors, Inc.
343 Hudson St.
New York, NY 10014

The M/G Financial Weekly
P.O. Box 26565
Dept. B-28
Richmond, VA 23261

Wall Street Journal
Dow Jones & Co., Inc.
22 Cortland St.
New York, NY 10007

American Council on Life Insurance
1850 K Street
Washington, DC 20006

Credit Union National Assn.
P.O. Box 431 ADJ
Madison, WI 53701

National Assn. of Securities Dealers
1735 K Street N.W.
Washington, DC 20006